JEAN-CHRISTOPHE

Romain Rolland's
JEAN-CHRISTOPHE

TRANSLATED FROM THE FRENCH

by

GILBERT CANNAN

HENRY HOLT AND COMPANY
NEW YORK

THE MARKET-PLACE

JEAN-CHRISTOPHE IN PARIS

I

DISORDER in order. Untidy officials offhanded in manner. Travelers protesting against the rules and regulations, to which they submitted all the same. Christophe was in France.

After having satisfied the curiosity of the customs, he took his seat again in the train for Paris. Night was over the fields that were soaked with the rain. The hard lights of the stations accentuated the sadness of the interminable plain buried in darkness. The trains, more and more numerous, that passed, rent the air with their shrieking whistles, which broke upon the torpor of the sleeping passengers. The train was nearing Paris.

Christophe was ready to get out an hour before they ran in; he had jammed his hat down on his head; he had buttoned his coat up to his neck for fear of the robbers, with whom he had been told Paris was infested; twenty times he had got up and sat down; twenty times he had moved his bag from the rack to the seat, from the seat to the rack, to the exasperation of his fellow-passengers, against whom he knocked every time with his usual clumsiness.

Just as they were about to run into the station the train suddenly stopped in the darkness. Christophe flattened his nose against the window and tried vainly to look out. He turned towards his fellow-travelers, hoping to find a friendly glance which would encourage him to ask where they were. But they were all asleep or pretending to be so: they were bored and scowling: not one of them made any attempt to

3

discover why they had stopped. Christophe was surprised by their indifference: these stiff, somnolent creatures were so utterly unlike the French of his imagination! At last he sat down, discouraged, on his bag, rocking with every jolt of the train, and in his turn he was just dozing off when he was roused by the noise of the doors being opened. . . . Paris! . . . His fellow-travelers were already getting out.

Jostling and jostled, he walked towards the exit of the station, refusing the porter who offered to carry his bag. With a peasant's suspiciousness he thought every one was going to rob him. He lifted his precious bag on to his shoulder and walked straight ahead, indifferent to the curses of the people as he forced his way through them. At last he found himself in the greasy streets of Paris.

He was too much taken up with the business in hand, the finding of lodgings, and too weary of the whirl of carriages into which he was swept, to think of looking at anything. The first thing was to look for a room. There was no lack of hotels: the station was surrounded with them on all sides: their names were flaring in gas letters. Christophe wanted to find a less dazzling place than any of these: none of them seemed to him to be humble enough for his purse. At last in a side street he saw a dirty inn with a cheap eating-house on the ground floor. It was called *Hôtel de la Civilisation*. A fat man in his shirt-sleeves was sitting smoking at a table: he hurried forward as he saw Christophe enter. He could not understand a word of his jargon: but at the first glance he marked and judged the awkward childish German, who refused to let his bag out of his hands, and struggled hard to make himself understood in an incredible language. He took him up an evil-smelling staircase to an airless room which opened on to a closed court. He vaunted the quietness of the room, to which no noise from outside could penetrate: and he asked a good price for it. Christophe only half understood him; knowing nothing of the conditions of life in Paris, and with his shoulder aching with the weight of his bag, he ac-

cepted everything: he was eager to be alone. But hardly was
he left alone when he was struck by the dirtiness of it all: and
to avoid succumbing to the melancholy which was creeping
over him, he went out again very soon after having dipped
his face in the dusty water, which was greasy to the touch.
He tried hard not to see and not to feel, so as to escape
disgust.

He went down into the street. The October mist was thick
and keenly cold: it had that stale Parisian smell, in which
are mingled the exhalations of the factories of the outskirts
and the heavy breath of the town. He could not see ten yards
in front of him. The light of the gas-jets flickered like a
candle on the point of going out. In the semi-darkness there
were crowds of people moving in all directions. Carriages
moved in front of each other, collided, obstructed the road,
stemming the flood of people like a dam. The oaths of the
drivers, the horns and bells of the trams, made a deafening
noise. The roar, the clamor, the smell of it all, struck fearfully
on the mind and heart of Christophe. He stopped for a moment, but was at once swept on by the people behind him and
borne on by the current. He went down the *Boulevard de
Strasbourg,* seeing nothing, bumping awkwardly into the
passers-by. He had eaten nothing since morning. The cafés,
which he found at every turn, abashed and revolted him, for
they were all so crowded. He applied to a policeman; but
he was so slow in finding words that the man did not even
take the trouble to hear him out, and turned his back on him
in the middle of a sentence and shrugged his shoulders. He
went on walking mechanically. There was a small crowd in
front of a shop-window. He stopped mechanically. It was a
photograph and picture-postcard shop: there were pictures of
girls in chemises, or without them: illustrated papers displayed
obscene jests. Children and young girls were looking at them
calmly. There was a slim girl with red hair who saw Christophe lost in contemplation and accosted him. He looked at her
and did not understand. She took his arm with a silly smile.

He shook her off, and rushed away, blushing angrily. There were rows of café concerts: outside the doors were displayed grotesque pictures of the comedians. The crowd grew thicker and thicker. Christophe was struck by the number of vicious faces, prowling rascals, vile beggars, painted women sickeningly scented. He was frozen by it all. Weariness, weakness, and the horrible feeling of nausea, which more and more came over him, turned him sick and giddy. He set his teeth and walked on more quickly. The fog grew denser as he approached the Seine. The whirl of carriages became bewildering. A horse slipped and fell on its side: the driver flogged it to make it get up: the wretched beast, held down by its harness, struggled and fell down again, and lay still as though it were dead. The sight of it—common enough—was the last drop that made the wretchedness that filled the soul of Christophe flow over. The miserable struggles of the poor beast, surrounded by indifferent and careless faces, made him feel bitterly his own insignificance among these thousands of men and women—the feeling of revulsion, which for the last hour had been choking him, his disgust with all these human beasts, with the unclean atmosphere, with the morally repugnant people, burst forth in him with such violence that he could not breathe. He burst into tears. The passers-by looked in amazement at the tall young man whose face was twisted with grief. He strode along with the tears running down his cheeks, and made no attempt to dry them. People stopped to look at him for a moment: and if he had been able to read the soul of the mob, which seemed to him to be so hostile, perhaps in some of them he might have seen—mingled, no doubt, with a little of the ironic feeling of the Parisians for any sorrow so simple and ridiculous as to show itself—pity and brotherhood. But he saw nothing: his tears blinded him.

He found himself in a square, near a large fountain. He bathed his hands and dipped his face in it. A little news-vendor watched him curiously and passed comment on him, waggishly though not maliciously: and he picked up his hat for him—Christophe had let it fall. The icy coldness of the water revived Christophe. He plucked up courage again. He retraced his steps, but did not look about him: he did not even think of eating: it would have been impossible for him to speak to anybody: it needed the merest trifle to set him off weeping again. He was worn out. He lost his way, and wandered about aimlessly until he found himself in front of his hotel, just when he had made up his mind that he was lost. He had forgotten even the name of the street in which he lodged.

He went up to his horrible room. He was empty, and his eyes were burning: he was aching body and soul as he sank down into a chair in the corner of the room: he stayed like that for a couple of hours and could not stir. At last he wrenched himself out of his apathy and went to bed. He fell into a fevered slumber, from which he awoke every few minutes, feeling that he had been asleep for hours. The room was stifling: he was burning from head to foot: he was horribly thirsty: he suffered from ridiculous nightmares, which clung to him even after he had opened his eyes: sharp pains thudded in him like the blows of a hammer. In the middle of the night he awoke, overwhelmed by despair, so profound that he all but cried out: he stuffed the bedclothes into his mouth so as not to be heard: he felt that he was going mad. He sat up in bed, and struck a light. He was bathed in sweat. He got up, opened his bag to look for a handkerchief. He laid his hand on an old Bible, which his mother had hidden in his linen. Christophe had never read much of the Book: but it was a comfort beyond words for him to find it at that moment. The Bible had belonged to his grandfather and to his grandfather's father. The heads of the family had inscribed on a blank page at the end their names and the important dates of their lives—births, marriages, deaths. His grandfather had written in pencil, in his large hand, the dates when he had read and re-read each chapter: the Book was full of tags of yellowed paper, on which the old man had jotted down his simple thoughts. The Book used to rest on a shelf above his bed, and he used often to take it down during the long, sleepless nights and hold converse with it rather than read it. It had been with him to the hour of his death, as it had been with his father. A century of the joys and sorrows of the family was breathed forth from the pages of the Book. Holding it in his hands, Christophe felt less lonely.

He opened it at the most somber words of all:

Is there not an appointed time to man upon earth? Are not his days also like the days of an hireling?

When I lie down, I say, When shall I arise and the night be gone? and I am full of tossings to and fro unto the dawn of the day.

When I say, My bed shall comfort me, my couch shall ease my complaint, then Thou scarest me with dreams and terrifiest me through visions. . . . How long wilt Thou not depart from me, nor let me alone till I swallow down my spittle? I have sinned; what shall I do unto Thee, O Thou preserver of men?

Though He slay me yet will I trust in Him.

All greatness is good, and the height of sorrow tops deliverance. What casts down and overwhelms and blasts the soul beyond all hope is mediocrity in sorrow and joy, selfish and niggardly suffering that has not the strength to be rid of the lost pleasure, and in secret lends itself to every sort of degradation to steal pleasure anew. Christophe was braced up by the bitter savor that he found in the old Book: the wind of Sinai coming from vast and lonely spaces and the mighty sea to sweep away the steamy vapors. The fever in Christophe subsided. He was calm again, and lay down and slept peacefully until the morrow. When he opened his eyes again it was day. More acutely than ever he was conscious of the horror of his room: he felt his loneliness and wretchedness: but he faced them. He was no longer disheartened: he was left only with a sturdy melancholy. He read over now the words of Job:

Even though God slay me yet would I trust in Him.

He got up. He was ready calmly to face the fight.

He made up his mind there and then to set to work. He knew only two people in Paris: two young fellow-countrymen: his old friend Otto Diener, who was in the office of his uncle, a cloth merchant in the *Mail* quarter: and a young Jew from Mainz, Sylvain Kohn, who had a post in a great publishing house, the address of which Christophe did not know.

He had been very intimate with Diener when he was fourteen or fifteen. He had had for him one of those childish friendships which precede love, and are themselves a sort of love.[1] Diener had loved him too. The shy, reserved boy had been attracted by Christophe's gusty independence: he had tried hard to imitate him, quite ridiculously: that had both irritated and flattered Christophe. Then they had made plans for the overturning of the world. In the end Diener had gone abroad for his education in business, and they did not see each other again: but Christophe had news of him from time to time from the people in the town with whom Diener remained on friendly terms.

As for Sylvain Kohn, his relation with Christophe had been of another kind altogether. They had been at school together, where the young monkey had played many pranks on Christophe, who thrashed him for it when he saw the trap into which he had fallen. Kohn did not put up a fight: he let Christophe knock him down and rub his face in the dust, while he howled; but he would begin again at once with a malice that never tired—until the day when he became really afraid, Christophe having seriously threatened to kill him.

Christophe went out early. He stopped to breakfast at a café. In spite of his self-consciousness, he forced himself to lose no opportunity of speaking French. Since he had to live in Paris, perhaps for years, he had better adapt himself as quickly as possible to the conditions of life there, and overcome his repugnance. So he forced himself, although he suffered horribly, to take no notice of the sly looks of the waiter as he listened to his horrible lingo. He was not discouraged, and

[1] See *Jean-Christophe*—I: " The Morning."

went on obstinately constructing ponderous, formless sentences
and repeating them until he was understood.

He set out to look for Diener. As usual, when he had an
idea in his head, he saw nothing of what was going on about
him. During that first walk his only impression of Paris
was that of an old and ill-kept town. Christophe was accustomed to the towns of the new German Empire, that were
both very old and very young, towns in which there is expressed a new birth of pride: and he was unpleasantly surprised by the shabby streets, the muddy roads, the hustling
people, the confused traffic—vehicles of every sort and shape:
venerable horse omnibuses, steam trams, electric trams, all sorts
of trams—booths on the pavements, merry-go-rounds of wooden
horses (or monsters and gargoyles) in the squares that were
choked up with statues of gentlemen in frock-coats: all sorts of
relics of a town of the Middle Ages endowed with the privilege
of universal suffrage, but quite incapable of breaking free from
its old vagabond existence. The fog of the preceding day had
turned to a light, soaking rain. In many of the shops the gas
was lit, although it was past ten o'clock.

Christophe lost his way in the labyrinth of streets round
the *Place des Victoires,* but eventually found the shop he was
looking for in the *Rue de la Banque.* As he entered he thought
he saw Diener at the back of the long, dark shop, arranging
packages of goods, together with some of the assistants. But
he was a little short-sighted, and could not trust his eyes, although it was very rarely that they deceived him. There was
a general movement among the people at the back of the shop
when Christophe gave his name to the clerk who approached
him: and after a confabulation a young man stepped forward
from the group, and said in German:

"Herr Diener is out."

"Out? For long?"

"I think so. He has just gone."

Christophe thought for a moment; then he said:

"Very well. I will wait."

The clerk was taken aback, and hastened to add:

"But he won't be back before two or three."

"Oh! That's nothing," replied Christophe calmly. "I haven't anything to do in Paris. I can wait all day if need be."

The young man looked at him in amazement, and thought he was joking. But Christophe had forgotten him already. He sat down quietly in a corner, with his back turned towards the street: and it looked as though he intended to stay there.

The clerk went back to the end of the shop and whispered to his colleagues: they were most comically distressed, and cast about for some means of getting rid of the insistent Christophe.

After a few uneasy moments, the door of the office was opened and Herr Diener appeared. He had a large red face, marked with a purple scar down his cheek and chin, a fair mustache, smooth hair, parted on one side, a gold-rimmed eyeglass, gold studs in his shirt-front, and rings on his fat fingers. He had his hat and an umbrella in his hands. He came up to Christophe in a nonchalant manner. Christophe, who was dreaming as he sat, started with surprise. He seized Diener's hands, and shouted with a noisy heartiness that made the assistants titter and Diener blush. That majestic personage had his reasons for not wishing to resume his former relationship with Christophe: and he had made up his mind from the first to keep him at a distance by a haughty manner. But he had no sooner come face to face with Christophe than he felt like a little boy again in his presence: he was furious and ashamed. He muttered hurriedly:

"In my office. . . . We shall be able to talk better there."

Christophe recognized Diener's habitual prudence.

But when they were in the office and the door was shut, Diener showed no eagerness to offer him a chair. He remained standing, making clumsy explanations:

"Very glad. . . . I was just going out. . . . They thought I had gone. . . . But I must go . . . I have only a minute . . . a pressing appointment. . . ."

Christophe understood that the clerk had lied to him, and that the lie had been arranged by Diener to get rid of him. His blood boiled: but he controlled himself, and said dryly:

"There is no hurry."

Diener drew himself up. He was shocked by such off-handedness.

"What!" he said. "No hurry! In business . . ." Christophe looked him in the face.

"No."

Diener looked away. He hated Christophe for having so put him to shame. He murmured irritably. Christophe cut him short:

"Come," he said. "You know . . ."

(He used the *"Du,"* which maddened Diener, who from the first had been vainly trying to set up between Christophe and himself the barrier of the *"Sie."*)

"You know why I am here?"

"Yes," said Diener. "I know."

(He had heard of Christophe's escapade, and the warrant out against him, from his friends.)

"Then," Christophe went on, "you know that I am not here for fun. I have had to fly. I have nothing. I must live."

Diener was waiting for that, for the request. He took it with a mixture of satisfaction—(for it made it possible for him to feel his superiority over Christophe)—and embarrassment—(for he dared not make Christophe feel his superiority as much as he would have liked).

"Ah!" he said pompously. "It is very tiresome, very tiresome. Life here is hard. Everything is so dear. We have enormous expenses. And all these assistants . . ."

Christophe cut him short contemptuously:

"I am not asking you for money."

Diener was abashed. Christophe went on:

"Is your business doing well? Have you many customers?"

"Yes. Yes. Not bad, thank God! . . ." said Diener cautiously. (He was on his guard.)

Christophe darted a look of fury at him, and went on:

"You know many people in the German colony?"

"Yes."

"Very well: speak for me. They must be musical. They have children. I will give them lessons."

Diener was embarrassed at that.

"What is it?" asked Christophe. "Do you think I'm not competent to do the work?"

He was asking a service as though it were he who was rendering it. Diener, who would not have done a thing for Christophe except for the sake of putting him under an obligation, was resolved not to stir a finger for him.

"It isn't that. You're a thousand times too good for it. Only . . ."

"What, then?"

"Well, you see, it's very difficult—very difficult—on account of your position."

"My position?"

"Yes. . . . You see, that affair, the warrant. . . . If that were to be known. . . . It is difficult for me. It might do me harm."

He stopped as he saw Christophe's face go hot with anger: and he added quickly:

"Not on my own account. . . . I'm not afraid. . . . Ah! If I were alone! . . . But my uncle . . . you know, the business is his. I can do nothing without him. . . ."

He grew more and more alarmed at Christophe's expression, and at the thought of the gathering explosion he said hurriedly—(he was not a bad fellow at bottom: avarice and vanity were struggling in him: he would have liked to help Christophe, at a price):

"Can I lend you fifty francs?"

Christophe went crimson. He went up to Diener, who stepped back hurriedly to the door and opened it, and held himself in readiness to call for help, if necessary. But Christophe only thrust his face near his and bawled:

"You swine!"

And he flung him aside and walked out through the little throng of assistants.   At the door he spat in disgust.

He strode along down the street.   He was blind with fury. The rain sobered him.   Where was he going?   He did not know.   He did not know a soul.   He stopped to think outside a book-shop, and he stared stupidly at the rows of books. He was struck by the name of a publisher on the cover of one of them.   He wondered why.   Then he remembered that it was the name of the house in which Sylvain Kohn was employed. He made a note of the address. . . .   But what was the good? He would not go. . . .   Why should he not go? . . .   If that scoundrel Diener, who had been his friend, had given him such a welcome, what had he to expect from a rascal whom he had handled roughly, who had good cause to hate him?   Vain humiliations!   His blood boiled at the thought.   But his native pessimism, derived perhaps from his Christian education, urged him on to probe to the depths of human baseness.

"I have no right to stand on ceremony.   I must try everything before I give in."

And an inward voice added:

"And I shall not give in."

He made sure of the address, and went to hunt up Kohn. He made up his mind to hit him in the eye at the first show of impertinence.

The publishing house was in the neighborhood of the Madeleine.   Christophe went up to a room on the second floor, and asked for Sylvain Kohn.   A man in livery told him that "Kohn was not known."   Christophe was taken aback, and thought his pronunciation must be at fault, and he repeated his question: but the man listened attentively, and repeated that no one of that name was known in the place. Quite out of countenance, Christophe begged pardon, and was turning to go when a door at the end of the corridor opened, and he saw Kohn himself showing a lady out.   Still suffering from the affront put upon him by Diener, he was inclined to think that everybody was having a joke at his expense. His first thought was that Kohn had seen him, and had given orders to the man to say that he was not there. His gorge rose at the impudence of it. He was on the point of going in a huff, when he heard his name: Kohn, with his sharp eyes, had recognized him: and he ran up to him, with a smile on his lips, and his hands held out with every mark of extraordinary delight.

Sylvain Kohn was short, thick-set, clean-shaven, like an American; his complexion was too red, his hair too black; he had a heavy, massive face, coarse-featured; little darting, wrinkled eyes, a rather crooked mouth, a heavy, cunning smile. He was modishly dressed, trying to cover up the defects of his figure, high shoulders, and wide hips. That was the only thing that touched his vanity: he would gladly have put up with any insult if only he could have been a few inches taller and of a better figure. For the rest, he was very well pleased with himself: he thought himself irresistible, as indeed he was. The little German Jew, clod as he was, had made himself the chronicler and arbiter of Parisian fashion and smartness. He wrote insipid society paragraphs and articles in a delicately involved manner. He was the champion of French style, French smartness, French gallantry, French wit—Regency, red heels, Lauzun. People laughed at him: but that did not prevent his success. Those who say that in Paris ridicule kills do not know Paris: so far from dying of it, there are people who live on it: in Paris ridicule leads to everything, even to fame and fortune. Sylvain Kohn was far beyond any need to reckon the good-will that every day accumulated to him through his Frankfortian affectations.

He spoke with a thick accent through his nose.

"Ah! What a surprise!" he cried gaily, taking Christophe's hands in his own clumsy paws, with their stubby fingers that looked as though they were crammed into too tight a skin. He could not let go of Christophe's hands. It was as

though he were encountering his best friend. Christophe was
so staggered that he wondered again if Kohn was not making
fun of him. But Kohn was doing nothing of the kind—or,
rather, if he was joking, it was no more than usual. There was
no rancor about Kohn: he was too clever for that. He had
long ago forgotten the rough treatment he had suffered at
Christophe's hands: and if ever he did remember it, it did
not worry him. He was delighted to have the opportunity of
showing his old schoolfellow his importance and his new duties,
and the elegance of his Parisian manners. He was not lying in
expressing his surprise: a visit from Christophe was the last
thing in the world that he expected: and if he was too worldly-
wise not to know that the visit was of set material purpose,
he took it as a reason the more for welcoming him, as it was,
in fact, a tribute to his power.

"And you have come from Germany? How is your
mother?" he asked, with a familiarity which at any other time
would have annoyed Christophe, but now gave him comfort in
the strange city.

"But how was it," asked Christophe, who was still inclined
to be suspicious, "that they told me just now that Herr Kohn
did not belong here?"

"Herr Kohn doesn't belong here," said Sylvain Kohn, laughing. "My name isn't Kohn now. My name is Hamilton."

He broke off.

"Excuse me," he said.

He went and shook hands with a lady who was passing and
smiled grimacingly. Then he came back. He explained that
the lady was a writer famous for her voluptuous and passionate novels. The modern Sappho had a purple ribbon on
her bosom, a full figure, bright golden hair round a painted
face; she made a few pretentious remarks in a mannish fashion
with the accent of Franche-Comté.

Kohn plied Christophe with questions. He asked about all
the people at home, and what had become of so-and-so, pluming
himself on the fact that he remembered everybody. Christophe

had forgotten his antipathy; he replied cordially and gratefully, giving a mass of detail about which Kohn cared nothing at all, and presently he broke off again.

"Excuse me," he said.

And he went to greet another lady who had come in.

"Dear me!" said Christophe. "Are there only women writers in France?"

Kohn began to laugh, and said fatuously:

"France is a woman, my dear fellow. If you want to succeed, make up to the women."

Christophe did not listen to the explanation, and went on with his own story. To put a stop to it, Kohn asked:

"But how the devil do you come here?"

"Ah!" thought Christophe, "he doesn't know. That is why he was so amiable. He'll be different when he knows."

He made it a point of honor to tell everything against himself: the brawl with the soldiers, the warrant out against him, his flight from the country.

Kohn rocked with laughter.

"Bravo!" he cried. "Bravo! That's a good story!"

He shook Christophe's hand warmly. He was delighted by any smack in the eye of authority: and the story tickled him the more as he knew the heroes of it: he saw the funny side of it.

"I say," he said, "it is past twelve. Will you give me the pleasure . . .? Lunch with me?"

Christophe accepted gratefully. He thought:

"This is a good fellow—decidedly a good fellow. I was mistaken."

They went out together. On the way Christophe put forward his request:

"You see how I am placed. I came here to look for work —music lessons—until I can make my name. Could you speak for me?"

"Certainly," said Kohn. "To any one you like. I know everybody here. I'm at your service."

He was glad to be able to show how important he was.

Christophe covered him with expressions of gratitude. He felt that he was relieved of a great weight of anxiety.

At lunch he gorged with the appetite of a man who has not broken fast for two days. He tucked his napkin round his neck, and ate with his knife. Kohn-Hamilton was horribly shocked by his voracity and his peasant manners. And he was hurt, too, by the small amount of attention that his guest gave to his bragging. He tried to dazzle him by telling of his fine connections and his prosperity: but it was no good: Christophe did not listen, and bluntly interrupted him. His tongue was loosed, and he became familiar. His heart was full, and he overwhelmed Kohn with his simple confidences of his plans for the future. Above all, he exasperated him by insisting on taking his hand across the table and pressing it effusively. And he brought him to the pitch of irritation at last by wanting to clink glasses in the German fashion, and, with sentimental speeches, to drink to those at home and to *Vater Rhein*. Kohn saw, to his horror, that he was on the point of singing. The people at the next table were casting ironic glances in their direction. Kohn made some excuse on the score of pressing business, and got up. Christophe clung to him: he wanted to know when he could have a letter of introduction, and go and see some one, and begin giving lessons.

" I'll see about it. To-day—this evening," said Kohn. " I'll talk about you at once. You can be easy on that score."

Christophe insisted.

" When shall I know? "

" To-morrow . . . to-morrow . . . or the day after."

" Very well. I'll come back to-morrow."

" No, no! " said Kohn quickly. " I'll let you know. Don't you worry."

" Oh! it's no trouble. Quite the contrary. Eh? I've nothing else to do in Paris in the meanwhile."

" Good God! " thought Kohn. . . . " No," he said aloud

" But I would rather write to you. You wouldn't find me the next few days. Give me your address."

Christophe dictated it.

" Good. I'll write you to-morrow."

" To-morrow? "

" To-morrow. You can count on it."

He cut short Christophe's hand-shaking, and escaped.

" Ugh! " he thought. " What a bore! "

As he went into his office he told the boy that he would not be in when " the German " came to see him. Ten minutes later he had forgotten him.

Christophe went back to his lair. He was full of gentle thoughts.

" What a good fellow! What a good fellow! " he thought. " How unjust I was about him. And he bears me no ill-will! "

He was remorseful, and he was on the point of writing to tell Kohn how sorry he was to have misjudged him, and to beg his forgiveness for all the harm he had done him. The tears came to his eyes as he thought of it. But it was harder for him to write a letter than a score of music: and after he had cursed and cursed the pen and ink of the hotel—which were, in fact, horrible—after he had blotted, criss-crossed, and torn up five or six sheets of paper, he lost patience and dropped it.

The rest of the day dragged wearily: but Christophe was so worn out by his sleepless night and his excursions in the morning that at length he dozed off in his chair. He only woke up in the evening, and then he went to bed: and he slept for twelve hours on end.

Next day from eight o'clock on he sat waiting for the promised letter. He had no doubt of Kohn's sincerity. He did not go out, telling himself that perhaps Kohn would come round by the hotel on his way to his office. So as not to be out, about midday he had his lunch sent up from the eating-house downstairs. Then he sat waiting again. He was sure Kohn would come on his way back from lunch. He paced up and down his room, sat down, paced up and down again, opened his door whenever he heard footsteps on the stairs. He had no desire to go walking about Paris to stay his anxiety. He lay down on his bed. His thoughts went back and back to his old mother, who was thinking of him too—she alone thought of him. He had an infinite tenderness for her, and he was remorseful at having left her. But he did not write to her. He was waiting until he could tell her that he had found work. In spite of the love they had for each other, it would never have occurred to either of them to write just to tell their love: letters were for things more definite than that. He lay on the bed with his hands locked behind his head, and dreamed. Although his room was away from the street, the roar of Paris invaded the silence: the house shook. Night came again, and brought no letter.

Came another day like unto the last.

On the third day, exasperated by his voluntary seclusion, Christophe decided to go out. But from the impression of his first evening he was instinctively in revolt against Paris. He had no desire to see anything: no curiosity: he was too much taken up with the problem of his own life to take any pleasure in watching the lives of others: and the memories of lives past, the monuments of a city, had always left him cold. And so, hardly had he set foot out of doors, than, although he had made up his mind not to go near Kohn for a week, he went straight to his office.

The boy obeyed his orders, and said that M. Hamilton had left Paris on business. It was a blow to Christophe. He gasped and asked when M. Hamilton would return. The boy replied at random:

" In ten days."

Christophe went back utterly downcast, and buried himself in his room during the following days. He found it impossible to work. His heart sank as he saw that his small supply of money—the little sum that his mother had sent him, carefully wrapped up in a handkerchief at the bottom of his bag—

was rapidly decreasing. He imposed a severe régime on himself. He only went down in the evening to dinner in the little pot-house, where he quickly became known to the frequenters of it as the " Prussian," or " Sauerkraut." With frightful effort, he wrote two or three letters to French musicians whose names he knew hazily. One of them had been dead for ten years. He asked them to be so kind as to give him a hearing. His spelling was wild, and his style was complicated by those long inversions and ceremonious formulæ which are the custom in Germany. He addressed his letters: " To the Palace of the Academy of France." The only man to read his gave it to his friends as a joke.

After a week Christophe went once more to the publisher's office. This time he was in luck. He met Sylvain Kohn going out, on the doorstep. Kohn made a face as he saw that he was caught: but Christophe was so happy that he did not see that. He took his hands in his usual uncouth way, and asked gaily:

" You've been away? Did you have a good time? "

Kohn said that he had had a very good time, but he did not unbend. Christophe went on:

" I came, you know. . . . They told you, I suppose? . . . Well, any news? You mentioned my name? What did they say? "

Kohn looked blank. Christophe was amazed at his frigid manner: he was not the same man.

" I mentioned you," said Kohn: " but I haven't heard yet. I haven't had time. I have been very busy since I saw you—up to my ears in business. I don't know how I can get through. It is appalling. I shall be ill with it all."

" Aren't you well? " asked Christophe anxiously and solicitously.

Kohn looked at him slyly, and replied:

" Not at all well. I don't know what's the matter, the last few days. I'm very unwell."

" I'm so sorry," said Christophe, taking his arm. " Do be

careful. You must rest. I'm so sorry to have been a bother
to you. You should have told me. What is the matter with
you, really?"

He took Kohn's sham excuses so seriously that the little
Jew was hard put to it to hide his amusement, and disarmed by
his funny simplicity. Irony is so dear a pleasure to the Jews
—(and a number of Christians in Paris are Jewish in this respect)—that they are indulgent with bores, and even with
their enemies, if they give them the opportunity of tasting it
at their expense. Besides, Kohn was touched by Christophe's
interest in himself. He felt inclined to help him.

"I've got an idea," he said. "While you are waiting for
lessons, would you care to do some work for a music publisher?"

Christophe accepted eagerly.

"I've got the very thing," said Kohn. "I know one of the
partners in a big firm of music publishers—Daniel Hecht. I'll
introduce you. You'll see what there is to do. I don't know
anything about it, you know. But Hecht is a real musician.
You'll get on with him all right."

They parted until the following day. Kohn was not sorry
to be rid of Christophe by doing him this service.

Next day Christophe fetched Kohn at his office. On his
advice, he had brought several of his compositions to show
to Hecht. They found him in his music-shop near the Opéra.
Hecht did not put himself out when they went in: he coldly
held out two fingers to take Kohn's hand, did not reply to Christophe's ceremonious bow, and at Kohn's request he took them
into the next room. He did not ask them to sit down. He
stood with his back to the empty chimney-place, and stared at
the wall.

Daniel Hecht was a man of forty, tall, cold, correctly
dressed, a marked Phenician type; he looked clever and disagreeable: there was a scowl on his face: he had black hair
and a beard like that of an Assyrian King, long and square-cut.
He hardly ever looked straight forward, and he had an icy

brutal way of talking which sounded insulting even when he only said "Good-day." His insolence was more apparent than real. No doubt it emanated from a contemptuous strain in his character: but really it was more a part of the automatic and formal element in him. Jews of that sort are quite common: opinion is not kind towards them: that hard stiffness of theirs is looked upon as arrogance, while it is often in reality the outcome of an incurable boorishness in body and soul.

Sylvain Kohn introduced his protégé, in a bantering, pretentious voice, with exaggerated praises. Christophe was abashed by his reception, and stood shifting from one foot to the other, holding his manuscripts and his hat in his hand. When Kohn had finished, Hecht, who up to then had seemed to be unaware of Christophe's existence, turned towards him disdainfully, and, without looking at him, said:

"Krafft . . . Christophe Krafft. . . . Never heard the name."

To Christophe it was as though he had been struck, full in the chest. The blood rushed to his cheeks. He replied angrily:

"You'll hear it later on."

Hecht took no notice, and went on imperturbably, as though Christophe did not exist:

"Krafft . . . no, never heard it."

He was one of those people for whom not to be known to them is a mark against a man.

He went on in German:

"And you come from the *Rhine-land?* . . . It's wonderful how many people there are there who dabble in music! But I don't think there is a man among them who has any claim to be a musician."

He meant it as a joke, not as an insult: but Christophe did not take it so. He would have replied in kind if Kohn had not anticipated him.

"Oh, come, come!" he said to Hecht. "You must do me the justice to admit that I know nothing at all about it."

"That's to your credit," replied Hecht.

"If I am to be no musician in order to please you," said Christophe dryly, "I am sorry, but I'm not that."

Hecht, still looking aside, went on, as indifferently as ever.

"You have written music? What have you written? *Lieder,* I suppose?"

"*Lieder,* two symphonies, symphonic poems, quartets, piano suites, theater music," said Christophe, boiling.

"People write a great deal in Germany," said Hecht, with scornful politeness.

It made him all the more suspicious of the newcomer to think that he had written so many works, and that he, Daniel Hecht, had not heard of them.

"Well," he said, "I might perhaps find work for you as you are recommended by my friend Hamilton. At present we are making a collection, a 'Library for Young People,' in which we are publishing some easy pianoforte pieces. Could you 'simplify' the *Carnival* of Schumann, and arrange it for six and eight hands?"

Christophe was staggered.

"And you offer that to me, to me—me . . . ?"

His naïve "Me" delighted Kohn: but Hecht was offended.

"I don't see that there is anything surprising in that," he said. "It is not such easy work as all that! If you think it too easy, so much the better. We'll see about that later on. You tell me you are a good musician. I must believe you. But I've never heard of you."

He thought to himself:

"If one were to believe all these young sparks, they would knock the stuffing out of Johannes Brahms himself."

Christophe made no reply—(for he had vowed to hold himself in check)—clapped his hat on his head, and turned towards the door. Kohn stopped him, laughing:

"Wait, wait!" he said. And he turned to Hecht: "He has brought some of his work to give you an idea."

"Ah!" said Hecht warily. "Very well, then: let us see them."

Without a word Christophe held out his manuscripts. Hecht cast his eyes over them carelessly.

"What's this? *A suite for piano* . . . (reading): *A Day.* . . . Ah! Always program music! . . ."

In spite of his apparent indifference he was reading carefully. He was an excellent musician, and knew his job: he knew nothing outside it: with the first bar or two he gauged his man. He was silent as he turned over the pages with a scornful air: he was struck by the talent revealed in them: but his natural reserve and his vanity, piqued by Christophe's manner, kept him from showing anything. He went on to the end in silence, not missing a note.

"Yes," he said, in a patronizing tone of voice, "they're well enough."

Violent criticism would have hurt Christophe less.

"I don't need to be told that," he said irritably.

"I fancy," said Hecht, "that you showed me them for me to say what I thought."

"Not at all."

"Then," said Hecht coldly, "I fail to see what you have come for."

"I came to ask for work, and nothing else."

"I have nothing to offer you for the time being, except what I told you. And I'm not sure of that. I said it was possible, that's all."

"And you have no other work to offer a musician like myself?"

"A musician like you?" said Hecht ironically and cuttingly. "Other musicians at least as good as yourself have not thought the work beneath their dignity. There are men whose names I could give you, men who are now very well known in Paris, have been very grateful to me for it."

"Then they must have been—swine!" bellowed Christophe. —(He had already learned certain of the most useful words in the French language)—"You are wrong if you think you have to do with a man of that kidney. Do you think you can take

me in with looking anywhere but at me, and clipping your
words? You didn't even deign to acknowledge my bow when
I came in. . . . But what the hell are you to treat me like
that? Are you even a musician? Have you ever written anything? . . . And you pretend to teach me how to write—
me, to whom writing is life! . . . And you can find nothing
better to offer me, when you have read my music, than a
hashing up of great musicians, a filthy scrabbling over their
works to turn them into parlor tricks for little girls! . . .
You go to your Parisians who are rotten enough to be taught
their work by you! I'd rather die first!"

It was impossible to stem the torrent of his words.

Hecht said icily:

"Take it or leave it."

Christophe went out and slammed the doors. Hecht
shrugged, and said to Sylvain Kohn, who was laughing:

"He will come to it like the rest."

At heart he valued Christophe. He was clever enough to
feel not only the worth of a piece of work, but also the worth
of a man. Behind Christophe's outburst he had marked a
force. And he knew its rarity—in the world of art more than
anywhere else. But his vanity was ruffled by it: nothing would
ever induce him to admit himself in the wrong. He desired
loyally to be just to Christophe, but he could not do it unless
Christophe came and groveled to him. He expected Christophe to return: his melancholy skepticism and his experience
of men had told him how inevitably the will is weakened and
worn down by poverty.

Christophe went home. Anger had given place to despair.
He felt that he was lost. The frail prop on which he had
counted had failed him. He had no doubt but that he had
made a deadly enemy, not only of Hecht, but of Kohn, who had
introduced him. He was in absolute solitude in a hostile city.
Outside Diener and Kohn he knew no one. His friend Corinne,
the beautiful actress whom he had met in Germany, was not

in Paris: she was still touring abroad, in America, this time on her own account: the papers published clamatory descriptions of her travels. As for the little French governess whom he had unwittingly robbed of her situation,—the thought of her had long filled him with remorse—how often had he vowed that he would find her when he reached Paris.[1] But now that he was in Paris he found that he had forgotten one important thing: her name. He could not remember it. He could only recollect her Christian name: Antoinette. And then, even if he remembered, how was he to find a poor little governess in that ant-heap of human beings?

He had to set to work as soon as possible to find a livelihood. He had five francs left. In spite of his dislike of him, he forced himself to ask the innkeeper if he did not know of anybody in the neighborhood to whom he could give music-lessons. The innkeeper, who had no great opinion of a lodger who only ate once a day and spoke German, lost what respect he had for him when he heard that he was only a musician. He was a Frenchman of the old school, and music was to him an idler's job. He scoffed:

"The piano! . . . I don't know. You strum the piano! Congratulations! . . . But 'tis a queer thing to take to that trade as a matter of taste! When I hear music, it's just for all the world like listening to the rain. . . . But perhaps you might teach me. What do you say, you fellows?" he cried, turning to some fellows who were drinking.

They laughed loudly.

"It's a fine trade," said one of them. "Not dirty work. And the ladies like it."

Christophe did not rightly understand the French or the jest: he floundered for his words: he did not know whether to be angry or not. The innkeeper's wife took pity on him:

"Come, come, Philippe, you're not serious," she said to her husband. "All the same," she went on, turning to Christophe, "there is some one who might do for you."

[1] See *Jean-Christophe*—I: "Revolt."

" Who ? " asked her husband.

" The Grasset girl. You know, they've bought a piano."

" Ah! Those stuck-up folk! So they have."

They told Christophe that the girl in question was the daughter of a butcher: her parents were trying to make a lady of her; they would perhaps like her to have lessons, if only for the sake of making people talk. The innkeeper's **wife** promised to see to it.

Next day she told Christophe that the butcher's wife would like to see him. He went to her house, and found her in the shop, surrounded with great pieces of meat. She was a pretty, rather florid woman, and she smiled sweetly, but stood on her dignity when she heard why he had come. Quite abruptly she came to the question of payment, and said quickly that she did not wish to give much, because the piano is quite an agreeable thing, but not necessary: she offered him fifty centimes an hour. In any case, she would not pay more than four francs a week. After that she asked Christophe a little doubtfully if he knew much about music. She was reassured, and became more amiable when he told her that not only did he know about music, but wrote it into the bargain: that flattered her vanity: it would be a good thing to spread about the neighborhood that her daughter was taking lessons with a composer.

Next day, when Christophe found himself sitting by the piano—a horrible instrument, bought second-hand, which sounded like a guitar—with the butcher's little daughter, whose short, stubby fingers fumbled with the keys; who was unable to tell one note from another; who was bored to tears; who began at once to yawn in his face; and he had to submit to the mother's superintendence, and to her conversation, and to her ideas on music and the teaching of music—then he felt so miserable, so wretchedly humiliated, that he had not even the strength to be angry about it. He relapsed into a state of despair: there were evenings when he could not eat. If in a few weeks he had fallen so low, where would he end? What

good was it to have rebelled against Hecht's offer? The thing
to which he had submitted was even more degrading.

One evening, as he sat in his room, he could not restrain his
tears: he flung himself on his knees by his bed and prayed.
. . . To whom did he pray? To whom could he pray? He
did not believe in God; he believed that there was no God. . . .
But he had to pray—he had to pray within his soul. Only the
mean of spirit never need to pray. They never know the need
that comes to the strong in spirit of taking refuge within the
inner sanctuary of themselves. As he left behind him the
humiliations of the day, in the vivid silence of his heart Christophe felt the presence of his eternal Being, of his God. The
waters of his wretched life stirred and shifted above Him and
never touched Him: what was there in common between that
and Him? All the sorrows of the world rushing on to destruction dashed against that rock. Christophe heard the blood beating in his veins, beating like an inward voice, crying:

"Eternal . . . I am . . . I am. . . ."

Well did he know that voice: as long as he could remember
he had heard it. Sometimes he forgot it: often for months together he would lose consciousness of its mighty monotonous
rhythm: but he knew that it was there, that it never ceased, like
the ocean roaring in the night. In the music of it he found
once more the same energy that he gained from it whenever
he bathed in its waters. He rose to his feet. He was fortified.
No: the hard life that he led contained nothing of which he
need be ashamed: he could eat the bread he earned, and never
blush for it: it was for those who made him earn it at such a
price to blush and be ashamed. Patience! Patience! The
time would come. . . .

But next day he began to lose patience again: and, in spite
of all his efforts, he did at last explode angrily, one day during
a lesson, at the silly little ninny, who had been maddeningly impertinent and laughed at his accent, and had taken a malicious
delight in doing exactly the opposite of what he told her.
The girl screamed in response to Christophe's angry shouts.

She was frightened and enraged at a man whom she paid daring to show her no respect. She declared that he had struck her—(Christophe had shaken her arm rather roughly). Her mother bounced in on them like a Fury, and covered her daughter with kisses and Christophe with abuse. The butcher also appeared, and declared that he would not suffer any infernal Prussian to take upon himself to touch his daughter. Furious, pale with rage, itching to choke the life out of the butcher and his wife and daughter, Christophe rushed away. His host and hostess, seeing him come in in an abject condition, had no difficulty in worming the story out of him: and it fed the malevolence with which they regarded their neighbors. But by the evening the whole neighborhood was saying that the German was a brute and a child-beater.

Christophe made fresh advances to the music-vendors: but in vain. He found the French lacking in cordiality: and the whirl and confusion of their perpetual agitation crushed him. They seemed to him to live in a state of anarchy, directed by a cunning and despotic bureaucracy.

One evening, he was wandering along the boulevards, discouraged by the futility of his efforts, when he saw Sylvain Kohn coming from the opposite direction. He was convinced that they had quarreled irrevocably and looked away and tried to pass unnoticed. But Kohn called to him:

"What became of you after that great day?" he asked with a laugh. "I've been wanting to look you up, but I lost your address. . . . Good Lord, my dear fellow, I didn't know you! You were epic: that's what you were, epic!"

Christophe stared at him. He was surprised and a little ashamed.

"You're not angry with me?"

"Angry? What an idea!"

So far from being angry, he had been delighted with the way in which Christophe had trounced Hecht: it had been a treat to him. It really mattered nothing to him whether Christophe or Hecht was right: he only regarded people as source of entertainment: and he saw in Christophe a spring of high comedy, which he intended to exploit to the full.

"You should have come to see me," he went on. "I was expecting you. What are you doing this evening? Come to dinner. I won't let you off. Quite informal: just a few artists: we meet once a fortnight. You should know these people. Come. I'll introduce you."

In vain did Christophe beg to be excused on the score of his clothes. Sylvain Kohn carried him off.

They entered a restaurant on one of the boulevards, and went up to the second floor. Christophe found himself among about thirty young men, whose ages ranged from twenty to thirty-five, and they were all engaged in animated discussion. Kohn introduced him as a man who had just escaped from a German prison. They paid no attention to him and did not stop their passionate discussion, and Kohn plunged into it at once.

Christophe was shy in this select company, and said nothing: but he was all ears. He could not grasp—he had great difficulty in following the volubility of the French—what great artistic interests were in dispute. He listened attentively, but he could only make out words like "trust," "monopoly," "fall in prices," "receipts," mixed up with phrases like "the dignity of art," and the "rights of the author." And at last he saw that they were talking business. A certain number of authors, it appeared, belonged to a syndicate and were angry about certain attempts which had been made to float a rival concern, which, according to them, would dispute their monopoly of exploitation. The defection of certain of their members who had found it to their advantage to go over bag and baggage to the rival house had roused them to the wildest fury. They talked of decapitation. ". . . Burked. . . . Treachery. . . . Shame. . . . Sold. . . ."

Others did not worry about the living: they were incensed against the dead, whose sales without royalties choked up the

market. It appeared that the works of De Musset had just
become public property, and were selling far too well. And
so they demanded that the State should give them rigorous
protection, and heavily tax the masterpieces of the past so as
to check their circulation at reduced prices, which, they declared, was unfair competition with the work of living artists.

They stopped each other to hear the takings of such and
such a theater on the preceding evening. They all went into
ecstasies over the fortune of a veteran dramatist, famous in
two continents—a man whom they despised, though they en-
vied him even more. From the incomes of authors they passed
to those of the critics. They talked of the sum—(pure cal-
umny, no doubt)—received by one of their colleagues for every
first performance at one of the theaters on the boulevards, the
consideration being that he should speak well of it. He was
an honest man: having made his bargain he stuck to it: but his
great secret lay—(so they said)—in so eulogizing the piece that
it would be taken off as quickly as possible so that there might be
many new plays. The tale—(or the account)—caused laughter,
but nobody was surprised.

And mingled with all that talk they threw out fine phrases:
they talked of "poetry" and "art for art's sake." But through
it all there rang "art for money's sake"; and this jobbing
spirit, newly come into French literature, scandalized Christophe. As he understood nothing at all about their talk of
money he had given it up. But then they began to talk of letters, or rather of men of letters.—Christophe pricked up his
ears as he heard the name of Victor Hugo.

They were debating whether he had been cuckolded: they
argued at length about the love of Sainte-Beuve and Madame
Hugo. And then they turned to the lovers of George Sand
and their respective merits. That was the chief occupation of
criticism just then: when they had ransacked the houses of
great men, rummaged through the closets, turned out the
drawers, ransacked the cupboards, they burrowed down to their
inmost lives. The attitude of Monsieur de Lauzun lying flat

under the bed of the King and Madame de Montespan was the attitude of criticism in its cult of history and truth— (everybody just then, of course, made a cult of truth). These young men were subscribers to the cult: no detail was too small for them in their search for truth. They applied it to the art of the present as well as to that of the past: and they analyzed the private life of certain of the more notorious of their contemporaries with the same passion for exactness. It was a queer thing that they were possessed of the smallest details of scenes which are usually enacted without witnesses. It was really as though the persons concerned had been the first to give exact information to the public out of their great devotion to the truth.

Christophe was more and more embarrassed and tried to talk to his neighbors of something else; but nobody listened to him. At first they asked him a few vague questions about Germany— questions which, to his amazement, displayed the almost complete ignorance of these distinguished and apparently cultured young men concerning the most elementary things of their work —literature and art—outside Paris; at most they had heard of a few great names: Hauptmann, Sudermann, Liebermann, Strauss (David, Johann, Richard), and they picked their way gingerly among them for fear of getting mixed. If they had questioned Christophe it was from politeness rather than from curiosity: they had no curiosity: they hardly seemed to notice his replies: and they hurried back at once to the Parisian topics which were regaling the rest of the company.

Christophe timidly tried to talk of music. Not one of these men of letters was a musician. At heart they considered music an inferior art. But the growing success of music during the last few years had made them secretly uneasy: and since it was the fashion they pretended to be interested in it. They frothed especially about a new opera and declared that music dated from its performance, or at least the new era in music. This idea made things easy for their ignorance and snobbishness, for it relieved them of the necessity of knowing anything else.

The author of the opera, a Parisian, whose name Christophe heard for the first time, had, said some, made a clean sweep of all that had gone before him, cleaned up, renovated, and recreated music. Christophe started at that. He asked nothing better than to believe in genius. But such a genius as that, a genius who had at one swoop wiped out the past. . . . Good heavens! He must be a lusty lad: how the devil had he done it? He asked for particulars. The others, who would have been hard put to it to give any explanation and were disconcerted by Christophe, referred him to the musician of the company, Théophile Goujart, the great musical critic, who began at once to talk of sevenths and ninths. Goujart knew music much as Sganarelle knew Latin. . . .

". . . *You don't know Latin?*"

"*No.*"

(*With enthusiasm*) "*Cabricias, arci thuram, catalamus, singulariter . . . bonus, bona, bonum.*"

Finding himself with a man who "understood Latin" he prudently took refuge in the chatter of esthetics. From that impregnable fortress he began to bombard Beethoven, Wagner, and classical art, which was not before the house (but in France it is impossible to praise an artist without making as an offering a holocaust of all those who are unlike him). He announced the advent of a new art which trampled under foot the conventions of the past. He spoke of a new musical language which had been discovered by the Christopher Columbus of Parisian music, and he said it made an end of the language of the classics: that was a dead language.

Christophe reserved his opinion of this reforming genius to wait until he had seen his work before he said anything: but in spite of himself he felt an instinctive distrust of this musical Baal to whom all music was sacrificed. He was scandalized to hear the Masters so spoken of: and he forgot that he had said much the same sort of thing in Germany. He who at home had thought himself a revolutionary in art, he who had scandalized others by the boldness of his judgments and the

frankness of his expressions, felt, as soon as he heard these
words spoken in France, that he was at heart a conservative.
He tried to argue, and was tactless enough to speak, not like a
man of culture, who advances arguments without exposition,
but as a professional, bringing out disconcerting facts. He
did not hesitate to plunge into technical explanations: and his
voice, as he talked, struck a note which was well calculated
to offend the ears of a company of superior persons to whom
his arguments and the vigor with which he supported them
were alike ridiculous. The critic tried to demolish him with
an attempt at wit, and to end the discussion which had shown
Christophe to his stupefaction that he had to deal with a man
who did not in the least know what he was talking about. And
so they came to the opinion that the German was pedantic and
superannuated: and without knowing anything about it they
decided that his music was detestable. But Christophe's bizarre
personality had made an impression on the company of young
men, and with their quickness in seizing on the ridiculous they
had marked the awkward, violent gestures of his thin arms
with their enormous hands, and the furious glances that darted
from his eyes as his voice rose to a falsetto. Sylvain Kohn saw
to it that his friends were kept amused.

Conversation had deserted literature in favor of women. As
a matter of fact they were only two aspects of the same subject:
for their literature was concerned with nothing but women,
and their women were concerned with nothing but literature,
they were so much taken up with the affairs and men of letters.

They spoke of one good lady, well known in Parisian society,
who had, it was said, just married her lover to her daughter,
the better to keep him. Christophe squirmed in his chair, and
tactlessly made a face of disgust. Kohn saw it, and nudged his
neighbor and pointed out that the subject seemed to excite
the German—that no doubt he was longing to know the lady.
Christophe blushed, muttered angrily, and finally said hotly
that such women ought to be whipped. His proposition was
received with a shout of Homeric laughter: and Sylvain Kohn

cooingly protested that no man should touch a woman, even
with a flower, etc., etc. (In Paris he was the very Knight of
Love.) Christophe replied that a woman of that sort was
neither more nor less than a bitch, and that there was only one
remedy for vicious dogs: the whip. They roared at him.
Christophe said that their gallantry was hypocritical, and that
those who talked most of their respect for women were those
who possessed the least of it: and he protested against these
scandalous tales. They replied that there was no scandal in
it, and that it was only natural: and they were all agreed
that the heroine of the story was not only a charming woman,
but *the* Woman, *par excellence.* The German waxed indignant.
Sylvain Kohn asked him slyly what he thought Woman was
like. Christophe felt that they were pulling his leg and laying
a trap for him: but he fell straight into it in the violent expression of his convictions. He began to explain his ideas on
love to these bantering Parisians. He could not find his words,
floundered about after them, and finally fished up from the
phrases he remembered such impossible words, such enormities,
that he had all his hearers rocking with laughter, while all the
time he was perfectly and admirably serious, never bothered
about them, and was touchingly impervious to their ridicule: for
he could not help seeing that they were making fun of him.
At last he tied himself up in a sentence, could not extricate
himself, brought his fist down on the table, and was silent.

They tried to bring him back into the discussion: he scowled
and did not flinch, but sat with his elbows on the table,
ashamed and irritated. He did not open his lips again, except to eat and drink, until the dinner was over. He drank
enormously, unlike the Frenchmen, who only sipped their wine.
His neighbor wickedly encouraged him, and went on filling his
glass, which he emptied absently. But, although he was not
used to these excesses, especially after the weeks of privation
through which he had passed, he took his liquor well, and did
not cut so ridiculous a figure as the others hoped. He sat there
lost in thought: they paid no attention to him: they thought he

was made drowsy by the wine. He was exhausted by the effort of following the conversation in French, and tired of hearing about nothing but literature—actors, authors, publishers,
the chatter of the *coulisses* and literary life : everything seemed
to be reduced to that. Amid all these new faces and the buzz
of words he could not fix a single face, nor a single thought.
His short-sighted eyes, dim and dreamy, wandered slowly round
the table, and they rested on one man after another without
seeming to see them. And yet he saw them better than any one,
though he himself was not conscious of it. He did not, like
these Jews and Frenchmen, peck at the things he saw and dis-
sect them, tear them to rags, and leave them in tiny, tiny pieces.
Slowly, like a sponge, he sucked up the essence of men and
women, and bore away their image in his soul. He seemed
to have seen nothing and to remember nothing. It was only
long afterwards—hours, often days—when he was alone, gazing
in upon himself, that he saw that he had borne away a whole
impression.

But for the moment he seemed to be just a German boor,
stuffing himself with food, concerned only with not missing a
mouthful. And he heard nothing clearly, except when he
heard the others calling each other by name, and then, with a
silly drunken insistency, he wondered why so many Frenchmen have foreign names: Flemish, German, Jewish, Levantine,
Anglo- or Spanish-American.

He did not notice when they got up from the table. He
went on sitting alone: and he dreamed of the Rhenish hills,
the great woods, the tilled fields, the meadows by the waterside, his old mother. Most of the others had gone. At last
he thought of going, and got up, too, without looking at anybody, and went and took down his hat and cloak, which were
hanging by the door. When he had put them on he was turning away without saying good-night, when through a half-open
door he saw an object which fascinated him: a piano. He had
not touched a musical instrument for weeks. He went in and
lovingly touched the keys, sat down just as he was, with his

hat on his head and his cloak on his shoulders, and began to play. He had altogether forgotten where he was. He did not notice that two men crept into the room to listen to him. One was Sylvain Kohn, a passionate lover of music—God knows why! for he knew nothing at all about it, and he liked bad music just as well as good. The other was the musical critic, Théophile Goujart. He—it simplifies matters so much—neither understood nor loved music: but that did not keep him from talking about it. On the contrary: nobody is so free in mind as the man who knows nothing of what he is talking about: for to such a man it does not matter whether he says one thing more than another.

Théophile Goujart was tall, strong, and muscular: he had a black beard, thick curls on his forehead, which was lined with deep inexpressive wrinkles, short arms, short legs, a big chest: a type of woodman or porter of the Auvergne. He had common manners and an arrogant way of speaking. He had gone into music through politics, at that time the only road to success in France. He had attached himself to the fortunes of a Minister to whom he had discovered that he was distantly related—a son "of the bastard of his apothecary." Ministers are not eternal, and when it seemed that the day of his Minister was over Théophile Goujart deserted the ship, taking with him all that he could lay his hands on, notably several orders: for he loved glory. Tired of politics, in which for some time past he had received various snubs, both on his own account and on that of his patron, he looked out for a shelter from the storm, a restful position in which he could annoy others without being himself annoyed. Everything pointed to criticism. Just at that moment there fell vacant the post of musical critic to one of the great Parisian papers. The previous holder of the post, a young and talented composer, had been dismissed because he insisted on saying what he thought of the authors and their work. Goujart had never taken any interest in music, and knew nothing at all about it: he was chosen without a moment's hesitation. They had had enough of competent critics: with

Goujart there was at least nothing to fear: he did not attach
an absurd importance to his opinions: he was always at the
editor's orders, and ready to comply with a slashing article or
enthusiastic approbation. That he was no musician was a
secondary consideration. Everybody in France knows a little
about music. Goujart quickly acquired the requisite knowledge. His method was quite simple: it consisted in sitting at
every concert next to some good musician, a composer if possible, and getting him to say what he thought of the works
performed. At the end of a few months of this apprenticeship,
he knew his job: the fledgling could fly. He did not, it is true,
soar like an eagle: and God knows what howlers Goujart committed with the greatest show of authority in his paper! He
listened and read haphazard, stirred the mixture up well in his
sluggish brains, and arrogantly laid down the law for others;
he wrote in a pretentious style, interlarded with puns, and
plastered over with an aggressive pedantry: he had the mind of
a schoolmaster. Sometimes, every now and then, he drew
down on himself cruel replies: then he shammed dead, and
took good care not to answer them. He was a mixture of cunning and thick-headedness, insolent or groveling as circumstances demanded. He cringed to the masters who had an official position or an established fame (he had no other means
of judging merit in music). He scorned everybody else, and
exploited writers who were starving. He was no fool.

In spite of his reputation and the authority he had acquired, he knew in his heart of hearts that he knew nothing
about music: and he recognized that Christophe knew a great
deal about it. Nothing would have induced him to say so:
but it was borne in upon him. And now he heard Christophe
play: and he made great efforts to understand him, looking absorbed, profound, without a thought in his head: he could
not see a yard ahead of him through the fog of sound, and he
wagged his head solemnly as one who knew and adjusted th
outward and visible signs of his approval to the flutter
the eyelids of Sylvain Kohn, who found it hard to stan

At last Christophe, emerging to consciousness from the fumes of wine and music, became dimly aware of the pantomime going on behind his back: he turned and saw the two amateurs of music. They rushed at him and violently shook hands with him Sylvain Kohn gurgling that he had played like a god, Goujart declaring solemnly that he had the left hand of Rubinstein and the right hand of Paderewski (or it might be the other way round). Both agreed that such talent ought not to be hid under a bushel, and they pledged themselves to reveal it. And, incidentally, they were both resolved to extract from it as much honor and profit as possible.

From that day on Sylvain Kohn took to inviting Christophe to his rooms, and put at his disposal his excellent piano, which he never used himself. Christophe, who was bursting with suppressed music, did not need to be urged, and accepted: and for a time he made good use of the invitation.

At first all went well. Christophe was only too happy to play: and Sylvain Kohn was tactful enough to leave him to play in peace. He enjoyed it thoroughly himself. By one of those queer phenomena which must be in everybody's observation, the man, who was no musician, no artist, cold-hearted and devoid of all poetic feeling and real kindness, was enslaved sensually by Christophe's music, which he did not understand, though he found in it a strongly voluptuous pleasure. Unfortunately, he could not hold his tongue. He had to talk, loudly, while Christophe was playing. He had to underline the music with affected exclamations, like a concert snob, or else he passed ridiculous comment on it. Then Christophe would thump the piano, and declare that he could not go on like that. Kohn would try hard to be silent: but he could not do it: at once he would begin again to sniffle, sigh, whistle, beat time, hum, imitate the various instruments. And when the piece was ended he would have burst if he had not given Christophe the nefit of his inept comment.

was a queer mixture of German sentimentality, Parisian ·· and intolerable fatuousness. Sometimes he expressed second-hand precious opinions; sometimes he made extravagant comparisons; and then he would make dirty, obscene remarks, or propound some insane nonsense. By way of praising Beethoven, he would point out some trickery, or read a lasciv-ious sensuality into his music. The *Quartet in C Minor* seemed to him jolly spicy. The sublime *Adagio of the Ninth Symphony* made him think of Cherubino. After the three crashing chords at the opening of the *Symphony in C Minor*, he called out: "Don't come in! I've some one here." He ad-mired the Battle of *Heldenleben* because he pretended that it was like the noise of a motor-car. And always he had some image to explain each piece, a puerile incongruous image. Really, it seemed impossible that he could have any love for music. However, there was no doubt about it: he really did love it: at certain passages to which he attached the most ridiculous meanings the tears would come into his eyes. But after having been moved by a scene from Wagner, he would strum out a gallop of Offenbach, or sing some music-hall ditty after the *Ode to Joy*. Then Christophe would bob about and roar with rage. But the worst of all to bear was not when Sylvain Kohn was absurd so much as when he was trying to be profound and subtle, when he was trying to impress Chris-tophe, when it was Hamilton speaking, and not Sylvain Kohn. Then Christophe would scowl blackly at him, and squash him with cold contempt, which hurt Hamilton's vanity: very often these musical evenings would end in a quarrel. But Kohn would forget it next day, and Christophe, sorry for his rude-ness, would make a point of going back.

That would not have mattered much if Kohn had been able to refrain from inviting his friends to hear Christophe. But he could not help wanting to show off his musician. The first time Christophe found in Kohn's rooms three or four little Jews and Kohn's mistress—a large florid woman, all paint and powder, who repeated idiotic jokes and talked about her food, and thought herself a musician because she showed her legs every evening in the Revue of the Variétés—Christophe looked black. Next time he told Sylvain Kohn curtly that he would never again play in his rooms. Sylvain Kohn swore by all his gods that he would not invite anybody again. But he did so by stealth, and hid his guests in the next room. Naturally, Christophe found that out, and went away in a fury, and this time did not return.

And yet he had to accommodate Kohn, who had introduced him to various cosmopolitan families, and found him pupils.

A few days after Théophile Goujart hunted Christophe up in his lair. He did not seem to mind his being in such a horrible place. On the contrary, he was charming. He said :

"I thought perhaps you would like to hear a little music from time to time: and as I have tickets for everything. I came to ask if you would care to come with me."

Christophe was delighted. He was glad of the kindly attention, and thanked him effusively. Goujart was a different man from what he had been at their first meeting. He had dropped his conceit, and, man to man, he was timid, docile, anxious to learn. It was only when they were with others that he resumed his superior manner and his blatant tone of voice. His eagerness to learn had a practical side to it. He had no curiosity about anything that was not actual. He wanted to know what Christophe thought of a score he had received which he would have been hard put to it to write about, for he could hardly read a note.

They went to a symphony concert. They had to go in by the entrance to a music-hall. They went down a winding passage to an ill-ventilated hall: the air was stifling: the seats were very narrow, and placed too close together: part of the audience was standing and blocking up every way out:—the uncomfortable French. A man who looked as though he were hopelessly bored was racing through a Beethoven symphony as though he were in a hurry to get to the end of it. The voluptuous strains of a stomach-dance coming from the music-hall next door were mingled with the funeral march of the *Eroica*. People kept coming in and taking their seats, and turning their glasses on the audience. As soon as the last person had arrived, they began to go out again. Christophe strained every nerve to try and follow the thread of the symphony through the babel: and he did manage to wrest some pleasure from it— (for the orchestra was skilful, and Christophe had been deprived of symphony music for a long time)—and then Goujart took his arm and, in the middle of the concert, said:

" Now let us go. We'll go to another concert."

Christophe frowned: but he made no reply and followed his guide. They went half across Paris, and then reached another hall, that smelled of stables, in which at other times fairy plays and popular pieces were given—(in Paris music is like those poor workingmen who share a lodging: when one of them leaves the bed, the other creeps into the warm sheets). No air, of course: since the reign of Louis XIV the French have considered air unhealthy: and the ventilation of the theaters, like that of old at Versailles, makes it impossible for people to breathe. A noble old man, waving his arms like a lion-tamer, was letting loose an act of Wagner: the wretched beast —the act—was like the lions of a menagerie, dazzled and cowed by the footlights, so that they have to be whipped to be reminded that they are lions. The audience consisted of female Pharisees and foolish women, smiling inanely. After the lion had gone through its performance, and the tamer had bowed, and they had both been rewarded by the applause of the audience, Goujart suggested that they should go to yet another concert. But this time Christophe gripped the arms of his stall, and declared that he would not budge: he had had enough of running from concert to concert, picking up the crumbs of a symphony and scraps of a concert on the way. In vain did Goujart try to explain to him that musical criticism in Paris was a trade in which it was more important to see than to hear. Christophe protested that music was not written to be heard in a cab, and needed more concentration. Such a hotch-potch of concerts was sickening to him: one at a time was enough for him.

He was much surprised at the extraordinary number of concerts in Paris. Like most Germans, he thought that music held a subordinate place in France: and he expected that it would be served up in small delicate portions. By way of a beginning, he was given fifteen concerts in seven days. There was one for every evening in the week, and often two or three an evening at the same time in different quarters of the city. On Sundays there were four, all at the same time. Christophe marveled at this appetite for music. And he was no less amazed at the length of the programs. Till then he had thought that his fellow-countrymen had a monopoly of these orgies of sound which had more than once disgusted him in Germany. He saw now that the Parisians could have given them points in the matter of gluttony. They were given full measure: two symphonies, a concerto, one or two overtures, an act from an opera. And they came from all sources: German, Russian, Scandinavian, French—beer, champagne, orgeat, wine —they gulped down everything without winking. Christophe was amazed that these indolent Parisians should have had such capacious stomachs. They did not suffer for it at all. It was the cask of the Danaïdes. It held nothing.

It was not long before Christophe perceived that this mass of music amounted to very little really. He saw the same faces and heard the same pieces at every concert. Their copious programs moved in a circle. Practically nothing earlier than Beethoven. Practically nothing later than Wagner. And what gaps between them! It seemed as though music were reduced to five or six great German names, three or four French names, and, since the Franco-Russian alliance, half a dozen Muscovites. None of the old French Masters. None of the great Italians. None of the German giants of the seventeenth and eighteenth centuries. No contemporary German music, with the single exception of Richard Strauss, who was more acute than the rest, and came once a year to plant his new

works on the Parisian public. No Belgian music. No Tschek
music. But, most surprising of all, practically no contemporary French music. And yet everybody was talking about
it mysteriously as a thing that would revolutionize the world.
Christophe was yearning for an opportunity of hearing it: he
was very curious about it, and absolutely without prejudice: he
was longing to hear new music, and to admire the works of
genius. But he never succeeded in hearing any of it: for he
did not count a few short pieces, quite cleverly written, but cold
and brain-spun, to which he had not listened very attentively.

While he was waiting to form an opinion, Christophe tried
to find out something about it from musical criticism.

That was not easy. It was like the Court of King Pétaud.
Not only did the various papers lightly contradict each other:
but they contradicted themselves in different articles—almost on
different pages. To read them all was enough to drive a man
crazy. Fortunately, the critics only read their own articles, and
the public did not read any of them. But Christophe, who
wanted to gain a clear idea about French musicians, labored
hard to omit nothing: and he marveled at the agility of the
critics, who darted about in a sea of contradictions like fish in
water.

But amid all these divergent opinions one thing struck him:
the pedantic manner of most of the critics. Who was it said
that the French were amiable fantastics who believed in nothing?
Those whom Christophe saw were more hag-ridden by the
science of music—even when they knew nothing—than all the
critics on the other side of the Rhine.

At that time the French musical critics had set about learning what music was. There were even a few who knew something about it: they were men of original thought, who had
taken the trouble to think about their art, and to think for
themselves. Naturally, they were not very well known: they
were shelved in their little reviews: with only one or two exceptions. the newspapers were not for them. They were honest

men—intelligent, interesting, sometimes driven by their isolation to paradox and the habit of thinking aloud, intolerance, and garrulity. The rest had hastily learned the rudiments of harmony: and they stood gaping in wonder at their newly acquired knowledge. Like Monsieur Jourdain when he learned the rules of grammar, they marvelled at their knowledge:

"*D, a, Da; F, a, Fa; R, a, Ra. . . . Ah! How fine it is! . . . Ah! How splendid it is to know something! . . .*"

They only babbled of theme and counter-theme, of harmonies and resultant sounds, of consecutive ninths and tierce major. When they had labeled the succeeding harmonies which made up a page of music, they proudly mopped their brows: they thought they had explained the music, and almost believed that they had written it. As a matter of fact, they had only repeated it in school language, like a boy making a grammatical analysis of a page of Cicero. But it was so difficult for the best of them to conceive music as a natural language of the soul that, when they did not make it an adjunct to painting, they dragged it into the outskirts of science, and reduced it to the level of a problem in harmonic construction. Some who were learned enough took upon themselves to show a thing or two to past musicians. They found fault with Beethoven, and rapped Wagner over the knuckles. They laughed openly at Berlioz and Gluck. Nothing existed for them just then but Johann Sebastian Bach, and Claude Debussy. And Bach, who had lately been roundly abused, was beginning to seem pedantic, a periwig, and in fine, a hack. Quite distinguished men extolled Rameau in mysterious terms—Rameau and Couperin, called the Great.

There were tremendous conflicts waged between these learned men. They were all musicians: but as they all affected different styles, each of them claimed that his was the only true style, and cried "Raca!" to that of their colleagues. They accused each other of sham writing and sham culture, and hurled at each other's heads the words "idealism" and "materialism," "symbolism" and "verism," "subjectivism" and "objectivism." Christophe thought it was hardly worth while leaving Germany to find the squabbles of the Germans in Paris. Instead of being grateful for having good music presented in so many different fashions, they would only tolerate their own particular fashion: and a new *Lutrin,* a fierce war, divided musicians into two hostile camps, the camp of counterpoint and the camp of harmony. Like the *Gros-boutiens* and the *Petits-boutiens,* one side maintained with acrimony that music should be read horizontally, and the other that it should be read vertically. One party would only hear of full-sounding chords, melting concatenations, succulent harmonies: they spoke of music as though it were a confectioner's shop. The other party would not hear of the ear, that trumpery organ, being considered: music was for them a lecture, a Parliamentary assembly, in which all the orators spoke at once without bothering about their neighbors, and went on talking until they had done: if people could not hear, so much the worse for them! They could read their speeches next day in the *Official Journal:* music was made to be read, and not to be heard. When Christophe first heard of this quarrel between the *Horizontalists* and the *Verticalists,* he thought they were all mad. When he was summoned to join in the fight between the army of *Succession* and the army of *Superposition,* he replied, with his usual formula, which was very different from that of Sosia:

" Gentlemen, I am everybody's enemy."

And when they insisted, saying:

" Which matters most in music, harmony or counterpoint? "
He replied:

" Music. Show me what you have done."

They were all agreed about their own music. These intrepid warriors who, when they were not pummeling each other, were whacking away at some dead Master whose fame had endured too long, were reconciled by the one passion which was common to them all: an ardent musical patriotism. France was to them *the* great musical nation. They were perpetually proclaiming the decay of Germany. That did not hurt Christophe. He had declared so himself, and therefore was not in a

position to contradict them. But he was a little surprised to
hear of the supremacy of French music: there was, in fact, very
little trace of it in the past. And yet French musicians maintained that their art had been admirable from the earliest
period. By way of glorifying French music, they set to work
to throw ridicule on the famous men of the last century, with
the exception of one Master, who was very good and very pure—
and a Belgian. Having done that amount of slaughter, they
were free to admire the archaic Masters, who had been forgotten, while a certain number of them were absolutely unknown.
Unlike the lay schools of France which date the world from the
French Revolution, the musicians regarded it as a chain of
mighty mountains, to be scaled before it could be possible to
look back on the Golden Age of music, the Eldorado of art.
After a long eclipse the Golden Age was to emerge again: the
hard wall was to crumble away: a magician of sound was to
call forth in full flower a marvelous spring: the old tree of
music was to put forth young green leaves: in the bed of harmony thousands of flowers were to open their smiling eyes upon
the new dawn: and silvery trickling springs were to bubble forth
with the vernal sweet song of streams—a very idyl.

Christophe was delighted. But when he looked at the bills
of the Parisian theaters, he saw the names of Meyerbeer,
Gounod, Massenet, and Mascagni and Leoncavallo—names with
which he was only too familiar: and he asked his friends if all
this brazen music, with its girlish rapture, its artificial flowers,
like nothing so much as a perfumery shop, was the garden of
Armide that they had promised him. They were hurt and
protested: if they were to be believed, these things were the
last vestiges of a moribund age: no one attached any value to
them. But the fact remained that *Cavalleria Rusticana* flourished at the Opéra Comique, and *Pagliacci* at the Opéra: Massenet and Gounod were more frequently performed than anybody else, and the musical trinity—*Mignon, Les Huguenots,*
and *Faust*—had safely crossed the bar of the thousandth performance. But these were only trivial accidents: there was

no need to go and see them. When some untoward fact upsets a theory, nothing is more simple than to ignore it. The French critics shut their eyes to these blatant works and to the public which applauded them: and only a very little more was needed to make them ignore the whole music-theater in France. The music-theater was to them a literary form, and therefore impure. (Being all literary men, they set a ban on literature.) Any music that was expressive, descriptive, suggestive—in short, any music with any meaning—was condemned as impure. In every Frenchman there is a Robespierre. He must be for ever chopping the head off something or somebody to purify it. The great French critics only recognized pure music: the rest they left to the rabble.

Christophe was rather mortified when he thought how vulgar his taste must be. But he found some comfort in the discovery that all these musicians who despised the theater spent their time in writing for it: there was not one of them who did not compose operas. But no doubt that was also a trivial accident. They were to be judged, as they desired, by their pure music. Christophe looked about for their pure music.

Théophile Goujart took him to the concerts of a Society dedicated to the national art. There the new glories of French music were elaborated and carefully hatched. It was a club, a little church, with several side-chapels. Each chapel had its saint, each saint his devotees, who blackguarded the saint in the next chapel. It was some time before Christophe could differentiate between the various saints. Naturally enough, being accustomed to a very different sort of art, he was at first baffled by the new music, and the more he thought he understood it, the farther was he from a real understanding.

It all seemed to him to be bathed in a perpetual twilight. It was a dull gray ground on which were drawn lines, shading off and blurring into each other, sometimes starting from the mist, and then sinking back into it again. Among all these

lines there were stiff, crabbed, and cramped designs, as though
they were drawn with a set-square—patterns with sharp corners, like the elbow of a skinny woman. There were patterns
in curves floating and curling like the smoke of a cigar. But
they were all enveloped in the gray light. Did the sun never
shine in France? Christophe had only had rain and fog since
his arrival, and was inclined to believe so; but it is the artist's
business to create sunshine when the sun fails. These men lit
up their little lanterns, it is true: but they were like the glow-
worm's lamp, giving no warmth and very little light. The
titles of their works were changed: they dealt with Spring, the
South, Love, the Joy of Living, Country Walks; but the music
never changed: it was uniformly soft, pale, enervated, anemic,
wasting away. It was then the mode in France, among the
fastidious, to whisper in music. And they were quite right:
for as soon as they tried to talk aloud they shouted: there
was no mean. There was no alternative but distinguished
somnolence and melodramatic declamation.

Christophe shook off the drowsiness that was creeping over
him, and looked at his program; and he was surprised to read
that the little puffs of cloud floating across the gray sky claimed
to represent certain definite things. For, in spite of theory, all
their pure music was almost always program music, or at least
music descriptive of a certain subject. It was in vain that they
denounced literature: they needed the support of a literary
crutch. Strange crutches they were, too, as a rule! Christophe observed the odd puerility of the subjects which they
labored to depict—orchards, kitchen-gardens, farmyards, musical menageries, a whole Zoo. Some musicians transposed for
orchestra or piano the pictures in the Louvre, or the frescoes
of the Opéra: they turned into music Cuyp, Baudry, and Paul
Potter: explanatory notes helped the hearer to recognize the
apple of Paris, a Dutch inn, or the crupper of a white horse.
To Christophe it was like the production of children obsessed
by images, who, not knowing how to draw, scribble down in
their exercise-books anything that comes into their heads, and

naïvely write down under it in large letters an inscription to the effect that it is a house or a tree.

But besides these blind image-fanciers who saw with their ears, there were the philosophers: they discussed metaphysical problems in music: their symphonies were composed of the struggle between abstract principles and stated symbols or religions. And in their operas they affected to study the judicial and social questions of the day: the Declaration of the Rights of Woman and the Citizen, elaborated by the metaphysicians of the Butte and the Palais-Bourbon. They did not shrink from bringing the question of divorce on to the platform together with the inquiry into the birth-rate and the separation of the Church and State. Among them were to be found lay ' symbolists and clerical symbolists. They introduced philosophic rag-pickers, sociological grisettes, prophetic bakers, and apostolic fishermen to the stage. Goethe spoke of the artists of his day, "who reproduced the ideas of Kant in allegorical pictures." The artists of Christophe's day wrote sociology in semi-quavers. Zola, Nietzsche, Maeterlinck, Barrès, Jaurès, Mendès, the Gospel, and the Moulin Rouge, all fed the cistern whence the writers of operas and symphonies drew their ideas. Many of them, intoxicated by the example of Wagner, cried: "And I, too, am a poet!" And with perfect assurance they tacked on to their music verses in rhyme, or unrhymed, written in the style of an elementary school or a decadent feuilleton.

All these thinkers and poets were partisans of pure music. But they preferred talking about it to writing it. And yet they did sometimes manage to write it. Then they wrote music that was not intended to say anything. Unfortunately, they often succeeded: their music was meaningless—at least, to Christophe. It is only fair to say that he had not the key to it.

In order to understand the music of a foreign nation a man must take the trouble to learn the language, and not make up his mind beforehand that he knows it. Christophe, like

every good German, thought he knew it. That was excusable.
Many Frenchmen did not understand it any more than he.
Like the Germans of the time of Louis XIV, who tried so
hard to speak French that in the end they forgot their own
language, the French musicians of the nineteenth century had
taken so much pains to unlearn their language that their music
had become a foreign lingo. It was only of recent years that a
movement had sprung up to speak French in France. They
did not all succeed: the force of habit was very strong: and
with a few exceptions their French was Belgian, or still smacked
faintly of Germany. It was quite natural, therefore, that a
German should be mistaken, and declare, with his usual assurance, that it was very bad German, and meant nothing, since
he could make nothing of it.

Christophe was in exactly that case. The symphonies of the
French seemed to him to be abstract, dialectic, and musical
themes were opposed and superposed arithmetically in them:
their combinations and permutations might just as well have
been expressed in figures or the letters of the alphabet. One
man would construct a symphony on the progressive development of a sonorous formula which did not seem to be complete
until the last page of the last movement, so that for nine-
tenths of the work it never advanced beyond the grub stage of
its existence. Another would erect variations on a theme which
was not stated until the end, so that the symphony gradually
descended from the complex to the simple. They were very
clever toys. But a man would need to be both very old and
very young to be able to enjoy them. They had cost their inventors untold effort. They took years to write a fantasy.
They worried their hair white in the search for new combinations of chords—to express . . .? No matter! New expressions. As the organ creates the need, they say, so the expression must in the end create the idea: the chief thing is
that the expression should be novel. Novelty at all costs!
They had a morbid horror of anything that " had been said."
The best of them were paralyzed by it all. They seemed always

to be keeping a fearful guard on themselves, and crossing out what they had written, wondering: " Good Lord! Where did I read that?" . . . There are some musicians—especially in Germany—who spend their time in piecing together other people's music. The musicians of France were always looking out at every bar to see that they had not included in their catalogues melodies that had already been used by others, and erasing, erasing, changing the shape of the note until it was like no known note, and even ceased to be like a note at all.

But they did not take Christophe in: in vain did they muffle themselves up in a complicated language, and make superhuman and prodigious efforts, go into orchestral fits, or cultivate inorganic harmonies, an obsessing monotony, declamations à la Sarah Bernhardt, beginning in a minor key, and going on for hours plodding along like mules, half asleep, along the edge of the slippery slope—always under the mask Christophe found the souls of these men, cold, weary, horribly scented, like Gounod and Massenet, but even less natural. And he repeated the unjust comment on the French of Gluck:

" Let them be: they always go back to their giddy-go-round."

Only they did try so hard to be learned. They took popular songs as themes for learned symphonies, like dissertations for the Sorbonne. That was the great game at the time. All sorts and kinds of popular songs, songs of all nations, were pressed into the service. And they worked them up into things like the *Ninth Symphony* and the *Quartet* of César Franck, only much more difficult. A musician would conceive quite a simple air. At once he would mix it up with another, which meant nothing at all, though it jarred hideously with the first. And all these people were obviously so calm, so perfectly balanced! . . .

And there was a young conductor, properly haggard and dressed for the part, who produced these works: he flung himself about, darted lightnings, made Michael Angelesque gestures as though he were summoning up the armies of Beethoven or Wagner. The audience, which was composed of society people, was bored to tears, though nothing would have induced them to renounce the honor of paying a high price for such glorious boredom: and there were young tyros who were only too glad to bring their school knowledge into play as they picked up the threads of the music, and they applauded with an enthusiasm as frantic as the gestures of the conductor, and the fearful noise of the music. . . .

"What rot!" said Christopher. (For he was well up in Parisian slang by now.)

But it is easier to penetrate the mystery of Parisian slang than the mystery of Parisian music. Christophe judged it with the passion which he brought to bear on everything, and the native incapacity of the Germans to understand French art. At least, he was sincere, and only asked to be put right if he was mistaken. And he did not regard himself as bound by his judgment, but left it open to any new impression that might alter it.

As matters stood, he readily admitted that there was much talent in the music he heard, interesting stuff, certain odd happy rhythms and harmonies, an assortment of fine materials, mellow and brilliant, glittering colors, a perpetual outpouring of invention and cleverness. Christophe was entertained by it, and learned a thing or two. All these small masters had infinitely more freedom of thought than the musicians of Germany: they bravely left the highroad and plunged through the woods. They did their best to lose themselves. But they were so clever that they could not manage it. Some of them found themselves on the road again in twenty yards. Others tired at once, and stopped wherever they might be. There were a few who almost discovered new paths, but instead of following them up they sat down at the edge of the wood and fell to musing under a tree. What they most lacked was willpower, force: they had all the gifts save one—vigor and life. And all their multifarious efforts were confusedly directed, and were lost on the road. It was only rarely that these artists became conscious of the nature of their efforts, and could join forces to a common and a given end. It was the usual result of French anarchy, which wastes the enormous wealth of talent and good intentions through the paralyzing influence of its uncertainty and contradictions. With hardly an exception, all the great French musicians, like Berlioz and Saint-Saens—to mention only the most recent—have been hopelessly muddled, self-destructive, and forsworn, for want of energy, want of faith, and, above all, for want of an inward guide.

Christophe, with the insolence and disdain of the latter-day German, thought:

"The French do no more than fritter away their energy in inventing things which they are incapable of using. They need a master of another race, a Gluck or a Napoleon, to turn their Revolutions to any account."

And he smiled at the notion of an Eighteenth of Brumaire.

And yet, in the midst of all this anarchy, there was a group striving to restore order and discipline to the minds of artists and public. By way of a beginning, they had taken a Latin name reminiscent of a clerical institution which had flourished thirteen or fourteen centuries ago at the time of the great Invasion of the Goths and Vandals. Christophe was rather surprised at their going back so far. It was a good thing, certainly, to dominate one's generation. But it looked as though a watch-tower fourteen centuries high might be a little inconvenient, and more suitable perhaps for observing the movements of the stars than those of the men of the present day. But Christophe was soon reassured when he saw that the sons of St. Gregory spent very little time on their tower: they only went up it to ring the bells, and spent the rest of their time in the church below. It was some time before Christophe, who attended some of their services, saw that it was a Catholic cult: he had been sure at the outset that their rites were those of some little Protestant sect. The audience groveled: the disciples were pious, intolerant, aggressive on the

smallest provocation: at their head was a man of a cold sort
of purity, rather childish and wilful, maintaining the integrity
of his doctrine, religious, moral, and artistic, explaining in
abstract terms the Gospel of music to the small number of the
Elect, and calmly damning Pride and Heresy. To these two
states of mind he attributed every defect in art and every vice
of humanity: the Renaissance, the Reformation, and present-
day Judaism, which he lumped together in one category. The
Jews of music were burned in effigy after being ignominiously
dressed. The colossal Handel was soundly trounced. Only
Johann Sebastian Bach attained salvation by the grace of the
Lord, who recognized that he had been a Protestant by mistake.

The temple of the *Rue Saint-Jacques* fulfilled an apostolic
function: souls and music found salvation there. The rules
of genius were taught there most methodically. Laborious
pupils applied the formulæ with infinite pains and absolute
certainty. It looked as though by their pious labors they
were trying to regain the criminal levity of their ancestors:
the Aubers, the Adams, and the trebly damned, the diabolical
Berlioz, the devil himself, *diabolus in musica*. With laudable
ardor and a sincere piety they spread the cult of the acknowledged masters. In ten years the work they had to show
was considerable: French music was transformed. Not only
the French critics, but the musicians themselves had learned
something about music. There were now composers, and even
virtuosi, who were acquainted with the works of Bach. And
that was not so common even in Germany! But, above all, a
great effort had been made to combat the stay-at-home spirit
of the French, who will shut themselves up in their homes,
and cannot be induced to go out. So their music lacks air:
it is sealed-chamber music, sofa music, music with no sort of
vigor. Think of Beethoven composing as he strode across country, rushing down the hillsides, swinging along through sun
and rain, terrifying the cattle with his wild shouts and gestures!
There was no danger of the musicians of Paris upsetting their
neighbors with the noise of their inspiration, like the bear of

Bonn. When they composed they muted' the strings of their thought: and the heavy hangings of their rooms prevented any sound from outside breaking in upon them.

The *Schola* had tried to let in fresh air, and had opened the windows upon the past. But only on the past. The windows were opened upon a courtyard, not into the street. And it was not much use. Hardly had they opened the windows than they closed the shutters, like old women afraid of catching cold. And there came up a gust or two of the Middle Ages, Bach, Palestrina, popular songs. But what was the good of that? The room still smelt of stale air. But really that suited them very well: they were afraid of the great modern draughts of air. And if they knew more than other people, they also denied more in art. Their music took on a doctrinal character: there was no relaxation: their concerts were history lectures, or a string of edifying examples. Advanced ideas became academic. The great Bach, he whose music is like a torrent, was received into the bosom of the Church and then tamed. His music was submitted to a transformation in the minds of the *Schola* very like the transformation to which the savagely sensual Bible has been submitted in the minds of the English. As for modern music, the doctrine promulgated was aristocratic and eclectic, an attempt to compound the distinctive characteristics of the three or four great periods of music from the sixth to the twentieth century. If it had been possible to carry it out, the resulting music would have been like those hybrid structures raised by a Viceroy of India on his return from his travels, with rare materials collected in every corner of the earth. But the good sense of the French saved them from any such barbarically erudite excesses: they carefully avoided any application of their theories: they treated them as Molière treated his doctors: they took their prescriptions, but did not carry them out. The best of them went their own way. The rest of them contented themselves in practice with very intricate and difficult exercises in counterpoint: they called them sonatas, quartets, and symphonies. . . . " Sonata, what do you desire of me?" The poor thing desired nothing at all except to be a sonata. The idea behind it was abstract and anonymous, heavy and joyless. So might a lawyer conceive an art. Christophe, who had at first been by way of being pleased with the French for not liking Brahms, now thought that there were many, many little Brahms in France. These laborious, conscientious, honest journeymen had many qualities and virtues. Christophe left them edified, but bored to distraction. It was all very good, very good. . . .

How fine it was outside!

And yet there were a few independent musicians in Paris, men belonging to no school. They alone were interesting to Christophe. It was only through them that he could gauge the vitality of the art. Schools and coteries only express some superficial fashion or manufactured theory. But the independent men who stand apart have more chance of really discovering the ideas of their race and time. It is true that that makes them all the more difficult for a foreigner to understand.

That was, in fact, what happened when Christophe first heard the famous work which the French had so extravagantly praised, while some of them were announcing the coming of the greatest musical revolution of the last ten centuries. (It was easy for them to talk about centuries: they knew hardly anything of any except their own.)

Théophile Goujart and Sylvain Kohn took Christophe to the Opéra Comique to hear *Pelleas and Melisande*. They were proud to display the opera to him—as proud as though they had written it themselves. They gave Christophe to understand that it would be the road to Damascus for him. And they went on eulogizing it even after the piece had begun. Christophe shut them up and listened intently. After the first act he turned to Sylvain Kohn, who asked him, with glittering eyes:

" Well, old man, what do you think of it?"

And he said:

" Is it like that all through? "

" Yes."

" But it's nothing."

Kohn protested loudly, and called him a Philistine.

" Nothing at all," said Christophe. " No music. No development. No sequence. No cohesion. Very nice harmony. Quite good orchestral effects, quite good. But it's nothing—nothing at all. . . ."

He listened through the second act. Little by little the lantern gathered light and glowed: and he began to perceive something through the twilight. Yes: he could understand the sober-minded rebellion against the Wagnerian ideal which swamped the drama with floods of music; but he wondered a little ironically if the ideal of sacrifice did not mean the sacrifice of something which one does not happen to possess. He felt the easy fluency of the opera, the production of an effect with the minimum of trouble, the indolent renunciation of the sturdy effort shown in the vigorous Wagnerian structures. And he was quite struck by the unity of it, the simple, modest, rather dragging declamation, although it seemed monotonous to him, and, to his German ears, it sounded false:—(and it even seemed to him that the more it aimed at truth the more it showed how little the French language was suited to music: it is too logical, too precise, too definite,—a world perfect in itself, but hermetically sealed).—However, the attempt was interesting, and Christophe gladly sympathized with the spirit of revolt and reaction against the over-emphasis and violence of Wagnerian art. The French composer seemed to have devoted his attention discreetly and ironically to all the things that sentiment and passion only whisper. He showed love and death inarticulate. It was only by the imperceptible throbbing of a melody, a little thrill from the orchestra that was no more than a quivering of the corners of the lips, that the drama passing through the souls of the characters was brought home to the audience. It was as though the artist were fearful of letting himself go. He had the genius of taste—except at certain moments when the Massenet slumbering in the heart of every Frenchman awoke and waxed lyrical. Then there showed hair that was too golden, lips that were too red—the Lot's wife of the Third Republic playing the lover. But such moments were the exception: they were a relaxation of the writer's self-imposed restraint: throughout the rest of the opera there reigned a delicate simplicity, a simplicity which was not so very simple, a deliberate simplicity, the subtle flower of an ancient society. That young Barbarian, Christophe, only half liked it. The whole scheme of the play, the poem, worried him. He saw a middle-aged Parisienne posing childishly and having fairy-tales told to her. It was not the Wagnerian sickliness, sentimental and clumsy, like a girl from the Rhine provinces. But the Franco-Belgian sickliness was not much better, with its simpering parlor-tricks:—" the hair," " the little father," " the doves,"—and the whole trick of mystery for the delectation of society women. The soul of the Parisienne was mirrored in the little piece, which, like a flattering picture, showed the languid fatalism, the boudoir Nirvana, the soft, sweet melancholy. Nowhere a trace of willpower. No one knew what he wanted. No one knew what he was doing.

" It is not my fault! It is not my fault! " these grown-up children groaned. All through the five acts, which took place in a perpetual half-light—forests, caves, cellars, death-chambers—little sea-birds struggled: hardly even that. Poor little birds! Pretty birds, soft, pretty birds. . . . They were so afraid of too much light, of the brutality of deeds, words, passions—life! Life is not soft and pretty. Life is no kid-glove matter. . . .

Christophe could hear in the distance the rumbling of cannon, coming to batter down that worn-out civilization, that perishing little Greece.

Was it that proud feeling of melancholy and pity that made him in spite of all sympathize with the opera? It interested

him more than he would admit. Although he went on telling
Sylvain Kohn, as they left the theater, that it was " very fine,
very fine, but lacking in *Schwung* (impulse), and did not con-
tain enough music for him," he was careful not to confound
Pelleas with the other music of the French. He was attracted
by the lamp shining through the fog. And then he saw other
lights, vivid and fantastic, flickering round it. His attention
was caught by these will-o'-the-wisps: he would have liked to
go near them to find out how it was that they shone: but they
were not easy to catch. These independent musicians, whom
Christophe did not understand, were not very approachable.
They seemed to lack that great need of sympathy which possessed Christophe. With a few exceptions they seemed to read
very little, know very little, desire very little. They almost
all lived in retirement, some outside Paris, others in Paris, but
isolated, by circumstances or purposely, shut up in a narrow
circle—from pride, shyness, disgust, or apathy. There were
very few of them, but they were split up into rival groups,
and could not tolerate each other. They were extremely
susceptible, and could not bear with their enemies, or their
rivals, or even their friends, when they dared to admire any
other musician than themselves, or when they admired too
coldly, or too fervently, or in too commonplace or too ec-
centric a manner. It was extremely difficult to please them.
Every one of them had actually sanctioned a critic, armed
with letters patent, who kept a jealous watch at the foot of
the statue. Visitors were requested not to touch. They did
not gain any greater understanding from being understood
only by their own little groups. They were deformed by the
adulation and the opinion that their partisans and they themselves held of their work, and they lost grip of their art and
their genius. Men with a pleasing fantasy thought themselves
reformers, and Alexandrine artists posed as rivals of Wagner.
They were almost all the victims of competition. Every day
they had to leap a little higher than the day before, and,
especially, higher than their rivals. These exercises in high

jumping were not always successful, and were certainly not attractive except to professionals. They took no account of
the public, and the public never bothered about them. Their
art was out of touch with the people, music which was only fed
from music. Now, Christophe was under the impression,
rightly or wrongly, that there was no music that had a greater
need of outside support than French music. That supple
climbing plant needed a prop: it could not do without literature, but did not find in it enough of the breath of life. French
music was breathless, bloodless, will-less. It was like a woman
languishing for her lover. But, like a Byzantine Empress, slender and feeble in body, laden with precious stones, it was
surrounded with eunuchs: snobs, esthetes, and critics. The
nation was not musical: and the craze, so much talked of during the last twenty years, for Wagner, Beethoven, Bach, or
Debussy, never reached farther than a certain class. The
enormous increase in the number of concerts, the flowing tide
of music at all costs, found no real response in the development of public taste. It was just a fashionable craze confined
to the few, and leading them astray. There was only a handful
of people who really loved music, and these were not the
people who were most occupied with it, composers and critics.
There are so few musicians in France who really love music!

So thought Christophe: but it did not occur to him that
it is the same everywhere, that even in Germany there are not
many more real musicians, and that the people who matter in
art are not the thousands who understand nothing about it,
but the few who love it and serve it in proud humility. Had
he ever set eyes on them in France? Creators and critics—
the best of them were working in silence, far from the racket,
as César Franck had done, and the most gifted composers of
the day were doing, and a number of artists who would live
out their lives in obscurity, so that some day in the future
some journalist might have the glory of discovering them and
posing as their friend—and the little army of industrious and
obscure men of learning who, without ambition and careless

of their fame, were building stone by stone the greatness of
the past history of France, or, being vowed to the musical education of the country, were preparing the greatness of the
France of the future. There were minds there whose wealth
and liberty and world-wide curiosity would have attracted Christophe if he had been able to discover them! But at most he
only caught a cursory glimpse of two or three of them: he
only made their acquaintance in the villainous caricatures of
their ideas. He saw only their defects copied and exaggerated
by the apish mimics of art and the bagmen of the Press.

But what most disgusted him with these vulgarians of music
was their formalism. They never seemed to consider anything
but form. Feeling, character, life—never a word of these!
It never seemed to occur to them that every real musician
lives in a world of sound, as other men live in a visible world,
and that his days are lived in and borne onward by a flood
of music. Music is the air he breathes, the sky above him.
Nature wakes answering music in his soul. His soul itself is
music: music is in all that it loves, hates, suffers, fears, hopes.
And when the soul of a musician loves a beautiful body, it
sees music in that, too. The beloved eyes are not blue, or
brown, or gray: they are music: their tenderness is like caressing
notes, like a delicious chord. That inward music is a thousand times more rich than the music that finds expression, and
the instrument is inferior to the player. Genius is measured
by the power of life, by the power of evoking life through the
imperfect instrument of art. But to how many men in France
does that ever occur? To these chemists music seems to be no
more than the art of resolving sounds. They mistake the
alphabet for a book. Christophe shrugged his shoulders when
he heard them say complacently that to understand art it must
be abstracted from the man. They were extraordinarily pleased
with this paradox: for by it they fancied they were proving their
own musical quality. And even Goujart subscribed to it—
Goujart, the idiot who had never been able to understand how
people managed to learn by heart a piece of music—(he had

tried to get Christophe to explain the mystery to him)—and had tried to prove to him that Beethoven's greatness of soul and Wagner's sensuality had no more to do with their music than a painter's model has to do with his portraits.

Christophe lost patience with him, and said:

"That only proves that a beautiful body is of no more artistic value to you than a great passion. Poor fellow! . . . You have no notion of the beauty given to a portrait by the beauty of a perfect face, or of the glow of beauty given to music by the beauty of the great soul which is mirrored in it? . . . Poor fellow! . . . You are interested only in the handiwork? So long as it is well done you are not concerned with the meaning of a piece of work. . . . Poor fellow! . . . You are like those people who do not listen to what an orator says, but only to the sound of his voice, and watch his gestures without understanding them, and then say he speaks devilish well. . . . Poor fellow! Poor wretch! . . . Oh, you rotten swine!"

But it was not only a particular theory that irritated Christophe; it was all their theories. He was appalled by their unending arguments, their Byzantine discussions, the everlasting talk, talk, talk, of musicians about music, and nothing else. It was enough to make the best of musicians heartily sick of music. Like Moussorgski, Christophe thought that it would be as well for musicians every now and then to leave their counterpoint and harmony in favor of books or experience of life. Music is not enough for a present-day musician; not thus will he dominate his age and raise his head above the stream of time. . . . Life! All life! To see everything, to know everything, to feel everything. To love, to seek, to grasp Truth—the lovely Penthesilea, Queen of the Amazons, whose teeth bite in answer to a kiss!

Away with your musical discussion-societies, away with your chord-factories! Not all the twaddle of the harmonic kitchens would ever help him to find a new harmony that was alive, alive, and not a monstrous birth.

He turned his back on these Doctor Wagners, brooding on their alembics to hatch out some homunculus in bottle: and, running away from French music, he sought to enter literary circles and Parisian society. Like many millions of people in France, Christophe made his first acquaintance with modern French literature through the newspapers. He wanted to get the measure of Parisian thought as quickly as possible, and at the same time to perfect his knowledge of the language. And so he set himself conscientiously to read the papers which he was told were most Parisian. On the first day after a horrific chronicle of events, which filled several pages with paragraphs and snapshots, he read a story about a father and a daughter, a girl of fifteen: it was narrated as though it were a matter of course, and even rather moving. Next day, in the same paper, he read a story about a father and a son, a boy of twelve, and the girl was mixed up in it again. On the following day he read a story about a brother and a sister. Next day, the story was about two sisters. On the fifth day . . . On the fifth day he hurled the paper away with a shudder, and said to Sylvain Kohn:

"But what's the matter with you all? Are you ill?"

Sylvain Kohn began to laugh, and said:

"That is art."

Christophe shrugged his shoulders:

"You're pulling my leg."

Kohn laughed once more:

"Not at all. Read a little more."

And he pointed to the report of a recent inquiry into Art and Morality, which set out that "Love sanctified everything," that "Sensuality was the leaven of Art," that "Art could not be Immoral," that "Morality was a convention of Jesuit education," and that nothing mattered except "the greatness of Desire." A number of letters from literary men witnessed the artistic purity of a novel depicting the life of bawds. Some of the signatories were among the greatest names in contemporary literature, or the most austere of critics. A domestic poet, *bourgeois* and a Catholic, gave his blessing as an artist to a detailed description of the decadence of the Greeks. There were enthusiastic praises of novels in which the course of Lewdness was followed through the ages: Rome, Alexandria, Byzantium, the Italian and French Renaissance, the Age of Greatness . . . Nothing was omitted. Another cycle of studies was devoted to the various countries of the world: conscientious writers had devoted their energies, with a monkish patience, to the study of the low quarters of the five continents. And it was no matter for surprise to discover among these geographers and historians of Pleasure distinguished poets and very excellent writers. They were only marked out from the rest by their erudition. In their most impeccable style they told archaic stories, highly spiced.

But what was most alarming was to see honest men and real artists, men who rightly enjoyed a high place in French literature, struggling in such a traffic, for which they were not at all suited. Some of them with great travail wrote, like the rest, the sort of trash that the newspapers serialize. They had to produce it by a fixed time, once or twice a week: and it had been going on for years. They went on producing and producing, long after they had ceased to have anything to say, racking their brains to find something new, something more sensational, more bizarre: for the public was surfeited and sick of everything, and soon wearied of even the most wanton imaginary pleasures: they had always to go one better—better than the rest, better than their own best—and they squeezed out their very life-blood, they squeezed out their guts: it was a pitiable sight, a grotesque spectacle.

Christophe, who did not know the ins and outs of that melancholy traffic, and if he had known them would not have been more indulgent; for in his eyes nothing in the world could excuse an artist for selling his art for thirty pieces of silver. . . .

(Not even to assure the well-being of those whom he loves? Not even then.

That is not human.

It is not a question of being human; it is a question of being a man. . . . Human! . . . May God have mercy on your white-livered humanitarianism, it is so bloodless! . . . No man loves twenty things at once, no man can serve many gods! . . .)

. . . Christophe, who, in his hard-working life, had hardly yet seen beyond the limits of his little German town, could have no idea that this artistic degradation, which showed so rawly in Paris, was common to nearly all the great towns: and the hereditary prejudices of chaste Germany against Latin immorality awoke in him once more. And yet Sylvain Kohn might easily have pointed to what was going on by the banks of the Spree, and the impurity of Imperial Germany, where brutality made shame and degradation even more repulsive. But Sylvain Kohn never thought of it: he was no more shocked by that than by the life of Paris. He thought ironically: "Every nation has its little ways," and the ways of the world in which he lived seemed so natural to him that Christophe could be excused for thinking it was in the nature of the people. And so, like so many of his compatriots, he saw in the secret sore which is eating away the intellectual aristocracies of Europe the vice proper to French art, and the bankruptcy of the Latin races.

Christophe was hurt by his first encounter with French literature, and it took him some time to get over it. And yet there were plenty of books which were not solely occupied with what one of these writers has nobly called "the taste for fundamental entertainments." But he never laid hands on the best and finest of them. Such books were not written for the like of Sylvain Kohn and his friends: they did not bother about them, and certainly Kohn and the rest never bothered about the better class of books: they ignored each other. Sylvain Kohn would never have thought of mentioning them to Christophe. He was quite sincerely convinced that his friends and himself were the incarnation of French

Art, and thought there was no talent, no art, no France outside the men who had been consecrated as great by their opinion and the press of the boulevards. Christophe knew nothing about the poets who were the glory of French literature, the very crown of France. Very few of the novelists reached him, or emerged from the ocean of mediocre writers: a few books of Barrès and Anatole France. But he was not sufficiently familiar with the language to be able to enjoy the universal dilettantism, and erudition, and irony of the one, or the unequal but superior art of the other. He spent some time in watching the little orange-trees in tubs growing in the hothouse of Anatole France, and the delicate, perfect flowers clambering over the gravelike soul of Barrès. He stayed for a moment or two before the genius, part sublime, part silly, of Maeterlinck: from that there issued a polite mysticism, monotonous, numbing like some vague sorrow. He shook himself, and plunged into the heavy, sluggish stream, the muddy romanticism of Zola, with whom he was already acquainted, and when he emerged from that it was to sink back and drown in a deluge of literature.

The submerged lands exhaled an *odor di femina*. The literature of the day teemed with effeminate men and women. It is well that women should write if they are sincere enough to describe what no man has yet seen: the depths of the soul of a woman. But only very few dared do that: most of them only wrote to attract the men: they were as untruthful in their books as in their drawing-rooms: they jockeyed their facts and flirted with the reader. Since they were no longer religious, and had no confessor to whom to tell their little lapses, they told them to the public. There was a perfect shower of novels, almost all scabrous, all affected, written in a sort of lisping style, a style scented with flowers and fine perfumes—sometimes too fine—sometimes not fine at all—and the eternal stale, warm, sweetish smell. Their books reeked of it. Christophe thought, like Goethe: " Let women do what they like with poetry and writing: but men must not write like women! That I cannot stand." He could not help being disgusted by their tricks, their sly coquetry, their sentimentality, which seemed to expend itself by preference upon creatures hardly worthy of interest, their style crammed with metaphor, their love-making and sensuality, their hotch-potch of subtlety and brutality.

But Christophe was ready to admit that he was not in a position to judge. He was deafened by the row of this babel of words. It was impossible to hear the little fluting sounds that were drowned in it all. For even among such books as these there were some, from the pages of which, behind all the nonsense, there shone the limpid sky and the harmonious outline of the hills of Attica—so much talent, so much grace, a sweet breath of life, and charm of style, a thought like the voluptuous women or the languid boys of Perugino and the young Raphael, smiling, with half-closed eyes, at their dream of love. But Christophe was blind to that. Nothing could reveal to him the dominant tendencies, the currents of public opinion. Even a Frenchman would have been hard put to it to see them. And the only definite impression that he had at this time was that of a flood of writing which looked like a national disaster. It seemed as though everybody wrote: men, women, children, officers, actors, society people, blackguards. It was an epidemic.

For the time being Christophe gave it up. He felt that such a guide as Sylvain Kohn must lead him hopelessly astray. His experience of a literary coterie in Germany gave him very properly a profound distrust of the people whom he met: it was impossible to know whether or no they only represented the opinion of a few hundred idle people, or even, in certain cases, whether or no the author was his own public. The theater gave a more exact idea of the society of Paris. It played an enormous part in the daily life of the city. It was an enormous kitchen, a Pantagruelesque restaurant, which could not cope with the appetite of the two million inhabitants. There were thirty leading theaters, without counting the local houses, café concerts, all sorts of shows—a hundred halls, all

giving performances every evening, and, every evening, almost
all full. A whole nation of actors and officials. Vast sums
were swallowed up in the gulf. The four State-aided theaters
gave work to three thousand people, and cost the country ten
million francs. The whole of Paris re-echoed with the glory
of the play-actors. It was impossible to go anywhere without
seeing innumerable photographs, drawings, caricatures, repro-
ducing their features and mannerisms, gramophones reproduc-
ing their voices, and the newspapers their opinions on art and
politics. They had special newspapers devoted to them. They
published their heroic and domestic Memoirs. These big self-
conscious children, who spent their time in aping each other,
these wonderful apes reigned and held sway over the Parisians:
and the dramatic authors were their chief ministers. Christophe asked Sylvain Kohn to conduct him into the kingdom
of shadows and reflections.

But Sylvain Kohn was no safer as a guide in that world
than in the world of books, and, thanks to him, Christophe's
first impression was almost as repulsive as that of his first
essay in literature. It seemed that there was everywhere the
same spirit of mental prostitution.

The pleasure-mongers were divided into two schools. On
the one hand there was the good old way, the national way, of
providing a coarse and unclean pleasure, quite frankly; a delight in ugliness, strong meat, physical deformities, a show of
drawers, barrack-room jests, risky stories, red pepper, high
game, private rooms—"a manly frankness," as those people say
who try to reconcile looseness and morality by pointing out that,
after four acts of dubious fun, order is restored and the Code
triumphs by the fact that the wife is really with the husband
whom she thinks she is deceiving—(so long as the law is observed, then virtue is all right):—that vicious sort of virtue
which defends marriage by endowing it with all the charm of
lewdness:—the Gallic way.

The other school was in the modern style. It was much

more subtle and much more disgusting. The Parisianized Jews and the Judaicized Christians who frequented the theater had introduced into it the usual hash of sentiment which is the distinctive feature of a degenerate cosmopolitanism. Those sons who blushed for their fathers set themselves to abnegate their racial conscience: and they succeeded only too well. Having plucked out the soul that was their birthright, all that was left them was a mixture of the moral and intellectual values of other races: they made a *macédoine* of them, an *olla podrida*: it was their way of taking possession of them. The men who who were at that time in control of the theaters in Paris were extraordinarily skilful at beating up filth and sentiment, and giving virtue a flavoring of vice, vice a flavoring of virtue, and turning upside down every human relation of age, sex, the family, and the affections. Their art, therefore, had an odor *sui generis,* which smelt both good and bad at once—that is to say, it smelled very bad indeed: they called it "amoralism."

One of their favorite heroes at that time was the amorous old man. Their theaters presented a rich gallery of portraits of the type: and in painting it they introduced a thousand pretty touches. Sometimes the sexagenarian hero would take his daughter into his confidence, and talk to her about his mistress: and she would talk about her lovers: and they would give each other friendly advice: the kindly father would aid his daughter in her indiscretions: and the precious daughter would intervene with the unfaithful mistress, beg her to return, and bring her back to the fold. Sometimes the good old man would listen to the confidences of his mistress: he would talk to her about her lovers, or, if nothing better was forthcoming, he would listen to the tale of her gallantries, and even take a delight in them. And there were portraits of lovers, distinguished gentlemen, who presided in the houses of their former mistresses, and helped them in their nefarious business. Society women were thieves. The men were bawds, the girls were Lesbian. And all these things happened in the highest society: the society of rich people—the only society that mattered. For that made it possible to offer the patrons of the theater damaged goods under cover of the delights of luxury. So tricked out, it was displayed in the market, to the joy of old gentlemen and young women. And it all reeked of death and the seraglio.

Their style was not less mixed than their sentiments. They had invented a composite jargon of expressions from all classes of society and every country under the sun—pedantic, slangy, classical, lyrical, precious, prurient, and low—a mixture of bawdy jests, affectations, coarseness, and wit, all of which seemed to have a foreign accent. Ironical, and gifted with a certain clownish humor, they had not much natural wit: but they were clever enough, and they manufactured their goods in imitation of Paris. If the stone was not always of the first water, and if the setting was always strange and overdone, at least it shone in artificial light, and that was all it was meant to do. They were intelligent, keen, though short-sighted observers—their eyes had been dulled by centuries of the life of the counting-house—turning the magnifying-glass on human sentiments, enlarging small things, not seeing big things. With a marked predilection for finery, they were incapable of depicting anything but what seemed to their upstart snobbishness the ideal of polite society: a little group of worn-out rakes and adventurers, who quarreled among themselves for the possession of certain stolen moneys and a few virtueless females.

And yet upon occasion the real nature of these Jewish writers would suddenly awake, come to the surface from the depths of their being, in response to some mysterious echo called forth by some vivid word or sensation. Then there appeared a strange hotch-potch of ages and races, a breath of wind from the Desert, bringing over the seas to their Parisian rooms the musty smell of a Turkish bazaar, the dazzling shimmer of the sands, the mirage, blind sensuality, savage invective, nervous disorder only a hair's-breadth away from epilepsy, a destructive frenzy —Samson, suddenly rising like a lion—after ages of squatting in the shade—and savagely tearing down the columns of the

Temple, which comes crashing down on himself and on his enemies.

Christophe blew his nose and said to Sylvain Kohn:

" There's power in it: but it stinks. That's enough! Let's go and see something else."

" What? " asked Sylvain Kohn.

" France."

" That's it! " said Kohn.

" Can't be," replied Christophe. " France isn't like that."

" It's France, and Germany, too."

" I don't believe it. A nation that was anything like that wouldn't last for twenty years: why, it's decomposing already. There must be something else."

" There's nothing better."

" There must be something else," insisted Christophe.

" Oh, yes," said Sylvain Kohn. " We have fine people, of course, and theaters for them, too. Is that what you want? We can give you that."

He took Christophe to the Théâtre Français.

That evening they happened to be playing a modern comedy, in prose, dealing with some legal problem.

From the very beginning Christophe was baffled to make out in what sort of world the action was taking place. The voices of the actors were out of all reason, full, solemn, slow, formal: they rounded every syllable as though they were giving a lesson in elocution, and they seemed always to be scanning Alexandrines with tragic pauses. Their gestures were solemn and almost hieratic. The heroine, who wore her gown as though it were a Greek peplus, with arm uplifted, and head lowered, was nothing else but Antigone, and she smiled with a smile of eternal sacrifice, carefully modulating the lower notes of her beautiful contralto voice. The heavy father walked about like a fencing-master, with automatic gestures, a funereal dignity,—romanticism in a frock-coat. The juvenile lead gulped and gasped and squeezed out a sob or two. The piece was written in the style of a tragic serial story: abstract phrases, bureaucratic epithets, academic periphrases. No movement, not a sound unrehearsed. From beginning to end it was clockwork, a set problem, a scenario, the skeleton of a play, with not a scrap of flesh, only literary phrases. Timid ideas lay behind discussions that were meant to be bold: the whole spirit of the thing was hopelessly middle-class and respectable.

The heroine had divorced an unworthy husband, by whom she had had a child, and she had married a good man whom she loved. The point was, that even in such a case as this divorce was condemned by Nature, as it is by prejudice. Nothing could be easier than to prove it: the author contrived that the woman should be surprised, for one occasion only, into yielding to the first husband. After that, instead of a perfectly natural remorse, perhaps a profound sense of shame, together with a greater desire to love and honor the second and good husband, the author trotted out an heroic case of conscience, altogether beyond Nature. French writers never seem to be on good terms with virtue: they always force the note when they talk of it: they make it quite incredible. They always seem to be dealing with the heroes of Corneille, and tragedy Kings. And are they not Kings and Queens, these millionaire heroes, and these heroines who would not be interesting unless they had at least a mansion in Paris and two or three country-houses? For such writers and such a public wealth itself is a beauty, and almost a virtue.

The audience was even more amazing than the play. They were never bored by all the tiresomely repeated improbabilities. They laughed at the good points, when the actors said things that were *meant* to be laughed at: it was made obvious that they were coming, so that the audience could be ready to laugh. They mopped their eyes and coughed, and were deeply moved when the puppets gasped, and gulped, and roared, and fainted away in accordance with the hallowed tragic ritual.

"And people say the French are gay!" exclaimed Christophe as they left the theater.

"There's a time for everything," said Sylvain Kohn chaffingly. "You wanted virtue. You see, there's still virtue in France."

"But that's not virtue!" cried Christophe. "That's rhetoric!"

"In France," said Sylvain Kohn. "Virtue in the theater is always rhetorical."

"A pretorium virtue," said Christophe, "and the prize goes to the best talker. I hate lawyers. Have you no poets in France?"

Sylvain Kohn took him to the poetic drama.

There were poets in France. There were even great poets. But the theater was not for them. It was for the versifiers. The theater is to poetry what the opera is to music. As Berlioz said: *Sicut amori lupanar.*

Christophe saw Princesses who were virtuously promiscuous, who prostituted themselves for their honor, who were compared with Christ ascending Calvary:—friends who deceived their friends out of devotion to them:—glorified triangular relations:—heroic cuckoldry: (the cuckold, like the blessed prostitute, had become a European commodity: the example of King Mark had turned the heads of the poets: like the stag of Saint Hubert, the cuckold never appeared without a halo.) And Christophe saw also lovely damsels torn between passion and duty: their passion bade them follow a new lover: duty bade them stay with the old one, an old man who gave them money and was deceived by them. And in the end they plumped heroically for Duty. Christophe could not see how Duty differed from sordid interest: but the public was satisfied. The word Duty was enough for them: they did not insist on having the thing itself; they took the author's word for it.

The summit of art was reached and the greatest pleasure was given when, most paradoxically, sexual immorality and Corneillian heroics could be combined. In that way every need of the Parisian public was satisfied: mind, senses, rhetoric. But it is only just to say that the public was fonder even of words than of lewdness. Eloquence could send it into ecstasies. It would have suffered anything for a fine tirade. Virtue or vice, heroics hobnobbing with the basest prurience, there was no pill that it would not swallow if it were gilded with sonorous rhymes and redundant words. Anything that came to hand was ground into couplets, antitheses, arguments: love, suffering, death. And when that was done, they thought they had felt love, suffering, and death. Nothing but phrases. It was all a game. When Hugo brought thunder on to the stage, at once (as one of his disciples said) he muted it so as not to frighten even a child. (The disciple fancied he was paying him a compliment.) It was never possible to feel any of the forces of Nature in their art. They made everything polite. Just as in music—and even more than in music, which was a younger art in France, and therefore relatively more simple—they were terrified of anything that had been "already said." The most gifted of them coldly devoted themselves to working contrariwise. The process was childishly simple: they pitched on some beautiful legend or fairy-story, and turned it upside down. Thus, Bluebeard was beaten by his wives, or Polyphemus was kind enough to pluck out his eye by way of sacrificing himself to the happiness of Acis and Galatea. And they thought of nothing but form. And once more it seemed to Christophe (though he was not a good judge) that these masters of form were rather coxcombs and imitators than great writers creating their own style and giving breadth and depth to their work.

They played at being artists. They played at being poets. Nowhere was the poetic lie more insolently reared than in the heroic drama. They put up a burlesque conception of a hero:

> "*The great thing is to have a soul magnificent,*
> *An eagel's eye ; broad brow like portico ; present*
> *An air of strength, grave mien, most touchingly to show*
> *A heart that throbs, eyes full of dreams of worlds they know.*"

Verses like that were taken seriously. Behind the hocus-pocus of such fine-sounding words, the bombast, the theatrical clash and clang of the swords and pasteboard helmets, there was always the incurable futility of a Sardou, the intrepid vaudevillist, playing Punch and Judy with history. When in the world was the like of the heroism of Cyrano ever to be found? These writers moved heaven and earth; they summoned from their tombs the Emperor and his legions, the bandits of the Ligue, the *condottieri* of the Renaissance, called up the human cyclones that once devastated the universe:—just to display a puppet, standing unmoved through frightful massacres, surrounded by armies, soldiers, and whole hosts of captive women, dying of a silly calfish love for a woman whom he had seen ten or fifteen years before—or King Henri IV submitting to assassination because his mistress no longer loved him.

So, and no otherwise, did these good people present their parlor Kings, and *condottieri,* and heroic passion. They were worthy scions of the illustrious nincompoops of the days of *Grand Cyrus,* those Gascons of the ideal—Scudéry, La Calprenède—an everlasting brood, the songsters of sham heroism, impossible heroism, which is the enemy of truth. Christophe observed to his amazement that the French, who are said to be so clever, had no sense of the ridiculous.

He was lucky when religion was not dragged in to fit the fashion! Then, during Lent, certain actors read the sermons of Bossuet at the Gaîté to the accompaniment of an organ. Jewish authors wrote tragedies about Saint Theresa for Jewish actresses. The *Way of the Cross* was acted at the Bodinière, the *Child Jesus* at the Ambigu, the *Passion* at the Porte-Saint-Martin, *Jesus* at the Odéon, orchestral suites on the subject of *Christ* at the Botanical Gardens. And a certain brilliant talker —a poet who wrote passionate love-songs—gave a lecture on the *Redemption* at the Châtelet. And, of course, the passages of the Gospel that were most carefully preserved by these people were those relating to Pilate and Mary Magdalene:—" *What is truth?"* and the story of the blessed foolish virgin.—And their boulevard Christs were horribly loquacious and well up in all the latest tricks of worldly casuistry.

Christophe said:

"That is the worst yet. It is untruth incarnate. I'm stifling. Let's get out."

And yet there was a great classic art that held its ground among all these modern industries, like the ruins of the splendid ancient temples among all the pretentious buildings of modern Rome. But, outside Molière, Christophe was not yet able to appreciate it. He was not yet familiar enough with the language, and, therefore, could not grasp the genius of the race. Nothing baffled him so much as the tragedy of the seventeenth century—one of the least accessible provinces of French art to foreigners, precisely because it lies at the very heart of France. It bored him horribly; he found it cold, dry, and revolting in its tricks and pedantry. The action was thin or forced, the characters were rhetorical abstractions or as insipid as the conversation of society women. They were caricatures of the ancient legends and heroes: a display of reason, arguments, quibbling, and antiquated psychology and archeology. Speeches, speeches, speeches; the eternal loquacity of the French. Christophe ironically refused to say whether it was beautiful or not: there was nothing to interest him in it: whatever the arguments put forward in turn by the orators of *Cinna*, he did not care a rap which of the talking-machines won in the end.

However, he had to admit that the French audience was not of his way of thinking, and that they did applaud these plays that bored him. But that did not help to dissipate his confusion: he saw the plays through the audience: and he recognized in the modern French certain of the features, distorted, of the classics. So might a critical eye see in the faded charms of an old coquette the clear, pure features of her daughter:—(such a discovery is not calculated to foster the illusion of love). Like the members of a family who are used to seeing each other, the French could not see the resemblance.

But Christophe was struck by it, and exaggerated it: he could see nothing else. Every work of art he saw seemed to him to be full of old-fashioned caricatures of the great ancestors of the French: and he saw these same great ancestors also in caricature. He could not see any difference between Corneille and the long line of his followers, those rhetorical poets whose mania it was to present nothing but sublime and ridiculous cases of conscience. And Racine he confounded with his offspring of pretentiously introspective Parisian psychologists.

None of these people had really broken free from the classics. The critics were for ever discussing *Tartuffe* and *Phèdre*. They never wearied of hearing the same plays over and over again. They delighted in the same old words, and when they were old men they laughed at the same jokes which had been their joy when they were children. And so it would be while the French nation endured. No country in the world has so firmly rooted a cult of its great-great-grandfathers. The rest of the universe did not interest them. There were many, many men and women, even intelligent men and women, who had never read anything, and never wanted to read anything outside the works that had been written in France under the Great King! Their theaters presented neither Goethe, nor Schiller, nor Kleist, nor Grillparzer, nor Hebbel, nor any of the great dramatists of other nations, with the exception of the ancient Greeks, whose heirs they declared themselves to be—(like every other nation in Europe). Every now and then they felt they ought to include Shakespeare. That was the touchstone. There were two schools of Shakespearean interpreters: the one played *King Lear,* with a commonplace realism, like a comedy of Emile Augier: the other turned *Hamlet* into an opera, with bravura airs and vocal exercises à la Victor Hugo. It never occurred to them that reality could be poetic or that poetry was the spontaneous language of hearts bursting with life. Shakespeare seemed false. They very quickly went back to Rostand.

And yet, during the last twenty years, there had been sturdy efforts made to vitalize the theater: the narrow circle of subjects drawn from Parisian literature had been widened: the theater laid hands on everything with a show of audacity. Two or three times even the outer world, public life, had torn down the curtain of convention. But the theatrists made haste to piece it together again. They lived in blinkers, and were afraid of seeing things as they are. A sort of clannishness, a classical tradition, a routine of form and spirit, and a lack of real seriousness, held them back from pushing their audacity to its logical extremity. They turned the acutest problems into ingenious games: and they always came back to the problem of women—women of a certain class. And what a sorry figure did the phantoms of great men cut on their boards: the heroic Anarchy of Ibsen, the Gospel of Tolstoy, the Superman of Nietzsche! . . .

The literary men of Paris took a great deal of trouble to seem to be advanced thinkers. But at heart they were all conservative. There was no literature in Europe in which the past, the old, the "eternal yesterday," held a completer and more unconscious sway: in the great reviews, in the great newspapers, in the State-aided theaters, in the Academy, Paris was in literature what London was in Politics: the check on the mind of Europe. The French Academy was a House of Lords. A certain number of the institutions of the *Ancien Régime* forced the spirit of the old days on the new society. Every revolutionary element was rejected or promptly assimilated. They asked nothing better. In vain did the Government pretend to a socialistic polity. In art it truckled under to the Academies and the Academic Schools. Against the Academies there was no opposition save from a few coteries, and they put up a very poor fight. For as soon as a member of a coterie could, he fell into line with an Academy, and became more academic than the rest. And even if a writer were in the advance guard or in the van of the army, he was almost always trammeled by his group and the ideas of his group. Some of them were hidebound by their academic *Credo*, others by their revolutionary *Credo:* and, when all was done, they both amounted to the same thing.

By way of rousing Christophe, on whom academic art had acted as a soporific, Sylvain Kohn proposed to take him to certain eclectic theaters,—the very latest thing. There they saw murder, rape, madness, torture, eyes plucked out, bellies gutted —anything to thrill the nerves, and satisfy the barbarism lurking beneath a too civilized section of the people. It had a great attraction for pretty women and men of the world—the people who would go and spend whole afternoons in the stuffy courts of the Palais de Justice, listening to scandalous cases, laughing, talking, and eating chocolates. But Christophe indignantly refused. The more closely he examined that sort of art, the more acutely he became aware of the odor that from the very first he had detected, faintly in the beginning, then more strongly, and finally it was suffocating: the odor of death.

Death: it was everywhere beneath all the luxury and uproar. Christophe discovered the explanation of the feeling of repugnance with which certain French plays had filled him. It was not their immorality that shocked him. Morality, immorality, amorality,—all these words mean nothing. Christophe had never invented any moral theory: he loved the great poets and great musicians of the past, and they were no saints: when he came across a great artist he did not inquire into his morality: he asked him rather:

" Are you healthy? "

To be healthy was the great thing. "If the poet is ill, let him first of all cure himself," as Goethe says. "When he is cured, he will write."

The writers of Paris were unhealthy: or if one of them happened to be healthy, the chances were that he was ashamed of it: he disguised it, and did his best to catch some disease. Their sickness was not shown in any particular feature of their art:—the love of pleasure, the extreme license of mind, or the universal trick of criticism which examined and dissected every idea that was expressed. All these things could be—and were, as the case might be—healthy or unhealthy. If death was there, it did not come from the material, but from the use that these people made of it: it was in the people themselves. And Christophe himself loved pleasure. He, too, loved liberty. He had drawn down upon himself the displeasure of his little German town by his frankness in defending many things, which he found here, promulgated by these Parisians, in such a way as to disgust him. And yet they were the same things. But nothing sounded the same to the Parisians and to himself. When Christophe impatiently shook off the yoke of the great Masters of the past, when he waged war against the esthetics and the morality of the Pharisees, it was not a game to him as it was to these men of intellect: and his revolt was directed only towards life, the life of fruitfulness, big with the centuries to come. With these people all tended to sterile enjoyment. Sterile, Sterile, Sterile. That was the key to the enigma. Mind and senses were fruitlessly debauched. A brilliant art, full of wit and cleverness—a lovely form, in truth, a tradition of beauty, impregnably seated, in spite of foreign alluvial deposits—a theater which was a theater, a style which was a style, authors who knew their business, writers who could write, the fine skeleton of an art, and a thought that had been great. But a skeleton. Sonorous words, ringing phrases, the metallic clang of ideas hurtling down the void, witticisms, minds haunted by sensuality, and senses numbed with thought. It was all useless, save for the sport of egoism. It led to death. It was a phenomenon analogous to the frightful decline in the birth-rate of France, which Europe was observing—and reckoning—in silence. So much wit, so much cleverness, so many acute senses, all wasted and wasting in a sort of shameful onanism! They had no notion of it, and wished to have none. They laughed. That was the only thing that comforted Christophe a little: these people could still laugh: all was not lost. He liked them even less when they tried to take themselves seriously: and nothing hurt him more than to see writers, who regarded art as no more than an instrument of pleasure, giving themselves airs as priests of a disinterested religion:

"We are artists," said Sylvain Kohn once more complacently. "We follow art for art's sake. Art is always pure: everything in art is chaste. We explore life as tourists, who find everything amusing. We are amateurs of rare sensations, lovers of beauty."

"You are hypocrites," replied Christophe bluntly. "Excuse my saying so. I used to think my own country had a monopoly. In Germany our hypocrisy consists in always talking about idealism while we think of nothing but our interests, and we even believe that we are idealists while we think of nothing but ourselves. But you are much worse: you cover your national lewdness with the names of Art and Beauty (with capitals)—when you do not shield your Moral Pilatism behind the names of Truth, Science, Intellectual Duty, and you wash your hands of the possible consequences of your haughty inquiry. Art for art's sake! . . . That's a fine faith! But it is the faith of the strong. Art! To grasp life, as the eagle claws its prey, to bear it up into the air, to rise with it into the serenity of space! . . . For that you need talons, great wings, and a strong heart. But you are nothing but sparrows who, when they find a piece of carrion, rend it here and there, squabbling for it, and twittering. . . . Art for art's sake! . . . Oh! wretched men! Art is no common ground for the feet of all who pass it by. Why, it is a pleasure, it is the most intoxicating of all. But it is a pleasure which is only won at the cost of a strenuous fight: it is the laurel-wreath that crowns the victory of the strong. Art is life tamed. Art is the Emperor of life. To be Cæsar a man must have the soul of Cæsar. But you are only limelight Kings: you are playing a part, and do not even deceive yourselves. And, like those actors, who turn to profit their deformities, you manufacture literature out of your own deformities and those of your public. Lovingly do you cultivate the diseases of your people, their fear of effort, their love of pleasure, their sensual minds, their chimerical humanitarianism, everything in them that drugs the will, everything in them that saps their power for action. You deaden their minds with the fumes of opium. Behind it all is death: you know it: but you will not admit it. Well, I tell you: Where death is, there art is not. Art is the spring of life. But even the most honest of your writers are so cowardly that even when the bandage is removed from their eyes they pretend not to see: they have the effrontery to say:

"'It is dangerous, I admit: it is poisonous: but it is full of talent.'

"It is as if a judge, sentencing a hooligan, were to say:

"'He's a blackguard, certainly: but he has so much talent! . . .'"

Christophe wondered what was the use of French criticism. There was no lack of critics: they swarmed all over and about French art. It was impossible to see the work of the artists: they were swamped by the critics.

Christophe was not indulgent towards criticism in general. He found it difficult to admit the utility of these thousands of artists who formed a Fourth or Fifth Estate in the modern community: he read in it the signs of a worn-out generation which relegates to others the business of regarding life—feeling vicariously. And, to go farther, it seemed to him not a little shameful that they could not even see with their own eyes the reflection of life, but must have yet more intermediaries, reflections of the reflection—the critics. At least, they ought to have seen to it that the reflections were true. But the critics reflected nothing but the uncertainty of the mob that moved round them. They were like those trick mirrors which reflect again and again the faces of the sightseers who gaze into them against a painted background.

There had been a time when the critics had enjoyed a tremendous authority in France. The public bowed down to their decrees: and they were not far from regarding them as superior to the artists, as artists with intelligence:—(apparently the two words do not go together naturally). Then they had multiplied too rapidly: there were too many oracles: that spoiled the trade. When there are so many people, each of whom declares that he is the sole repository of truth, it is impossible to believe them: and in the end they cease to believe it themselves. They were discouraged: in the passage from night to day, according to the French custom, they passed from one extreme to the other. Where they had before professed to know everything, they now professed to know nothing. It was a point of honor with them, quite fatuously. Renan had taught those milksop generations that it is not correct to affirm anything without denying it at once, or at least casting a doubt on it. He was one of those men of whom St. Paul speaks: "For whom there is always Yes, Yes, and then No, No." All the superior persons in France had wildly embraced this amphibious *Credo*. It exactly suited their indolence of mind and weakness of character. They no longer said of a work of art that it was good or bad, true or false, intelligent or idiotic. They said:

"It may be so. . . . Nothing is impossible. . . . I don't know. . . . I wash my hands of it."

If some objectionable piece were put up, they did not say:

"That is nasty rubbish!"

They said:

"Sir Sganarelle, please do not talk like that. Our philosophy bids us talk of everything open-mindedly: and therefore you ought not to say: 'That is nasty rubbish!' but: 'It seems to me that that is nasty rubbish. . . . But it is not certain that it is so. It may be a masterpiece. Who can say that it is not?'"

There was no danger of their being accused of tyranny over the arts. Schiller once taught them a lesson when he reminded the petty tyrants of the Press of his time of what he called bluntly:

"The Duty of Servants.

"First, the house must be clean that the Queen is to enter. Bustle about, then! Sweep the rooms. That is what you are there for, gentlemen!

"But as soon as She appears, out you go! Let not the serving-wench sit in her lady's chair!"

But, to be just to the critics of that time, it must be said that they never did sit in their lady's chair. It was ordered that they should be servants: and servants they were. But bad servants: they never took a broom in their hands: the room was thick with dust. Instead of cleaning and tidying, they folded their arms, and left the work to be done by the master, the divinity of the day:—Universal Suffrage.

In fact, there had been for some time a wave of reaction passing through the popular conscience. A few people had set out—feebly enough—on a campaign of public health: but Christophe could see no sign of it among the people with whom he lived. They gained no hearing, and were laughed at. When every now and then some honest man did raise a protest against unclean art, the authors replied haughtily that they were in the right, since the public was satisfied. That was enough to silence every objection. The public had spoken: that was the supreme law of art! It never occurred to anybody to impeach the evidence of a debauched public in favor of those who had debauched them, or that it was the artist's business to lead the public, not the public the artist. A numerical religion— the number of the audience, and the sum total of the receipts— dominated the artistic thought of that commercialized democracy. Following the authors, the critics docilely declared that the essential function of a work of art was to please. Success is law: and when success endures, there is nothing to be done but to bow to it. And so they devoted their energies to anticipating the fluctuations of the Exchange of pleasure, in trying to find out what the public thought of the various plays. The joke of it was that the public was always trying frantically to find out what the critics thought. And so there they were.

looking at each other: and in each other's eyes they saw nothing but their own indecision.

And yet never had there been such crying need of a fearless critic. In an anarchical Republic, fashion, which is all-powerful in art, very rarely looks backward, as it does in a conservative State: it goes onwards always: and there is a perpetual competition of libertinism which hardly anybody dare resist. The mob is incapable of forming an opinion: at heart it is shocked: but nobody dares to say what everybody secretly feels. If the critics were strong, if they dared to be strong, what a power they would have! A vigorous critic would in a few years become the Napoleon of public taste, and sweep away all the diseases of art. But there is no Napoleon in France. All the critics live in that vitiated atmosphere, and do not notice it. And they dare not speak. They all know each other. They are a more or less close company, and they have to consider each other: not one of them is independent. To be so, they would have to renounce their social life, and even their friendships. Who is there that would have the courage, in such a knock-kneed time, when even the best critics doubt whether a just notice is worth the annoyance it may cause to the writer and the object of it? Who is there so devoted to duty that he would condemn himself to such a hell on earth: dare to stand out against opinion, fight the imbecility of the public, expose the mediocrity of the successes of the day, defend the unknown artist who is alone and at the mercy of the beasts of prey, and subject the minds of those who were born to obey to the dominion of the master-mind? Christophe actually heard the critics at a first night in the vestibule of the theater say: "H'm! Pretty bad, isn't it? Utter rot!" And next day in their notices they talked of masterpieces, Shakespeare, the wings of genius beating above their heads.

"It is not so much talent that your art lacks as character," said Christophe to Sylvain Kohn. "You need a great critic, a Lessing, a . . ."

"A Boileau?" said Sylvain quizzically.

"A Boileau, perhaps, more than these artists of genius."

"If we had a Boileau," said Sylvain Kohn, "no one would listen to him."

"If they did not listen to him," replied Christophe, "he would not be a Boileau. I bet you that if I set out and told you the truth about yourselves, quite bluntly, however clumsy I might be, you would have to gulp it down."

"My dear good fellow!" laughed Sylvain Kohn.

That was all the reply he made.

He was so cocksure and so satisfied with the general flabbiness of the French that suddenly it occurred to Christophe that Kohn was a thousand times more of a foreigner in France than himself: and there was a catch at his heart.

"It is impossible," he said once more, as he had said that evening when he had left the theater on the boulevards in disgust. "There must be something else."

"What more do you want?" asked Sylvain Kohn.

"France."

"We are France," said Sylvain Kohn, gurgling with laughter.

Christophe stared hard at him for a moment, then shook his head, and said once more:

"There must be something else."

"Well, old man, you'd better look for it," said Sylvain Kohn, laughing louder than ever.

Christophe had to look for it. It was well hidden.

II

THE more clearly Christophe saw into the vat of ideas in which Parisian art was fermenting, the more strongly he was impressed by the supremacy of women in that cosmopolitan community. They had an absurdly disproportionate importance. It was not enough for woman to be the helpmeet of man. It was not even enough for her to be his equal. Her pleasure must be law both for herself and for man. And man

truckled to it. When a nation is growing old, it renounces
its will, its faith, the whole essence of its being, in favor of the
giver of pleasure. Men make works of art: but women make
men,—(except when they tamper with the work of the men, as
happened in France at that time) :—and it would be more
just to say that they unmake what they make. No doubt the
Eternal Feminine has been an uplifting influence on the best
of men: but for the ordinary men, in ages of weariness and
fatigue, there is, as some one has said, another Feminine, just
as eternal, who drags them down. This other Feminine was
the mistress of Parisian thought, the Queen of the Republic.

Christophe closely observed the Parisian women at the houses
at which Sylvain Kohn's introduction or his own skill at the
piano had made him welcome. Like most foreigners, he gen-
eralized freely and unsparingly about French women from the
two or three types he had met: young women, not very tall,
and not at all fresh, with neat figures, dyed hair, large hats
on their pretty heads that were a little too large for their bodies:
they had trim features, but their faces were just a little too
fleshy: good noses, vulgar sometimes, characterless always: quick
eyes without any great depth, which they tried to make as
brilliant and large as possible: well-cut lips that were perfectly
under control: plump little chins; and the lower part of their
faces revealed their utter materialism; they were elegant little
creatures who, amid all their preoccupations with love and intrigue, never lost sight of public opinion and their domestic
affairs. They were pretty, but they belonged to no race.
In all these polite ladies there was the savor of the respectable woman perverted, or wanting to be so, together
with all the traditions of her class; prudence, economy, coldness, practical common sense, egoism. A poor sort of life.
A desire for pleasure emanating rather from a cerebral
curiosity than from a need of the senses. Their will was
mediocre in quality, but firm. They were very well dressed,
and had little automatic gestures. They were always patting

their hair or their gowns with the backs or the palms of their
hands, with little delicate movements. And they always managed to sit so that they could admire themselves—and watch
other women—in a mirror, near or far, not to mention, at
tea or dinner, the spoons, knives, silver coffee-pots, polished
and shining, in which they always peeped at the reflections of
their faces, which were more interesting to them than anything
or anybody else. At meals they dieted sternly: drinking water
and depriving themselves altogether of any food that might
stand in the way of their ideal of a complexion of a floury
whiteness.

There was a fairly large proportion of Jewesses among
Christophe's acquaintance: and he was always attracted by
them, although, since his encounter with Judith Mannheim,
he had hardly any illusions about them. Sylvain Kohn had
introduced him to several Jewish houses where he was received with the usual intelligence of the race, which loves intelligence. Christophe met financiers there, engineers, newspaper proprietors, international brokers, slave-dealers of a sort
from Algiers—the men of affairs of the Republic. They were
clear-headed and energetic, indifferent to other people, smiling,
affable, and secretive. Christophe felt sometimes that behind
their hard faces was the knowledge of crime in the past, and
the future, of these men gathered round the sumptuous table
laden with food, flowers, and wine. They were almost all ugly.
But the women, taken as a whole, were quite brilliant, though
it did not do to look at them too closely: in most of them there
was a want of subtlety in their coloring. But brilliance there
was, and a fair show of material life, beautiful shoulders generously exposed to view, and a genius for making their beauty
and even their ugliness a lure for the men. An artist would
have recognized in some of them the old Roman type, the women
of the time of Nero, down to the time of Hadrian. And there
were Palmaesque faces, with a sensual expression, heavy chins
solidly modeled with the neck, and not without a certain bestial
beauty. Some of them had thick curly hair, and bold, fiery

eyes: they seemed to be subtle, incisive, ready for everything, more virile than other women. And also more feminine. Here and there a more spiritual profile would stand out. Those pure features came from beyond Rome, from the East, the country of Laban: there was expressed in them the poetry of silence, of the Desert. But when Christophe went nearer, and listened to the conversations between Rebecca and Faustina the Roman, or Saint Barbe the Venetian, he found her to be just a Parisian Jewess, just like the others, even more Parisian than the Parisian women, more artificial and sophisticated, talking quietly, and maliciously stripping the assembled company, body and soul, with her Madonna's eyes.

Christophe wandered from group to group, but could identify himself with none of them. The men talked savagely of hunting, brutally of love, and only of money with any sort of real appreciation. And that was cold and cunning. They talked business in the smoking-room. Christophe heard some one say of a certain fop who was sauntering from one lady to another, with a buttonhole in his coat, oozing heavy compliments:

"So! He is free again?"

In a corner of the room two ladies were talking of the love-affairs of a young actress and a society woman. There was occasional music. Christophe was asked to play. Large women, breathless and heavily perspiring, declaimed in an apocalyptic tone verses of Sully-Prudhomme or Auguste Dorchain. A famous actor solemnly recited a *Mystic Ballad* to the accompaniment of an American organ. Words and music were so stupid that they turned Christophe sick. But the Roman women were delighted, and laughed heartily to show their magnificent teeth. Scenes from Ibsen were performed. It was a fine epilogue to the struggle of a great man against the Pillars of Society that it should be used for their diversion!

And then they all began, of course, to prattle about art. That was horrible. The women especially began to talk of Ibsen, Wagner, Tolstoy, flirtatiously, politely, boredly, or idiotically. Once the conversation had started, there was no stopping it.

The disease was contagious. Christophe had to listen to the ideas of bankers, brokers, and slave-dealers on art. In vain did he refuse to speak or try to turn the conversation: they insisted on talking about music and poetry. As Berlioz said: "Such people use the words quite coolly: just as though they were talking of wine, women, or some such trash." An alienist physician recognized one of his patients in an Ibsen heroine, though to his way of thinking she was infinitely more silly. An engineer quite sincerely declared that the husband was the sympathetic character in the *Doll's House.* The famous actor —a well-known Comedian—brayed his profound ideas on Nietzsche and Carlyle: he assured Christophe that he could not see a picture of Velasquez—(the idol of the hour)—" without the tears coursing down his cheeks." And he confided—still to Christophe's private ear—that, though he esteemed art very highly, yet he esteemed still more highly the art of living, acting, and that if he were asked to choose what part he would play, it would be that of Bismarck. . . . Sometimes there would be of the company a professed wit, but the level of the conversation was not appreciably higher for that. Generally they said nothing; they confined themselves to a jerky remark or an enigmatic smile: they lived on their reputations, and were saved further trouble. But there were a few professional talkers, generally from the South. They talked about anything and everything. They had no sense of proportion: everything came alike to them. One was a Shakespeare. Another a Molière. Another a Pascal, if not a Jesus Christ. They compared Ibsen with Dumas *fils,* Tolstoy with George Sand: and the gist of it all was that everything came from France. Generally they were ignorant of foreign languages. But that did not disturb them. It mattered so little to their audience whether they told the truth or not! What did matter was that they should say amusing things, things as flattering as possible to national vanity. Foreigners had to put up with a good deal—with the exception of the idol of the hour: for there was always a fashionable idol: Grieg, or Wagner, or

Nietzsche, or Gorki, or D'Annunzio. It never lasted long, and the idol was certain one fine morning to be thrown on to the rubbish-heap.

For the moment the idol was Beethoven. Beethoven—save the mark!—was in the fashion: at least, among literary and polite persons: for musicians had dropped him at once, in accordance with the see-saw system which is one of the laws of artistic taste in France. A Frenchman needs to know what his neighbor thinks before he knows what he thinks himself, so that he can think the same thing or the opposite. Thus, when they saw Beethoven in popular favor, the most distinguished musicians began to discover that he was not distinguished enough for them: they claimed to lead opinion, not to follow it: and rather than be in agreement with it they turned their backs on it. They began to regard Beethoven as a man afflicted with deafness, crying in a voice of bitterness: and some of them declared that he might be an excellent moralist, but that he was certainly overpraised as a musician. That sort of joke was not at all to Christophe's taste. Still less did he like the enthusiasm of polite society. If Beethoven had come to Paris just then, he would have been the lion of the hour: it was such a pity that he had been dead for more than a century. His vogue grew not so much out of his music as out of the more or less romantic circumstances of his life which had been popularized by sentimental and virtuous biographies. His rugged face and lion's mane had become a romantic figure. Ladies wept for him: they hinted that if they had known him he should not have been so unhappy: and in their greatness of heart they were the more ready to sacrifice all for him, in that there was no danger of Beethoven taking them at their word: the old fellow was beyond all need of anything. That was why the virtuosi, the conductors, and the *impresarii* bowed down in pious worship before him: and, as the representatives of Beethoven, they gathered the homage destined for him. There were sumptuous festivals at exorbitant prices, which afforded society people an opportunity of showing their generosity—and incidentally also of discovering Beethoven's symphonies. There were committees of actors, men of the world, Bohemians, and politicians, appointed by the Republic to preside over the destinies of art, and they informed the world of their intention to erect a monument to Beethoven: and on these committees, together with a few honest men whose names guaranteed the rest, were all the riffraff who would have stoned Beethoven if he had been alive, if Beethoven had not crushed the life out of them. Christophe watched and listened. He ground his teeth to keep himself from saying anything outrageous. He was on tenterhooks the whole evening. He could not talk, nor could he keep silent. It seemed to him humiliating and shameful to talk neither for pleasure nor from necessity, but out of politeness, because he had to talk. He was not allowed to say what he thought, and it was impossible for him to make conversation. And he did not even know how to be polite without talking. If he looked at anybody, he glared too fixedly and intently: in spite of himself he studied that person, and that person was offended. If he spoke at all, he believed too much in what he was saying; and that was disturbing for everybody, and even for himself. He quite admitted that he was out of his element: and, as he was clever enough to sound the general note of the company, in which his presence was a discord, he was as upset by his manners as his hosts. He was angry with himself and with them.

When at last he stood in the street once more, very late at night, he was so worn out with the boredom of it all that he could hardly drag himself home: he wanted to lie down just where he was, in the street, as he had done many times when he was returning as a boy from his performances at the Palace of the Grand Duke. Although he had only five or six francs to take him to the end of the week, he spent two of them on a cab. He flung himself into it the more quickly to escape: and as he drove along he groaned aloud from sheer exhaustion. When he reached home and got to bed, he groaned in his sleep. . . . And then, suddenly, he roared with laughter as he remembered some ridiculous saying. He woke up repeating it, and imitating the features of the speaker. Next day, and for several days after, as he walked about, he would suddenly bellow like a bull. . . . Why did he visit these people? Why did he go on visiting them? Why force himself to gesticulate and make faces, like the rest, and pretend to be interested in things that did not appeal to him in the very least? Was it true that he was not in the least interested? A year ago he would not have been able to put up with them for a moment. Now, at heart, he was amused by it all, while at the same time it exasperated him. Was a little of the indifference of the Parisians creeping over him? He would sometimes wonder fearfully whether he had lost strength. But, in truth, he had gained in strength. He was more free in mind in strange surroundings. In spite of himself, his eyes were opened to the great Comedy of the world.

Besides, whether he liked it or not, he had to go on with it if he wanted his art to be recognized by Parisian society, which is only interested in art in so far as it knows the artist. And he had to make himself known if he were to find among these Philistines the pupils necessary to keep him alive.

And, then, Christophe had a heart: his heart must have affection: wherever he might be, there he would find food for his affections: without it he could not live.

Among the few girls of that class of society—few enough —whom Christophe taught, was the daughter of a rich motor-car manufacturer, Colette Stevens. Her father was a Belgian, a naturalized Frenchman, the son of an Anglo-American settled at Antwerp, and a Dutchwoman. Her mother was an Italian. A regular Parisian family. To Christophe—and to many others —Colette Stevens was the type of French girl.

She was eighteen, and had velvety, soft black eyes, which she used skilfully upon young men—regular Spanish eyes, with enormous pupils; a rather long and fantastic nose, which wrinkled up and moved at the tip as she talked, with little fractious pouts and shrugs; rebellious hair; a pretty little face; rather sallow complexion, dabbed with powder; heavy, rather thick features: altogether she was like a plump kitten.

She was slight, very well dressed, attractive, provoking: she had sly, affected, rather silly manners: her pose was that of a little girl, and she would sit rocking her chair for hours at a time, and giving little exclamations like: "No? Impossible.-. -. -."

At meals she would clap her hands when there was a dish she loved: in the drawing-room she would smoke cigarette after cigarette, and, when there were men present, display an exuberant affection for her girl-friends, flinging her arms round their necks, kissing their hands, whispering in their ears, making ingenuous and naughty remarks, doing it most brilliantly, in a soft, twittering voice; and in the lightest possible way she would say improper things, without seeming to do more than hint at them, and was even more skilful in provoking them from others; she had the ingenuous air of a little girl, who knows perfectly well what she is about, with her large brilliant eyes, slyly and voluptuously looking sidelong, maliciously taking in all the gossip, and catching at all the dubious remarks of the conversation, and all the time angling for hearts.

All these tricks and shows, and her sophisticated ingenuity, were not at all to Christophe's liking. He had better things to do than to lend himself to the practices of an artful little girl, and did not even care to look on at them for his amusement. He had to earn his living, to keep his life and ideas from death. He had no interest in these drawing-room parakeets beyond the gaining of a livelihood. In return for their money, he gave them lessons, conscientiously concentrating all his energies on the task, to keep the boredom of it from mastering him, and his attention from being distracted by the tricks of his pupils when they were coquettes, like Colette Stevens. He paid no more attention to her than to Colette's little cousin, a child of twelve, shy and silent, whom the Stevens had adopted, to whom also Christophe gave lessons on the piano.

But Colette was too clever not to feel that all her charms were lost on Christophe, and too adroit not to adapt herself at once to his character. She did not even need to do so deliberately. It was a natural instinct with her. She was a woman. She was like water, formless. The soul of every man she met was a vessel, whose form she took immediately out of curiosity. It was a law of her existence that she should always be some one else. Her whole personality was for ever shifting. She was for ever changing her vessel.

Christophe attracted her for many reasons, the chief of which was that he was not attracted by her. He attracted her also because he was different from all the young men of her acquaintance: she had never tried to pour herself into a vessel of such a rugged form. And, finally, he attracted her, because, being naturally and by inheritance expert in the valuation at the first glance of men and vessels, she knew perfectly well that what he lacked in polish Christophe made up in a solidity of character which none of her smart young Parisians could offer her.

She played as well and as badly as most idle young women. She played a great deal and very little—that is to say, that she was always working at it, but knew nothing at all about it. She strummed on her piano all day long, for want of anything else to do, or from affectation, or because it gave her pleasure. Sometimes she rattled along mechanically. Sometimes she would play well, very well, with taste and soul—(it was almost as though she had a soul: but, as a matter of fact, she only borrowed one). Before she knew Christophe, she was capable of liking Massenet, Grieg, Thomé. But after she met Christophe she ceased to like them. Then she played Bach and Beethoven very correctly—(which is not very high praise): but the great thing was that she loved them. At bottom it was not Beethoven, nor Thomé, nor Bach, nor Grieg that she loved, but the notes, the sounds, the fingers running over the keys, the thrills she got from the chords which tickled her nerves and made her wriggle with pleasure.

In the drawing-room of the great house, decorated with faded tapestry, and on an easel in the middle room, a portrait of the stout Madame Stevens by a fashionable painter who had represented her in a languishing attitude, like a flower dying for want of water, with a die-away expression in her eyes, and her body draped in impossible curves, by way of expressing the rare quality of her millionaire soul—in the great drawing-room, with its bow-windows looking on to a clump of old trees powdered with snow, Christophe would find Colette sitting at her piano, repeating the same passage over and over again, delighting her ear with mellifluous dissonance.

"Ah!" Christophe would say as he entered, "the cat is still purring!"

"How wicked of you!" she would laugh. . . . (And she would hold out her soft little hand.)

". . . Listen. Isn't it pretty?"

"Very pretty," he would say indifferently.

"You aren't listening! . . . Will you please listen?"

"I am listening. . . . It's the same thing over and over again."

"Ah! you are no musician," she would say pettishly.

"As if that were music or anything like it!"

"What! Not music! . . . What is it, then, if you please?"

"You know quite well: I won't tell you, because it would not be polite."

"All the more reason why you should say it."

"You want me to? . . . So much the worse for you! . . . Well, do you know what you are doing with your piano? . . . You are flirting with it."

"Indeed!"

"Certainly. You say to it: 'Dear piano, dear piano, say pretty things to me; kiss me; give me just one little kiss!'"

"You need not say any more," said Colette, half vexed, half laughing. "You haven't the least idea of respect."

" Not the least."

" You are impertinent. . . . And then, even if it were so, isn't that the right way to love music? "

" Oh, come, don't mix music up with that."

" But that is music! A beautiful chord is a kiss."

" I never told you that."

" But isn't it true? . . . Why do you shrug your shoulders and make faces? "

" Because it annoys me."

" So much the better."

" It annoys me to hear music spoken of as though it were a sort of indulgence. . . . Oh, it isn't your fault. It's the fault of the world you live in. The stale society in which you live regards music as a sort of legitimate vice. . . . Come, sit down! Play me your sonata."

" No. Let us talk a little longer."

" I'm not here to talk. I'm here to teach you the piano. . . . Come, play away! "

" You're so rude! " said Colette, rather vexed—but at heart delighted to be handled so roughly.

She played her piece carefully: and, as she was clever, she succeeded fairly well, and sometimes even very well. Christophe, who was not deceived, laughed inwardly at the skill " of the little beast, who played as though she felt what she was playing, while really she felt nothing at all." And yet he had a sort of amused sympathy for her. Colette, on her part, seized every excuse for going on with the conversation, which interested her much more than her lesson. It was no good Christophe drawing back on the excuse that he could not say what he thought without hurting her feelings: she always wheedled it out of him: and the more insulting it was, the less she was hurt by it: it was an amusement for her. But, as she was quick enough to see that Christophe liked nothing so much as sincerity, she would contradict him flatly, and argue tenaciously. They would part very good friends.

However, Christophe would never have had the least illusion
about their friendship, and there would never have been the
smallest intimacy between them, had not Colette one day taken
it into her head, out of sheer instinctive coquetry, to confide in
him.

The evening before her parents had given an At Home. She
had laughed, chattered, flirted outrageously: but next morning,
when Christophe came for her lesson, she was worn out, drawn-
looking, gray-faced, and haggard. She hardly spoke: she
seemed utterly depressed. She sat at the piano, played softly,
made mistakes, tried to correct them, made them again, stopped
short, and said:

"I can't. . . . Please forgive me. . . . Please wait a
little. . . ."

He asked if she were unwell. She said: "No. . . . She
was out of sorts. . . . She had bouts of it. . . . It was
absurd, but he must not mind."

He proposed to go away and come again another day: but
she insisted on his staying:

"Just a moment. . . . I shall be all right presently. . . .
It's silly of me, isn't it?"

He felt that she was not her usual self: but he did not
question her: and, to turn the conversation, he said:

"That's what comes of having been so brilliant last night.
You took too much out of yourself."

She smiled a little ironically.

"One can't say the same of you," she replied.

He laughed.

"I don't believe you said a word," she went on.

"Not a word."

"But there were interesting people there."

"Oh yes. All sorts of lights and famous people, all talking
at once. But I'm lost among all your boneless Frenchmen who
understand everything, and explain everything, and excuse
everything—and feel nothing at all. People who talk for hours
together about art and love! Isn't it revolting?"

" But you ought to be interested in art if not in love."

" One doesn't talk about these things : one does them."

" But when one cannot do them ? " said Colette, pouting.
Christophe replied with a laugh :

" Well, leave it to others.   Everybody is not fit for art."

" Nor for love ? "

" Nor for love."

" How awful !   What is left for us ? "

" Housekeeping."

" Thanks," said Colette, rather annoyed.   She turned to the
piano and began again, made mistakes, thumped the keyboard.
and moaned :

" I can't ! . . .   I'm no good at all.   I believe you are right.
Women aren't any good."

" It's something to be able to say so," said Christophe
genially.

She looked at him rather sheepishly, like a little girl who
has been scolded, and said :

" Don't be so hard."

" I'm not saying anything hard about good women," replied
Christophe gaily.   " A good woman is Paradise on earth.   Only,
Paradise on earth . . ."

" I know.   No one has ever seen it."

" I'm not so pessimistic.   I say only that I have never seen
it : but that's no reason why it should not exist.   I'm determined to find it, if it does exist.   But it is not easy.   A good
woman and a man of genius are equally rare."

" And all the other men and women don't count ? "

" On the contrary, it is only they who count—for the
world."

" But for you ? "

" For me, they don't exist."

" You *are* hard," repeated Colette.

" A little.   Somebody has to be hard, if only in the interest
of the others ! . . .   If there weren't a few pebbles here and
there in the world, the whole thing would go to pulp."

"Yes. You are right. It is a good thing for you that you are strong," said Colette sadly. "But you must not be too hard on men,—and especially on women who aren't strong. . . . You don't know how terrible our weakness is to us. Because you see us flirting, and laughing, and doing silly things, you think we never dream of anything else, and you despise us. Ah! if you could see all that goes on in the minds of the girls of from fifteen to eighteen as they go out into society, and have the sort of success that comes to their youth and freshness—when they have danced, and talked smart nonsense, and said bitter things at which people laugh because they laugh, when they have given themselves to imbeciles, and sought in vain in their eyes the light that is nowhere to be found, —if you could see them in their rooms at night, in silence, alone, kneeling in agony to pray! . . ."

"Is it possible?" said Christophe, altogether amazed. "What! you, too, have suffered?"

Colette did not reply: but tears came to her eyes. She tried to smile and held out her hand to Christophe: he grasped it warmly.

"What would you have us do? There is nothing to do. You men can free yourselves and do what you like. But we are bound for ever and ever within the narrow circle of the duties and pleasures of society: we cannot break free."

"There is nothing to prevent your freeing yourselves, finding some work you like, and winning your independence just as we do."

"As you do? Poor Monsieur Krafft! Your work is not so very certain! . . . But at least you like your work. But what sort of work can we do? There isn't any that we could find interesting—for, I know, we dabble in all sorts of things, and pretend to be interested in a heap of things that do not concern us: we do so want to be interested in something! I do what the others do. I do charitable work and sit on social work committees. I go to lectures at the Sorbonne by Bergson and Jules Lemaître, historical concerts, classical matinées, and I

take notes and notes. . . . I never know what I am writing!
. . . and I try to persuade myself that I am absorbed by it,
or at least that it is useful. Ah! but I know that it is not true.
I know that I don't care a bit, and that I am bored by it all!
. . . Don't despise me because I tell you frankly what everybody thinks in secret. I'm no sillier than the rest. But what
use are philosophy, history, and science to me? As for art,—
you see,—I strum and daub and make messy little water-color
sketches;—but is that enough to fill a woman's life? There is
only one end to our life: marriage. But do you think there is
much fun in marrying this or that young man whom I know
as well as you do? I see them as they are. I am not for-
tunate enough to be like your German Gretchens, who can always create an illusion for themselves. . . . That is terrible,
isn't it? To look around and see girls who have married and
their husbands, and to think that one will have to do as they
have done, be cramped in body and mind, and become dull like
them! . . . One needs to be stoical, I tell you, to accept such
a life with such obligations. All women are not capable of it.
. . . And time passes, the years go by, youth fades: and yet
there were lovely things and good things in us—all useless, for
day by day they die, and one has to surrender them to the fools
and people whom one despises, people who will despise oneself!
. . . And nobody understands! One would think that we
were sphinxes. One can forgive the men who find us dull and
strange! But the women ought to understand us! They have
been like us: they have only to look back and remember. . . .
But no. There is no help from them. Even our mothers ignore us, and actually try not to know what we are. They only
try to get us married. For the rest, they say, live, die, do as
you like! Society absolutely abandons us."

"Don't lose heart," said Christophe. "Every one has to
face the experience of life all over again. If you are brave.
it will be all right. Look outside your own circle. There
must be a few honest men in France."

"There are. I know. But they are so tedious! . . . And

then, I tell you, I detest the circle in which I live: but I don't
think I could live outside it, now. It has become a habit. I
need a certain degree of comfort, certain refinements of luxury
and comfort, which, no doubt, money alone cannot provide,
though it is an indispensable factor. That sounds pretty poor,
I know. But I know myself: I am weak. . . . Please, please,
don't draw away from me because I tell you of my cowardice.
Be kind and listen to me. It helps me so to talk to you! I
feel that you are strong and sound: I have such confidence in
you. Will you be my friend?"

"Gladly," said Christophe. "But what can I do?"

"Listen to me, advise me, give me courage. I am often
so depressed! And then I don't know what to do. I say to
myself: 'What is the good of fighting? What's the good of
tormenting myself? One way or the other, what does it matter? Nothing and nobody matters!' That is a dreadful condition to be in. I don't want to get like that. Help me.
Help me."

She looked utterly downcast; she looked older by ten years:
she looked at Christophe with abject, imploring eyes. He promised what she asked. Then she revived, smiled, and was gay
once more.

And in the evening she was laughing and flirting as usual.

Thereafter they had many intimate conversations. They
were alone together: she confided in him: he tried hard to
understand and advise her: she listened to his advice, or, if
necessary, to his remonstrances, gravely, attentively, like a good
little girl: it was a distraction, an interest, even a support for
her: she thanked him coquettishly with a depth of feeling in her
eyes.—But her life was changed in nothing: it was only a distraction the more.

Her day was passed in a succession of metamorphoses. She
got up very late, about midday, after a sleepless night: for she
rarely went to sleep before dawn. All day long she did nothing.
She would vaguely call to mind a poem, an idea, a scrap of an

idea, or a face that had pleased her. She was never quite awake until about four or five in the afternoon. Till then her eyelids were heavy, her face was puffy, and she was sulky and sleepy. She would revive on the arrival of a few girl-friends as talkative as herself, and all sharing the same interest in the gossip of Paris. They chattered endlessly about love. The psychology of love: that was the unfailing topic, mixed up with dress, the indiscretions of others, and scandal. She had also a circle of idle young men to whom it was necessary to spend three hours a day among skirts: they ought to have worn them really, for they had the souls and the conversation of girls. Christophe had his hour as her confessor. At once Colette would become serious and intense. She was like the young Frenchwoman, of whom Bodley speaks, who, at the confessional, " developed a calmly prepared essay, a model of clarity and order, in which everything that was to be said was properly arranged in distinct categories."—And after that she flung herself once more into the business of amusement. As the day went on she grew younger. In the evening she went to the theater: and there was the eternal pleasure of recognizing the same eternal faces in the audience:—her pleasure lay not in the play that was performed, but in the actors whom she knew, whose familiar mannerisms she remarked once more. And she exchanged spiteful remarks with the people who came to see her in her box about the people in the other boxes and about the actresses. The *ingénue* was said to have a thin voice " like sour mayonnaise," or the great comédienne was dressed " like a lampshade."—Or else she went out to a party: and there the pleasure, for a pretty girl like Colette, lay in being seen:—(but there were bad days: nothing is more capricious than good looks in Paris) :—and she renewed her store of criticisms of people, and their dresses, and their physical defects. There was no conversation.—She would go home late, and take her time about going to bed (that was the time when she was most awake). She would dawdle about her dressing-table: skim through a book: laugh to herself at the memory of something said or done. She was bored and very unhappy. She could not go to sleep, and in the night there would come frightful moments of despair.

Christophe, who only saw Colette for a few hours at intervals, and could only be present at a few of these transformations, found it difficult to understand her at all. He wondered when she was sincere,—or if she were always sincere—or if she were never sincere. Colette herself could not have told him. Like most girls who are idle and circumscribed in their desires, she was in darkness. She did not know what she was, because she did not know what she wanted, because she could not know what she wanted without having tried it. She would try it, after her fashion, with the maximum of liberty and the minimum of risk, trying to copy the people about her and to take their moral measure. She was in no hurry to choose. She would have liked to try everything, and turn everything to account.

But that did not work with a friend like Christophe. He was perfectly willing to allow her to prefer people whom he did not admire, even people whom he despised; but he would not suffer her to put him on the same level with them. Everybody to his own taste: but at least let everybody have his own taste.

He was the less inclined to be patient with Colette, as she seemed to take a delight in gathering round herself all the young men who were most likely to exasperate Christophe: disgusting little snobs, most of them wealthy, all of them idle, or jobbed into a sinecure in some government office—which amounts to the same thing. They all wrote—or pretended to write. That was an itch of the Third Republic. It was a sort of indolent vanity,—intellectual work being the hardest of all to control, and most easily lending itself to the game of bluff. They never gave more than a discreet, though respectful hint, of their great labors. They seemed to be convinced of the importance of their work, staggering under the weight of it. At first Christophe was a little embarrassed by the fact that he had never heard of them or their works. He tried bashfully to ask about them: he was especially anxious to know what one of them had written, a young man who was declared by the others to be a master of the theater. He was surprised to hear that this great dramatist had written a one-act play taken from a novel, which had been pieced together from a number of short stories, or, rather, sketches, which he had published in one of the Reviews during the past ten years. The baggage of the others was not more considerable: a few one-act plays, a few short stories, a few verses. Some of them had won fame with an article, others with a book "which they were going to write." They professed scorn for long-winded books. They seemed to attach extreme importance to the handling of words. And yet the word "thought" frequently occurred in their conversation: but it did not seem to have the same meaning as is usually given to it: they applied it to the details of style. However, there were among them great thinkers, and great ironists, who, when they wrote, printed their subtle and profound remarks in *italics*, so that there might be no mistake.

They all had the cult of the letter *I:* it was the only cult they had. They tried to proselytize. But, unfortunately, other people were subscribers to the cult. They were always conscious of their audience in their way of speaking, walking, smoking, reading a paper, carrying their heads, looking, bowing to each other.—Such players' tricks are natural to young people, and the more insignificant—that is to say, unoccupied —they are, the stronger hold do they have on them. They are more especially paraded before women: for they covet women, and long—even more—to be coveted by them. But even on a chance meeting they will trot out their bag of tricks: even for a passer-by from whom they can expect only a glance of amazement. Christophe often came across these young strutting peacocks: budding painters, and musicians, art-students who modeled their appearance on some famous portrait: Van Dyck, Rembrandt, Velasquez, Beethoven; or fitted it to the parts they wish to play:-painter, musician, workman, the profound thinker, the jolly fellow, the Danubian peasant, the

natural man. . . . They were always on the lookout to see
if they were attracting attention. When Christophe met them
in the street he took a malicious pleasure in looking the other
way and ignoring them. But their discomfiture never lasted
long: a yard or so farther on they would start strutting for the
next comer.—But the young men of Colette's little circle were
rather more subtle: their coxcombry was mental: they had two
or three models. who were not themselves original. Or else
they would mimic an idea: Force, Joy, Pity, Solidarity, Socialism, Anarchism, Faith, Liberty: all these were parts for their
playing. They were horribly clever in making the dearest and
rarest thoughts mere literary stuff, and in degrading the most
heroic impulses of the human soul to the level of drawing-room
commodities, fashionable neckties.

But in love they were altogether in their element: that was
their special province. The casuistry of pleasure had no secrets
for them: they were so clever that they could invent new problems so as to have the honor of solving them. That has always been the occupation of people who have nothing else to
do: in default of love, they "make love": above all, they explain it. Their notes took up far more room than their text,
which, as a matter of fact, was very short. Sociology gave a
relish to the most scabrous thoughts: everything was sheltered
beneath the flag of sociology: though they might have had
pleasure in indulging their vices, there would have been something lacking if they had not persuaded themselves that they
were laboring in the cause of the new world. That was an
eminently Parisian sort of socialism: erotic socialism.

Among the problems that were then exercising the little
Court of Love was the equality of men and women in marriage, and their respective rights in love. There had been
young men, honest, protestant, and rather ridiculous,—Scan-
dinavians and Swiss—who had based equality on virtue: saying that men should come to marriage as chaste as women.
The Parisian casuists looked for another sort of equality, an
equality based on loss of virtue, saying that women should

come to marriage as besmirched as men,—the right to take lovers. The Parisians had carried adultery, in imagination and practice, to such a pitch that they were beginning to find it rather insipid: and in the world of letters attempts were being made to support it by a new invention: the prostitution of young girls,—I mean regularized, universal, virtuous, decent, domestic, and, above all, social prostitution.—There had just appeared a book on the question, full of talent, which apparently said all there was to be said: through four hundred pages of playful pedantry, "strictly in accordance with the rules of the Baconian method," it dealt with the "best method of controlling the relations of the sexes." It was a lecture on free love, full of talk about manners, propriety, good taste, nobility, beauty, truth, modesty, morality,—a regular Berquin for young girls who wanted to go wrong.—It was, for the moment, the Gospel in which Colette's little court rejoiced, while they paraphrased it. It goes without saying, that, like all disciples, they discarded all the justice, observation, and even humanity that lay behind the paradox, and only retained the evil in it. They plucked all the most poisonous flowers from the little bed of sweetened blossoms,—aphorisms of this sort: "The taste for pleasure can only sharpen the taste for work":—"It is monstrous that a girl should become a mother before she has tasted the sweets of life."—"To have had the love of a worthy and pure-souled man as a girl is the natural preparation of a woman for a wise and considered motherhood":—"Mothers," said this author, "should organize the lives of their daughters with the same delicacy and decency with which they control the liberty of their sons."—"The time would come when girls would return as naturally from their lovers as now they return from a walk or from taking tea with a friend."

Colette laughingly declared that such teaching was very reasonable.

Christophe had a horror of it. He exaggerated its importance and the evil that it might do. The French are too clever to bring their literature into practice. These Diderots in miniature are, in ordinary life, like the genial Panurge of the encyclopedia, honest citizens, not really a whit less timorous than the rest. It is precisely because they are so timid in action that they amuse themselves with carrying action (in thought) to the limit of possibility. It is a game without any risk.

But Christophe was not a French dilettante.

Among the young men of Colette's circle, there was one whom she seemed to prefer, and, of course, he was the most objectionable of all to Christophe.

He was one of those young parvenus of the second generation who form an aristocracy of letters, and are the patricians of the Third Republic. His name was Lucien Lévy-Cœur. He had quick eyes, set wide apart, an aquiline nose, a fair Van Dyck beard clipped to a point: he was prematurely bald, which did not become him: and he had a silky voice, elegant manners, and fine soft hands, which he was always rubbing together. He always affected an excessive politeness, an exaggerated courtesy, even with people he did not like, and even when he was bent on snubbing them.

Christophe had met him before at the literary dinner, to which he was taken by Sylvain Kohn: and though they had not spoken to each other, the sound of Lévy-Cœur's voice had been enough to rouse a dislike which he could not explain, and he was not to discover the reason for it until much later. There are sudden outbursts of love: and so there are of hate,—or—(to avoid hurting those tender souls who are afraid of the word as of every passion)—let us call it the instinct of health scenting the enemy, and mounting guard against him.

Lévy-Cœur was exactly the opposite of Christophe, and represented the spirit of irony and decay which fastened gently, politely, inexorably, on all the great things that were left of the dying society: the family, marriage, religion, patriotism: in art, on everything that was manly, pure, healthy, of the people: faith in ideas, feelings, great men, in Man. Behind that mode of thought there was only the mechanical pleasure of analysis, analysis pushed to extremes, a sort of animal desire to nibble at thought, the instinct of a worm. And side by side with that ideal of intellectual nibbling was a girlish sensuality, the sensuality of a blue-stocking: for to Lévy-Cœur everything became literature. Everything was literary copy to him: his own adventures, his vices and the vices of his friends. He had written novels and plays in which, with much talent, he described the private life of his relations, and their most intimate adventures, and those of his friends, his own, his *liaisons,* among others one with the wife of his best friend: the portraits were well-drawn: everybody praised them, the public, the wife, and his friend. It was impossible for him to gain the confidence or the favors of a woman without putting them into a book.—One would have thought that his indiscretions would have produced strained relations with his "friends." But there was nothing of the kind; they were hardly more than a little embarrassed: they protested as a matter of form: but at heart they were delighted at being held up to the public gaze, *en déshabille:* so long as their faces were masked, their modesty was undisturbed. But there was never any spirit of vengeance, or even of scandal, in his tale-telling. He was no worse a man or lover than the majority. In the very chapters in which he exposed his father and mother and his mistress, he would write of them with a poetic tenderness and charm. He was really extremely affectionate: but he was one of those men who have no need to respect when they love: quite the contrary: they rather love those whom they can despise a little: that makes the object of their affection seem nearer to them and more human. Such men are of all the least capable of understanding heroism and purity. They are not far from considering them lies or weakness of mind. It goes without saying that such men are convinced that they understand better than anybody else the heroes of art whom they judge with a patronizing familiarity.

He got on excellently well with the young women of the

rich, idle middle-class. He was a companion for them, a sort of depraved servant, only more free and confidential, who gave them instruction and roused their envy. They had hardly any constraint with him: and, with the lamp of Psyche in their hands, they made a careful study of the hermaphrodite, and he suffered them.

Christophe could not understand how a girl like Colette, who seemed to have so refined a nature and a touching eagerness to escape from the degrading round of her life, could find pleasure in such company. Christophe was no psychologist. Lucien Lévy-Cœur could easily beat him on that score. Christophe was Colette's confidant: but Colette was the confidante of Lucien Lévy-Cœur. That gave him a great advantage. It is very pleasant to a woman to feel that she has to deal with a man weaker than herself. She finds food in it at once for her lower and higher instincts: her maternal instinct is touched by it. Lucien Lévy-Cœur knew that perfectly: one of the surest means of touching a woman's heart is to sound that mysterious chord. But in addition, Colette felt that she was weak, and cowardly, and possessed of instincts of which she was not proud, though she was not inclined to deny them. It pleased her to allow herself to be persuaded by the audacious and nicely calculated confessions of her friend that others were just the same, and that human nature must be taken for what it is. And so she gave herself the satisfaction of not resisting inclinations that she found very agreeable, and the luxury of saying that it must be so, and that it was wise not to rebel and to be indulgent with what one could not—" alas! "—prevent. There was a wisdom in that, the practice of which contained no element of pain.

For any one who can envisage life with serenity, there is a peculiar relish in remarking the perpetual contrast which exists in the very bosom of society between the extreme refinement of apparent civilization and its fundamental animalism. In every gathering that does not consist only of fossils and petrified souls, there are, as it were, two conversational strata.

one above the other: one—which everybody can hear—between mind and mind: the other—of which very few are conscious, though it is the greater of the two—between instinct and instinct, the beast in man and woman. Often these two strata of conversation are contradictory. While mind and mind are passing the small change of convention, body and body say: Desire, Aversion, or, more often: Curiosity, Boredom, Disgust. The beast in man and woman, though tamed by centuries of civilization, and as cowed as the wretched lions in the tamer's cage, is always thinking of its food.

But Christophe had not yet reached that disinterestedness which comes only with age and the death of the passions. He had taken himself very seriously as adviser to Colette. She had asked for his help: and he saw her in the lightness of her heart exposed to danger. So he made no effort to conceal his dislike of Lucien Lévy-Cœur. At first that gentleman maintained towards Christophe an irreproachable and ironical politeness. He, too, scented the enemy: but he thought he had nothing to fear from him: he made fun of him without seeming to do so. If only he could have had Christophe's admiration he would have been on quite good terms with him, but that he never could obtain: he saw that clearly, for Christophe had not the art of disguising his feelings. And so Lucien Lévy-Cœur passed insensibly from an abstract intellectual antagonism to a little, carefully veiled, war, of which Colette was to be the prize.

She held the balance evenly between her two friends. She appreciated Christophe's talent and moral superiority: but she also appreciated Lucien Lévy-Cœur's amusing immorality and wit: and, at bottom, she found more pleasure in it. Christophe did not mince his protestations: she listened to him with a touching humility which disarmed him. She was quite a good creature, but she lacked frankness, partly from weakness, partly from her very kindness. She was half play-acting: she pretended to think with Christophe. As a matter of fact, she knew the worth of such a friend: but she was not ready to make any sacrifice for a friendship: she was not ready to sacrifice anything for anybody: she just wanted everything to go smoothly and pleasantly. And so she concealed from Christophe the fact that she went on receiving Lucien Lévy-Cœur: she lied with the easy charm of the young women of her class who, from their childhood, are expert in the practice which is so necessary for those who wish to keep their friends and please everybody. She excused herself by pretending that she wished to avoid hurting Christophe: but in reality it was because she knew that he was right and wanted to go on doing as she liked without quarreling with him. Sometimes Christophe suspected her tricks: then he would scold her, and wax indignant. She would go on playing the contrite little girl, and be affectionate and sorry: and she would look tenderly at him —*feminæ ultima ratio.*—And really it did distress her to think of losing Christophe's friendship: she would be charmingly serious and in that way succeed in disarming Christophe for a little while longer. But sooner or later there had to be an explosion. Christophe's irritation was fed unconsciously by a little jealousy. And into Colette's coaxing tricks there crept a little, a very little, love, all of which made the rupture only the more violent.

One day when Christophe had caught Colette out in a flagrant lie he gave her a definite alternative: she must choose between Lucien Lévy-Cœur and himself. She tried to dodge the question: and, finally, she vindicated her right to have whatever friends she liked. She was perfectly right: and Christophe admitted that he had been absurd: but he knew also that he had not been exacting from egoism: he had a sincere affection for Colette: he wanted to save her even against her will. He insisted awkwardly. She refused to answer. He said:

"Colette, do you want us not to be friends any more?"

She replied:

"No, no. I should be sorry if you ceased to be my friend."

"But you will not sacrifice the smallest thing for our friendship."

"Sacrifice! What a silly word!" she said. "Why should one always be sacrificing one thing for another? It's just a stupid Christian idea. You're nothing but an old parson at heart."

"Maybe," he said. "I want one thing or another. I allow nothing between good and evil, not so much as the breadth of a hair."

"Yes, I know," she said. "That is why I love you. For I do love you: but . . ."

"But you love the other fellow too?"

She laughed, and said, with a soft look in her eyes and a tender note in her voice:

"Stay!"

He was just about to give in once more when Lucien Lévy-Cœur came in: and he was welcomed with the same soft look in her eyes and the same tender note in her voice. Christophe sat for some time in silence watching Colette at her tricks: then he went away, having made up his mind to break with her. He was sick and sorry at heart. It was so stupid to grow so fond, always to be falling into the trap!

When he reached home he toyed with his books, and idly opened his Bible and read:

"*. . . The Lord saith, Because the daughters of Zion are haughty and walk with stretched forth necks and wanton eyes, walking and mincing as they go, and making a tinkling with their feet,*

"*Therefore the Lord will smite with a scab the crown of the head of the daughters of Zion, and the Lord will discover their secret parts . . .*"

He burst out laughing as he thought of Colette's little tricks: and he went to bed well pleased with himself. Then he thought that he too must have become tainted with the corruption of Paris for the Bible to have become a humorous work to him. But he did not stop saying over and over again the judgment of the great judiciary humorist: and he tried to imagine its effect on the head of his young friend. He went to sleep laughing like a child. He had lost all thought of his new sorrow. One more or less. . . . He was getting used to it.

He did not give up Colette's music-lessons: but he refused to take the opportunities she gave him of continuing their intimate conversations. It was no use her being sorry about it or offended, and trying all sorts of tricks: he stuck to his guns: they were rude to each other: of her own accord she took to finding excuses for missing the lessons: and he also made excuses for declining the Stevens' invitations.

He had had enough of Parisian society: he could not bear the emptiness of it, the idleness, the moral impotence, the neurasthenia, its aimless, pointless, self-devouring hypercriticism. He wondered how people could live in such a stagnant atmosphere of art for art's sake and pleasure for pleasure's sake. And yet the French did live in it: they had been a great nation, and they still cut something of a figure in the world: at least, they seemed to do so to the outside spectator. But where were the springs of their life? They believed in nothing, nothing but pleasure. . . .

Just as Christophe reached this point in his reflections, he ran into a crowd of young men and women, all shouting at the tops of their voices, dragging a carriage in which was sitting an old priest casting blessings right and left. A little farther on he found some French soldiers battering down the doors of a church with axes, and there were men attacking them with chairs. He saw that the French did still believe in something —though he could not understand in what. He was told that the State and the Church were separated after a century of living together, and that as the Church had refused to go with a good grace, standing on its rights and its power, it was being evicted. To Christophe the proceeding seemed ungallant: but he was so sick of the anarchical dilettantism of the Parisian artists that he was delighted to find men ready to have their heads broken for a cause, however foolish it might be.

It was not long before he discovered that there were many such people in France. The political journals plunged into the fight like the Homeric heroes: they published daily calls to civil war. It is true that it got no farther than words, and that they very rarely came to blows. But there was no lack of simple souls to put into action what the others declared in words. Strange things happened: departments threatened to break away from France, regiments deserted, prefectures were burned, tax-collectors were on horseback at the head of a company of gendarmes, peasants were armed with scythes, and put their kettles on to boil to defend the churches, which the Free Thinkers were demolishing in the name of liberty: there were popular redeemers who climbed trees to address the provinces of Wine, that had risen against the provinces of Alcohol. Everywhere there were millions of men shaking hands, all red in the face from shouting, and in the end all going for each other. The Republic flattered the people: and then turned arms against them. The people on their side broke the heads of a few of their own young men—officers and soldiers.—And so every one proved to everybody else the excellence of his cause and his fists. Looked at from a distance, through the newspapers, it was as though the country had gone back a few centuries, Christophe discovered that France—skeptical France—was a nation of fanatics. But it was impossible for him to find out the meaning of their fanaticism. For or against religion? For or against Reason? For or against the country?—They were for and against everything. They were fanatics for the pleasure of it.

He spoke about it one evening to a Socialist deputy whom he met sometimes at the Stevens'. Although he had spoken to him before, he had no idea what sort of man he was: till then they had only talked about music. Christophe was very surprised to learn that this man of the world was the leader of a violent party.

Achille Roussin was a handsome man, with a fair beard, a

burring way of talking, a florid complexion, affable manners,
a certain polish on his fundamental vulgarity, certain peasant
tricks which from time to time he used in spite of himself:—
a way of paring his nails in public, a vulgar habit of catching
hold of the coat of the man he was talking to, or gripping him
by the arm:—he was a great eater, a heavy drinker, a high
liver with a gift of laughter, and the appetite of a man of the
people pushing his way into power: he was adaptable, quick
to alter his manners to sort with his surroundings and the person he was talking to, full of ideas, and reasonable in expound-
ing them, able to listen, and to assimilate at once everything he
heard: for the rest he was sympathetic, intelligent, interested
in everything, naturally, or as a matter of acquired habit, or
merely out of vanity: he was honest so far as was compatible
with his interests, or when it was dangerous not to be so.

He had quite a pretty wife, tall, well made, and well set
up, with a charming figure which was a little too much shown
off by her tight dresses, which accentuated and exaggerated
the rounded curves of her anatomy: her face was framed in
curly black hair: she had big black eyes, a long, pointed chin:
her face was big, but quite charming in its general effect, though
it was spoiled by the twitch of her short-sighted eyes, and her
silly little pursed-up mouth. She had an affected precise manner, like a bird, and a simpering way of talking: but she was
kindly and amiable. She came of a rich shopkeeping family,
broad-minded and virtuous, and she was devoted to the countless duties of society, as to a religion, not to mention the
duties, social and artistic, which she imposed on herself: she
had her *salon,* dabbled in University Extension movements, and
was busy with philanthropic undertakings and researches into
the psychology of childhood,—all without any enthusiasm or
profound interest,—from a mixture of natural kindness, snobbishness, and the harmless pedantry of a young woman of education, who always seems to be repeating a lesson, and taking
a pride in showing that she has learned it well. She needed to
be busy, but she did not need to be interested in what she was

doing. It was like the feverish industry of those women who always have a piece of knitting in their hands, and never stop clicking their needles, as though the salvation of the world depended on their work, which they themselves do not know what to do with. And then there was in her—as in women who knit—the vanity of the good woman who sets an example to other women.

The Deputy had an affectionate contempt for her. He had chosen well both as regards his pleasure and his peace of mind. He enjoyed her beauty and asked no more of her: and she asked no more of him. He loved her and deceived her. She put up with that, provided she had her share of his attention. Perhaps also it gave her a sort of pleasure. She was placid and sensual. She had the attitude of mind of a woman of the harem.

They had two fine children of four and five years old, whom she looked after, like a good mother, with the same amiable, cold attentiveness with which she followed her husband's political career, and the latest fashions in dress and art. And it produced in her the most odd mixture of advanced ideas, ultra-decadent art, polite restlessness, and bourgeois sentiment.

They invited Christophe to go and see them. Madame Roussin was a good musician, and played the piano charmingly: she had a delicate, firm touch: with her little head bowed over the keyboard, and her hands poised above it and darting down, she was like a pecking hen. She was talented and knew more about music than most Frenchwomen, but she was as insensible as a fish to the deeper meaning of music: to her it was only a succession of notes, rhythms, and degrees of sound, to which she listened or reproduced carefully: she never looked for the soul in it, having no use for it herself. This amiable, intelligent, simple woman, who was always ready to do any one a kindness, gave Christophe the graceful welcome which she extended to everybody. Christophe was not particularly grateful to her for it: he was not much in sympathy with her: she hardly existed for him. Perhaps it was that unconsciously

he could not forgive her acquiescence in her husband's infidel-
ities, of which she was by no means ignorant. Passive acceptance was of all the vices that which he could least excuse.

He was more intimate with Achille Roussin. Roussin loved
music, as he loved the other arts, crudely but sincerely. When
he liked a symphony, it became a thing that he could take
into his arms. He had a superficial culture and turned it to
good account: his wife had been useful to him there. He was
interested in Christophe because he saw in him a vigorous
vulgarian such as he was himself. And he found it absorbing
to study an original of his stamp—(he was unwearying in his
observation of humanity)—and to discover his impressions of
Paris. The frankness and rudeness of Christophe's remarks
amused him. He was skeptic enough to admit their truth.
He was not put out by the fact that Christophe was a German.
On the contrary: he prided himself on being above national
prejudice. And, when all was said and done, he was sincerely
" human "—(that was his chief quality) ;—he sympathized
with everything human. But that did not prevent his being
quite convinced of the superiority of the French—an old race,
and an old civilization—over the Germans, and making fun of
the Germans.

At Achille Roussin's Christophe met other politicians, the
Ministers of yesterday, and the Ministers of to-morrow. He
would have been only too glad to talk to each of them individually, if these illustrious persons had thought him worthy. In
spite of the generally accepted opinion he found them much
more interesting than the other Frenchmen of his acquaintance.
They were more alive mentally, more open to the passions and
the great interests of humanity. They were brilliant talkers,
mostly men from the South, and they were amazingly dilettante :
individually they were almost as much so as the men of letters.
Of course, they were very ignorant about art, and especially
about foreign art: but they all pretended more or less to some
knowledge of it: and often they really loved it. There were

Councils which were very like the coterie of some little Review. One of them would be a playwright: another would scrape on the violin; another would be a besotted Wagnerian. And they all collected Impressionist pictures, read decadent books, and prided themselves on a taste for some ultra-aristocratic art, which was almost always in direct opposition to their ideas. It puzzled Christophe to find these Socialist or Radical-Socialist Ministers, these apostles of the poor and down-trodden, posing as connoisseurs of eclectic art. No doubt they had a perfect right to do so: but it seemed to him rather disloyal.

But the odd thing was when these men who in private conversation were skeptics, sensualists, Nihilists, and anarchists, came to action: at once they became fanatics. Even the most dilettante of them when they came into power became like Oriental despots: they had a mania for ordering everything, and let nothing alone: they were skeptical in mind and tyrannical in temper. The temptation to use the machinery of administrative centralization created by the greatest of despots was too great, and it was difficult not to abuse it. The result was a sort of republican imperialism on to which there had latterly been grafted an atheistic catholicism.

For some time past the politicians had made no claim to do anything but control the body—that is to say, money:—they hardly troubled the soul at all, since the soul could not be converted into money. Their own souls were not concerned with politics: they passed above or below politics, which in France are thought of as a branch—a lucrative, though not very exalted branch—of commerce and industry: the intellectuals despised the politicians, the politicians despised the intellectuals. —But lately there had been a closer understanding, then an alliance, between the politicians and the lowest class of intellectuals. A new power had appeared upon the scene, which had arrogated to itself the absolute government of ideas: the Free Thinkers. They had thrown in their lot with the other power, which had seen in them the perfect machinery of political despotism. They were trying not so much to destroy the

Church as to supplant it: and, in fact, they created a Church of Free Thought which had its catechisms, and ceremonies, its baptisms, its confirmations, its marriages, its regional councils, if not its œcumenicals at Rome. It was most pitifully comic to see these thousands of poor wretches having to band themselves together in order to be able to "think freely." True, their freedom of thought consisted in setting a ban on the thought of others in the name of Reason: for they believed in Reason as the Catholics believed in the Blessed Virgin without ever dreaming for a moment that Reason, like the Virgin, was in itself nothing, or that the real thing lay behind it. And, just as the Catholic Church had its armies of monks and its congregations stealthily creeping through the veins of the nation, propagating its views and destroying every other sort of vitality, so the Anti-Catholic Church had its Free Masons, whose chief Lodge, the Grand-Orient, kept a faithful record of all the secret reports with which their pious informers in all quarters of France supplied them. The Republican State secretly encouraged the sacred espionage of these mendicant friars and Jesuits of Reason, who terrorized the army, the University, and every branch of the State: and it was never noticed that while they pretended to serve the State, they were all the time aiming at supplanting it, and that the country was slowly moving towards an atheistic theocracy; very little, if anything, different from that of the Jesuits of Paraguay.

Christophe met some of these gentry at Roussin's. They were all blind fetish-worshippers. At that time they were rejoicing at having removed Christ from the Courts of Law. They thought they had destroyed religion because they had destroyed a few pieces of wood and ivory. Others were concentrating on Joan of Arc and her banner of the Virgin, which they had just wrested from the Catholics. One of the Fathers of the new Church, a general who was waging war on the French of the old Church, had just given utterance to an anti-clerical speech in honor of Vercingetorix: he proclaimed the ancient Gaul, to whom Free Thought had erected a statue, to be a son of the

people, and the first champion against (the Church of) Rome.
The Ministers of the Marine, by way of purifying the fleet
and showing their horror of war, called their cruisers *Descartes*
and *Ernest Renan*. Other Free Thinkers had set themselves
to purify art. They expurgated the classics of the seventeenth
century, and did not allow the name of God to sully the *Fables*
of La Fontaine. They did not allow it in music either: and
Christophe heard one of them, an old radical,—("*To be a
radical in old age,*" says Goethe, "*is the height of folly*")—
wax indignant at the religious *Lieder* of Beethoven having been
given at a popular concert. He demanded that other words
should be used instead of " God."

"What?" asked Christophe in exasperation. " The Republic?"

Others who were even more radical would accept no compromise and wanted purely and simply to suppress all religious
music and all schools in which it was taught. In vain did a
director of the University of Fine Arts, who was considered
an Athenian in that Bœotia, try to explain that musicians must
be taught music: for, as he said, with great loftiness of thought,
" when you send a soldier to the barracks, you teach him how
to use a gun and then how to shoot. And so it is with a young
composer: his head is buzzing with ideas: but he has not yet
learned to put them in order." And, being a little scared by
his own courage, he protested with every sentence: " I am an
old Free Thinker. . . . I am an old Republican . . ."
and he declared audaciously that " he did not care much whether
the compositions of Pergolese were operas or Masses: all that he
wanted to know was, were they human works of art?"—But
his adversary with implacable logic answered " the old Free
Thinker and Republican " that " there were two sorts of music:
that which was sung in churches and that which was sung in
other places." The first sort was the enemy of Reason and the
State: and the Reason of the State ought to suppress it.

All these silly people would have been more ridiculous than
dangerous if behind them there had not been men of real worth,

supporting them, who were, like them—and perhaps even more —fanatics of Reason. Tolstoy speaks somewhere of those "epidemic influences" which prevail in religion, philosophy, politics, art, and science, "insensate influences, the folly of which only becomes apparent to men when they are clear of them, while as long as they are under their dominion they seem so true to them that they think them beyond all argument." Instances are the craze for tulips, belief in sorcery, and the aberrations of literary fashions.—The religion of Reason was such a craze. It was common to the most ignorant and the most cultured, to the "sub-veterinaries" of the Chamber, and certain of the keenest intellects of the University. It was even more dangerous in the latter than in the former: for with the latter it was mixed up with a credulous and stupid optimism, which sapped its energy: while with the others it was fortified and given a keener edge by a fanatical pessimism which was under no illusion as to the fundamental antagonism of Nature and Reason, and they were only the more desperately resolved to wage the war of abstract Liberty, abstract Justice, abstract Truth, against the malevolence of Nature. There was behind it all the idealism of the Calvinists, the Jansenists, and the Jacobins, the old belief in the fundamental perversity of mankind, which can and must be broken by the implacable pride of the Elect inspired by the breath of Reason,—the Spirit of God. It was a very French type, the type of intelligent Frenchman, who is not at all "human." A pebble as hard as iron: nothing can penetrate it: it breaks everything that it touches.

Christophe was appalled by the conversations that he had at Achille Roussin's with some of these fanatics. It upset all his ideas about France. He had thought, like so many people, that the French were a well-balanced, sociable, tolerant, liberty-loving people. And he found them lunatics with their abstract ideas, their diseased logic, ready to sacrifice themselves and everybody else for one of their syllogisms. They were always talking of liberty, but there never were men less able to understand it or to stand it. Nowhere in the world were there characters more coldly and atrociously despotic in their passion for intellect or their passion for always being in the right.

And it was not only true of one party. Every party was the same. They could not—they would not—see anything above or beyond their political or religious formula, or their country, their province, their group, or their own narrow minds. There were anti-Semites who expended all the forces of their being in a blind, impotent hatred of all the privileges of wealth: for they hated all Jews, and called those whom they hated "Jews." There were nationalists who hated—(when they were kinder they stopped short at despising)—every other nation, and even among their own people, they called everybody who did not agree with them foreigners, or renegades, or traitors. There were anti-protestants who persuaded themselves that all Protestants were English or Germans, and would have them all expelled from France. There were men of the West who denied the existence of anything east of the Rhine: men of the North who denied the existence of everything south of the Loire: men of the South who called all those who lived north of the Loire Barbarians: and there were men who boasted of being of Gallic descent: and, craziest of all, there were "Romans" who prided themselves on the defeat of their ancestors: and Bretons, and Lorrainians, and Félibres, and Albigeois; and men from Carpentras, and Pontoise, and Quimper-Corentin: they all thought only of themselves, the fact of being themselves was sufficient patent of nobility, and they could not put up with the idea of people being anything else. There is nothing to be done with such people: they will not listen to argument from any other point of view: they must burn everybody else at the stake, or be burned themselves.

Christophe thought that it was lucky that such people should live under a Republic: for all these little despots did at least annihilate each other. But if any one of them had become Emperor or King, it would have been the end of him.

He did not know that there is one virtue left to work the salvation of people of that temper of mind:—inconsequence.

The French politicians were no exception. Their despotism was tempered with anarchy: they were for ever swinging between two poles. On one hand they relied on the fanatics of thought, on the other they relied on the anarchists of thought. Mixed up with them was a whole rabble of dilettante Socialists, mere opportunists, who held back from taking any part in the fight until it was won, though they followed in the wake of the army of Free Thought, and, after every battle won, they swooped down on the spoils. These champions of Reason did not labor in the cause of Reason. . . . *Sic vos non vobis* . . . but in the cause of the Citizens of the World, who with glad shouts trampled under foot the traditions of the country, and had no intention of destroying one Faith in order to set up another, but in order to set themselves up and break away from all restraint.

There Christophe marked the likeness of Lucien Lévy-Cœur. He was not surprised to learn that Lucien Lévy-Cœur was a Socialist. He only thought that Socialists must be fairly on the road to success to have enrolled Lucien Lévy-Cœur. But he did not know that Lucien Lévy-Cœur had also contrived to figure in the opposite camp, where he had succeeded in allying himself with men of the most anti-Liberal opinions, if not anti-Semite, in politics and art. He asked Achille Roussin:

"How can you put up with such men?"

Roussin replied:

"He is so clever! And he is working for us; he is destroying the old world."

"He is doing that all right," said Christophe. "He is destroying it so thoroughly that I don't see what is going to be left for you to build up again. Do you think there'll be timber enough left for your new house? And are you even sure that the worms have not crept into your building-yard?"

Lucien Lévy-Cœur was not the only nibbler at Socialism. The Socialist papers were staffed by these petty men of letters, with their art for art's sake, these licentious anarchists who had fastened on all the roads that might lead to success. They barred the way to others, and filled the papers, which styled themselves the organs of the people, with their dilettante decadence and their *struggle for life*. They were not content with being jobbed into positions: they wanted fame. Never had there been a time when there were so many premature statues, or so many speeches delivered at the unveiling of them. But queerest of all were the banquets that were periodically offered to one or other of the great men of the fraternity by the sycophants of fame, not in celebration of any of their deeds, but in celebration of some honor given to them: for those were the things that most appealed to them. Esthetes, supermen, Socialist Ministers, they were all agreed when it was a question of feasting to celebrate some promotion in the Legion of Honor founded by the Corsican officer.

Roussin laughed at Christophe's amazement. He did not think the German far out in his estimation of the supporters of his party. When they were alone together he would handle them severely himself. He knew their stupidity and their knavery better than any one: but that did not keep him from supporting them in order to retain their support. And if in private he never hesitated to speak of the people in terms of contempt, on the platform he was a different man. Then he would assume a high-pitched voice, shrill, nasal, labored, solemn tones, a tremolo, a bleat, wide, sweeping, fluttering gestures like the beating of wings: exactly like Mounet-Sully.

Christophe tried hard to discover exactly how far Roussin believed in his Socialism. It was obvious that at heart he did not believe in it at all: he was too skeptical. And yet he did believe in it, to a certain extent: and though he knew perfectly well that it was only a part of his mind that believed in it—(perhaps the most important part)—he had arranged his life and conduct in accordance with it, because it suited him best. It was not only his practical interest that was served by it, but also his vital interests, the foundations of his being and all his actions. His Socialistic Faith was to him a sort of

State religion.—Most people live like that. Their lives are based on religious, moral, social, or purely practical beliefs,—(belief in their profession, in their work, in the utility of the part they play in life)—in which they do not, at heart, believe. But they do not wish to know it: for they must have this apparent faith, this " State religion," of which every man is priest, to live.

Roussin was not one of the worst. There were many, many others who called themselves Socialists and Radicals, from—it can hardly be called ambition, for their ambition was so short-sighted, and did not go beyond immediate plunder and their re-election! They pretended to believe in a new order of society. Perhaps there was a time when they believed in it: and they went on pretending to do so: but, in fact, they had no idea beyond living on the spoils of the dying order of society. This predatory Nihilism was saved by a short-sighted opportunism. The great interests of the future were sacrificed to the egoism of the present. They cut down the army; they would have dislocated the country to please the electors. They were not lacking in cleverness: they knew perfectly well what they ought to have done: but they did not do it, because it would have cost them too much effort, and they were incapable of effort. They wanted to arrange their own lives and the life of the nation with the least possible amount of trouble and sacrifice. All down the scale the point was to get the maximum of pleasure with the minimum of effort. That was their morality, immoral enough, but it was the only guide in the political muddle, in which the leaders set the example of anarchy, and the disordered pack of politicians were chasing ten hares at once, and letting them all escape one after the other, and an aggressive Foreign Office was yoked with a pacific War Office, and Ministers of War were cutting down the army in order to purify it, Naval Ministers were inciting the workmen in the arsenals, military instructors were preaching the horrors of war, and all the officials, judges, revolutionaries, and patriots were dilettante. The political demoralization was universal. Every man was expecting the State to provide him with office, honors, pensions, indemnities: and the Government did, as a matter of fact, feed the appetite of its supporters: honors and pensions were made the quarry of the sons, nephews, grand-nephews, and valets of those in power: the deputies were always voting an increase in their own salaries: revenues, posts, titles, all the possessions of the State, were being blindly squandered.—And, like a sinister echo of the example of the upper classes, the lower classes were always on the verge of a strike: they had men teaching contempt of authority and revolt against the established order; post-office employés burned letters and despatches, workers in factories threw sand or emery-powder into the gears of the machines, men working in the arsenals sacked them, ships were burned, and artisans deliberately made a horrible mess of their work,—the destruction not of riches, but of the wealth of the world.

And to crown it all the intellectuals amused themselves by discovering that this national suicide was based on reason and right, in the sacred right of every human being to be happy. There was a morbid humanitarianism which broke down the distinction between Good and Evil, and developed a sentimental pity for the "sacred and irresponsible human" in the criminal, the doting sentimentality of an old man:—it was a capitulation to crime, the surrender of society to its mercies.

Christophe thought:

"France is drunk with liberty. When she has raved and screamed, she will fall down dead-drunk. And when she wakes up she will find herself in prison."

What hurt Christophe most in this demagogy was to see the most violent political measures coldly carried through by these men whose fundamental instability he knew perfectly well. The disproportion between the shiftiness of these men and the rigorous Acts that they passed or authorized was too scandalous. It was as though there were in them two contradictory things: an inconsistent character, believing in nothing, and discursive Reason, intent on truncating, mowing down, and crushing life, without regard for anything. Christophe wondered why the peaceful middle-class, the Catholics, the officials who were harassed in every conceivable way, did not throw them all out by the window. He dared not tell Roussin what he thought: but, as he was incapable of concealing anything, Roussin had no difficulty in guessing it. He laughed and said:

"No doubt that is what you or I would do. But there is no danger of them doing it. They are just a set of poor devils who haven't the energy: they can't do much more than grumble. They're just the fag end of an aristocracy, idiotic, stultified by their clubs and their sport, prostituted by the Americans and the Jews, and, by way of showing how up to date they are, they play the degraded parts allotted to them in fashionable plays, and support those who have degraded them. They're an apathetic and surly middle-class: they read nothing, understand nothing, don't want to understand anything; they only know how to vilify, vilify, vaguely, bitterly, futilely—and they have only one passion: sleep, to lie huddled in sleep on their money-bags, hating anybody who disturbs them, and even anybody whose tastes differ from theirs, for it does upset them to think of other people working while they are snoozing! If you knew them you would sympathize with us."

But Christophe could find nothing but disgust with both: for he did not hold that the baseness of the oppressed was any excuse for that of the oppressor. Only too frequently had he met at the Stevens' types of the rich dull middle-class that Roussin described,

> " . . . L'anime triste di coloro,
> Che visser senza infamia esenza lodo, . . ."

He saw only too clearly the reason why Roussin and his friends were sure not only of their power over these people, but of their right to abuse it. They had to hand all the instruments of tyranny. Thousands of officials, who had renounced their will and every vestige of personality, and obeyed blindly. A loose, vulgar way of living, a Republic without Republicans: Socialist papers and Socialist leaders groveling before Royalties when they visited Paris: the souls of servants gaping at titles, and gold lace, and orders: they could be kept quiet by just having a bone to gnaw, or the Legion of Honor flung at them. If the Kings had ennobled all the citizens of France, all the citizens of France would have been Royalist.

The politicians were having a fine time. Of the Three Estates of '89 the first was extinct: the second was proscribed, suspect, or had emigrated: the third was gorged by its victory and slept. And, as for the Fourth Estate, which had come into existence at a later date, and had become a public menace in its jealousy, there was no difficulty about squaring that. The decadent Republic treated it as decadent Rome treated the barbarian hordes, that she no longer had the power to drive from her frontiers; she assimilated them, and they quickly became her best watch-dogs. The Ministers of the middle-class called themselves Socialists, lured away and annexed to their own party the most intelligent and vigorous of the working-class: they robbed the proletariat of their leaders, infused their new blood into their own system, and, in return, gorged them with indigestible science and middle-class culture.

One of the most curious features of these attempts at distraint by the middle-class on the people were the Popular Universities. They were little jumble-sales of scraps of knowledge of every period and every country. As one syllabus declared, they set out to teach "every branch of physical, biological, and sociological science: astronomy, cosmology, anthropology, ethnology, physiology, psychology, psychiatry, geography, languages, esthetics, logic, etc." Enough to split the skull of Pico della Mirandola.

In truth there had been originally, and still was in some of them, a certain grand idealism, a keen desire to bring truth, beauty, and morality within the reach of all, which was a very fine thing. It was wonderful and touching to see workmen, after a hard day's toil, crowding into narrow, stuffy lecture-rooms, impelled by a thirst for knowledge that was stronger than fatigue and hunger. But how the poor fellows had been tricked! There were a few real apostles, intelligent human beings, a few upright warm-hearted men, with more good intentions than skill to accomplish them; but, as against them, there were hundreds of fools, idiots, schemers, unsuccessful authors, orators, professors, parsons, speakers, pianists, critics, anarchists, who deluged the people with their productions. Every man jack of them was trying to unload his stock-in-trade. The most thriving of them were naturally the nostrum-mongers, the philosophical lecturers who ladled out general ideas, leavened with a few facts, a scientific smattering, and cosmological conclusions.

The Popular Universities were also an outlet for the ultra-aristocratic works of art: decadent etchings, poetry, and music. The aim was the elevation of the people for the rejuvenation of thought and the regeneration of the race. They began by inoculating them with all the fads and cranks of the middle-class. They gulped them down greedily, not because they liked them, but because they were middle-class. Christophe, who was taken to one of these Popular Universities by Madame Roussin, heard her play Debussy to the people between *la Bonne Chanson* of Gabriel Fauré and one of the later quartets of Beethoven. He who had only begun to grasp the meaning of the later works of Beethoven after many years, and long weary labor, asked some one who sat near him pityingly:

" Do you understand it? "

The man drew himself up like an angry cock, and said:

"Certainly. Why shouldn't I understand it as well as you?"

And by way of showing that he understood it he encored a fugue, glaring defiantly at Christophe.

Christophe went away. He was amazed. He said to himself that the swine had succeeded in poisoning even the living wells of the nation: the People had ceased to be—"People yourselves!" as a working-man said to one of the would-be founders of the Theaters of the People. "I am as much of the middle-class as you."

One fine evening when above the darkening town the soft sky was like an Oriental carpet, rich in warm faded colors, Christophe walked along by the river from Notre Dame to the Invalides. In the dim fading light the tower of the cathedral rose like the arms of Moses held up during the battle. The carved golden spire of the Sainte-Chapelle, the flowering Holy Thorn, flashed out of the labyrinth of houses. On the other side of the water stretched the royal front of the Louvre, and its windows were like weary eyes lit up with the last living rays of the setting sun. At the back of the great square of the Invalides behind its trenches and proud walls, majestic, solitary, floated the dull gold dome, like a symphony of bygone victories. And at the top of the hill there stood the Arc de Triomphe, bestriding the hill with the giant stride of the Imperial legions. And suddenly Christophe thought of it all as of a dead giant lying prone upon the plain. The terror of it clutched at his heart; he stopped to gaze at the gigantic fossils of a fabulous race, long since extinct, that in its life had made the whole earth ring with the tramp of its armies,—the race whose helmet was the dome of the Invalides, whose girdle was the Louvre, the thousand arms of whose cathedrals had clutched at the heavens, who traversed the whole world with the triumphant stride of the Arch of Napoleon, under whose heel there now swarmed Lilliput.

III

WITHOUT any deliberate effort on his part, Christophe had gained a certain celebrity in the Parisian circles to which he had been introduced by Sylvain Kohn and Goujart. He was seen everywhere with one or other of his friends at first nights,

and at concerts, and his extraordinary face, his ugliness, the
absurdity of his figure and costume, his brusque, awkward manners, the paradoxical opinions to which he gave vent from time
to time, his undeveloped, but large and healthy intellect, and
the romantic stories spread by Sylvain Kohn about his escapades
in Germany, and his complications with the police and flight
to France, had marked him out for the idle, restless curiosity
of the great cosmopolitan hotel drawing-room that Paris has
become. As long as he held himself in check, observing, listening, and trying to understand before expressing any opinion,
as long as nothing was known of his work or what he really
thought, he was tolerated. The French were pleased with him
for having been unable to stay in Germany. And the French
musicians especially were delighted with Christophe's unjust
pronouncements on German music, and took them all as
homage to themselves:—(as a matter of fact, they heard only
his old youthful opinions, to many of which he would no longer
have subscribed: a few articles published in a German Review
which had been amplified and circulated by Sylvain Kohn).—
Christophe was interesting and did not interfere with anybody: there was no danger of his supplanting anybody. He
needed only to become the great man of a coterie. He needed
only not to write anything, or as little as possible, and not to
have anything performed, and to supply Goujart and his like
with ideas, Goujart and the whole set of men whose motto is the
famous quip—adapted a little:

"My glass is small: but I drink . . . the wine of others."

A strong personality sheds its rays especially on young people who are more concerned with feeling than with action.
There were plenty of young people about Christophe. They
were for the most part idle, will-less, aimless, purposeless.
Young men, living in dread of work, fearful of being left
alone with themselves, who sought an armchair immortality,
wandering from café to theater, from theater to café, finding
all sorts of excuses for not going home, to avoid coming face
to face with themselves. They came and stayed for hours,

dawdling, talking, making aimless conversation, and going away empty, aching, disgusted, satiated, and yet famishing, forced to go on with it in spite of loathing. They surrounded Christophe, like Goethe's water-spaniel, the "lurking specters," that lie in wait and seize upon a soul and fasten upon its vitality.

A vain fool would have found pleasure in such a circle of parasites. But Christophe had no taste for pedestals. He was revolted by the idiotic subtlety of his admirers, who read into anything he did all sorts of absurd meanings, Renanian, Nietzschean, hermaphroditic. He kicked them out. He was not made for passivity. Everything in him cried aloud for action. He observed so as to understand: he wished to understand so as to act. He was free of the constraint of any school, and of any prejudice, and he inquired into everything, read everything, and studied all the forms of thought and the resources of the expression of other countries and other ages in his art. He seized on all those which seemed to him effective and true. Unlike the French artists whom he studied, who were ingenious inventors of new forms, and wore themselves out in the unceasing effort of invention, and gave up the struggle half-way, he endeavored not so much to invent a new musical language as to speak the authentic language of music with more energy: his aim was not to be particular, but to be strong. His passion for strength was the very opposite of the French genius of subtlety and moderation. He scorned style for the sake of style and art for art's sake. The best French artists seemed to him to be no more than pleasure-mongers. One of the most perfect poets in Paris had amused himself with drawing up a "list of the workers in contemporary French poetry, with their talents, their productions, and their earnings": and he enumerated "the crystals, the Oriental fabrics, the gold and bronze medals, the lace for dowagers, the polychromatic sculpture, the painted porcelain." which had been produced in the workshops of his various colleagues. He pictured himself "in the corner of a vast factory of letters, mending old tapestry, or polishing up rusty halberds."—Such a conception of

the artist as a good workman, thinking only of the perfection of
his craft, was not without an element of greatness. But it did
not satisfy Christophe: and while he admitted in it a certain
professional dignity, he had a contempt for the poor quality of
life which most often it disguised. He could not **understand**
writing for the sake of writing, or talking for the sake of
talking. He never said words; he said—or wanted to say—
the things themselves.

"*Ei dice cose, e voi dite parole . . .*"

After a long period of rest, during which he had been entirely occupied with taking in a new world, Christophe suddenly became conscious of an imperious need for creation.
The antagonism which he felt between himself and Paris
called up all his reserve of force by its challenge of his personality. All his passions were brimming in him, and imperi-
ously demanding expression. They were of every kind: and
they were all equally insistent. He tried to create, to fashion
music, into which to turn the love and hatred that were
swelling in his heart, and the will and the renunciation, and
all the daimons struggling within him, all of whom had an
equal right to live. Hardly had he assuaged one passion in
music,—(sometimes he hardly had the patience to finish it)—
than he hurled himself at the opposite passion. But the contradiction was only apparent: if they were always changing,
they were in truth always the same. He beat out roads in
music, roads that led to the same goal: his soul was a mountain:
he tried every pathway up it; on some he wound easily, dally-
ing in the shade: on others he mounted toilsomely with the hot
sun beating up from the dry, sandy track: they all led to God
enthroned on the summit. Love, hatred, evil, renunciation, all
the forces of humanity at their highest pitch, touched eternity,
and were a part of it. For every man the gateway to eternity
is in himself: for the believer as for the atheist, for him who
sees life everywhere as for him who everywhere denies it, and
for him who doubts both life and the denial of it,—and for
Christophe in whose soul there met all these opposing views of

life. All the opposites become one in eternal Force. For Christophe the chief thing was to wake that Force within himself and in others, to fling armfuls of wood upon the fire, to feed the flames of Eternity, and make them roar and flicker. Through the voluptuous night of Paris a great flame darted in his heart. He thought himself free of Faith, and he was a living torch of Faith.

Nothing was more calculated to outrage the French spirit of irony. Faith is one of the feelings which a too civilized society can least forgive: for it has lost it and hates others to possess it. In the blind or mocking hostility of the majority of men towards the dreams of youth there is for many the bitter thought that they themselves were once even as they, and had ambitions and never realized them. All those who have denied their souls, all those who had the seed of work within them, and have not brought it forth rather to accept the security of an easy, honorable life, think:

"Since I could not do the thing I dreamed, why should they do the things they dream? I will not have them do it."

How many Hedda Gablers are there among men! What a relentless struggle is there to crush out strength in its new freedom, with what skill is it killed by silence, irony, wear and tear, discouragement,—and, at the crucial moment, betrayed by some treacherous seductive art! . . .

The type is of all nations. Christophe knew it, for he had met it in Germany. Against such people he was armed. His method of defense was simple: he was the first to attack; pounced on the first move, and declared war on them: he forced these dangerous friends to become his enemies. But if such a policy of frankness was an excellent safeguard for his personality, it was not calculated to advance his career as an artist. Once more Christophe began his German tactics. It was too strong for him. Only one thing was altered: his temper: he was in fine fettle.

Lightheartedly, for the benefit of anybody who cared to listen, he expressed his unmeasured criticism of French artists:

and so he made many enemies. He did not take the precaution. as a wise man would have done. of surrounding himself with a little coterie. He would have found no difficulty in gathering about him a number of artists who would gladly have admired him if he had admired them. There were some who admired him in advance, investing admiration as it were. They considered any man they praised as a debtor, of whom, at a given moment, they could demand repayment. But it was a good investment.—But Christophe was a very bad investment. He never paid back. Worse than that, he was barefaced enough to consider poor the works of men who thought his good. Unavowedly they were rancorous, and engaged themselves on the next opportunity to pay him back in kind.

Among his other indiscretions Christophe was foolish enough to declare war on Lucien Lévy-Cœur. He found him in the way, everywhere, and he could not conceal an extraordinary antipathy for the gentle, polite creature who was doing no apparent harm, and even seemed to be kinder than himself, and was, at any rate, far more moderate. He provoked him into argument: and, however insignificant the subject of it might be, Christophe always brought into it a sudden heat and bitterness which surprised their hearers. It was as though Christophe were seizing every opportunity of battering at Lucien Lévy-Cœur, head down: but he could never reach him. His enemy had an extraordinary skill, even when he was most obviously in the wrong, in carrying it off well: he would defend himself with a courtesy which showed up Christophe's bad manners. Christophe still spoke French very badly, interlarding it with slang, and often with very coarse expressions which he had picked up, and, like many foreigners, used wrongly, and he was incapable of outwitting the tactics of Lucien Lévy-Cœur: and he raged furiously against his gentle irony. Everybody thought him in the wrong, for they could not see what Christophe vaguely felt: the hypocrisy of that gentleness, which, when it was brought up against a force which it could not hold in check, tried quietly to stifle it by silence. He was in no hurry, for, like Christophe, he counted on time, not, as Christophe did, to build, but to destroy. He had no difficulty in detaching Sylvain Kohn and Goujart from Christophe, just as he had gradually forced him out of the Stevens' circle. He was isolating Christophe.

Christophe himself helped him. He pleased nobody, for he would not join any party, but was rather against all parties. He did not like the Jews: but he liked the anti-Semites even less. He was revolted by the cowardice of the masses stirred up against a powerful minority, not because it was bad, but because it was powerful, and by the appeal to the basest instincts of jealousy and hatred. The Jews came to regard him as an anti-Semite, and the anti-Semites looked on him as a Jew. As for the artists, they felt his hostility. Instinctively Christophe made himself more German than he was, in art. Revolting against the voluptuous ataraxia of a certain class of Parisian music, he set up, with violence, a manly, healthy pessimism. When joy appeared in his music, it was with a want of taste, a vulgar ardor, which were well calculated to disgust even the aristocratic patrons of popular art. An erudite, crude form. In his reaction he was not far from affecting an apparent carelessness in style and a disregard of external originality, which were bound to be offensive to the French musicians. And so those of them, to whom he sent some of his work, without any careful consideration, visited on it the contempt they had for the belated Wagnerism of the contemporary German school. Christophe did not care: he laughed inwardly, and repeated the lines of a charming musician of the French Renaissance—adapted to his own case:

*　　　*　　　*　　　*　　　*

> " *Come, come, don't worry about those who will say:*
> ' *Christophe has not the counterpoint of A,*
> *And he has not such harmony as Monsieur B.'*
> *I have something else which they never will see.*"

But when he tried to have some of his music performed, he found the doors shut against him. They had quite enough to do to play—or not to play—the works of young French musicians, and could not bother about those of an unknown German.

Christophe did not go on trying. He shut himself up in his room and went on writing. He did not much care whether the people of Paris heard him or not. He wrote for his own pleasure and not for success. The true artist is not concerned with the future of his work. He is like those painters of the Renaissance who joyously painted mural decorations, knowing full well that in ten years nothing would be left of them. So Christophe worked on in peace, quite good-humoredly resigned to waiting for better times, when help would come to him from some unexpected source.

Christophe was then attracted by the dramatic form. He dared not yet surrender freely to the flood of his own lyrical impulse. He had to run it into definite channels. And, no doubt, it is a good thing for a young man of genius, who is not yet master of himself, and does not even know exactly what he is, to set voluntary bounds upon himself, and to confine therein the soul of which he has so little hold. They are the dikes and sluices which allow the course of thought to be directed.—Unfortunately Christophe had not a poet: he had himself to fashion his subjects out of legend and history.

Among the visions which had been floating before his mind for some months past were certain figures from the Bible.— That Bible, which his mother had given him as a companion in his exile, had been a source of dreams to him. Although he did not read it in any religious spirit, the moral, or, rather, vital energy of that Hebraic Iliad had been to him a spring in which, in the evenings, he washed his naked soul of the smoke and mud of Paris. He was concerned with the sacred meaning of the book: but it was not the less a sacred book to him, for the breath of savage nature and primitive in- dividualities that he found in its pages. He drew in its hymns of the earth, consumed with faith, quivering mountains, exultant skies, and human lions.

One of the characters in the book for whom he had an especial tenderness was the young David. He did not give him the ironic smile of the Florentine boy, or the tragic intensity of the sublime works of Michael Angelo and Verrochio: he knew them not. His David was a young shepherd-poet, with a virgin soul, in which heroism slumbered, a Siegfried of the South, of a finer race, and more beautiful, and of greater harmony in mind and body.—For his revolt against the Latin spirit was in vain: unconsciously he had been permeated by that spirit. Not only art influences art, not only mind and thought, but everything about the artist:—people, things, gestures, movements, lines, the light of each town. The atmosphere of Paris is very powerful: it molds even the most rebellious souls. And the soul of a German is less capable than any other of resisting it: in vain does he gird himself in his national pride: of all Europeans the German is the most easily denationalized. Unwittingly the soul of Christophe had already begun to assimilate from Latin art a clarity, a sobriety, an understanding of the emotions, and even, up to a point, a plastic beauty, which otherwise it never would have had. His *David* was the proof of it.

He had endeavored to recreate certain episodes of the youth of David: the meeting with Saul, the fight with Goliath: and he had written the first scene. He had conceived it as a symphonic picture with two characters.

On a deserted plateau, on a moor covered with heather in bloom, the young shepherd lay dreaming in the sun. The serene light, the hum and buzz of tiny creatures, the sweet whispering of the waving grass, the silvery tinkling of the grazing sheep, the mighty beat and rhythm of the earth sang through the dreaming boy unconscious of his divine destiny. Drowsing, his voice and the notes of his flute joined the harmonious silence: and his song was so calmly, so limpidly joyous, that, hearing it, there could be no thought of joy or sorrow, only the feeling

that it must be so and could not be otherwise.—Suddenly over
the moor reached great shadows: the air was still: life seemed
to withdraw into the veins of the earth. Only the music of
the flute went on calmly. Saul, with his crazy thoughts, passed.
The mad King, racked by his fancy, burned like a flame, devouring itself, flung this way and that by the wind. He breathed
prayers and violent abuse, hurling defiance at the void about
him, the void within himself. And when he could speak no
more and fell breathless to the ground, there rang through the
silence the smiling peace of the song of the young shepherd,
who had never ceased. Then, with a furious beating in his
heart, came Saul in silence up to where the boy lay in the
heather: in silence he gazed at him: he sat down by his side
and placed his fevered hand on the cool brows of the shepherd.
Untroubled, David turned, and smiled, and looked at the King.
He laid his hand on Saul's knees, and went on singing and
playing his flute. Evening came: David went to sleep in the
middle of his song, and Saul wept. And through the starry
night there rose once more the serene joyous hymn of nature
refreshed, the song of thanksgiving of the soul relieved of its
burden.

When he wrote the scene, Christophe had thought of nothing
but his own joy: he had never given a thought to the manner
of its performance: and it had certainly never occurred to him
that it might be produced on the stage. He meant it to be sung
at a concert at such time as the concert-halls should be open
to him.

One evening he spoke of it to Achille Roussin, and when,
by request, he had tried to give him an idea of it on the piano,
he was amazed to see Roussin burst into enthusiasm, and declare
that it must at all costs be produced at one of the theaters,
and that he would see to it. He was even more amazed when,
a few days later, he saw that Roussin was perfectly serious:
and his amazement grew to stupefaction when he heard that
Sylvain Kohn, Goujart, and Lucien Lévy-Cœur were taking it
up. He had to admit that their personal animosity had

yielded to their love of art: and he was much surprised. The only man who was not eager to see his work produced was himself. It was not suited to the theater: it was nonsense, and almost hurtful to stage it. But Roussin was so insistent, Sylvain Kohn so persuasive, and Goujart so positive, that Christophe yielded to the temptation. He was weak. He was so longing to hear his music!

It was quite easy for Roussin. Manager and artist rushed to please him. It happened that a newspaper was organizing a benefit matinée for some charity. It was arranged that the *David* should be produced. A good orchestra was got together. As for the singers, Roussin claimed that he had found the ideal representative of David.

The rehearsals were begun. The orchestra came through the first reading fairly well, although, as usual in France, there was not much discipline about it. Saul had a good, though rather tired, voice: and he knew his business. The David was a handsome, tall, plump, solid lady with a sentimental vulgar voice which she used heavily, with a melodramatic tremolo and all the café-concert tricks. Christophe scowled. As soon as she began to sing it was obvious that she could not be allowed to play the part. After the first pause in the rehearsal he went to the impresario, who had charge of the business side of the undertaking, and was present, with Sylvain Kohn, at the rehearsal. The impresario beamed and said:

" Well, are you satisfied? "

" Yes," said Christophe. " I think it can be made all right. There's only one thing that won't do: the singer. She must be changed. Tell her as gently as you can: you're used to it. . . . It will be quite easy for you to find me another."

The impresario looked disgruntled: he looked at Christophe as though he could not believe that he was serious; and he said:

" But that's impossible! "

" Why is it impossible? " asked Christophe.

The impresario looked cunningly at Sylvain Kohn, and replied:

" But she has so much talent! "

" Not a spark," said Christophe.

" What! . . . She has a fine voice! "

" Not a bit of it."

" And she is beautiful."

" I don't care a damn."

" That won't hurt the part," said Sylvain Kohn, laughing.

" I want a David, a David who can sing: I don't want Helen of Troy," said Christophe.

The impresario rubbed his nose uneasily.

" It's a pity, a great pity . . ." he said. " She is an excellent artist. . . . I give you my word for it! Perhaps she is not at her best to-day. You must give her another trial."

" All right," said Christophe. " But it is a waste of time."

He went on with the rehearsal. It was worse than ever. He found it hard to go on to the end: it got on his nerves: his remarks to the singer, from cold and polite, became dry and cutting, in spite of the obvious pains she was taking to satisfy him, and the way she ogled him by way of winning his favor. The impresario prudently stopped the rehearsal just when it seemed to be hopeless. By way of softening the bad effect of Christophe's remarks, he bustled up to the singer and paid her heavy compliments. Christophe, who was standing by, made no attempt to conceal his impatience, called the impresario, and said:

" There's no room for argument. I won't have the woman. It's unpleasant, I know: but I did not choose her. Do what you can to arrange the matter."

The impresario bowed frigidly, and said coldly:

" I can't do anything. You must see M. Roussin."

" What has it got to do with M. Roussin? I don't want to bother him with this business," said Christophe.

" That won't bother him," said Sylvain Kohn ironically.

And he pointed to Roussin, who had just come in.

Christophe went up to him. Roussin was in high good humor, and cried:

"What! Finished already? I was hoping to hear a bit of it. Well, maestro, what do you say? Are you satisfied?"

"It's going quite well," said Christophe. "I don't know how to thank you . . ."

"Not at all! Not at all!"

"There is only one thing wrong."

"What is it? We'll put it right. I am determined to satisfy you."

"Well . . . the singer. Between ourselves she is detestable."

The beaming smile on Roussin's face froze suddenly. He said, with some asperity:

"You surprise me, my dear fellow."

"She is useless, absolutely useless," Christophe went on. "She has no voice, no taste, no knowledge of her work, no talent. You're lucky not to have heard her! . . ."

Roussin grew more and more acid. He cut Christophe short, and said cuttingly:

"I know Mlle. de Sainte-Ygraine. She is a very talented artiste. I have the greatest admiration for her. Every man of taste in Paris shares my opinion."

And he turned his back on Christophe, who saw him offer his arm to the actress and go out with her. He was dumfounded, and Sylvain Kohn, who had watched the scene delightedly, took his arm and laughed, and said as they went down the stairs of the theater:—

"Didn't you know that she was his mistress?"

Christophe understood. So it was for her sake and not for his own that his piece was to be produced! That explained Roussin's enthusiasm, the money he had laid out, and the eagerness of his sycophants. He listened while Sylvain Kohn told him the story of the Sainte-Ygraine: a music-hall singer, who, after various successes in the little vaudeville theaters, had, like so many of her kind, been fired with the ambition to

be heard on a stage more worthy of her talent. She counted on
Roussin to procure her an engagement at the Opéra or the
Opéra-Comique: and Roussin, who asked nothing better, had
seen in the performance of *David* an opportunity of revealing
to the Parisian public at no very great risk the lyrical gifts
of the new tragedienne, in a part which called for no particular
dramatic acting, and gave her an excellent opportunity of
displaying the elegance of her figure.

Christophe heard the story through to the end: then he
shook off Sylvain Kohn and burst out laughing. He laughed
and laughed. When he had done, he said:

"You disgust me. You all disgust me. Art is nothing to
you. It's always women, nothing but women. An opera is
put on for a dancer, or a singer, for the mistress of M. So-
and-So, or Madame Thingummy. You think of nothing but
your dirty little intrigues. Bless you, I'm not angry with
you: you are like that: very well then, be so and wallow in
your mire. But we must part company: we weren't made to
live together. Good-night."

He left him, and when he reached home, wrote to Roussin,
saying that he withdrew the piece, and did not disguise his reasons for doing so.

It meant a breach with Roussin and all his gang. The consequences were felt at once. The newspapers had made a
certain amount of talk about the forthcoming piece, and the
story of the quarrel between the composer and the singer appeared in due course. A certain conductor was adventurous
enough to play the piece at a Sunday afternoon concert. His
good fortune was disastrous for Christophe. The *David* was
played—and hissed. All the singer's friends had passed the
word to teach the insolent musician a lesson: and the outside
public, who had been bored by the symphonic poem, added their
voices to the verdict of the critics. To crown his misfortunes,
Christophe was ill-advised enough to accept the invitation to
display his talents as a pianist at the same concert by giving a
Fantasia for piano and orchestra. The unkindly disposition

of the audience, which had been to a certain extent restrained during the performance of the *David,* out of consideration for the interpreters, broke loose, when they found themselves face to face with the composer,—whose playing was not all that it might have been. Christophe was unnerved by the noise in the hall, and stopped suddenly half-way through a movement: and he looked jeeringly at the audience, who were startled into silence, and played *Malbrouck s'en va-t-en guerre!*—and said insolently:

" That is all you are fit for."

Then he got up and went away.

There was a terrific row. The audience shouted that he had insulted them, and that he must come and apologize. Next day the papers unanimously slaughtered the grotesque German to whom justice had been meted out by the good taste of Paris.

And then once more he was left in absolute isolation. Once more Christophe found himself alone, more solitary than ever, in that great, hostile, stranger city. He did not worry about it. He began to think that he was fated to be so, and would be so all his life.

He did not know that a great soul is never alone, that, however Fortune may cheat him of friendship, in the end a great soul creates friends by the radiance of the love with which it is filled, and that even in that hour, when he thought himself for ever isolated, he was more rich in love than the happiest men and women in the world.

Living with the Stevens was a little girl of thirteen or fourteen, to whom Christophe had given lessons at the same time as Colette. She was a distant cousin of Colette's, and her name was Grazia Buontempi. She was a little girl with a golden-brown complexion, with cheeks delicately tinged with red: healthy-looking: she had a little aquiline nose, a large well-shaped mouth, always half-open, a round chin, very white, calm clear eyes, softly smiling, a round forehead framed in masses of long, silky hair, which fell in long, waving locks loosely down to her shoulders. She was like a little Virgin of Andrea del Sarto, with her wide face and serenely gazing eyes.

She was Italian. Her parents lived almost all the year round in the country on an estate in the North of Italy: plains, fields, little canals. From the loggia on the housetop they looked down on golden vines, from which here and there the black spikes of the cypress-trees emerged. Beyond them were fields, and again fields. Silence. The lowing of the oxen returning from the fields, and the shrill cries of the peasants at the plow were to be heard:

"*Ihi! . . . Fat innanz'! . . .*"

Grasshoppers chirruped in the trees, frogs croaked by the waterside. And at night there was infinite silence under the silver beams of the moon. In the distance, from time to time, the watchers by the crops, sleeping in huts of branches, fired their guns by way of warning thieves that they were awake. To those who heard them drowsily, these noises meant no more than the chiming of a dull clock in the distance, marking the hours of the night. And silence closed again, like a soft cloak, about the soul.

Round little Grazia life seemed asleep. Her people did not give her much attention. In the calmness and beauty that was all about her she grew up peacefully without haste, without fever. She was lazy, and loved to dawdle and to sleep. For hours together she would lie in the garden. She would let herself be borne onward by the silence like a fly on a summer stream. And sometimes, suddenly, for no reason, she would begin to run. She would run like a little animal, head and shoulders a little leaning to the right, moving easily and supply. She was like a kid climbing and slithering among the stones for the sheer joy of leaping about. She would talk to the dogs, the frogs, the grass, the trees, the peasants, and the beasts in the farmyard. She adored all the creatures about her, great and small: but she was less at her ease with the great. She saw very few people. The estate was isolated and far from any town. Very rarely there came along the dusty road some trudging, solemn peasant, or lovely country woman, with bright eyes and sunburnt face, walking with a slow rhythm, head high and chest well out. For days together Grazia lived alone in the silence of the garden: she saw no one: she was never bored: she was afraid of nothing.

One day a tramp came, stealing fowls. He stopped dead when he saw the little girl lying on the grass, eating a piece of bread and butter and humming to herself. She looked up at him calmly, and asked him what he wanted. He said:

"Give me something, or I'll hurt you."

She held out her piece of bread and butter and smiled, and said:

"You must not do harm."

Then he went away.

Her mother died. Her father, a kind, weak man, was an old Italian of a good family, robust, jovial, affectionate, but rather childish, and he was quite incapable of bringing up his child. Old Buontempi's sister, Madame Stevens, came to the funeral, and was struck by the loneliness of the child, and decided to take her back to Paris for a while, to distract her from her grief. Grazia and her father wept: but when Madame Stevens had made up her mind to anything, there was nothing for it but to give in: nobody could stand out against her. She had the brains of the family: and, in her house in Paris, she directed everything, dominated everybody: her husband, her daughter, her lovers:—for she had not denied herself in the matter of love: she went straight at her duties, and her pleasures: she was a practical woman and a passionate—very worldly and very restless.

Transplanted to Paris, Grazia adored her pretty cousin Colette, whom she amused. The pretty little savage was taken out into society and to the theater. They treated her as a child, and she regarded herself as a child, although she was a child no longer. She had feelings which she hid away, for she was fearful of them: accesses of tenderness for some person or thing. She was secretly in love with Colette, and would steal a ribbon or a handkerchief that belonged to her: often in her presence, she could not speak a word: and when she expected her, when she knew that she was going to see her, she would tremble with impatience and happiness. At the theater when she saw her pretty cousin, in evening dress, come into the box and attract general attention, she would smile humbly, affectionately, lovingly: and her heart would leap when Colette spoke to her. Dressed in white, with her beautiful black hair loose and hanging over her shoulders, biting the fingers of her long white cotton gloves, and idly poking her fingers through the holes,—every other minute during the play she would turn towards Colette in the hope of meeting a friendly look, to share the pleasure she was feeling, and to say with her clear brown eyes:

"I love you."

When they were out together in the Bois, outside Paris, she would walk in Colette's shadow, sit at her feet; run in front of her, break off branches that might be in her way, place stones in the mud for her to walk on. And one evening in the garden, when Colette shivered and asked for her shawl, she gave a little cry of delight—she was at once ashamed of it—to think that her beloved would be wrapped in something of hers, and would give it back to her presently filled with the scent of her body.

There were books, certain passages in the poets, which she read in secret—(for she was still given children's books)—which gave her delicious thrills. And there were more even in certain passages in music, although she was told that she could not understand them: and she persuaded herself that she did not understand them:—but she would turn pale and cold with emotion. No one knew what was happening within her at such moments.

Outside that she was just a docile little girl, dreamy, lazy, greedy, blushing on the slightest provocation, now silent for hours together, now talking volubly, easily touched to tears and laughter, breaking suddenly into fits of sobbing or childish laughter. She loved to laugh, and silly little things would amuse her. She never tried to be grown up. She remained a child. She was, above all, kind and could not bear to hurt anybody, and she was hurt by the least angry word addressed to herself. She was very modest and retiring, ready to love and admire anything that seemed good and beautiful to her, and so she attributed to others qualities which they did not possess.

She was being educated, for she was very backward. And that was how she came to be taught music by Christophe.

She saw him for the first time at a crowded party in her aunt's house. Christophe, who was incapable of adapting himself to his audience, played an interminable *adagio* which made everybody yawn: when it seemed to be over he began again: and everybody wondered if it was ever going to end. Madame Stevens was boiling with impatience: Colette was highly amused: she was enjoying the absurdity of it, and rather pleased with Christophe for being so insensible of it: she felt that he was a force, and she liked that: but it was comic too: and she would have been the last person to defend him. Grazia alone was moved to tears by the music. She hid herself away in a corner of the room. When it was over she went away, so that no one should see her emotion, and also because she could not bear to see people making fun of Christophe.

A few days later, at dinner, Madame Stevens in her presence spoke of her having music-lessons from Christophe. Grazia was so upset that she let her spoon drop into her soup-plate, and splashed herself and her neighbor. Colette said she ought first to have lessons in table-manners. Madame Stevens added that Christophe was not the person to go to for that. Grazia was glad to be scolded in Christophe's company.

Christophe began to teach her. She was stiff and frozen, and held her arms close to her sides, and could not stir: and when Christophe placed his hand on hers, to correct the

position of her fingers, and stretched them over the keys, she
nearly fainted. She was fearful of playing badly for him:
but in vain did she practise until she nearly made herself ill,
and evoked impatient protests from her cousin: she always
played vilely when Christophe was present: she was breathless, and her fingers were as stiff as pieces of wood, or as flabby
as cotton: she struck the wrong notes and gave the emphasis
all wrong: Christophe would lose his temper, scold her, and
go away: then she would long to die.

He paid no attention to her, and thought only of Colette.
Grazia was envious of her cousin's intimacy with Christophe:
but, although it hurt her, in her heart she was glad both for
Colette and for Christophe. She thought Colette so superior to
herself that it seemed natural to her that she should monopolize
attention.—It was only when she had to choose between her
cousin and Christophe that she felt her heart turn against
Colette. With her girlish intuition she saw that Christophe
was made to suffer by Colette's coquetry, and the persistent
courtship of her by Lucien Lévy-Cœur. Instinctively she disliked Lévy-Cœur, and she detested him as soon as she knew
that Christophe detested him. She could not understand how
Colette could admit him as a rival to Christophe. She began
secretly to judge him harshly. She discovered certain of his
small hypocrisies, and suddenly changed her manner towards
him. Colette saw it, but did not guess the cause: she pretended
to ascribe it to a little girl's caprice. But it was very certain
that she had lost her power over Grazia: as was shown by a
trifling incident. One evening, when they were walking together in the garden, a gentle rain came on, and Colette,
tenderly, though coquettishly, offered Grazia the shelter of her
cloak: Grazia, for whom, a few weeks before, it would have been
happiness ineffable to be held close to her beloved cousin,
moved away coldly, and walked on in silence at a distance of
some yards. And when Colette said that she thought a piece
of music that Grazia was playing was ugly, Grazia was not
kept from playing and loving it.

She was only concerned with Christophe. She had the insight of her tenderness, and saw that he was suffering, without his saying a word. She exaggerated it in her childish, uneasy regard for him. She thought that Christophe was in love with Colette, when he had really no more than an exacting friendship. She thought he was unhappy, and she was unhappy for him, and she had little reward for her anxiety. She paid for it when Colette had infuriated Christophe: then he was surly and avenged himself on his pupil, waxing wrathful with her mistakes. One morning when Colette had exasperated him more than usual, he sat down by the piano so savagely that Grazia lost the little nerve she had: she floundered: he angrily scolded her for her mistakes: then she lost her head altogether: he fumed, wrung his hands, declared that she would never do anything properly, and that she had better occupy herself with cooking, sewing, anything she liked, only, in Heaven's name, she must not go on with her music! It was not worth the trouble of torturing people with her mistakes. With that he left her in the middle of her lesson. He was furious. And poor Grazia wept, not so much for the humiliation of anything he had said to her, as for despair at not being able to please Christophe, when she longed to do so, and could only succeed in adding to his sufferings. The greatest grief was when Christophe ceased to go to the Stevens' house. Then she longed to go home. The poor child, so healthy, even in her dreams, in whom there was much of the sweet peace of the country, felt ill at ease in the town, among the neurasthenic, restless women of Paris. She never dared say anything, but she had come to a fairly accurate estimation of the people about her. But she was shy, and, like her father, weak, from kindness, modesty, distrust of herself. She submitted to the authority of her domineering aunt and her cousin, who was used to tyrannizing over everybody. She dared not write to her father, to whom she wrote regularly long, affectionate letters:

"Please, please, take me home!"

And her father dared not take her home, in spite of his

own longing: for Madame Stevens had answered his timid advances by saying that Grazia was very well off where she was, much better off than she would be with him, and that she must stay for the sake of her education.

But there came a time when her exile was too hard for the little southern creature, a time when she had to fly back towards the light.—That was after Christophe's concert. She went to it with the Stevens: and she was tortured by the hideous sight of the rabble amusing themselves with insulting an artist. . . . An artist? The man who, in Grazia's eyes, was the very type of art, the personification of all that was divine in life! She was on the point of tears; she longed to get away. She had to listen to all the caterwauling, the hisses, the howls, and, when they reached home, to the laughter of Colette as she exchanged pitying remarks with Lucien Lévy-Cœur. She escaped to her room, and through part of the night she sobbed: she spoke to Christophe, and consoled him: she would gladly have given her life for him, and she despaired of ever being able to do anything to make him happy. It was impossible for her to stay in Paris any longer. She begged her father to take her away, saying:

"I cannot live here any longer; I cannot: I shall die if you leave me here any longer."

Her father came at once, and though it was very painful to them both to stand up to her terrible aunt, they screwed up their courage for it by a desperate effort of will.

Grazia returned to the sleepy old estate. She was glad to get back to Nature and the creatures that she loved. Every day she gathered comfort for her sorrow, but in her heart there remained a little of the melancholy of the North, like a veil of mist, that very slowly melted away before the sun. Sometimes she thought of Christophe's wretchedness. Lying on the grass, listening to the familiar frogs and grasshoppers, or sitting at her piano, which now she played more often than before, she would dream of the friend her heart had chosen: she would talk to him, in whispers, for hours together, and it seemed

not impossible to her that one day he would open the door
and come in to her. She wrote to him, and, after long hesitation, she sent the letter, unsigned, which, one day, with beating
heart, she went secretly and dropped into the box in the village
two miles away, beyond the long plowed fields,—a kind, good,
touching letter, in which she told him that he was not alone,
that he must not be discouraged, that there was one who thought
of him, and loved him, and prayed to God for him,—a poor
little letter, which was lost in the post, so that he never received it.

Then the serene, monotonous days succeeded each other in the
life of his distant friend. And the Italian peace, the genius of
tranquillity, calm happiness, silent contemplation, once more
took possession of that chaste and silent heart, in whose depths
there still burned, like a little constant flame, the memory of
Christophe.

But Christophe never knew of the simple love that watched
over him from afar, and was later to fill so great a room in his
life. Nor did he know that at that same concert, where he
had been insulted, there sat the woman who was to be the
beloved, the dear companion, destined to walk by his side,
shoulder to shoulder, hand in hand.

He was alone. He thought himself alone. But he did not
suffer overmuch. He did not feel that bitter anguish that had
given him such great agony in Germany. He was stronger,
riper: he knew that it must be so. His illusions about Paris
were destroyed: men were everywhere the same: he must be a
law unto himself, and not waste strength in a childish struggle
with the world: he must be himself, calmly, tranquilly. As
Beethoven had said, "If we surrender the forces of our lives to
life, what, then, will be left for the noblest and highest?" He
had firmly grasped a knowledge of his nature and the temper
of his race, which formerly he had so harshly judged. The
more he was oppressed by the atmosphere of Paris, the more
keenly did he feel the need of taking refuge in his own coun-

try, in the arms of the poets and musicians, in whom the best of Germany is garnered and preserved. As soon as he opened their books his room was filled with the sound of the sunlit Rhine and lit by the loving smiles of old friends new found.

How ungrateful he had been to them! How was it he had failed to feel the treasure of their goodness and honesty? He remembered with shame all the unjust, outrageous things he had said of them when he was in Germany. Then he saw only their defects, their awkward ceremonious manners, their tearful idealism, their little mental hypocrisies, their cowardice. Ah! How small were all these things compared with their great virtues! How could he have been so hard upon their weaknesses, which now made them even more moving in his eyes: for they were more human for them! In his reaction he was the more attracted to those of them to whom he had been most unjust. What things he had said about Schubert and Bach! And now he felt so near to them. Now it was as though these noble souls, whose foibles he had so scorned, leaned over him, now that he was in exile and far from his own people, and smiled kindly and said:

"Brother, we are here! Courage! We too have had more than our share of misery. . . . Bah! one wins through it. . . ."

He heard the soul of Johann Sebastian Bach roaring like the sea: hurricanes, winds howling, the clouds of life scudding, —men and women drunk with joy, sorrow, fury, and the Christ, all meekness, the Prince of Peace, hovering above them,—towns awakened by the cries of the watchmen, running with glad shouts, to meet the divine Bridegroom, whose footsteps shake the earth,—the vast store of thoughts, passions, musical forms, heroic life, Shakespearean hallucinations, Savonarolaesque prophecies, pastoral, epic, apocalyptic visions, all contained in the stunted body of the little Thuringian *cantor*, with his double chin, and little shining eyes under the wrinkled lids and the raised eyebrows . . .—he could see him so clearly! somber, jovial, a little absurd, with his head stuffed full of allegories and symbols, Gothic and rococo, choleric, obstinate, serene, with a passion for life, and a great longing for death . . .—he saw him in his school, a genial pedant, surrounded by his pupils, dirty, coarse, vagabond, ragged, with hoarse voices, the ragamuffins with whom he squabbled, and sometimes fought like a navvy, one of whom once gave him a mighty thrashing . . .—he saw him with his family, surrounded by his twenty-one children, of whom thirteen died before him, and one was an idiot, and the rest were good musicians who gave little concerts. . . . Sickness, burial, bitter disputes, want, his genius misunderstood:—and through and above it all, his music, his faith, deliverance and light, joy half seen, felt, desired, grasped,—God, the breath of God kindling his bones, thrilling through his flesh, thundering from his lips. . . . O Force! Force! Thrice joyful thunder of Force! . . .

Christophe took great draughts of that force. He felt the blessing of that power of music which issues from the depths of the German soul. Often mediocre, and even coarse, what does it matter? The great thing is that it is so, and that it flows plenteously. In France music is gathered carefully, drop by drop, and passed through Pasteur filters into bottles, and then corked. And the drinkers of stale water are disgusted by the rivers of German music! They examine minutely the defects of the German men of genius!

"Poor little things!"—thought Christophe, forgetting that he himself had once been just as absurd—"they find fault with Wagner and Beethoven! They must have faultless men of genius! . . . As though, when the tempest rages, it would take care not to upset the existing order of things! . . ."

He strode about Paris rejoicing in his strength. If he were misunderstood, so much the better! He would be all the freer. To create, as genius must, a whole world, organically constituted according to his own inward laws, the artist must live in it altogether. An artist can never be too much alone. What is terrible is to see his ideas reflected in a mirror which deforms and stunts them. He must say nothing to others of

what he is doing until he has done it: otherwise he would never
have the courage to go on to the end: for it would no longer be
his idea, but the miserable idea of others that would live in him.

Now that there was nothing to disturb his dreams, they
bubbled forth like springs from all the corners of his soul,
and from every stone of the roads by which he walked. He
was living in a visionary state. Everything he saw and heard
called forth in him creatures and things different from those
he saw and heard. He had only to live to find everywhere about
him the life of his heroes. Their sensations came to him of
their own accord. The eyes of the passers-by, the sound of a
voice borne by the wind, the light on a lawn, the birds singing
in the trees of the Luxembourg, a convent-bell ringing so far
away, the pale sky, the little patch of sky seen from his room,
the sounds and shades of sound of the different hours of the
day, all these were not in himself, but in the creatures of his
dreams.—Christophe was happy.

But his material position was worse than ever. He had lost
his few pupils, his only resource. It was September, and rich
people were out of town, and it was difficult to find new pupils.
The only one he had was an engineer, a crazy, clever fellow,
who had taken it into his head, at forty, to become a great
violinist. Christophe did not play the violin very well: but
he knew more about it than his pupil: and for some time he
gave him three hours a week at two francs an hour. But at
the end of six weeks the engineer got tired of it, and suddenly discovered that painting was his vocation.—When he im-
parted his discovery to Christophe, Christophe laughed heartily:
but, when he had done laughing, he reckoned up his finances,
and found that he had in hand the twelve francs which his
pupil had just paid him for his last lessons. That did not
worry him: he only said to himself that he must certainly set
about finding some other means of living, and start once more
going from publisher to publisher. That was not very pleasant.
. . . Pff! . . . It was useless to torment himself in advance. It was a jolly day. He went to Meudon.

He had a sudden longing for a walk. As he walked there rose in him scraps of music. He was as full of it as a hive of honey: and he laughed aloud at the golden buzzing of his bees. For the most part it was changing music. And lively leaping rhythms, insistent, haunting. . . . Much good it is to create and fashion music buried within four walls! There you can only make combinations of subtle, hard, unyielding harmonies, like the Parisians!

When he was weary he lay down in the woods. The trees were half in leaf, the sky was periwinkle blue. Christophe dozed off dreamily, and in his dreams there was the color of the sweet light falling from October clouds. His blood throbbed. He listened to the rushing flood of his ideas. They came from all corners of the earth: worlds, young and old, at war, rags and tatters of dead souls, guests and parasites that once had dwelled within him, as in a city. The words that Gottfried had spoken by the grave of Melchior returned to him: he was a living tomb, filled with the dead, striving in him,—all his unknown forefathers. He listened to those countless lives, it delighted him to set the organ roaring, the roaring of that age-old forest, full of monsters, like the forest of Dante. He was no longer fearful of them as he had been in his youth. For the master was there: his will. It was a great joy to him to crack his whip and make the beasts howl, and feel the wealth of living creatures in himself. He was not alone. There was no danger of his ever being alone. He was a host in himself. Ages of Kraffts, healthy and rejoicing in their health. Against hostile Paris, against a hostile people, he could set a whole people: the fight was equal.

He had left the modest room—it was too expensive—which he occupied and taken an attic in the Montrouge district. It was well aired, though it had no other advantage. There was a continual draught. But he wanted to breathe. From his window he had a wide view over the chimneys of Paris to Montmartre in the background. It had not taken him long to move:

a handcart was enough: Christophe pushed it himself. Of all
his possessions the most precious to him, after his old bag,
was one of those casts, which have lately become so popular,
of the death-mask of Beethoven. He packed it with as much
care as though it were a priceless work of art. He never let
it out of his sight. It was an oasis in the midst of the desert
of Paris. And also it served him as a moral thermometer.
The death-mask indicated more clearly than his own conscience
the temperature of his soul, the character of his most secret
thoughts: now a cloudy sky, now the gusty wind of the passions,
now fine calm weather.

He had to be sparing with his food. He only ate once a
day, at one in the afternoon. He bought a large sausage, and
hung it up in his window: a thick slice of it, a hunk of bread,
and a cup of coffee that he made himself were a feast for the
gods. He would have preferred two such feasts. He was angry
with himself for having such a good appetite. He called himself to task, and thought himself a glutton, thinking only of his
stomach. He lost flesh: he was leaner than a famished dog.
But he was solidly built, he had an iron constitution, and his
head was clear.

He did not worry about the morrow, though he had good reason for doing so. As long as he had in hand money enough
for the day he never bothered about it. When he came to the
end of his money he made up his mind to go the round of the
publishers once more. He found no work. He was on his way
home, empty, when, happening to pass the music-shop where he
had been introduced to Daniel Hecht by Sylvain Kohn, he went
in without remembering that he had already been there under
not very pleasant circumstances. The first person he saw was
Hecht. He was on the point of turning tail: but he was too
late: Hecht had seen him. Christophe did not wish to seem to
be avoiding him: he went up to Hecht, not knowing what to
say to him, and fully prepared to stand up to him as arrogantly as need be: for he was convinced that Hecht would be
unsparingly insolent. But he was nothing of the kind. Hecht

coldly held out his hand, muttered some conventional inquiry
after his health, and, without waiting for any request from
Christophe, he pointed to the door of his office, and stepped
aside to let him pass. He was secretly glad of the visit,
which he had foreseen, though he had given up expecting it.
Without seeming to do so, he had carefully followed Christophe's doings: he had missed no opportunity of hearing his
music: he had been at the famous performance of the *David:*
and, despising the public, he had not been greatly surprised
at its hostile reception, since he himself had felt the beauty of
the work. There were probably not two people in Paris more
capable than Hecht of appreciating Christophe's artistic originality. But he took care not to say anything about it, not only
because his vanity was hurt by Christophe's attitude towards
himself, but because it was impossible for him to be amiable:
it was the peculiarly ungracious quality of his nature. He was
sincerely desirous of helping Christophe: but he would not
have stirred a finger to do so: he was waiting for Christophe to
come and ask it of him. And now that Christophe had come,—
instead of generously seizing the opportunity of wiping out the
memory of their previous misunderstanding by sparing his
visitor any humiliation, he gave himself the satisfaction of
hearing him make his request at length: and he even went so
far as to offer Christophe, at least for the time being, the
work which he had formerly refused. He gave him fifty pages
of music to transpose for mandoline and guitar by the next
day. After which, being satisfied that he had made him truckle
down, he found him less distasteful work, but always so un-
graciously that it was impossible to be grateful to him for it:
Christophe had to be ground down by necessity before he would
ever go to Hecht again. In any case he preferred to earn his
money by such work, however irritating it might be, than accept it as a gift from Hecht, as it was once more offered to
him:—and, indeed, Hecht meant it kindly: but Christophe had
been conscious of Hecht's original intention to humiliate him:
he was forced to accept his conditions, but nothing would in-

duce him to accept any favor from him: he was willing to work for him:—by giving and giving he squared the account: —but he would not be under any obligation to him. Unlike Wagner, that impudent mendicant where his art was concerned, he did not place his art above himself: the bread that he had not earned himself would have choked him.—One day, when he brought some work that he had sat up all night to finish, he found Hecht at table. Hecht, remarking his pallor and the hungry glances that involuntarily he cast at the dishes, felt sure that he had not eaten that day, and invited him to lunch. He meant kindly, but he made it so apparent that he had noticed Christophe's straits that his invitation looked like charity: Christophe would have died of hunger rather than accept. He could not refuse to sit down at the table—(Hecht said he wanted to talk to him):—but he did not touch a morsel: he pretended that he had just had lunch. His stomach was aching with hunger.

Christophe would gladly have done without Hecht: but the other publishers were even worse.—There were also wealthy amateurs who had conceived some scrap of a musical idea, and could not even write it down. They would send for Christophe, hum over their lucubrations, and say:

"Isn't it fine?"

Then they would give them to him for elaboration,—(to be written):—and then they would appear under their own names through some great publishing house. They were quite convinced that they had composed them themselves. Christophe knew such a one, a distinguished nobleman, a strange, restless creature, who would suddenly call him "Dear friend," grasp him by the arm, and burst into a torrent of enthusiastic demonstrations, talking and giggling, babbling and telling funny stories, interlarded with cries of ecstatic laughter: Beethoven, Verlaine, Fauré, Yvette Guilbert. . . . He made him work, and failed tc pay. He worked it out in invitations to lunch and handshakes. Finally he sent Christophe twenty francs, which Christophe gave himself the foolish luxury of returning. That day he had not twenty sous in the world: and he had to buy a twenty-five centimes stamp for a letter to his mother. It was Louisa's birthday, and Christophe would not for the world have failed her: the poor old creature counted on her son's letter, and could not have endured disappointment. For some weeks past she had been writing to him more frequently, in spite of the pain it caused her. She was suffering from her loneliness. But she could not bring herself to join Christophe in Paris: she was too timid, too much attached to her own little town, to her church, her house, and she was afraid of traveling. And besides, if she had wanted to come, Christophe had not enough money: he had not always enough for himself.

· He had been given a great deal of pleasure once by receiving a letter from Lorchen, the peasant girl for whose sake he had plunged into the brawl with the Prussian soldiers:[1] she wrote to tell him that she was going to be married: she gave him news of his mother, and sent him a basket of apples and a piece of cake to eat in her honor. They came in the nick of time. That evening with Christophe was a fast, Ember Days, Lent: only the butt end of the sausage hanging by the window was left. Christophe compared himself to the anchorite saints fed by a crow among the rocks. But no doubt the crow was hard put to it to feed all the anchorites, for he never came again.

In spite of all his difficulties Christophe kept his end up. He washed his linen in his basin, and cleaned his boots, whistling like a blackbird. He consoled himself with the saying of Berlioz: "Let us raise our heads above the miseries of life, and let us blithely sing the familiar gay refrain, *Dies iræ*. . . ."—He used to sing it sometimes, to the dismay of his neighbors, who were amazed and shocked to hear him break off in the middle and shout with laughter.

He led a life of stern chastity. As Berlioz remarked: "The lover's life is a life for the idle and the rich." Christophe's poverty, his daily hunt for bread, his excessive sobriety, and

[1] See *Jean-Christophe*—I, " Revolt."

his creative fever left him neither the time nor the taste for any thought of pleasure. He was more than indifferent about it: in his reaction against Paris he had plunged into a sort of moral asceticism. He had a passionate need of purity, a horror of any sort of dirtiness. It was not that he was rid of his passions. At other times he had been swept headlong by them. But his passions remained chaste even when he yielded to them: for he never sought pleasure through them but the absolute giving of himself and fulness of being. And when he saw that he had been deceived he flung them furiously from him. Lust was not to him a sin like any other. It was the great Sin, that which poisons the very springs of life. All those in whom the old Christian belief has not been crusted over with strange conceptions, all those who still feel in themselves the vigor and life of the races, which through the strengthening of an heroic discipline have built up Western civilization, will have no difficulty in understanding him. Christophe despised cosmopolitan society, whose only aim and creed was pleasure.—In truth it is good to seek pleasure, to desire pleasure for all men, to combat the cramping pessimistic beliefs, that have come to weigh upon humanity through twenty centuries of Gothic Christianity. But that can only be upon condition that it is a generous faith, earnestly desirous of the good of others. But instead of that, what happens? The most pitiful egoism. A handful of loose-living men and women trying to give their senses the maximum of pleasure with the minimum of risk, while they take good care that the rest shall drudge for it.—Yes, no doubt, they have their parlor Socialism! . . . But they know perfectly well that their doctrine of pleasure is only practicable for " well-fed " people, for a select pampered few, that it is poison to the poor. . . .

" The life of pleasure is a rich man's life."

Christophe was neither rich nor likely to become so. When he made a little money he spent it at once on music: he went without food to go to concerts. He would take cheap seats in the gallery of the *Théâtre du Châtelet:* and he would steep himself in music: he found both food and love in it. He had such a hunger for happiness and so great a power of enjoying it that the imperfections of the orchestra never worried him: he would stay for two or three hours, drowsy and beatific, and wrong notes or defective taste never provoked in him more than an indulgent smile: he left his critical faculty outside: he was there to love, not to judge. Around him the audience sat motionless, with eyes half closed, letting itself be borne on by the great torrent of dreams. Christophe fancied them as a mass of people curled up in the shade, like an enormous cat, weaving fantastic dreams of lust and carnage. In the deep golden shadows certain faces stood out, and their strange charm and silent ecstasy drew Christophe's eyes and heart: he loved them: he listened through them: he became them, body and soul. One woman in the audience became aware of it, and between her and Christophe during the concert there was woven one of those obscure sympathies, which touch the very depths, though never by one word are they translated into the region of consciousness, while, when the concert is over and the thread that binds soul to soul is snapped, nothing is left of it. It is a state familiar to lovers of music, especially when they are young and do most wholly surrender: the essence of music is so completely love, that the full savor of it is not won unless it be enjoyed through another, and so it is that, at a concert, we instinctively seek among the throng for friendly eyes, for a friend with whom to share a joy too great for ourselves alone.

Among such friends, the friends of one brief hour, whom Christophe marked out for choice of love, the better to taste the sweetness of the music, he was attracted by one face which he saw again and again, at every concert. It was the face of a little grisette who seemed to adore music without understanding it at all. She had an odd little profile, a short, straight nose, almost in line with her slightly pouting lips and delicately molded chin, fine arched eyebrows, and clear eyes: one

of those pretty little faces behind the veil of which one feels
joy and laughter concealed by calm indifference. It is perhaps in such light-hearted girls, little creatures working for
their living, that one finds most the old serenity that is no
more, the serenity of the antique statues and the faces of
Raphael. There is but one moment in their lives, the first
awakening of pleasure: all too soon their lives are sullied.
But at least they have lived for one lovely hour.

It gave Christophe an exquisite pleasure to look at her:
a pretty face would always warm his heart: he could enjoy
without desire: he found joy in it, force, comfort,—almost
virtue. It goes without saying that she quickly became aware
that he was watching her: and, unconsciously, there was set up
between them a magnetic current. And as they met at almost every concert, almost always in the same places, they
quickly learned each other's likes and dislikes. At certain
passages they would exchange meaning glances: when she particularly liked some melody she would just put out her tongue
as though to lick her lips: or, to show that she did not think
much of it, she would disdainfully wrinkle up her pretty nose.
In these little tricks of hers there was a little of that innocent
posing of which hardly any one can be free when he knows
that he is being watched. During serious music she would
sometimes try to look grave and serious: and she would turn
her profile towards him, and look absorbed, and smile to herself, and look out of the corner of her eye to see if he were
watching. They had become very good friends, without ex-
changing a word, and even without having attempted—at least
Christophe did not—to meet outside.

At last by chance at an evening concert they found themselves sitting next each other. After a moment of smiling
hesitation they began to talk amicably. She had a charming
voice and said many stupid things about music: for she knew
nothing about it and wanted to seem as if she knew: but she
loved it passionately. She loved the worst and the best. Massenet and Wagner: only the mediocre bored her. Music was a

physical pleasure to her: she drank it in through all the pores of her skin as Danaë did the golden rain. The prelude of *Tristan* made her blood run cold: and she loved feeling herself being carried away, like some warrior's prey, by the *Symphonia Eroica*. She told Christophe that Beethoven was deaf and dumb, and that, in spite of it all, if she had known him, she would have loved him, although he was precious ugly. Christophe protested that Beethoven was not so very ugly: then they argued about beauty and ugliness: and she agreed that it was a matter of taste: what was beautiful for one person was not so for another: "We're not golden louis and can't please every one." He preferred her when she did not talk: he understood her better. During the death of Isolde she held out her hand to him: her hand was warm and moist: he held it in his until the end of the piece: they could feel life coursing through the veins of their clasped hands.

They went out together: it was near midnight. They walked back to the Latin Quarter talking eagerly: she had taken his arm and he took her home: but when they reached the door, and she seemed to suggest that he should go up and see her room, he disregarded her smile and the friendliness in her eyes and left her. At first she was amazed, then furious: then she laughed aloud at the thought of his stupidity: and then, when she had reached her room and began to undress, she felt hurt and angry, and finally wept in silence. When next she met him at a concert she tried to be dignified and indifferent and crushing. But he was so kind to her that she could not hold to her resolution. They began to talk once more: only now she was a little reserved with him. He talked to her warmly but very politely and always about serious things, and the music to which they were listening and what it meant to him. She listened attentively and tried to think as he did. The meaning of his words often escaped her: but she believed him all the same. She was grateful to Christophe and had a respect for him which she hardly showed. By tacit agreement they only spoke to each other at concerts. He met her once surrounded with students. They bowed gravely. She never talked about him to any one. In the depths of her soul there was a little sanctuary, a quality of beauty, purity, consolation.

And so Christophe, by his presence, by the mere fact of his existence, exercised an influence that brought strength and solace. Wherever he passed he unconsciously left behind the traces of his inward light. He was the last to have any notion of it. Near him, in the house where he lived, there were people whom he had never seen, people who, without themselves suspecting it, gradually came under the spell of his beneficent radiance.

For several weeks Christophe had no money for concerts even by fasting: and in his attic under the roof, now that winter was coming in, he was numbed with the cold: he could not sit still at his table. Then he would get up and walk about Paris, trying to warm himself. He had the faculty of forgetting the seething town about him, and slipping away into space and the infinite. It was enough for him to see above the noisy street the dead, frozen moon, hung there in the abysm of the sky, or the sun, like a disc, rolling through the white mist; then Paris would sink down into the boundless void and all the life of it would seem to be no more than the phantom of a life that had been once, long, long ago . . . ages ago . . . The smallest tiny sign, imperceptible to the common lot of men, of the great wild life of Nature, so sparsely covered with the livery of civilization, was enough to make it all come rushing mightily up before his gaze. The grass growing between the stones of the streets, the budding of a tree strangled by its cast-iron cage, airless, earthless, on some bleak boulevard: a dog, a passing bird, the last relics of the beasts and birds that thronged the primeval world, which man has since destroyed: a whirling cloud of flies: the mysterious epidemic that raged through a whole district:—these were enough in the thick air of that human hothouse to bring the breath of the Spirit of the Earth up to slap his cheeks and whip his energy to action.

During those long walks, when he was often starving, and often had not spoken to a soul for days together, his wealth of dreams seemed inexhaustible. Privation and silence had aggravated his morbid heated condition. At night he slept feverishly, and had exhausting dreams: he saw once more and never ceased to see the old house and the room in which he had lived as a child: he was haunted by musical obsessions. By day he talked and never ceased to talk to the creatures within himself and the beings whom he loved, the absent and the dead.

One cold afternoon in December, when the grass was covered with frost, and the roofs of the houses and the great domes were glistening through the fog, and the trees, with their cold, twisted, naked branches, groping through the mist that hung about them, looked like great weeds at the bottom of the sea,— Christophe, who had been shivering all day and could not get warm again, went into the Louvre, which he hardly knew at all.

Till then painting had never moved him much. He was too much absorbed by the world within himself to grasp the world of color and form. They only acted on him through their music and rhythm, which only brought him an indistinguishable echo of their truth. No doubt his instinct did obscurely divine the selfsame laws that rule the harmony of visible form, as of the form of sounds, and the deep waters of the soul, from which spring the two rivers of color and sound, to flow down the two sides of the mountain of life. But he only knew one side of the mountain, and he was lost in the kingdom of the eye, which was not his. And so he missed the secret of the most exquisite, and perhaps the most natural charm of clear-eyed France, the queen of the world of light.

Even had he been interested in painting, Christophe was too German to adapt himself to so widely different a vision of things. He was not one of those up-to-date Germans who decry the German way of feeling, and persuade themselves that they admire and love French Impressionism or the artists of the eighteenth century,—except when they go farther and are convinced that they understand them better than the French. Christophe was a barbarian, perhaps: but he was frank about it. The pink flesh of Boucher, the fat chins of Watteau, the bored shepherds and plump, tight-laced shepherdesses, the whipped-cream souls, the virtuous oglings of Greuze, the tucked shirts of Fragonard, all that bare-legged poesy interested him no more than a fashionable, rather spicy newspaper. He did not see its rich and brilliant harmony; the voluptuous and sometimes melancholy dreams of that old civilization, the highest in Europe, were foreign to him. As for the French school of the seventeenth century, he liked neither its devout ceremony nor its pompous portraits: the cold reserve of the gravest of the masters, a certain grayness of soul that clouded the proud works of Nicolas Poussin and the pale faces of Philippe de Champaigne, repelled Christophe from old French art. And, once more, he knew nothing about it. If he had known anything about it he would have misunderstood it. The only modern painter whose fascination he had felt at all in Germany, Boecklin of Basle, had not prepared him much for Latin art. Christophe remembered the shock of his impact with that brutal genius, which smacked of earth and the musty smell of the heroic beasts that it had summoned forth. His eyes, seared by the raw light, used to the frantic motley of that drunken savage, could hardly adapt themselves to the half-tints, the dainty and mellifluous harmonies of French art.

But no man with impunity can live in a foreign land. Unknown to him it sets its seal upon him. In vain does he withdraw into himself: upon a day he must wake up to find that something has changed.

There was a change in Christophe on that evening when he wandered through the rooms of the Louvre. He was tired, cold, hungry; he was alone. Around him darkness was descending upon the empty galleries, and sleeping forms awoke. Christophe was very cold as he walked in silence among Egyptian sphinxes, Assyrian monsters, bulls of Persepolis, gleaming snakes from Palissy. He seemed to have passed into a magic world: and in his heart there was a strange, mysterious emotion. The dream of humanity wrapped him about,—the strange flowers of the soul. . . .

In the misty gilded light of the picture-galleries, and the gardens of rich brilliant hues, and painted airless fields, Christophe, in a state of fever, on the very brink of illness, was visited by a miracle.—He was walking, numbed by hunger, by the coldness of the galleries, by the bewildering mass of pictures: his head was whirling. When he reached the end of the gallery that looks on to the river, he stood before the *Good Samaritan* of Rembrandt, and leaned on the rail in front of the pictures to keep himself from falling: he closed his eyes for a moment. When he opened them on the picture in front of him—he was quite close to it—and he was held spellbound. . . .

Day was spent. Day was already far gone; it was already dead. The invisible sun was sinking down into the night. It was the magic hour when dreams and visions come mounting from the soul, saddened by the labors of the day, still, musing drowsily. All is silent, only the beating of the heart is heard. In the body there is hardly the strength to move, hardly to breathe; sadness; resignation; only an immense longing to fall into the arms of a friend, a hunger for some miracle, a feeling that some miracle must come. . . . It comes! A flood of golden light flames through the twilight, is cast upon the walls of the hovel, on the shoulder of the stranger bearing the dying man, touches with its warmth those humble objects, and those poor creatures, and the whole takes on a new gentleness, a divine glory. It is the very God, clasping in his terrible, tender arms the poor wretches, weak, ugly, poor, unclean, the poor down-at-heel rascal, the miserable creatures, with twisted haggard faces, thronging outside the window, the apathetic, silent creatures standing in mortal terror,—all the pitiful human beings of Rembrandt, the herd of obscure broken creatures who

know nothing, can do nothing, only wait, tremble, weep, and
pray.—But the Master is there. He will come: it is known
that He will come. Not He Himself is seen: only the light that
goes before, and the shadow of the light which He casts upon
all men. . . .

Christophe left the Louvre, staggering and tottering. His
head ached. He could not see. In the street it was raining,
but he hardly noticed the puddles between the flags and the
water trickling down from his shoes. Over the Seine the
yellowish sky was lit up, as the day waned, by an inward flame
—like the light of a lamp. Still Christophe was spellbound,
hypnotized. It seemed as though nothing existed: not the
carriages rattling over the stones with a pitiless noise: the
passers-by were not banging into him with their wet umbrellas:
he was not walking in the street: perhaps he was sitting at
home and dreaming: perhaps he had ceased to exist. . . .
And suddenly,—(he was so weak!)—he turned giddy and felt
himself falling heavily forward. . . . It was only for the
flash of a second: he clenched his fists, hurled himself backward, and recovered his balance.

At that very moment when he emerged into consciousness
his eyes met the eyes of a woman standing on the other side
of the street, who seemed to be looking for recognition. He
stopped dead, trying to remember when he had seen her before.
It was only after a moment or two that he could place those
sad, soft eyes: it was the little French governess whom, unwittingly, he had had dismissed in Germany, for whom he had
been looking for so long to beg her to forgive him. She had
stopped, too, in the busy throng, and was looking at him. Suddenly he saw her try to cross through the crowd of people and
step down into the road to come to him. He rushed to meet
her: but they were separated by a block in the traffic: he saw
her again for a moment struggling on the other side of that living wall: he tried to force his way through, was knocked over
by a horse, slipped and fell on the slippery asphalt, and was all
but run over. When he got up, covered with mud, and suc-

ceeded in reaching the other side of the street, she had disappeared.

He tried to follow her, but he had another attack of giddiness. and he had to give it up. Illness was close upon him: he felt that, but he would not submit to it. He set his teeth, and would not go straight home, but went far out of his way. It was just a useless torment to him: he had to admit that he was beaten: his legs ached, he dragged along. and only reached home with frightful difficulty. Half-way up the stairs he choked, and had to sit down. When he got to his icy room he refused to go to bed: he sat in his chair. wet through; his head was heavy and he could hardly breathe, and he drugged himself with music as broken as himself. He heard a few fugitive bars of the *Unfinished Symphony* of Schubert. Poor Schubert! He, too, was alone when he wrote that, feverish, somnolent, in that semitorpid condition which precedes the last great sleep: he sat dreaming by the fireside: all round him were heavy drowsy melodies, like stagnant water: he dwelt on them, like a child. half-asleep delighting in some self-told story, and repeating some passage in it twenty times: so sleep comes, then death. . . . And Christophe heard fleetingly that other music, with burning hands, closed eyes, a little weary smile, heart big with sighs, dreaming of the deliverance of death:—the first chorus in the Cantata of J. S. Bach: "*Dear God, when shall I die?*" . . . It was sweet to sink back into the soft melodies slowly floating by, to hear the distant, muffled clangor of the bells. . . . To die, to pass into the peace of earth! . . . *Und dann selber Erde werden.* . . . "And then himself to become earth. . . ."

Christophe shook off these morbid thoughts, the murderous smile of the siren who lies in wait for the hours of weakness of the soul. He got up, and tried to walk about his room: but he could not stand. He was shaking and shivering with fever. He had to go to bed. He felt that it was serious this time: but he did not lay down his arms: he never was of those who, when they are ill, yield utterly to their illness: he struggled,

he refused to be ill, and, above all, he was absolutely determined
not to die. He had his poor mother waiting for him in Germany. And he had his work to do: he would not yield to death.
He clenched his chattering teeth, and firmly grasped his will
that was oozing away: he was like a sturdy swimmer battling
with the waves dashing over him. At every moment, down he
plunged: his mind wandered, endless fancies haunted him,
memories of Germany and of Parisian society: he was obsessed
by rhythms and scraps of melody which went round, and round,
and round, like horses in a circus: the sudden shock of the
golden light of the *Good Samaritan*: the tense, stricken faces in
the shadow: and then, dark nothingness and night. Then up
he would come once more, wrenching away the grimacing mists,
clenching his fists, and setting his jaw. He clung to all those
whom he loved in the present and the past, to the face of the
friend he had just seen in the street, his dear mother, and to the
indestructible life within himself, that he felt was like a rock,
impervious to death. But once more the rock was covered
by the tide: the waves dashed over it, and tore his soul away
from its hold upon it: it was borne headlong and dashed by
the foam. And Christophe struggled in delirium, babbling
strangely, conducting and playing an imaginary orchestra:
trombones, horns, cymbals, timbals, bassoons, double-bass, . . .
he scraped, blew, beat the drum, frantically. The poor wretch
was bubbling over with suppressed music. For weeks he had
been unable to hear or play any music, and he was like a boiler
at high pressure, near bursting-point. Certain insistent phrases
bored into his brain like gimlets, pierced his skull, and made
him scream with agony. After these attacks he would fall back
on his pillow, dead tired, wet through, utterly weak, breathless, choking. He had placed his water-jug by his bedside, and
he took great draughts of it. The various noises of the adjoining rooms, the banging of the attic doors, made him start. He
was filled with a delirious disgust for the creatures swarming
round him. But his will fought on, sounded a warlike clarion-
note, declaring battle on all devils. . . . "*Und wenn die*

*Welt voll Teufel wär, und wollten uns verschlingen, so fürchten
wir uns nicht so sehr. . . ."* (" And even though the world
were full of devils, all seeking to devour us, we should not be
afraid. . . .").

And over the sea of scalding shadows that dashed over him
there came a sudden calm, glimpses of light, a gentle murmuring of violins and viols, the clear triumphant notes of trumpets
and horns, while, almost motionless, like a great wall, there rose
from the sick man's soul an indomitable song, like a choral of
J. S. Bach.

While he was fighting against the phantoms of fever and
the choking in his lungs, he was dimly aware that some one
had opened the door, and that a woman entered with a candle
in her hand. He thought it was another hallucination. He
tried to speak, but could not, and fell back on his pillow.
When, every now and then, he was brought for a moment back
to consciousness, he felt that his pillow had been raised, that his
feet had been wrapped up, that there was something burning
his back, or he would see the woman, whose face was not altogether unfamiliar, sitting at the foot of his bed. Then he saw
another face, that of a doctor using a stethoscope. Christophe
could not hear what they were saying, but he gathered that
they were talking of sending him to the hospital. He tried to
protest, to cry out that he would not go, that he would die
where he was, alone: but he could only frame incomprehensible
sounds. But the woman understood him: for she took his part,
and reassured him. He tried hard to find out who she was.
As soon as he could, with frightful effort, frame a sentence, he
asked her. She replied that she lived in the next attic and had
heard him moaning through the wall, and had taken the liberty
of coming in, thinking that he wanted help. She begged him
respectfully not to wear himself out with talking. He obeyed
her. He was worn out with the effort he had made: he lay
still and said nothing: but his brain went on working, pain-
fully gathering together its scattered memories. Where had

he seen her? . . . At last he remembered: yes, he had met her on the attic landing: she was a servant, and her name was Sidonie.

He watched her with half-closed eyes, so that she could not see him. She was little, and had a grave face, a wide forehead, hair drawn back, so that her temples were exposed; her cheeks were pale and high-boned; she had a short nose, pale blue eyes, with a soft, steady look in them, thick lips tightly pressed together, an anemic complexion, a humble, deliberate, and rather stiff manner. She looked after Christophe with busy silent devotion, without a spark of familiarity, and without ever breaking down the reserve of a servant who never forgets class differences.

However, little by little, when he was better and could talk to her, Christophe's affectionate cordiality made Sidonie talk to him a little more freely: but she was always on her guard: there were obviously certain things which she would not tell. She was a mixture of humility and pride. Christophe learned that she came from Brittany, where she had left her father, of whom she spoke very discreetly: but Christophe gathered that he did nothing but drink, have a good time, and live on his daughter: she put up with it, without saying anything, from pride: and she never failed to send him part of her month's wages: but she was not taken in. She had also a younger sister who was preparing for a teacher's examination, and she was very proud of her. She was paying almost all the expenses of her education. She worked frightfully hard, with grim determination.

"Have you a good situation?" asked Christophe.

"Yes. But I am thinking of leaving."

"Why? Aren't they good to you?"

"Oh! no. They're very good to me."

"Don't they pay you enough?"

"Yes. . . ."

He did not quite understand: he tried to understand, and encouraged her to talk. She had nothing to tell him but the monotony of her life, and the difficulty of earning a living: she did not lay any stress on it: she was not afraid of work: it was a necessity to her, almost a pleasure. She never spoke of the thing that tried her most: boredom. He guessed it. Little by little, with the intuition of perfect sympathy, he saw that her suffering was increasing, and it was made more acute for him by the memory of the trials supported by his own mother in a similar existence. He saw, as though he had lived it, the drab, unhealthy, unnatural existence—the ordinary existence imposed on servants by the middle-classes:—employers who were not so much unkind as indifferent, sometimes leaving her for days together without speaking a word outside her work. The hours and hours spent in the stuffy kitchen, the one small window, blocked up by a meat-safe, looking out on to a white wall. And her only pleasure was when she was told carelessly that her sauce was good or the meat well cooked. A cramped airless life with no prospect, with no ray of desire or hope, without interest of any kind.—The worst time of all for her was when her employers went away to the country. They economized by not taking her with them: they paid her wages for the month, but not enough to take her home: they gave her permission to go at her own expense. She would not, she could not do that. And so she was left alone in the deserted house. She had no desire to go out, and did not even talk to other servants, whose coarseness and immorality she despised. She never went out in search of amusement: she was naturally serious, economical, and afraid of misadventure. She sat in her kitchen, or in her room, from whence across the chimneys she could see the top of a tree in the garden of a hospital. She did not read, but tried to work listlessly: she would sit there dreaming, bored, bored to tears: she had a singular and infinite capacity for weeping: it was her only pleasure. But when her boredom weighed too heavily on her she could not even weep: she was frozen, sick at heart, and dead. Then she would pull herself together: or life would return of its own accord. She would think of her sister, listen to a barrel-organ in the distance, and dream, and slowly count the days until she had gained such and such a sum of money: she would be out in her reckoning, and begin to count all over again: she would fall asleep. So the days passed. . . .

The fits of depression alternated with outbursts of childish chatter and laughter. She would make fun of herself and other people. She watched and judged her employers, and their anxieties fed by their want of occupation, and her mistress's moods and melancholy, and the so-called interests of these so-called people of culture, how they patronized a picture, or a piece of music, or a book of verse. With her rude common sense, as far removed from the snobbishness of the very Parisian servants as from the crass stupidity of the very provincial girls, who only admire what they do not understand, she had a respectful contempt for their dabbling in music, their pointless chatter, and all those perfectly useless and tiresome intellectual smatterings which play so large a part in such hypocritical existences. She could not help silently comparing the real life, with which she grappled, with the imaginary pains and pleasures of that cushioned life, in which everything seems to be the product of boredom. She was not in revolt against it. Things were so: things were so. She accepted everything, knaves and fools alike. She said:

"It takes all sorts to make a world."

Christophe imagined that she was borne up by her religion: but one day she said, speaking of others who were richer and more happy:

"But in the end we shall all be equal."

"When?" asked Christophe. "After the social revolution?"

"The revolution?" said she. "Oh, there'll be much water flowing under bridges before that. I don't believe that stuff. Things will always be the same."

"When shall we all be equal, then?"

"When we're dead, of course! That's the end of everybody."

He was surprised by her calm materialism. He dared not say to her:

"Isn't it a frightful thing, in that case, if there is only one life, that it should be the like of yours, while there are so many others who are happy?"

But she seemed to have guessed his thought: she went on phlegmatically, resignedly, and a little ironically:

"One has to put up with it. Everybody cannot draw a prize. I've drawn a blank: so much the worse!"

She never even thought of looking for a more profitable place outside France. (She had once been offered a situation in America.) The idea of leaving the country never entered her head. She said:

"Stones are hard everywhere."

There was in her a profound, skeptical, and mocking fatalism. She was of the stock that has little or no faith, few considered reasons for living, and yet a tremendous vitality—the stock of the French peasantry, industrious and apathetic, riotous and submissive, who have no great love of life, but cling to it, and have no need of artificial stimulants to keep up their courage.

Christophe, who had not yet come across them, was astonished to find in the girl an absence of all faith: he marveled at her tenacious hold on life, without pleasure or purpose, and most of all he admired her sturdy moral sense that had no need of prop or support. Till then he had only seen the French people through naturalistic novels, and the theories of the mannikins of contemporary literature, who, reacting from the art of the century of pastoral scenes and the Revolution, loved to present natural man as a vicious brute, in order to sanctify their own vices. . . . He was amazed when he discovered Sidonie's uncompromising honesty. It was not a matter of morality but of instinct and pride. She had her aristocratic pride. For it is foolish to imagine that everybody belonging to the people is "popular." The people have their aristocrats just as the upper classes have their vulgarians. The aristocrats are those creatures whose instincts, and perhaps whose blood, are purer than those of the others: those who know and are conscious of what they are, and must be true to themselves. They are in the minority: but, even when they are forced to live apart, the others know that they are the salt of the earth: and the fact of their existence is a check upon the others, who are forced to model themselves upon them, or to pretend to do so. Every province, every village, every congregation of men, is, to a certain degree, what its aristocrats are: and public opinion varies accordingly, and is, in one place, severe, in another, lax. The present anarchy and upheaval of the majority will not change the unvoiced power of the minority. It is more dangerous for them to be uprooted from their native soil and scattered far and wide in the great cities. But even so, lost amid strange surroundings, living in isolation, yet the individualities of the good stock persist and never mix with those about them.—Sidonie knew nothing, wished to know nothing, of all that Christophe had seen in Paris. She was no more interested in the sentimental and unclean literature of the newspapers than in the political news. She did not even know that there were Popular Universities: and, if she had known, it is probable that she would have put herself out as little to go to them as she did to hear a sermon. She did her work, and thought for herself: she was not concerned with what other people thought. Christophe congratulated her.

"Why is that surprising?" she asked. "I am like everybody else. You haven't met any French people."

"I've been living among them for a year," said Christophe, "and I haven't met a single one who thought of anything but amusing himself or of aping those who amuse him."

"That's true," said Sidonie. "You have only seen rich people. The rich are the same everywhere. You've seen nothing at all."

"That's true," said Christophe. "I'm beginning."

For the first time he caught a glimpse of the people of France, men and women who seem to be built for eternity, who are one with the earth, who, like the earth, have seen so many conquering races, so many masters of a day, pass away, while they themselves endure and do not pass.

When he was getting better and was allowed to get up for a little, the first thing he thought of was to pay Sidonie back for the expenses she had incurred during his illness. It was impossible for him to go about Paris looking for work, and he had to bring himself to write to Hecht: he asked him for an advance on account of future work. With his amazing combination of indifference and kindliness Hecht made him wait a fortnight for a reply—a fortnight during which Christophe tormented himself and practically refused to touch any of the food Sidonie brought him, and would only accept a little bread and milk, which she forced him to take, and then he grumbled and was angry with himself because he had not earned it: then, without a word, Hecht sent him the sum he asked: and not once during the months of Christophe's illness did Hecht make any inquiry after him. He had a genius for making himself disliked even when he was doing a kindness. Even in his kindness Hecht could not be generous.

Sidonie came every day in the afternoon and again in the evening. She cooked Christophe's dinner for him. She made no noise, but went quietly about her business: and when she saw the dilapidated condition of his clothes she took them away to mend them. Insensibly there had crept an element of affection into their relation. Christophe talked at length about his mother: and that touched Sidonie: she would put herself in Louisa's place, alone in Germany: and she had a maternal feeling for Christophe, and when he talked to her he tried to trick his need of mothering and love, from which a man suffers most when he is weak and ill. He felt nearer Louisa with Sidonie than with anybody else. Sometimes he would confide his artistic troubles to her. She would pity him gently, though she seemed to regard such sorrows of the intellect ironically. That, too, reminded him of his mother and comforted him.

He tried to get her to confide in him: but she was much

less open than he. He asked her jokingly why she did not get married. And she would reply in her usual tone of mocking resignation that " it was not allowed for servants to marry: it complicates things too much. Besides, she was sure to make a bad choice, and that is not pleasant. Men are sordid creatures. They come courting when a woman has money, squeeze it out of her, and then leave her in the lurch. She had seen too many cases of that and was not inclined to do the same."—She did not tell him of her own unfortunate experience: her future husband had left her when he found that she was giving all her earnings to her family.—Christophe used to see her in the court-yard mothering the children of a family living in the house. When she met them alone on the stairs she would sometimes embrace them passionately. Christophe would fancy her occupying the place of a lady of his acquaintance: she was not a fool, and she was no plainer than many another woman: he declared that in the lady's place she would have been the better woman of the two. There are so many splendid lives hidden in the world, unknown and unsuspected! And, on the other hand, the hosts of the living dead, who encumber the earth, and take up the room and the happiness of others in the light of the sun! . . .

Christophe had no ulterior thought. He was fond, too fond of her: he let her coddle him like a child.

Some days Sidonie would be queer and depressed: but he attributed that to her work. Once when they were talking she got up suddenly and left him, making some excuse about her work. Finally, after a day when Christophe had been more confidential than usual, she broke off her visits for a time: and when she came back she would only talk to him constrainedly. He wondered what he could have done to offend her. He asked her. She replied quickly that he had not offended her: but she stayed away again. A few days later she told him that she was going away: she had given up her situation and was leaving the house. Coldly and reservedly she thanked him for all his kindness, told him she hoped he would soon recover, and that his mother would remain in good health, and then she said good-by.

He was so astonished at her abrupt departure that he did not know what to say: he tried to discover her reasons: she replied evasively. He asked her where she was going: she did not reply, and, to cut short his questions, she got up to go. As she reached the door he held out his hand: she grasped it warmly: but her face did not betray her, and to the end she maintained her stiff, cold manner. She went away.

He never understood why.

He dragged through the winter—a wet, misty, muddy winter. Weeks on end without sun. Although Christophe was better he was by no means recovered. He still had a little pain in his lungs, a lesion which healed slowly, and fits of coughing which kept him from sleeping at night. The doctor had forbidden him to go out. He might just as well have ordered him to go to the Riviera or the Canary Islands. He had to go out! If he did not go out to look for his dinner, his dinner would certainly not come to look for him.—And he was ordered medicines which he could not afford. And so he gave up consulting doctors: it was a waste of money: and besides he was always ill at ease with them: they could not understand each other: they lived in separate worlds. They had an ironical and rather contemptuous pity for the poor devil of an artist who claimed to be a world to himself, and was swept along like a straw by the river of life. He was humiliated by being examined, and prodded, and handled by these men. He was ashamed of his sick body, and thought:

" How glad I shall be when *it* is dead! "

In spite of loneliness, illness, poverty, and so many other causes of suffering, Christophe bore his lot patiently. He had never been so patient. He was surprised at himself. Illness is often a blessing. By ravaging the body it frees the soul and purifies it: during the nights and days of forced inaction thoughts arise which are fearful of the raw light of day, and are scorched by the sun of health. No man who has never been ill can have a thorough knowledge of himself.

His illness had, in a queer way, soothed Christophe. It had purged him of the coarser elements of his nature. Through his most subtle nerves he felt the world of mysterious forces which dwell in each of us, though the tumult of life prevents our hearing them. Since his visit to the Louvre, in his hours of fever, the smallest memories of which were graven upon his mind, he had lived in an atmosphere like that of the Rembrandt picture, warm, soft, profound. He too felt in his heart the magic beams of an invisible sun. And although he did not believe, he knew that he was not alone: a God was holding him by the hand, and leading him to the predestined goal of his endeavors. He trusted in Him like a little child.

For the first time for years he felt that he must rest. The lassitude of his convalescence was in itself a rest for him after the extraordinary tension of mind that had gone before his illness and had left him still exhausted. Christophe, who for many months had been continually on the alert and strained, upon his guard, felt the fixity of his gaze slowly relax. He was not less strong for it: he was more human. The great though rather monstrous quality of life of the man of genius had passed into the background: he found himself a man like the rest, purged of the fanaticism of his mind, and all the hardness and mercilessness of his actions. He hated nothing: he gave no thought to things that exasperated him, or, if he did, he shrugged them off: he thought less of his own troubles and more of the troubles of others. Since Sidonie had reminded him of the silent suffering of the lowly, fighting on without complaint, all over the world, he forgot himself in them. He who was not usually sentimental now had periods of that mystic tenderness which is the flower of weakness and sickness. In the evening, as he sat with his elbows on the window-sill, gazing down into the courtyard and listening to all the mysterious noises of the night, . . . a voice singing in a house near by, made moving by the distance, or a little girl artlessly strumming Mozart, . . . he thought:

"All you whom I love though I know you not! You whom

life has not sullied; you, who dream of great things, that you
know to be impossible, while you fight for them against the envious world,—may you be happy—it is so good to be happy!
. . . Oh, my friends, I know that you are there, and I
hold my arms out to you. . . . There is a wall between us.
Stone by stone I am breaking it down, but I am myself
broken in the labor of it. Shall we ever be together? Shall
I reach you before another wall is raised up between us: the
wall of death? . . . No matter! Though all my life I am
alone, so only I may work for you, do you good, and you
may love me a little, later on, when I am dead! . . ."

So the convalescent Christophe was nursed by those two
good foster-mothers *" Liebe und Noth "* (Love and Poverty).

While his will was thus in abeyance Christophe felt a longing to be with people. And, although he was still very weak,
and it was a very foolish thing to do, he used to go out early in
the morning when the stream of people poured out of the resi-
dential streets on their way to their work, or in the evening,
when they were returning. His desire was to plunge into the
refreshing bath of human sympathy. Not that he spoke to a
soul. He did not even try to do so. It was enough for him to
watch the people pass, and guess what they were, and love them.
With fond pity he used to watch the workers hurrying along,
all, as it were, already worn out by the business of the day,
—young men and girls, with pale faces, worn expressions, and
strange smiles,—thin, eager faces beneath which there passed
desires and anxieties, all with a changing irony,—all so intelligent, too intelligent, a little morbid, the dwellers in a great
city. They all hurried along, the men reading the papers, the
women nibbling and munching. Christophe would have given
a month of his life to let one poor girl, whose eyes were swollen with sleep, who passed near him with a little nervous,
mincing walk, sleep on for a few hours more. Oh! how she
would have jumped at it, if she had been offered the chance!

He would have loved to pluck all the idle rich people out of their rooms, hermetically sealed at that hour, where they were so ungratefully lying at their ease, and replace them in their beds, in their comfortable existence, with all these eager, weary bodies, these fresh souls, not abounding with life, but alive and greedy of life. In that hour he was full of kindness towards them: and he smiled at their alert, thin little faces, in which there were cunning and ingenuousness, a bold and simple desire for pleasure, and, behind all, honest little souls, true and industrious. And he was not hurt when some of the girls laughed in his face, or nudged each other to point out the strange young man staring at them so hard.

And he would lounge about the riverside, lost in dreams. That was his favorite walk. It did a little satisfy his longing for the great river that had sung the lullaby of his childhood. Ah! it was not *Vater Rhein!* It had none of his all-puissant might: none of the wide horizons, vast plains over which the mind soars and is lost. A river with gray eyes, gowned in pale green, with finely drawn, correct features, a graceful river, with supple movements, wearing with sparkling nonchalance the sumptuous and sober garb of her city, the bracelets of its bridges, the necklets of its monuments, and smiling at her own prettiness, like a lovely woman strolling through the town. . . . The delicious light of Paris! That was the first thing that Christophe had loved in the city: it filled his being sweetly, sweetly: and imperceptibly, slowly, it changed his heart. It was to him the most lovely music, the only music in Paris. He would spend hours in the evening walking by the river, or in the gardens of old France, tasting the harmonies of the light of day touching the tall trees bathed in purple mist, the gray statues and ruins, the worn stones of the royal monuments which had absorbed the light of centuries,—that smooth atmosphere, made of pale sunshine and milky vapor, in which, on a cloud of silvery dust, there floats the laughing spirit of the race.

One evening he was leaning over the parapet near the Saint-

Michel Bridge, and looking at the water and absently turning over the books in one of the little boxes. He chanced upon a battered old volume of Michelet and opened it at random. He had already read a certain amount of that historian, and had been put off by his Gallic boasting, his trick of making himself drunk with words, and his halting style. But that evening he was held from the very first words: he had lighted on the trial of Joan of Arc. He knew the Maid of Orleans through Schiller: but hitherto she had only been a romantic heroine who had been endowed with an imaginary life by a great poet. Suddenly the reality was presented to him and gripped his attention. He read on and on, his heart aching for the tragic horror of the glorious story: and when he came to the moment when Joan learns that she is to die that evening and faints from fear, his hands began to tremble, tears came into his eyes, and he had to stop. He was weak from his illness: he had become absurdly sensitive, and was himself exasperated by it.—When he turned once more to the book it was late and the bookseller was shutting up his boxes. He decided to buy the book and hunted through his pockets: he had exactly six sous. Such scantiness was not rare and did not bother him: he had paid for his dinner, and counted on getting some money out of Hecht next day for some copying he had done. But it was hard to have to wait a day! Why had he spent all he had on his dinner? Ah! if only he could offer the bookseller the bread and sausages that were in his pockets, in payment!

Next morning, very early, he went to Hecht's to get his money: but as he was passing the bridge which bears the name of the archangel of battle—" the brother in Paradise " of Joan of Arc—he could not help stopping. He found the precious book once more in the bookseller's box, and read it right through: he stayed reading it for nearly two hours and missed his appointment with Hecht: and he wasted the whole day waiting to see him. At last he managed to get his new commission and the money for the old. At once he rushed

back to buy the book, although he had read it. He was afraid
it might have been sold to another purchaser. No doubt that
would not have mattered much: it was quite easy to get another
copy: but Christophe did not know whether the book was rare
or not: and besides, he wanted that particular book and no other.
Those who love books easily become fetish worshipers. The
pages from which the well of dreams springs forth are sacred
to them, even when they are dirty and spotted.

In the silence of the night, in his room, Christophe read
once more the Gospel of the Passion of Joan of Arc: and
now there was nothing to make him restrain his emotion. He
was filled with tenderness, pity, infinite sorrow for the poor
little shepherdess in her coarse peasant clothes, tall, shy, soft-
voiced, dreaming to the sound of bells—(she loved them as he
did)—with her lovely smile, full of understanding and kindness, and her tears, that flowed so readily—tears of love, tears
of pity, tears of weakness: for she was at once so manlike and
so much a woman, the pure and valiant girl, who tamed the
savage lusts of an army of bandits, and calmly, with her intrepid sound good sense, her woman's subtlety, and her gentle
persistency, alone, betrayed on all hands, for months together
foiled the threats and hypocritical tricks of a gang of church-
men and lawyers,—wolves and foxes with bloody eyes and fangs
—who closed a ring about her.

What touched Christophe most nearly was her kindness,
her tenderness of heart,—weeping after her victories, weeping
over her dead enemies, over those who had insulted her, giving
them consolation when they were wounded, aiding them in
death, knowing no bitterness against those who sold her, and
even at the stake, when the flames roared about her, thinking
not of herself, thinking only of the monk who exorcised her,
and compelling him to depart. She was "gentle in the most
bitter fight, good even amongst the most evil, peaceful even
in war. Into war, the triumph of Satan, she brought the **very**
Spirit of God."

And Christophe, thinking of himself, said:

" And into my fight I have not brought enough of the Spirit of God."

He read the fine words of the evangelist of Joan of Arc:

" Be kind, and seek always to be kinder, amid all the injustice of men and the hardships of Fate. . . . Be gentle and of a good countenance even in bitter quarrels, win through experience, and never let it harm that inward treasure. . . ."

And he said within himself:

" I have sinned. I have not been kind. I have not shown good-will towards men. I have been too hard.—Forgive me. Do not think me your enemy, you against whom I wage war! For you too I seek to do good. . . . But you must be kept from doing evil. . . ."

And, as he was no saint, the thought of them was enough to kindle his anger again. What he could least forgive them was that when he saw them, and saw France, through them, he found it impossible to conceive such a flower of purity and poetic heroism ever springing from such a soil. And yet it was so. Who could say that such a flower would not spring from it a second time? The France of to-day could not be worse than that of Charles VII. the debauched and prostituted nation from which the Maid sprang. The temple was empty, fouled, half in ruins. No matter! God had spoken in it.

Christophe was seeking a Frenchman whom he could love for the love of France.

It was about the end of March. For months Christophe had not spoken to a soul nor had a single letter, except every now and then a few lines from his mother, who did not know that he was ill and did not tell him that she herself was ill. His relation with the outside world was confined to his journeys to the music shop to take or bring away his work. He arranged to go there at times when he knew that Hecht would be out—to avoid having to talk to him. The precaution was superfluous, for the only time he met Hecht, he hardly did more than ask him a few indifferent questions about his health.

He was immured in a prison of silence when, one morning, he received an invitation from Madame Roussin to a musical *soirée:* a famous quartet was to play. The letter was very friendly in tone, and Roussin had added a few cordial lines. He was not very proud of his quarrel with Christophe: the less so as he had since quarreled with the singer and now condemned her in no sparing terms. He was a good fellow: he never bore those whom he had wronged any grudge. And he would have thought it preposterous for any of his victims to be more thin-skinned than himself. And so, when he had the pleasure of seeing them again, he never hesitated about holding out his hand.

Christophe's first impulse was to shrug his shoulders and vow that he would not go. But he wavered as the day of the concert came nearer. He was stifling from never hearing a human voice or a note of music. But he vowed again that he would never set foot inside the Roussins' house. But when the day came he went, raging against his own cowardice.

He was ill rewarded. Hardly did he find himself once more in the gathering of politicians and snobs than he was filled with an aversion for them more violent than ever: for during his months of solitude he had lost the trick of such people. It was impossible to hear the music: it was a profanation; Christophe made up his mind to go as soon as the first piece was over.

He glanced round among the faces of those people who were even physically so antipathetic to him. At the other end of the room he saw a face, the face of a young man, looking at him, and then he turned away at once. There was in the face a strange quality of candor which among such bored, indifferent people was most striking. The eyes were timid, but clear and direct. French eyes, which, once they marked a man, went on looking at him with absolute truth, hiding nothing of the soul behind them, missing nothing of the soul of the man at whom they gazed. They were familiar to Christophe. And yet he did not know the face. It was that of a young man between twenty and twenty-five, short, slightly stooping, delicate-looking, beardless, and melancholy, with chestnut hair, irregular features, though fine, a certain crookedness which gave it an expression not so much of uneasiness as of bashfulness, which was not without charm, and seemed to contradict the tranquillity of the eyes. He was standing in an open door: and nobody was paying any attention to him. Once more Christophe looked at him: and once more he met his eyes, which turned away timidly with a delightful awkwardness: once more he "recognized" them: it seemed to him that he had seen them in another face.

Christophe, as usual, was incapable of concealing what he felt, and moved towards the young man: but as he made his way he wondered what he should say to him: and he hesitated and stood still looking to right and left, as though he were moving without any fixed object. But the young man was not taken in, and saw that Christophe was moving towards himself: he was so nervous at the thought of speaking to him that he tried to slip into the next room: but he was glued to his place by his very bashfulness. So they came face to face. It was some moments before they could find anything to say. And as they went on standing like that each thought the other must think him absurd. At last Christophe looked straight at the young man, and said with a smile, in a gruff voice:

"You're not a Parisian?"

In spite of his embarrassment the young man smiled at this unexpected question, and replied in the negative. His light voice, with its hint of a musical quality, was like some delicate instrument.

"I thought not," said Christophe. And, as he saw that he was a little confused by the singular remark, he added:

"It is no reproach."

But the young man's embarrassment was only increased.

There was another silence. The young man made an effort to speak: his lips trembled: it seemed that he had a sentence on the tip of his tongue, but he could not bring himself to

speak it. Christophe eagerly studied his mobile face, the
muscles of which he could see twitching under the clear skin:
he did not seem to be of the same clay as the people all about
him in the room, with their heavy, coarse faces, which were only
a continuation of their necks, part and parcel of their bodies.
In the young man's face the soul shone forth: in every part of it
there was a spiritual life.

He could not bring himself to speak. Christophe went on
genially:

"What are you doing among all these people?"

He spoke out loud with that strange freedom of manner
which made him hated. His friend blushed and could not
help looking round to see if he had been heard: and Christophe disliked the movement. Then, instead of answering,
he asked with a shy, sweet smile:

"And you?"

Christophe began to laugh as usual, rather loudly.

"Yes. And I," he said delightedly.

The young man at last summoned up his courage.

"I love your music so much!" he said, in a choking voice.

Then he stopped and tried once more, vainly, to get the
better of his shyness. He was blushing, and knew it: and he
blushed the more, up to his temples and round to his ears.
Christophe looked at him with a smile, and longed to take him
in his arms. The young man looked at him timidly.

"No," he said. "Of course, I can't . . . I can't talk about
that . . . not here. . . ."

Christophe took his hand with a grin. He felt the stranger's
thin fingers tremble in his great paw and press it with an involuntary tenderness: and the young man felt Christophe's paw
affectionately crush his hand. They ceased to hear the chatter
of the people round them. They were alone together and they
knew that they were friends.

It was only for a second, for then Madame Roussin touched
Christophe on the arm with her fan and said:

"I see that you have introduced yourselves and don't need

me to do so. The boy came on purpose to meet you this evening."

Then, rather awkwardly, they parted.

Christophe asked Madame Roussin:

"Who is he?"

"What?" said she. "You don't know him? He is a young poet and writes very prettily. One of your admirers. He is a good musician and plays the piano quite nicely. It is no good discussing you in his presence: he is mad about you. The other day he all but came to blows about you with Lucien Lévy-Cœur."

"Oh! Bless him for that!" said Christophe.

"Yes, I know you are unjust to poor Lucien. And yet he too loves your work."

"Ah! don't tell me that! I should hate myself."

"It is so, I assure you."

"Never! never! I will not have it. I forbid him to do so."

"Just what your admirer said. You are both mad. Lucien was just explaining one of your compositions to us. The shy boy you met just now got up, trembling with anger, and forbade him to mention your name. Think of it! . . . Fortunately I was there. I laughed it off: Lucien did the same: and the boy was utterly confused and relapsed into silence: and in the end he apologized."

"Poor boy!" said Christophe.

He was touched by it.

"Where did he go?" he asked, without listening to Madame Roussin, who had already begun to talk about something else.

He went to look for him. But his unknown friend had disappeared. Christophe returned to Madame Roussin:

"Tell me, what is his name?"

"Who?" she asked.

"The boy you were talking about just now."

"Your young poet?" she said. "His name is Olivier Jeannin."

The name rang in Christophe's ears like some familiar

melody. The shadowy figure of a girl floated for a moment before his eyes. But the new image, the image of his friend blotted it out at once.

Christophe went home. He strode through the streets of Paris mingling with the throng. He saw nothing, heard nothing; he was insensible to everything about him. He was like a lake cut off from the rest of the world by a ring of mountains. Not a breath stirred, not a sound was heard, all was still. Peace. He said to himself over and over again:

"I have a friend."

ANTOINETTE

I

THE Jeannins were one of those old French families who have remained stationary for centuries in the same little corner of a province, and have kept themselves pure from any infusion of foreign blood. There are more of them than one would think in France, in spite of all the changes in the social order: it would need a great upheaval to uproot them from the soil to which they are held by so many ties, the profound nature of which is unknown to them. Reason counts for nothing in their devotion to the soil, and interest for very little: and as for sentimental historic memories, they only hold good for a few literary men. What does bind them irresistibly is the obscure though very strong feeling, common to the dull and the intelligent alike, of having been for centuries past a parcel of the land, of living in its life, breathing the same air, hearing the heart of it beating against their own, like the heart of the beloved, feeling its slightest tremor, the changing hours and seasons and days, bright or dull, and hearing the voices and the silence of all things in Nature. It is not always the most beautiful country, nor that which has the greatest charm of life, that most strongly grips the affections, but rather it is the region where the earth seems simplest and most humble, nearest man, speaking to him in a familiar friendly tongue.

Such was the country in the center of France where the Jeannins lived. A flat, damp country, an old sleepy little town, wearily gazing at its reflection in the dull waters of a still canal: round about it were monotonous fields, plowed fields, meadows, little rivers, woods, and again monotonous fields. . . . No scenery, no monuments, no memories. Nothing attractive. It is all dull and oppressive. In its drowsy torpor is a hidden force. The soul tasting it for the first time suffers and revolts against it. But those who have lived with it for generations cannot break free: it eats into their very bones: and the stillness of it, the harmonious dullness, the monotony, have a charm for them and a sweet savor which they cannot analyze, which they malign, love, and can never forget.

The Jeannins had always lived there. The family could be traced back to the sixteenth century, living in the town or its neighborhood: for of course they had a great-uncle who had devoted his life to drawing up the genealogical tree of their obscure line of humble, industrious people: peasants, farmers, artisans, then clerks, country notaries, working in the sub-prefecture of the district, where Augustus Jeannin, the father of the present head of the house, had successfully established himself as a banker: he was a clever man, with a peasant's cunning and obstinacy, but honest as men go, not over-scrupulous, a great worker, and a good liver: he had made himself respected and feared everywhere by his genial malice, his bluntness of speech, and his wealth. Short, thick-set, vigorous, with little sharp eyes set in a big red face, pitted with smallpox, he had been known as a petticoat-hunter: and he had not altogether lost his taste for it. He loved a spicy yarn and good eating. It was a sight to see him at meals, with his son Antoine sitting opposite him, with a few old friends of their kidney: the district judge, the notary, the Archdeacon of the Cathedral:—(old Jeannin loved stuffing the priest: but also he could stuff with the priest, if the priest were good at it):—hearty old fellows built on the same Rabelaisian lines. There was a running fire of terrific stories to the accompaniment of thumps on the table and roars of laughter, and the row they made could be heard by the servants in the kitchen and the neighbors in the street. Then old Augustus caught a chill, which turned to pneumonia, through going down into his cellars one hot summer's day in his shirt-sleeves to bottle his wine. In less than twenty-four hours he had departed this life for the next world, in which he hardly believed, properly equipped with all the Sacraments of the Church, having, like a good Voltairian provincial, submitted to it at the last moment in order to pacify his women, and also because it did not matter one way or the other. . . . And then, one never knows. . . .

His son Antoine succeeded him in business. He was a fat little man, rubicund and expansive, clean-shaven, except for his mutton-chop whiskers, and he spoke quickly and with a slight stutter, in a loud voice, accompanying his remarks with little quick, curt gestures. He had not his father's grasp of finance: but he was quite a good manager. He had only to look after the established undertakings, which went on developing day by day, by the mere fact of their existence. He had the advantage of a business reputation in the district, although he had very little to do with the success of the firm's ventures. He only contributed method and industry. For the rest he was absolutely honorable, and was everywhere deservedly esteemed. His pleasant unctuous manners, though perhaps a little too familiar for some people, a little too expansive, and just a little common, had won him a very genuine popularity in the little town and the surrounding country. He was more lavish with his sympathy than with his money: tears came readily to his eyes: and the sight of poverty so sincerely moved him that the victim of it could not fail to be touched by it.

Like most men living in small towns, his thoughts were much occupied with politics. He was an ardent moderate Republican, an intolerant Liberal, a patriot, and, like his father, extremely anti-clerical. He was a member of the Municipal Council: and, like the rest of his colleagues, he delighted in playing tricks on the *curé* of the parish, or on the Lent preacher, who roused so much enthusiasm in the ladies of the town. It must not be forgotten that the anti-clericalism of the little towns in France is always, more or less, an episode in domestic warfare, and is a subtle form of that silent, bitter struggle between husbands and wives, which goes on in almost every house.

Antoine Jeannin had also some literary pretensions. Like all provincials of his generation, he had been brought up on the Latin Classics, many pages of which he knew by heart, and also a mass of proverbs, and on La Fontaine and Boileau,—the Boileau of *L'Art Poétique,* and, above all, of *Lutrin,*—on the author of *La Pucelle,* and the *poetœ minores* of the eighteenth century, in whose manner he squeezed out a certain number of poems. He was not the only man of his acquaintance possessed by that particular mania, and his reputation gained by it. His rhyming jests, his quatrains, couplets, acrostics, epigrams, and songs, which were sometimes rather risky, though they had a certain coarsely witty quality, were often quoted. He was wont to sing the mysteries of digestion: the Muse of the Loire districts is fain to blow her trumpet like the famous devil of Dante:

"*. . . Ed egli avea del cul fatto trombetta.*"

This sturdy, jovial, active little man had taken to wife a woman of a very different character,—the daughter of a country magistrate, Lucie de Villiers. The De Villiers—or rather Devilliers, for their name had split in its passage through time, like a stone which cracks in two as it goes hurtling down a hill-side—were magistrates from father to son; they were of that old parliamentary race of Frenchmen who had a lofty idea of the law, and duty, the social conventions, their personal, and especially their professional, dignity, which was fortified by perfect honesty, tempered with a certain conscious uprightness. During the preceding century they had been infected by non-conformist Jansenism, which had given them a grumbling pessimistic quality, as well as a contempt for the Jesuit attitude of mind. They did not see life as beautiful: and, rather than smooth away life's difficulties, they preferred to exaggerate them so as to have good reason to complain. Lucie de Villiers had certain of these characteristics, which were so directly opposed to the not very refined optimism of her husband. She was tall—taller than he by a head—slender, well made; she dressed well and elegantly, though in a rather sober fashion, which made her seem—perhaps designedly—older than she was: she was of a high moral quality: but she was hard on other people; she would countenance no fault, and hardly even a caprice: she was thought cold and disdainful. She was very pious, and that gave rise to perpetual disputes with her husband. For the rest, they were very fond of each other: and, in spite of their frequent disagreements, they could not have lived without each other. They were both rather unpractical: he from want of perception—(he was always in danger of being taken in by good looks and fine words),—she from her absolute inexperience of business—(she knew nothing about it: and having always been kept outside it, she took no interest in it).

They had two children: a girl, Antoinette, the elder by five years; and a boy, Olivier.

Antoinette was a pretty dark-haired child, with a charming, honest face of the French type, round, with sharp eyes, a round forehead, a fine chin, a little straight nose—" one of those very pretty, fine, noble noses " (as an old French portrait-painter says so charmingly) " in which there was a certain imperceptible play of expression, which animated the face, and revealed the subtlety of the workings of her mind as she talked or listened." She had her father's gaiety and carelessness.

Olivier was a delicate fair boy, short, like his father, but very different in character. His health had been undermined by one illness after another when he was a child: and although, as a result, he was petted by his family, his physical weakness had made him a melancholy, dreamy little boy, who was afraid of death and very poorly equipped for life. He was shy, and preferred to be alone: he avoided the society of other children: he was ill at ease with them: he hated their games and quarrels: their brutality filled him with horror. He let them strike him, not from want of courage, but from timidity, because he was afraid to defend himself, afraid of hurting them: they would have bullied the life out of him, but for the safeguard of his father's position. He was tender-hearted and morbidly sensitive: a word, a sign of sympathy, a reproach, were enough to make him burst into tears. His sister was much sturdier, and laughed at him, and called him a "little fountain."

The two children were devoted to each other: but they were too different to live together. They went their own ways and lived in their own dreams. As Antoinette grew up, she became prettier: people told her so, and she was well aware of it: it made her happy, and she wove romances about the future. Olivier, in his sickly melancholy, was always rubbed up the wrong way by contact with the outer world: and he withdrew into the circle of his own absurd little brain: and he told himself stories. He had a burning, almost feminine, longing to love and be loved: and, living alone, away from boys of his own age, he had invented two or three imaginary friends: one was called Jean, another Étienne, another François: he was always with them. He never slept well, and he was always dreaming. In the morning, when he was lifted out of bed, he would forget himself, and sit with his bare legs dangling down, or sometimes with two stockings on one leg. He would go off into a dream with his hands in the basin. He would forget himself at his desk in the middle of writing or learning a lesson: he would dream for hours on end: and then he would suddenly wake up, horrified to find that he had learned nothing. At dinner he was abashed if any one spoke to him: he would reply two minutes after he had been spoken to: he would forget what he was going to say in the middle of a sentence. He would doze off to the murmuring of his thoughts and the familiar sensations of the monotonous provincial days that marched so slowly by: the great half-empty house, only part of which they occupied: the vast and dreadful barns and cellars: the mysterious closed rooms, the fastened shutters, the covered furniture, veiled mirrors, and the chandeliers wrapped up: the old family portraits with their haunting smiles: the Empire engravings, with their virtuous, suave heroism: *Alcibiades and Socrates in the House of the Courtezan, Antiochus and Stratonice, The Story*

of Epaminondas, Belisarius Begging. . . . Outside, the sound
of the smith shoeing horses in the smithy opposite, the un-
even clink of the hammers on the anvil, the snorting of the
broken-winded horses, the smell of the scorched hoofs, the
slapping of the pats of the washerwomen kneeling by the water,
the heavy thuds of the butcher's chopper next door, the clatter
of a horse's hoofs on the stones of the street, the creaking of
a pump, or the drawbridge over the canal, the heavy barges
laden with blocks of wood, slowly passing at the end of the
garden, drawn along by a rope: the little tiled courtyard, with a
square patch of earth, in which two lilac-trees grew, in the
middle of a clump of geraniums and petunias: the tubs of laurel
and flowering pomegranate on the terrace above the canal:
sometimes the noise of a fair in the square hard by, with peasants in bright blue smocks, and grunting pigs. . . . And on
Sunday, at church, the precentor, who sang out of tune, and
the old priest, who went to sleep as he was saying Mass: the
family walk along the station road, where all the time he had to
take off his hat politely to other wretched beings, who were under the same impression of the necessity of going for a walk all
together,—until at last they reached the sunny fields, above
which larks soared invisible,—or along by the still mirror of
the canal, on both sides of which were poplars rustling in
line. . . . And then there was the great provincial Sunday
dinner, when they went on and on eating and talking about
food learnedly and with gusto: for everybody was a connoisseur:
and, in the provinces, eating is the chief occupation, the first
of all the arts. And they would talk business, and tell spicy
yarns, and every now and then discuss their neighbors' illnesses,
going into endless detail. . . . And the little boy, sitting
in his corner, would make no more noise than a little mouse,
pick at his food, eat hardly anything, and listen with all his
ears. Nothing escaped him: and when he did not understand,
his imagination supplied the deficiency. He had that singular
gift, which is often to be remarked in the children of old
families and an old stock, on which the imprint of the ages is

too strongly marked, of divining thoughts, which have never
passed through their minds before, and are hardly compre-
hensible to them.—Then there was the kitchen, where bloody
and succulent mysteries were concocted: and the old servant
who used to tell him frightful and droll stories. . . . At
last came evening, the silent flitting of the bats, the terror of
the monstrous creatures that were known to swarm in the dark
depths of the old house: huge rats, enormous hairy spiders:
and he would say his prayers, kneeling at the foot of his bed,
and hardly know what he was saying: the little cracked bell of
the convent hard by would sound the bed-time of the nuns;—
and so to bed, the Island of Dreams. . . .

The best times of the year were those that they spent in
spring and autumn at their country house some miles away
from the town. There he could dream at his ease: he saw nobody. Like most of the children of their class, the little Jeannins were kept apart from the common children: the children
of servants and farmers, who inspired them with fear and disgust. They inherited from their mother an aristocratic—or,
rather, essentially middle-class—disdain for all who worked with
their hands. Olivier would spend the day perched up in the
branches of an ash reading marvelous stories: delightful folk-
lore, the *Tales* of Musæus, or Madame d'Aulnoy, or the *Arabian
Nights*, or stories of travel. For he had that strange longing
for distant lands, "those oceanic dreams," which sometimes
possess the minds of boys in the little provincial towns
of France. A thicket lay between the house and himself, and
he could fancy himself very far away. But he knew that he
was really near home, and was quite happy: for he did not like
straying too far alone: he felt lost with Nature. Round him
the wind whispered through the trees. Through the leaves that
hid his nest he could see the yellowing vines in the distance,
and the meadows where the straked cows were at pasture, filling
the silence of the sleeping country-side with their plaintive
long-drawn lowing. The strident cocks crowed to each other
from farm to farm. There came up the irregular beat of the

flails in the barns. The fevered life of myriads of creatures swelled and flowed through the peace of inanimate Nature. Uneasily Olivier would watch the ever hurrying columns of the ants, and the bees big with their booty, buzzing like organ-pipes, and the superb and stupid wasps who know not what they want —the whole world of busy little creatures, all seemingly devoured by the desire to reach their destination. . . . Where is it? They do not know. No matter where! Somewhere. . . . Olivier was fearful amid that blind and hostile world. He would start, like a young hare, at the sound of a pine-cone falling, or the breaking of a rotten branch. . . . He would find his courage again when he heard the rattling of the chains of the swing at the other end of the garden, where Antoinette would be madly swinging to and fro.

She, too, would dream: but in her own fashion. She would spend the day prowling round the garden, eating, watching, laughing, picking at the grapes on the vines like a thrush, secretly plucking a peach from the trellis, climbing a plum-tree, or giving it a little surreptitious shake as she passed to bring down a rain of the golden mirabelles which melt in the mouth like scented honey. Or she would pick the flowers, although that was forbidden: quickly she would pluck a rose that she had been coveting all day, and run away with it to the arbor at the end of the garden. Then she would bury her little nose in the delicious scented flower, and kiss it, and bite it, and suck it: and then she would conceal her booty, and hide it in her bosom between her little breasts, at the wonder of whose coming she would gaze in eager fondness. . . . And there was an exquisite forbidden joy in taking off her shoes and stockings, and walking bare-foot on the cool sand of the paths, and on the dewy turf, and on the stones, cold in the shadow, burning in the sun, and in the little stream that ran along the outskirts of the wood, and kissing with her feet, and legs, and knees, water, earth, and light. Lying in the shadow of the pines, she would hold her hands up to the sun, and watch the light play through them, and she would press her lips

upon the soft satin skin of her pretty rounded arms. She would
make herself crowns and necklets and gowns of ivy-leaves and
oak-leaves: and she would deck them with the blue thistles, and
barberry and little pine-branches, with their green fruit: and
then she looked like a little savage Princess. And she would
dance for her own delight round and round the fountain: and,
with arms outstretched, she would turn and turn until her head
whirled, and she would slip down on the lawn and bury her
face in the grass, and shout with laughter for minutes on end,
unable to stop herself, without knowing why.

So the days slipped by for the two children, within hail of
each other, though neither ever gave a thought to the other,—
except when it would suddenly occur to Antoinette to play a
prank on her brother, and throw a handful of pine-needles
in his face, or shake the tree in which he was sitting, threatening to make him fall, or frighten him by springing suddenly
out upon him and yelling:

"Ooh! Ooh! . . ."

Sometimes she would be seized by a desire to tease him. She
would make him come down from his tree by pretending that
her mother was calling him. Then, when he had climbed down,
she would take his place and refuse to budge. Then Olivier
would whine and threaten to tell. But there was no danger
of Antoinette staying in the tree for long: she could not
keep still for two minutes. When she had done with taunting
Olivier from the top of his tree, when she had thoroughly
infuriated him and brought him almost to tears, then she
would slip down, fling her arms round him, shake him, and
laugh, and call him a "little muff," and roll him on the ground,
and rub his face with handfuls of grass. He would try to
struggle: but he was not strong enough. Then he would lie
still, flat on his black, like a cockchafer, with his thin arms
pinned to the ground by Antoinette's strong little hands: and
he would look piteous and resigned. Antoinette could not resist
that: she would look at her vanquished prisoner, and burst out
laughing and kiss him suddenly, and let him go—not without

the parting attention of a little gag of fresh grass in his mouth: and that he detested most of all, because it made him sick. And he would spit and wipe his mouth, and storm at her, while she ran away as hard as she could, pealing with laughter. She was always laughing. Even when she was asleep she laughed. Olivier, lying awake in the next room, would suddenly start up in the middle of the stories he was telling himself, at the sound of the wild laughter and the muttered words which she would speak in the silence of the night. Outside, the trees would creak with the wind, an owl would hoot, in the distant villages and the farms in the heart of the woods dogs would bark. In the dim phosphorescence of the night Olivier would see the dark, heavy branches of the pines moving like ghosts outside his window: and Antoinette's laughter would comfort him.

The two children were very religious, especially Olivier. Their father used to scandalize them with his anti-clerical professions of faith, but he did not interfere with them: and, at heart, like so many men of his class who are unbelievers, he was not sorry that his family should believe for him: for it is always good to have allies in the opposing camp, and one is never sure which way Fortune will turn. He was a Deist, and he reserved the right to summon a priest when the time came, as his father had done: even if it did no good, it could do no harm: one insures against fire, even if one has no reason to believe that the house will be burned down.

Olivier was morbidly inclined towards mysticism. There were times when he doubted whether he existed. He was credulous and soft-hearted, and needed a prop: he took a sorrowful delight in confession, in the comfort of confiding in the invisible Friend, whose arms are always open to you, to whom you can tell everything, who understands and forgives everything: he tasted the sweetness of the waters of humility and love, from which the soul issues pure, cleansed, and comforted. It was so natural to him to believe, that he could not understand how any one could doubt: he thought people did so from wickedness, and that God would punish them. He used to pray secretly that his father might find grace: and he was delighted when, one day, as they went into a little country church, he saw his father mechanically make the sign of the cross. The stories of the Gospel were mixed up in his mind with the marvelous tales of Rübezahl, and Gracieuse and Percinet, and the Caliph Haroun-al-Raschid. When he was a little boy he no more doubted the truth of the one than the other. And just as he was not sure that he did not know Shacabac of the cleft lips, and the loquacious barber, and the little hunchback of Casgar, just as when he was out walking he used to look about for the black woodpecker which bears in its beak the magic root of the treasure-seeker, so Canaan and the Promised Land became in his childish imagination certain regions in Burgundy or Berrichon. A round hill in the country, with a little tree, like a shabby old feather, at the summit, seemed to him to be like the mountain where Abraham had built his pyre. A large dead bush by the edge of a field was the Burning Bush, which the ages had put out. Even when he was older, and his critical faculty had been awakened, he loved to feed on the popular legends which enshrined his faith: and they gave him so much pleasure, though he no longer accepted them implicitly, that he would amuse himself by pretending to do so. So for a long time on Easter Saturday he would look out for the return of the Easter bells, which went away to Rome on the Thursday before, and would come floating through the air with little streamers. He did finally admit that it was not true: but he did not give up looking skywards when he heard them ringing: and once—though he knew perfectly well that it could not be—he fancied he saw one of them disappearing over the house with blue ribbons.

It was vitally necessary for him to steep himself in the world of legend and faith. He avoided life. He avoided himself. Thin, pale, puny, he suffered from being so, and could not bear its being talked about. He was naturally pessimistic, no doubt inheriting it from his mother, and his pessimism was fed by his morbidity. He did not know it: thought everybody must be like himself: and the queer little boy of ten, instead of romping in the gardens during his play-time, used to shut himself up in his room, and, carefully picking his words, wrote his will.

He used to write a great deal. Every evening he used laboriously and secretly to write his diary—he did not know why, for he had nothing to say, and he said nothing worth saying. Writing was an inherited mania with him, the age-old itch of the French provincial—the old indestructible stock—who every day, until the day of his death, with an idiotic patience which is almost heroic, writes down in detail what he has seen, said, done, heard, eaten, and drunk. For his own pleasure, entirely. It is not for other eyes. No one will ever read it: he knows that: he never reads it again himself.

Music, like religion, was for Olivier a shelter from the too vivid light of day. Both brother and sister were born musicians,—especially Olivier, who had inherited the gift from his mother. Their taste, as it needed to be, was excellent. There was no one capable of forming it in the province, where no music was ever heard but that of the local band, which played nothing but marches, or—on its good days—selections from Adolphe Adam, and the church organist who played romanzas, and the exercises of the young ladies of the town who strummed a few valses and polkas, the overture to the *Caliph of Bagdad, la Chasse du Jeune Henri,* and two or three sonatas of Mozart, always the same, and always with the same mistakes, on instruments that were sadly out of tune. These things were invariably included in the evening's program at parties. After dinner, those who had talent were asked to display it: at first they would blush and refuse, but then they would yield to the entreaties of the assembled company: and they would play their stock pieces without their music. Every one would then admire the artist's memory and her beautiful touch.

The ceremony was repeated at almost every party, and the thought of it would altogether spoil the children's dinner. When they had to play the *Voyage en Chine* of Bazin, or their pieces of Weber as a duet, they gave each other confidence, and were not very much afraid. But it was torture to them to have to play alone. Antoinette, as usual, was the braver of the two. Although it bored her dreadfully,—as she knew that there was no way out of it, she would go through with it, sit at the piano with a determined air, and gallop through her *rondo* at breakneck speed, stumbling over certain passages, make a hash of others, break off, turn her head, and say, with a smile :

" Oh ! I can't remember. . . ."

Then she would start off again a few bars farther on, and go on to the end. And she would make no attempt to conceal her pleasure at having finished : and when she returned to her chair, amid the general chorus of praise, she would laugh and say :

" I made such a lot of mistakes."

But Olivier was not so easy to handle. He could not bear making a show of himself in public, and being " the observed of all observers." It was bad enough for him to have to speak in company. But to have to play, especially for people who did not like music—(that was obvious to him)—for people whom music actually bored, people who only asked him to play as a matter of habit, seemed to him to be neither more nor less than tyranny, and he tried vainly to revolt against it. He would refuse obstinately. Sometimes he would escape and go and hide in a dark room, in a passage, or even in the barn, in spite of his horror of spiders. His refusal would make the guests only insist the more, and they would quiz him : and his parents would sternly order him to play, and even slap him when he was too impudently rebellious. And in the end he always had to play,—of course unwillingly and sulkily. And then he would suffer agonies all night because he had played

so badly, partly from vanity, and partly from his very genuine
love for music.

The taste of the little town had not always been so banal.
There had been a time when there were quite good chamber
concerts at several houses. Madame Jeannin used often to
speak of her grandfather, who adored the violoncello, and used
to sing airs of Gluck, and Dalayrac, and Berton. There was
a large volume of them in the house, and a pile of Italian
songs. For the old gentleman was like M. Andrieux, of whom
Berlioz said: "He *loved* Gluck." And he added bitterly: "He
also *loved* Piccinni."—Perhaps of the two he preferred Piccinni. At all events, the Italian songs were in a large majority
in her grandfather's collection. They had been Olivier's first
musical nourishment. Not a very substantial diet, rather like
those sweetmeats with which provincial children are stuffed:
they corrupt the palate, destroy the tissues of the stomach, and
there is always a danger of their killing the appetite for more
solid nutriment. But Olivier could not be accused of greedi-
ness. He was never offered any more solid food. Having no
bread, he was forced to eat cake. And so, by force of circumstance, it came about that Cimarosa, Paesiello, and Rossini fed
the mystic, melancholy little boy, who was more than a little
intoxicated by his draughts of the *Asti spumante* poured out
for him, instead of milk, by these bacchanalian Satyrs, and the
two lively, ingenuously, lasciviously smiling Bacchante of
Naples and Catania—Pergolesi and Bellini.

He played a great deal to himself, for his own pleasure. He
was saturated with music. He did not try to understand what
he was playing, but gave himself up to it. Nobody ever thought
of teaching him harmony, and it never occurred to him to learn
it. Science and the scientific mind were foreign to the nature
of his family, especially on his mother's side. All the lawyers,
wits, and humanists of the De Villiers were baffled by any sort
of problem. It was told of a member of the family—a distant
cousin—as a remarkable thing that he had found a post in the
Bureau des Longitudes. And it was further told how he had

gone mad. The old provincial middle-classes, robust and positive in temper, but dull and sleepy as a result of their gigantic
meals and the monotony of their lives, are very proud of their
common sense: they have so much faith in it that they boast that
there is no difficulty which cannot be resolved by it: and they
are never very far from considering men of science as artists
of a sort, more useful than the others, but less exalted, because at least artists serve no useful purpose, and there is a
sort of distinction about their lounging existence.—(Besides,
every business man flatters himself that he might have been
an artist if he had cared about it.)—While scientists are not
far from being manual laborers,—(which is degrading),—just
master-workmen with more education, though they are a little
cracked: they are mighty fine on paper: but outside their arith-
metic factories they're nobody. They would not be much use
without the guidance of common-sense people who have some
experience of life and business.

Unfortunately, it is not proven that their experience of life
and business goes so far as these people like to think. It is
only a routine, ringing the changes on a few easy cases. If any
unforeseen position arises, in which they have to decide quickly
and vigorously, they are always disgruntled.

Antoine Jeannin was that sort of man. Everything was so
nicely adjusted, and his business jogged along so comfortably
in its place in the life of the province, that he had never en-
countered any serious difficulty. He had succeeded to his
father's position without having any special aptitude for the
business: and, as everything had gone well, he attributed it to
his own brilliant talents. He loved to say that it was enough
to be honest, methodical, and to have common sense: and he intended handing down his business to his son, without any more
regard for the boy's tastes than his father had had for his own.
He did not do anything to prepare him for it. He let his children grow up as they liked, so long as they were good, and,
above all, happy: for he adored them. And so the two children
were as little prepared for the struggle of life as possible: they

were like hothouse flowers. But, surely, they would always live like that? In the soft provincial atmosphere, in the bosom of their wealthy, influential family, with a kindly, gay, jovial father, surrounded by friends, one of the leading men of the district, life was so easy, so bright and smiling.

Antoinette was sixteen. Olivier was about to be confirmed. His mind was filled with all kinds of mystic dreams. In her heart Antoinette heard the sweet song of new-born hope soaring, like the lark in April, in the springtime of her life. It was a joy to her to feel the flowering of her body and soul, to know that she was pretty, and to be told so. Her father's immoderate praises were enough to turn her head.

He was in ecstasies over her: he delighted in her little coquetries, to see her eying herself in her mirror, to watch her little innocent tricks. He would take her on his knees, and tease her about her childish love-affairs, and the conquests she had made, and the suitors that he pretended had come to him a-wooing: he would tell her their names: respectable citizens, each more old and ugly than the last. And she would cry out in horror, and break into rippling laughter, and put her arms about her father's neck, and press her cheek close to his. And he would ask which was the happy man of her choice: was it the District Attorney, who, the Jeannins' old maid used to say, was as ugly as the seven deadly sins? Or was it the fat notary? And she would slap him playfully to make him cease, or hold her hand over his mouth. He would kiss her little hands, and jump her up and down on his knees, and sing the old song

> " What would you, pretty maid?
> An ugly husband, eh? "

And she would giggle and tie his whiskers under his chin, and reply with the refrain:

> " A handsome husband I,
> No ugly man, madame."

She would declare her intention of choosing for herself. She knew that she was, or would be, very rich,—(her father

used to tell her so at every turn)—she was a " fine catch."
The sons of the distinguished families of the country were already courting her, setting a wide white net of flattery and
cunning snares to catch the little silver fish. But it looked
as though the fish would elude them all: for Antoinette saw
all their tricks, and laughed at them: she was quite ready to be
caught, but not against her will. She had already made up
her mind to marry.

The noble family of the district—(there is generally one
noble family to every district, claiming descent from the ancient
lords of the province, though generally its origin goes no farther
back than some purchaser of the national estates, some com-
missary of the eighteenth century, or some Napoleonic army-
contractor)—the Bonnivets, who lived some few miles away
from the town, in a castle with tall towers with gleaming slates,
surrounded by vast woods, in which were innumerable fish-
ponds, themselves proposed for the hand of Mademoiselle Jeannin. Young Bonnivet was very assiduous in his courtship of
Antoinette. He was a handsome boy, rather stout and heavy
for his age, who did nothing but hunt and eat, and drink and
sleep: he could ride, dance, had charming manners, and was not
more stupid than other young men. He would ride into the
town, or drive in his buggy and call on the banker, on some
business pretext: and sometimes he would bring some game or a
bouquet of flowers for the ladies. He would seize the opportunity to pay court to Antoinette. They would walk in the
garden together. He would pay her lumbering compliments,
and pull his mustache, and make jokes, and make his spurs
clatter on the tiles of the terrace. Antoinette thought him
charming. Her pride and her affections were both tickled.
She would swim in those first sweet hours of young love.
Olivier detested the young squire, because he was strong, heavy,
brutal, had a loud laugh, and hands that gripped like a vise,
and a disdainful trick of always calling him: "Boy . . ."
and pinching his cheeks. He detested him above all,—without
knowing it,—because he dared to love his sister: . . . his

sister, his very own, his, and she could not belong to any one
else! . . .

Disaster came. Sooner or later there must come a crisis
in the lives of the old middle-class families which for centuries have vegetated in the same little corner of the earth,
and have sucked it dry. They sleep in peace, and think themselves as eternal as the earth that bears them. But the soil
beneath them is dry and dead, their roots are sapped: just the
blow of an ax, and down they come. Then they talk of accidents and unforeseen misfortunes. There would have been
no accident if there had been more strength in the tree: or, at
least, would have been no more than a sudden storm, wrenching
away a few branches, but never shaking the tree.

Antoine Jeannin was weak, trustful, and a little vain. He
loved to throw dust in people's eyes, and easily confounded
" seeming " and " being." He spent recklessly, though his
extravagance, moderated by fits of remorse as the result of the
age-old habit of economy—(he would fling away pounds, and
haggle over a farthing)—never seriously impaired his capital.
He was not very cautious in business either. He never refused
to lend money to his friends: and it was not difficult to be a
friend of his. He did not always trouble to ask for a receipt:
he kept a rough account of what was owing to him, and never
asked for payment before it was offered him. He believed in
the good faith of other men, and supposed that they would
believe in his own. He was much more timid than his jocular,
easy-going manners led people to suppose. He would never
have dared to refuse certain importunate borrowers, or to let
his doubts of their solvency appear. That arose from a mixture
of kindness and pusillanimity. He did not wish to offend anybody, and he was afraid of being insulted. So he was always
giving way. And, by way of carrying it off, he would lend with
alacrity, as though his debtors were doing him a service by
borrowing his money. And he was not far from believing it:

his vanity and optimism had no difficulty in persuading him that every business he touched was good business.

Such ways of dealing were not calculated to alienate the sympathies of his debtors: he was adored by the peasants, who knew that they could always count on his good nature, and never hesitated to resort to him. But the gratitude of men— even of honest men—is a fruit that must be gathered in good season. If it is left too long upon the tree, it quickly rots. After a few months M. Jeannin's debtors would begin to think that his assistance was their right: and they were even inclined to think that, as M. Jeannin had been so glad to help them, it must have been to his interest to do so. The best of them considered themselves discharged—if not of the debt, at least of the obligation of gratitude—by the present of a hare they had killed, or a basket of eggs from their fowlyard, which they would come and offer to the banker on the day of the great fair of the year.

As hitherto only small sums had been lent, and M. Jeannin had only had to do with fairly honest people, there were no very awkward consequences: the loss of money—of which the banker never breathed a word to a soul—was very small. But it was a very different matter when M. Jeannin knocked up against a certain company promoter who was launching a great industrial concern, and had got wind of the banker's easy-going ways and financial resources. This gentleman, who wore the ribbon of the Legion of Honor, and pretended to be intimate with two or three Ministers, an Archbishop, an assortment of senators, and various celebrities of the literary and financial world, and to be in touch with an omnipotent newspaper, had a very imposing manner, and most adroitly assumed the authoritative and familiar tone most calculated to impress his man. By way of introduction and recommendation, with a clumsiness which would have aroused the suspicions of a quicker man than M. Jeannin, he produced certain ordinary complimentary letters which he had received from the illustrious persons of his acquaintance, asking him to dinner, or thanking him for some invitation they had received: for it is well known that the French are never niggardly with such epistolary small change, nor particularly chary of shaking hands with, and accepting invitations from, an individual whom they have only known for an hour—provided only that he amuses them and does not ask them for money: and even as regards that, there are many who would not refuse to lend their new friend money so long as others did the same. And it would be a poor lookout for a clever man bent on relieving his neighbor of his superfluous money if he could not find a sheep who could be induced to jump the fence so that all the rest would follow.—If other sheep had not taken the fence before him, M. Jeannin would have been the first. He was of the woolly tribe which is made to be fleeced. He was seduced by his visitor's exalted connections, his fluency and his trick of flattery, and also by the first fine results of his advice. He only risked a little at first, and won: then he risked much: finally he risked all: not only his own money, but that of his clients as well. He did not tell them about it: he was sure he would win: he wanted to overwhelm them with the great thing he had done for them.

The venture collapsed. He heard of it indirectly through one of his Parisian correspondents who happened to mention the new crash, without ever dreaming that Jeannin was one of the victims: for the banker had not said a word to anybody: with incredible irresponsibility, he had not taken the trouble—even avoided—asking the advice of men who were in a position to give him information: he had done the whole thing secretly, in the infatuated belief in his infallible common sense, and he had been satisfied with the vaguest knowledge of what he was doing. There are such moments of aberration in life: moments, it would seem, when a man is marked out for ruin, when he is fearful lest any one should come to his aid, when he avoids all advice that might save him, hides away, and rushes headlong, madly, shaking himself free for the fatal plunge.

M. Jeannin rushed to the station, utterly sick at heart, and took train for Paris. He went to look for his man. He flattered himself with the hope that the news might be false, or, at least, exaggerated. Naturally he did not find the fellow, and received further news of the collapse, which was as complete as possible. He returned distracted, and said nothing. No one had any idea of it yet. He tried to gain a few weeks, a few days. In his incurable optimism, he tried hard to believe that he would find a way to make good, if not his own losses, at least those of his clients. He tried various expedients, with a clumsy haste which would have removed any chance of succeeding that he might have had. He tried to borrow, but was everywhere refused. In his despair, he staked the little he had left on wildly speculative ventures, and lost it all. From that moment there was a complete change in his character. He relapsed into an alarming state of terror: still he said nothing: but he was bitter, violent, harsh, horribly sad. But still, when he was with strangers, he affected his old gaiety: but no one could fail to see the change in him: it was attributed to his health. With his family he was less guarded: and they saw at once that he was concealing some serious trouble. They hardly knew him. Sometimes he would burst into a room and ransack a desk, flinging all the papers higgledy-piggledy on to the floor, and flying into a frenzy because he could not find what he was looking for, or because some one offered to help him. Then he would stand stock still in the middle of it all, and when they asked him what he was looking for, he did not know himself. He seemed to have lost all interest in his family: or he would kiss them with tears in his eyes. He could not sleep. He could not eat.

Madame Jeannin saw that they were on the eve of a catastrophe: but she had never taken any part in her husband's affairs, and did not understand them. She questioned him: he repulsed her brutally: and, hurt in her pride, she did not persist. But she trembled, without knowing why.

The children could have no suspicion of the impending disaster. Antoinette, no doubt, was too intelligent not, like her mother, to have a presentiment of some misfortune: but she was absorbed in the delight of her budding love: she refused to think of unpleasant things: she persuaded herself that the clouds would pass—or that it would be time enough to see them when it was impossible to disregard them.

Of the three, the boy Olivier was perhaps the nearest to understanding what was going on in his unhappy father's soul. He felt that his father was suffering, and he suffered with him in secret. But he dared not say anything: naturally he could do nothing, and he was helpless. And then he, too, thrust back the thought of sad things, the nature of which he could not grasp: like his mother and sister, he was superstitiously inclined to believe that perhaps misfortune, the approach of which he did not wish to see, would not come. Those poor wretches who feel the imminence of danger do readily play the ostrich: they hide their heads behind a stone, and pretend that Misfortune will not see them.

Disturbing rumors began to fly. It was said that the bank's credit was impaired. In vain did the banker assure his clients that it was perfectly all right, on one pretext or another the more suspicious of them demanded their money. M. Jeannin felt that he was lost: he defended himself desperately, assuming a tone of indignation, and complaining loftily and bitterly of their suspicions of himself: he even went so far as to be violent and angry with some of his old clients, but that only let him down finally. Demands for payment came in a rush. On his beam-ends, at bay, he completely lost his head. He went away for a few days to gamble with his last few banknotes at a neighboring watering-place, was cleaned out in a quarter of an hour, and returned home. His sudden departure set the little town by the ears, and it was said that he had cleared out: and Madame Jeannin had had great difficulty in coping with the wild, anxious inquiries of the people: she begged them to be patient, and swore that her husband would return. They did not believe her, although they would have been only too glad to do so. And so, when it was known that he had returned, there was a general sigh of relief: there were many who almost believed that their fears had been baseless, and that the Jeannins were much too shrewd not to get out of a hole by admitting that they had fallen into it. The banker's attitude confirmed that impression. Now that he no longer had any doubt as to what he must do, he seemed to be weary, but quite calm. He chatted quietly to a few friends whom he met in the station road on his way home, talking about the drought and the country not having had any water for weeks, and the superb condition of the vines, and the fall of the Ministry, announced in the evening papers.

When he reached home he pretended not to notice his wife's excitement, who had run to meet him when she heard him come in, and told him volubly and confusedly what had happened during his absence. She scanned his features to try and see whether he had succeeded in averting the unknown danger: but, from pride, she did not ask him anything: she was waiting for him to speak first. But he did not say a word about the thing that was tormenting them both. He silently disregarded her desire to confide in him, and to get him to confide in her. He spoke of the heat, and of how tired he was, and complained of a racking headache: and they sat down to dinner as usual.

He talked little, and was dull, lost in thought, and his brows were knit: he drummed with his fingers on the table: he forced himself to eat, knowing that they were watching him, and looked with vague, unseeing eyes at his children, who were intimidated by the silence, and at his wife, who sat stiffly nursing her injured vanity, and, without looking at him, marking his every movement. Towards the end of dinner he seemed to wake up: he tried to talk to Antoinette and Olivier, and asked them what they had been doing during his absence: but he did not listen to their replies, and heard only the sound of their voices: and although he was staring at them, his gaze was elsewhere. Olivier felt it: he stopped in the middle of his prattle, and had no desire to go on. But, after a moment's embarrassment, Antoinette recovered her gaiety: she chattered merrily, like a magpie, laid her head on her father's shoulder, or tugged his sleeve to make him listen to what she was saying. M. Jeannin said nothing: his eyes wandered from Antoinette to Olivier, and the crease in his forehead grew deeper and deeper. In the middle of one of his daughter's stories he could bear it no longer, and got up and went and looked out of the window to conceal his emotion. The children folded their napkins, and got up too. Madame Jeannin told them to go and play in the garden: in a moment or two they could be heard chasing each other down the paths and screaming. Madame Jeannin looked at her husband, whose back was turned towards her, and she walked round the table as though to arrange something. Suddenly she went up to him, and, in a voice hushed by her fear of being overheard by the servants and by the agony that was in her, she said:

"Tell me, Antoine, what is the matter? There is something the matter. . . . You are hiding something. . . . Has something dreadful happened? Are you ill?"

But once more M. Jeannin put her off, and shrugged his shoulders, and said harshly:

"No! No, I tell you! Let me be!"

She was angry, and went away: in her fury, she declared that, no matter what happened to her husband, she would not bother about it any more.

M. Jeannin went down into the garden. Antoinette was still larking about, and tugging at her brother to make him run. But the boy declared suddenly that he was not going to play any more: and he leaned against the wall of the terrace a few yards away from his father. Antoinette tried to go on teasing him: but he drove her away and sulked: then she called him names: and when she found she could get no more fun out of him, she went in and began to play the piano.

M. Jeannin and Olivier were left alone.

"What's the matter with you, boy? Why won't you play?" asked the father gently

"I'm tired, father."

"Well, let us sit here on this seat for a little."

They sat down. It was a lovely September night. A dark, clear sky. The sweet scent of the petunias was mingled with the stale and rather unwholesome smell of the canal sleeping darkly below the terrace wall. Great moths, pale and sphinx-like, fluttered about the flowers, with a little whirring sound. The even voices of the neighbors sitting at their doors on the other side of the canal rang through the silent air. In the house Antoinette was playing a florid Italian cavatina. M. Jeannin held Olivier's hand in his. He was smoking. Through the darkness behind which his father's face was slowly disappearing the boy could see the red glow of the pipe, which gleamed, died away, gleamed again, and finally went out. Neither spoke. Then Olivier asked the names of the stars. M. Jeannin, like almost all men of his class, knew nothing of the things of Nature, and could not tell him the names of any save the great constellations, which are known to every one: but he pretended that the boy was asking their names, and told him. Olivier made no objection: it always pleased him to hear their beautiful mysterious names, and to repeat them in a whisper. Besides, he was not so much wanting to know their names as instinctively to come closer to his father. They said nothing more. Olivier looked at the stars, with his head thrown back and his mouth open: he was lost in drowsy thoughts: he could feel through all his veins the warmth of his father's hand. Suddenly the hand began to tremble. That seemed funny to Olivier, and he laughed and said sleepily:

"Oh, how your hand is trembling, father!"

M. Jeannin removed his hand.

After a moment Olivier, still busy with his **own thoughts** said:

"Are you tired, too, father?"

" Yes, my boy."

The boy replied affectionately:

" You must not tire yourself out so much, father."

M. Jeannin drew Olivier towards him, and held him to his breast and murmured:

" My poor boy! . . ."

But already Olivier's thoughts had flown off on another tack. The church clock chimed eight o'clock. He broke away, and said:

" I'm going to read."

On Thursdays he was allowed to read for an hour after dinner, until bedtime: it was his greatest joy: and nothing in the world could induce him to sacrifice a minute of it.

M. Jeannin let him go. He walked up and down the terrace for a little in the dark. Then he, too, went in.

In the room his wife and the two children were sitting round the lamp. Antoinette was sewing a ribbon on to a blouse, talking and humming the while, to Olivier's obvious discomfort, for he was stopping his ears with his fists so as not to hear, while he pored over his book with knitted brows, and his elbows on the table. Madame Jeannin was mending stockings and talking to the old nurse, who was standing by her side and giving an account of her day's expenditure, and seizing the opportunity for a little gossip: she always had some amusing tale to tell in her extraordinary lingo, which used to make them roar with laughter, while Antoinette would try to imitate her. M. Jeannin watched them silently. No one noticed him. He wavered for a moment, sat down, took up a book, opened it at random, shut it again, got up: he could not sit still. He lit a candle and said good-night. He went up to the children and kissed them fondly: they returned his kiss absently without looking up at him,—Antoinette being absorbed in her work, and Olivier in his book. Olivier did not even take his hands from his ears, and grunted " Goodnight," and went on reading:—(when he was reading even if one of his family had fallen into the fire, he would not have looked up).—M. Jeannin left the room. He lingered in the next room, for a moment. His wife came out soon, the old nurse having gone to arrange the linen-cupboard. She pretended not to see him. He hesitated, then came up to her, and said:

"I beg your pardon. I was rather rude just now."

She longed to say to him:

"My dear, my dear, that is nothing: but, tell me, what is the matter with you? Tell me, what is hurting you so?"

But she jumped at the opportunity of taking her revenge, and said:

"Let me be! You have been behaving odiously. You treat me worse than you would a servant."

And she went on in that strain, setting forth all her grievances volubly, shrilly, rancorously.

He raised his hands wearily, smiled bitterly, and left her.

No one heard the report of the revolver. Only, next day, when it was known what had happened, a few of the neighbors remembered that, in the middle of the night, when the streets were quiet, they had noticed a sharp noise like the cracking of a whip. They did not pay any attention to it. The silence of the night fell once more upon the town, wrapping both living and dead about with its mystery.

Madame Jeannin was asleep, but woke up an hour or two later. Not seeing her husband by her side she got up and went anxiously through all the rooms, and downstairs to the offices of the bank, which were in an annex of the house: and there, sitting in his chair in his office, she found M. Jeannin huddled forward on his desk in a pool of blood, which was still dripping down on to the floor. She gave a scream, dropped her candle, and fainted. She was heard in the house. The servants came running, picked her up, took care of her, and laid the body of M. Jeannin on a bed. The door of the children's room was locked. Antoinette was sleeping happily. Olivier heard the sound of voices and footsteps: he wanted to go and see what it was all about: but he was afraid of waking his sister, and presently he went to sleep again.

Next morning the news was all over the town before they knew anything. Their old nurse came sobbing and told them. Their mother was incapable of thinking of anything: her condition was critical. The two children were left alone in the presence of death. At first they were more fearful than sorrowful. And they were not allowed to weep in peace. The cruel legal formalities were begun the first thing in the morning. Antoinette hid away in her room, and with all the force of her youthful egoism clung to the only idea which could help her to thrust back the horror of the overwhelming reality: the thought of her lover: all day long she waited for him to come. Never had he been more ardent than the last time she had seen him, and she had no doubt that, as soon as he heard of the catastrophe, he would hasten to share her grief.—But nobody came, or wrote, or gave one sign of sympathy. As soon as the news of the suicide was out, people who had intrusted their money to the banker rushed to the Jeannins' house, forced their way in, and, with merciless cruelty, stormed and screamed at the widow and the two children.

In a few days they were faced with their utter ruin: the loss of a dear one, the loss of their fortune, their position, their public esteem, and the desertion of their friends. A total wreck. Nothing was left to provide for them. They had all three an uncompromising feeling for moral purity, which made their suffering all the greater from the dishonor of which they were innocent. Of the three Antoinette was the most distraught by their sorrow, because she had never really known suffering. Madame Jeannin and Olivier, though they were racked by it, were more inured to it. Instinctively pessimistic, they were overwhelmed but not surprised. The idea of death had always been a refuge to them, as it was now, more than ever: they longed for death. It is pitiful to be so resigned, but not so terrible as the revolt of a young creature, confident and happy, loving every moment of her life, who suddenly finds herself face to face with such unfathomable, irremediable sorrow, and death which is horrible to her. . . .

Antoinette discovered the ugliness of the world in a flash. Her eyes were opened: she saw life and human beings as they are: she judged her father, her mother, and her brother. While Olivier and Madame Jeannin wept together, in her grief she drew into herself. Desperately she pondered the past, the present, and the future: and she saw that there was nothing left for her, no hope, nothing to support her: she could count on no one.

The funeral took place, grimly, shamefully. The Church refused to receive the body of the suicide. The widow and orphans were deserted by the cowardice of their former friends. One or two of them came for a moment: and their embarrassment was even harder to bear than the absence of the rest. They seemed to make a favor of it, and their silence was big with reproach and pitying contempt. It was even worse with their relations: not only did they receive no single word of sympathy, but they were visited with bitter reproaches. The banker's suicide, far from removing ill-feeling, seemed to be hardly less criminal than his failure. Respectable people cannot forgive those who kill themselves. It seems to them monstrous that a man should prefer death to life with dishonor: and they would fain call down all the rigor of the law on him who seems to say:

"There is no misery so great as that of living with you."

The greatest cowards are not the least ready to accuse him of cowardice. And when, in addition, the suicide, by ending his life, touches their interests and their revenge, they lose all control.—Not for one moment did they think of all that the wretched Jeannin must have suffered to come to it. They would have had him suffer a thousand times more. And as he had escaped them, they transferred their fury to his family. They did not admit it to themselves: for they knew they were unjust. But they did it all the same, for they needed a victim.

Madame Jeannin, who seemed to be able to do nothing but

weep and moan, recovered her energy when her husband was attacked. She discovered then how much she had loved him: and she and her two children, who had no idea what would become of them in the future, all agreed to renounce their claim to her dowry, and to their own personal estate, in order, as far as possible, to meet M. Jeannin's debts. And, since it had become impossible for them to stay in the little town, they decided to go to Paris.

Their departure was something in the nature of a flight.

On the evening of the day before,—(a melancholy evening towards the end of September: the fields were disappearing behind the white veil of mist, out of which, as they walked along the road, on either side the fantastic shapes of the dripping, shivering bushes started forth, looking like the plants in an aquarium),—they went together to say farewell to the grave where he lay. They all three knelt on the narrow curbstone which surrounded the freshly turned patch of earth. They wept in silence; Olivier sobbed. Madame Jeannin mopped her eyes mournfully. She augmented her grief and tortured herself by saying to herself over and over again the words she had spoken to her husband the last time she had seen him alive. Olivier thought of that last conversation on the seat on the terrace. Antoinette wondered dreamily what would become of them. None of them ever dreamed of reproaching the wretched man who had dragged them down in his own ruin. But Antoinette thought:

"Ah! dear father, how we shall suffer!"

The mist grew more dense, the cold damp pierced through to their bones. But Madame Jeannin could not bring herself to go. Antoinette saw that Olivier was shivering and she said to her mother:

"I am cold."

They got up. Just as they were going, Madame Jeannin turned once more towards the grave, gazed at it for the last time, and said:

"My dear, my dear!"

They left the cemetery as night was falling.   Antoinette held Olivier's icy hand in hers.

They went back to the old house.   It was their last night under the roof-tree where they had always slept, where their lives and the lives of their parents had been lived—the walls, the hearth, the little patch of earth were so indissolubly linked with the family's joys and sorrows, as almost themselves to be part of the family, part of their life, which they could only leave to die.

Their boxes were packed.   They were to take the first train next day before the shops were opened: they wanted to escape their neighbors' curiosity and malicious remarks.—They longed to cling to each other and stay together: but they went instinctively to their rooms and stayed there: there they remained standing, never moving, not even taking off their hats and cloaks, touching the walls, the furniture, all the things they were going to leave, pressing their faces against the window-panes, trying to take away with them in memory the contact of the things they loved.   At last they made an effort to shake free from the absorption of their sorrowful thoughts and met in Madame Jeannin's room,—the family room, with a great recess at the back, where, in old days, they always used to fore-gather in the evening, after dinner, when there were no visitors. In old days! . . .   How far off they seemed now!—They sat silently round the meager fire: then they all knelt by the bed and said their prayers: and they went to bed very early, for they had to be up before dawn.   But it was long before they slept.

About four o'clock in the morning Madame Jeannin, who had looked at her watch every hour or so to see whether it was not time to get ready, lit her candle and got up.   Antoinette, who had hardly slept at all, heard her and got up too. Olivier was fast asleep.   Madame Jeannin gazed at him tenderly and could not bring herself to wake him.   She stole away on tiptoe and said to Antoinette:

"Don't make any noise: let the poor boy enjoy his last moments here!"

The two women dressed and finished their packing. About the house hovered the profound silence of the cold night, such a night as makes all living things, men and beasts, cower away for warmth into the depths of sleep. Antoinette's teeth were chattering: she was frozen body and soul.

The front door creaked upon the frozen air. The old nurse, who had the key of the house, came for the last time to serve her employers. She was short and fat, short-winded, and slow-moving from her portliness, but she was remarkably active for her age: she appeared with her jolly face muffled up, and her nose was red, and her eyes were wet with tears. She was heart-broken when she saw that Madame Jeannin had got up without waiting for her, and had herself lit the kitchen fire.— Olivier woke up as she came in. His first impulse was to close his eyes, turn over, and go to sleep again. Antoinette came and laid her hand gently on her brother's shoulder, and she said in a low voice:

"Olivier, dear, it is time to get up."

He sighed, opened his eyes, saw his sister's face leaning over him: she smiled sadly and caressed his face with her hand. She said:

"Come!"

He got up.

They crept out of the house, noiselessly, like thieves. They all had parcels in their hands. The old nurse went in front of them trundling their boxes in a wheelbarrow. They left behind almost all their possessions, and took away, so to speak, only what they had on their backs and a change of clothes. A few things for remembrance were to be sent after them by goods-train: a few books, portraits, the old grandfather's clock, whose tick-tock seemed to them to be the beating of their hearts.—The air was keen. No one was stirring in the town: the shutters were closed and the streets empty. They said nothing: only the old servant spoke. Madame Jeannin was striving to fix in her memory all the images which told her of all her past life.

At the station, out of vanity, Madame Jeannin took second-class tickets, although she had vowed to travel third: but she had not the courage to face the humiliation in the presence of the railway clerks who knew her. She hurried into an empty compartment with her two children and shut the door. Hiding behind the curtains they trembled lest they should see any one they knew. But no one appeared: the town was hardly awake by the time they left: the train was empty: there were only a few peasants traveling by it, and some oxen, who hung their heads out of their trucks and bellowed mournfully. After a long wait the engine gave a slow whistle, and the train moved on through the mist. The fugitives drew the curtains and pressed their faces against the windows to take a last long look at the little town, with its Gothic tower just appearing through the mist, and the hill covered with stubby fields, and the meadows white and steaming with the frost; already it was a distant dream-landscape, fading out of existence. And when the train turned a bend and passed into a cutting, and they could no longer see it, and were sure there was no one to see them, they gave way to their emotion. With her handkerchief pressed to her lips Madame Jeannin sobbed. Olivier flung himself into her arms and with his head on her knees he covered her hands with tears and kisses. Antoinette sat at the other end of the compartment and looked out of the window and wept in silence. They did not all weep for the same reason. Madame Jeannin and Olivier were thinking only of what they had left behind them. Antoinette was thinking rather of what they were going to meet: she was angry with herself: she, too, would gladly have been absorbed in her memories. . . .—She was right to think of the future: she had a truer vision of the world than her mother and brother. They were weaving dreams about Paris. Antoinette herself had little notion of what awaited them there. They had never been there. Madame Jeannin imagined that, though their position would be sad enough, there would be no reason for anxiety. She had a sister in Paris, the wife of a wealthy magistrate: and she counted on her assistance. She was convinced also that with the education her children had received and their natural gifts, which, like all mothers, she overestimated, they would have no difficulty in earning an honest living.

Their first impressions were gloomy enough. As they left the station they were bewildered by the jostling crowd of people in the luggage-room and the confused uproar of the carriages outside. It was raining. They could not find a cab, and had to walk a long way with their arms aching with their heavy parcels, so that they had to stop every now and then in the middle of the street at the risk of being run over or splashed by the carriages. They could not make a single driver pay any attention to them. At last they managed to stop a man who was driving an old and disgustingly dirty barouche. As they were handing in the parcels they let a bundle of rugs fall into the mud. The porter who carried the trunk and the cabman traded on their ignorance, and made them pay double. Madame Jeannin gave the address of one of those second-rate expensive hotels patronized by provincials who go on going to them, in spite of their discomfort, because their grandfathers went to them thirty years ago. They were fleeced there. They were told that the hotel was full, and they were accommodated with one small room for which they were charged the price of three. For dinner they tried to economize by avoiding the table d'hôte: they ordered a modest meal, which cost them just as much and left them famishing. Their illusions concerning Paris had come toppling down as soon as they arrived. And, during that first night in the hotel, when they were squeezed into one little, ill-ventilated room, they could not sleep: they were hot and cold by turns, and could not breathe, and started at every footstep in the corridor, and the banging of the doors, and the furious ringing of the electric bells: and their heads throbbed with the incessant roar of the carriages and heavy

drays: and altogether they felt terrified of the monstrous city
into which they had plunged to their utter bewilderment.

Next day Madame Jeannin went to see her sister, who lived
in a luxurious flat in the *Boulevard Haussmann*. She hoped,
though she did not say so, that they would be invited to stay
there until they had found their feet. The welcome she received was enough to undeceive her. The Poyet-Delormes
were furious at their relative's failure: especially Madame
Delorme, who was afraid that it would be set against her, and
might injure her husband's career, and she thought it shame-
less of the ruined family to come and cling to them, and compromise them even more. The magistrate was of the same
opinion: but he was a kindly man: he would have been more
inclined to help, but for his wife's intervention—to which he
knuckled under. Madame Poyet-Delorme received her sister
with icy coldness. It cut Madame Jeannin to the heart: but
she swallowed down her pride: she hinted at the difficulty of
her position and the assistance she hoped to receive from the
Poyets. Her sister pretended not to understand, and did not
even ask her to stay to dinner: they were ceremoniously invited
to dine at the end of the week. The invitation did not come
from Madame Poyet either, but from the magistrate, who was a
little put out at his wife's treatment of her sister, and tried to
make amends for her curtness: he posed as the good-natured
man: but it was obvious that it did not come easily to him
and that he was really very selfish. The unhappy Jeannins returned to their hotel without daring to say what they thought
of their first visit.

They spent the following days in wandering about Paris,
looking for a flat: they were worn out with going up stairs,
and disheartened by the sight of the great barracks crammed
full of people, and the dirty stairs, and the dark rooms, that
seemed so depressing to them after their own big house in the
country. They grew more and more depressed. And they were
always shy and timid in the streets, and shops, and restaurants,
so that they were cheated at every turn. Everything they asked

for cost an exorbitant sum: it was as though they had the faculty of turning everything they touched into gold: only, it was they who had to pay out the gold. They were incredibly simple and absolutely incapable of looking after themselves.

Though there was little left to hope for from Madame Jeannin's sister, the poor lady wove illusions about the dinner to which they were invited. They dressed for it with fluttering hearts. They were received as guests, and not as relations—though nothing more was expended on the dinner than the ceremonious manner. The children met their cousins, who were almost the same age as themselves, but they were not much more cordial than their father and mother. The girl was very smart and coquettish, and spoke to them with a lisp and a politely superior air, with affectedly honeyed manners which disconcerted them. The boy was bored by this duty-dinner with their poor relations: and he was as surly as could be. Madame Poyet-Delorme sat up stiffly in her chair, and, even when she handed her a dish, seemed to be reading her sister a lesson. Madame Poyet-Delorme talked trivialities to keep the conversation from becoming serious. They never got beyond talking of what they were eating for fear of touching upon any intimate and dangerous topic. Madame Jeannin made an effort to bring them round to the subject next her heart: Madame Poyet-Delorme cut her short with some pointless remark, and she had not the courage to try again.

After dinner she made her daughter play the piano by way of showing off her talents. The poor girl was embarrassed and unhappy and played execrably. The Poyets were bored and anxious for her to finish. Madame Poyet exchanged glances with her daughter, with an ironic curl of her lips: and as the music went on too long she began to talk to Madame Jeannin about nothing in particular. At last Antoinette, who had quite lost her place, and saw to her horror that, instead of going on, she had begun again at the beginning, and that there was no reason why she should ever stop, broke off suddenly, and ended with two inaccurate chords and a third which was absolutely dissonant. Monsieur Poyet said:

"Bravo!"

And he asked for coffee.

Madame Poyet said that her daughter was taking lessons with Pugno: and the young lady "who was taking lessons with Pugno" said:

"Charming, my dear . . . ."

And asked where Antoinette had studied.

The conversation dropped. They had exhausted the knick-knacks in the drawing-room and the dresses of Madame and Mademoiselle Poyet. Madame Jeannin said to herself:

"I must speak now. I must . . ."

And she fidgeted. Just as she had pulled herself together to begin, Madame Poyet mentioned casually, without any attempt at an apology, that they were very sorry but they had to go out at half-past nine: they had an invitation which they had been unable to decline. The Jeannins were at a loss, and got up at once to go. The Poyets made some show of detaining them. But a quarter of an hour later there was a ring at the door: the footman announced some friends of the Poyets, neighbors of theirs, who lived in the flat below. Poyet and his wife exchanged glances, and there were hurried whisperings with the servants. Poyet stammered some excuse, and hurried the Jeannins into the next room. (He was trying to hide from his friends the existence, and the presence in his house, of the compromising family.) The Jeannins were left alone in a room without a fire. The children were furious at the affront. Antoinette had tears in her eyes and insisted on their going. Her mother resisted for a little: but then, after they had waited for some time, she agreed. They went out. In the hall they were caught by Poyet, who had been told by a servant, and he muttered excuses: he pretended that he wanted them to stay: but it was obvious that he was only eager for them to go. He helped them on with their cloaks, and hurried them to the door with smiles and handshakes and whispered pleasantries, and

closed the door on them. When they reached their hotel the
children burst into angry tears. Antoinette stamped her
foot, and swore that she would never enter their house
again.

Madame Jeannin took a flat on the fourth floor near the
Jardin des Plantes. The bedrooms looked on to the filthy
walls of a gloomy courtyard: the dining-room and the drawing-
room—(for Madame Jeannin insisted on having a drawing-
room)—on to a busy street. All day long steam-trams went
by and hearses crawling along to the Ivry Cemetery. Filthy
Italians, with a horde of children, loafed about on the seats,
or spent their time in shrill argument. The noise made it impossible to have the windows open: and in the evening, on their
way home, they had to force their way through crowds of
bustling, evil-smelling people, cross the thronged and muddy
streets, pass a horrible pothouse, that was on the ground floor
of the next house, in the door of which there were always fat,
frowsy women with yellow hair and painted faces, eying the
passers-by.

Their small supply of money soon gave out. Every evening
with sinking hearts they took stock of the widening hole in their
purse. They tried to stint themselves: but they did not know
how to set about it: that is a science which can only be learned
by years of experimenting, unless it has been practised from
childhood. Those who are not naturally economical merely
waste their time in trying to be so: as soon as a fresh opportunity of spending money crops up, they succumb to the temptation: they are always going to economize next time: and when
they do happen to make a little money, or to think they have
made it, they rush out and spend ten times the amount on the
strength of it.

At the end of a few weeks the Jeannins' resources were exhausted. Madame Jeannin had to gulp down what was left
of her pride, and, unknown to her children, she went and asked
Poyet for money. She contrived to see him alone at his office,
and begged him to advance her a small sum until they had

found work to keep them alive. Poyet, who was weak and human enough, tried at first to postpone the matter, but finally acceded to her request. He gave her two hundred francs in a moment of emotion, which mastered him, and he repented of it immediately afterwards,—when he had to make his peace with Madame Poyet, who was furious with her husband's weakness, and her sister's slyness.

All day and every day the Jeannins were out and about in Paris, looking for work. Madame Jeannin, true to the prejudices of her class, would not hear of their engaging in any other profession than those which are called "liberal"—no doubt because they leave their devotees free to starve. She would even have gone so far as to forbid her daughter to take a post as a family governess. Only the official professions, in the service of the State, were not degrading in her eyes. They had to discover a means of letting Olivier finish his education so that he might become a teacher. As for Antoinette, Madame Jeannin's idea was that she should go to a school to teach, or to the Conservatoire to win the prize for piano playing. But the schools at which she applied already had teachers enough, who were much better qualified than her daughter with her poor little elementary certificate: and, as for music, she had to recognize that Antoinette's talent was quite ordinary compared with that of so many others who did not get on at all. They came face to face with the terrible struggle for life, and the blind waste of talent, great and small, for which Paris can find no use.

The two children lost heart and exaggerated their uselessness: they believed that they were mediocre, and did their best to convince themselves and their mother that it was so. Olivier, who had had no difficulty in shining at his provincial school, was crushed by his various rebuffs: he seemed to have lost possession of all his gifts. At the school for which he won a scholarship, the results of his first examinations were so disastrous that his scholarship was taken away from him. He thought himself utterly stupid. At the same time he had a horror of Paris, and its swarming inhabitants, and the disgusting immorality of his schoolfellows, and their shameful conversation, and the bestiality of a few of them who did not spare him from their abominable proposals. He was not even strong enough to show his contempt for them. He felt degraded by the mere thought of their degradation. With his mother and sister, he took refuge in the heartfelt prayers which they used to say every evening after the day of deceptions and private humiliations, which to their innocence seemed to be a taint, of which they dared not tell each other. But, in contact with the latent spirit of atheism which is in the air of Paris, Olivier's faith was beginning to crumble away, without his knowledge, like whitewash trickling down a wall under the beating of the rain. He went on believing: but all about him God was dying.

His mother and sister pursued their futile quest. Madame Jeannin turned once more to the Poyets, who were anxious to be quit of them, and offered them work. Madame Jeannin was to go as reader to an old lady who was spending the winter in the South of France. A post was found for Antoinette as governess in a family in the West, who lived all the year round in the country. The terms were not bad, but Madame Jeannin refused. It was not so much for herself that she objected to a menial position, but she was determined that Antoinette should not be reduced to it, and unwilling to part with her. However unhappy they might be, just because they were unhappy, they wished to be together.—Madame Poyet took it very badly. She said that people who had no means of living had no business to be proud. Madame Jeannin could not refrain from crying out upon her heartlessness. Madame Poyet spoke bitterly of the bankruptcy and of the money that Madame Jeannin owed her. They parted, and the breach between them was final. All relationship between them was broken off. Madame Jeannin had only one desire left: to pay back the money she had borrowed. But she was unable to do that.

They resumed their vain search for work. Madame Jeannin went to see the deputy and the senator of her department, men whom Monsieur Jeannin had often helped. Everywhere she was brought face to face with ingratitude and selfishness. The deputy did not even answer her letters, and when she called on him he sent down word that he was out. The senator commiserated her ponderously on her unhappy position, which he attributed to "the wretched Jeannin," whose suicide he stigmatized harshly. Madame Jeannin defended her husband. The senator said that of course he knew that the banker had acted, not from dishonesty, but from stupidity, and that he was a fool, a poor gull, who knew nothing, and would go his own way without asking anybody's advice or taking a warning from any one. If he had only ruined himself, there would have been nothing to say: that would have been his own affair. But—not to mention the ruin that he had brought on others,— that he should have reduced his wife and children to poverty and deserted them and left them to get out of it as best they could . . . it was Madame Jeannin's own business if she chose to forgive him, if she were a saint, but for his part, he, the senator, not being a saint—(s, a, i, n, t),—but, he flattered himself, just a plain man—(s, a, i, n),—a plain, sensible, reasonable human being,—he could find no reason for forgiveness: a man who, in such circumstances, could kill himself, was a wretch. The only extenuating circumstance he could find in Jeannin's case was that he was not responsible for his actions. With that he begged Madame Jeannin's pardon for having expressed himself a little emphatically about her husband: he pleaded the sympathy that he felt for her: and he opened his drawer and offered her a fifty-franc note,—charity—which she refused.

She applied for a post in the offices of a great Government department. She set about it clumsily and inconsequently, and all her courage oozed out at the first attempt. She returned home so demoralized that for several days she could not stir. And, when she resumed her efforts, it was too late. She did not find help either with the church-people, either because they saw there was nothing to gain by it, or because they took no interest in a ruined family, the head of which had been notoriously anti-clerical. After days and days of hunting for work Madame Jeannin could find nothing better than a post as music-teacher in a convent—an ungrateful task, ridiculously ill-paid. To eke out her earnings she copied music in the evenings for an agency. They were very hard on her. She was severely called to task for omitting words and whole lines, as she did in spite of her application, for she was always thinking of so many other things and her wits were wool-gathering. And so, after she had stayed up through the night till her eyes and her back ached, her copy was rejected. She would return home utterly downcast. She would spend days together moaning, unable to stir a finger. For a long time she had been suffering from heart trouble, which had been aggravated by her hard struggles, and filled her with dark forebodings. Sometimes she would have pains, and difficulty in breathing as though she were on the point of death. She never went out without her name and address written on a piece of paper in her pocket in case she should collapse in the street. What would happen if she were to disappear? Antoinette comforted her as best she could by affecting a confidence which she did not possess: she begged her to be careful and to let her go and work in her stead. But the little that was left of Madame Jeannin's pride stirred in her, and she vowed that at least her daughter should not know the humiliation she had to undergo.

In vain did she wear herself out and cut down their expenses: what she earned was not enough to keep them alive. They had to sell the few jewels which they had kept. And the worst blow of all came when the money, of which they were in such sore need, was stolen from Madame Jeannin the very day it came into her hands. The poor flustered creature took it into her head while she was out to go into the *Bon Marché,* which was on her way: it was Antoinette's birthday next day, and she wanted to give her a little present. She was carrying her purse in her hand so as not to lose it. She put it down mechanically on the counter for a moment while she looked at something. When she put out her hand for it the purse was gone. It was the last blow for her.

A few days later, on a stifling evening at the end of August, —a hot steaming mist hung over the town,—Madame Jeannin came in from her copying agency, whither she had been to deliver a piece of work that was wanted in a hurry. She was late for dinner, and had saved her three sous' bus fare by hurrying home on foot to prevent her children being anxious. When she reached the fourth floor she could neither speak nor breathe. It was not the first time she had returned home in that condition: the children took no notice of it. She forced herself to sit down at table with them. They were both suffering from the heat and did not eat anything: they had to make an effort to gulp down a few morsels of food, and a sip or two of stale water. To give their mother time to recover they did not talk—(they had no desire to talk)—and looked out of the window.

Suddenly Madame Jeannin waved her hands in the air, clutched at the table, looked at her children, moaned, and collapsed. Antoinette and Olivier sprang to their feet just in time to catch her in their arms. They were beside themselves, and screamed and cried to her:

"Mother! Mother! Dear, dear mother!"

But she made no sound. They were at their wit's end. Antoinette clung wildly to her mother's body, kissed her, called to her. Olivier ran to the door of the flat and yelled:

"Help! Help!"

The housekeeper came running upstairs, and when she saw what had happened she ran for a doctor. But when the doctor arrived, he could only say that the end had come. Death had been instantaneous—happily for Madame Jeannin—although it was impossible to know what thoughts might have been hers during the last moments when she knew that she was dying and leaving her children alone in such misery.

They were alone to bear the horror of the catastrophe, alone to weep, alone to perform the dreadful duties that follow upon death. The porter's wife, a kindly soul, helped them a little: and people came from the convent where Madame Jeannin had taught: but they were given no real sympathy.

The first moments brought inexpressible despair. The only thing that saved them was the very excess of that despair, which made Olivier really ill. Antoinette's thoughts were distracted from her own suffering, and her one idea was to save her brother: and her great, deep love filled Olivier and plucked him back from the violent torment of his grief. Locked in her arms near the bed where their mother was lying in the glimmer of a candle, Olivier said over and over again that they must die, that they must both die, at once: and he pointed to the window. In Antoinette, too, there was the dark desire: but she fought it down: she wished to live. . . .

" Why? Why? "

" For her sake," said Antoinette—(she pointed to her mother).—" She is still with us. Think . . . after all that she has suffered for our sake, we must spare her the crowning sorrow, that of seeing us die in misery. . . . Ah! " (she went on emphatically). . . . " And then, we must not give way. I will not! I refuse to give in. You must, you shall be happy, some day! "

" Never! "

" Yes. You shall be happy. We have had too much unhappiness. A change will come: it must. You shall live your life. You shall have children, you shall be happy, you shall, you shall! "

" How are we to live? We cannot do it. . . . "

" We can. What is it, after all? We have to live somehow until you can earn your living. I will see to that. You will see: I'll do it. Ah! If only mother had let me do it, as I could have done. . . . "

" What will you do? I will not have you degrading yourself. You could not do it."

"I can. . . . And there is nothing humiliating in working for one's living—provided it be honest work. Don't you worry about it, please. You will see, everything will come right. You shall be happy, we shall be happy: dear Olivier, *she* will be happy through us. . . ."

The two children were the only mourners at their mother's grave. By common consent they agreed not to tell the Poyets: the Poyets had ceased to exist for them: they had been too cruel to their mother: they had helped her to her death. And, when the housekeeper asked them if they had no other relations, they replied:

"No. Nobody."

By the bare grave they prayed hand in hand. They set their teeth in desperate resolve and pride and preferred their solitude to the presence of their callous and hypocritical relations.—They returned on foot through the throng of people who were strangers to their grief, strangers to their thoughts, strangers to their lives, and shared nothing with them but their common language. Antoinette had to support Olivier.

They took a tiny flat in the same house on the top floor—two little attics, a narrow hall, which had to serve as a dining-room, and a kitchen that was more like a cupboard. They could have found better rooms in another neighborhood: but it seemed to them that they were still with their mother in that house. The housekeeper took an interest in them for a time: but she was soon absorbed in her own affairs and nobody bothered about them. They did not know a single one of the other tenants: and they did not even know who lived next door.

Antoinette obtained her mother's post as music-teacher at the convent. She procured other pupils. She had only one idea: to educate her brother until he was ready for the *École Normale*. It was her own idea, and she had decided upon it after mature reflection: she had studied the syllabus and asked about it, and had also tried to find out what Olivier thought:—but he had no ideas, and she chose for him. Once at the *École Normale* he would be sure of a living for the rest of his life, and his future would be assured. He must get in, somehow; whatever it cost, they would have to keep alive till then. It meant five or six terrible years: they would win through. The idea possessed Antoinette, absorbed her whole life. The poor solitary existence which she must lead, which she saw clearly mapped out in front of her, was only made bearable through the passionate exaltation which filled her, her determination, by all means in her power, to save her brother and make him happy. The light-hearted, gentle girl of seventeen or eighteen was transfigured by her heroic resolution: there was in her an ardent quality of devotion, a pride of battle, which no one had suspected, herself least of all. In that critical period of a woman's life, during the first fevered days of spring, when love fills all her being, and like a hidden stream murmuring beneath the earth, laves her soul, envelops it, floods it with tenderness, and fills it with sweet obsessions, love appears in divers shapes: demanding that she should give herself, and yield herself up to be its prey: for love the least excuse is enough, and for its profound yet innocent sensuality any sacrifice is easy. Love made Antoinette the prey of sisterly devotion.

Her brother was less passionate and had no such stay. Besides, the sacrifice was made for him, it was not he who was sacrificed—which is so much easier and sweeter when one loves. He was weighed down with remorse at seeing his sister wearing herself out for him. He would tell her so, and she would reply:

"Ah! My dear! . . . But don't you see that that is what keeps me going? Without you to trouble me, what should I have to live for?"

He understood. He, too, in Antoinette's position, would have been jealous of the trouble he caused her: but to be the cause of it! . . . That hurt his pride and his affection. And what a burden it was for so weak a creature to bear such a responsibility, to be bound to succeed, since on his success his sister had staked her whole life! The thought of it was intolerable to him, and, instead of spurring him on, there were times when it robbed him of all energy. And yet she forced

him to struggle on, to work, to live, as he never would have
done without her aid and insistence. He had a natural pre-
disposition towards depression,—perhaps even towards suicide:
—perhaps he would have succumbed to it had not his sister
wished him to be ambitious and happy. He suffered from the
contradiction of his nature: and yet it worked his salvation.
He, too, was passing through a critical age, that fearful period
when thousands of young men succumb, and give themselves
up to the aberrations of their minds and senses, and for two or
three years' folly spoil their lives beyond repair. If he had
had time to yield to his thoughts he would have fallen into discouragement or perhaps taken to dissipation: always when he
turned in upon himself he became a prey to his morbid dreams,
and disgust with life, and Paris, and the impure fermentation
of all those millions of human beings mingling and rotting together. But the sight of his sister's face was enough to dispel
the nightmare: and since she was living only that he might
live, he would live, yes, he would be happy, in spite of himself.

So their lives were built on an ardent faith fashioned of
stoicism, religion, and noble ambition. All their endeavor was
directed towards the one end: Olivier's success. Antoinette
accepted every kind of work, every humiliation that was offered
her: she went as a governess to houses where she was treated
almost as a servant: she had to take her pupils out for walks,
like a nurse, wandering about the streets with them for hours
together under pretext of teaching them German. In her love
for her brother and her pride she found pleasure even in such
moral suffering and weariness.

She would return home worn out to look after Olivier, who
was a day-boarder at his school and only came home in the
evening. She would cook their dinner—a wretched dinner—
on the gas-stove or over a spirit-lamp. Olivier had never any
appetite and everything disgusted him, and his gorge would
rise at the food: and she would have to force him to eat, or
cudgel her brains to invent some dish that would catch his fancy,
and poor Antoinette was by no means a good cook. And when

she had taken a great deal of trouble she would have the mortification of hearing him declare that her cooking was uneatable. It was only after moments of despair at her cooking-stove,—those moments of silent despair which come to inexperienced young housekeepers and poison their lives and sometimes their sleep, unknown to everybody—that she began to understand it a little.

After dinner, when she had washed up the dishes—(he would offer to help her, but she would never let him),—she would take a motherly interest in her brother's work. She would hear him his lessons, read his exercises, and even look up certain words in the dictionary for him, always taking care not to ruffle up his sensitive little soul. They would spend the evening at their one table at which they had both to eat and write. He would do his homework, she would sew or do some copying. When he had gone to bed she would sit mending his clothes or doing some work of her own.

Although they had difficulty in making both ends meet, they were both agreed that every penny they could put by should be used in the first place to settle the debt which their mother owed to the Poyets. It was not that the Poyets were importunate creditors: they had given no sign of life: they never gave a thought to the money, which they counted as lost: they thought themselves very lucky to have got rid of their undesirable relatives so cheaply. But it hurt the pride and filial piety of the young Jeannins to think that their mother should have owed anything to these people whom they despised. They pinched and scraped: they economized on their amusements, on their clothes, on their food, in order to amass the two hundred francs—an enormous sum for them. Antoinette would have liked to have done the saving by herself. But when her brother found out what she was up to, nothing could keep him from doing likewise. They wore themselves out in the effort, and were delighted when they could set aside a few sous a day.

In three years, by screwing and scraping, sou by sou, they had succeeded in getting the sum together. It was a great joy

to them. Antoinette went to the Poyets one evening. She
was coldly received, for they thought she had come to ask for
help. They thought it advisable to take the initiative: and
reproached her for not letting them have any news of them: and
not having even told them of the death of her mother, and not
coming to them when she wanted help. She cut them short
calmly by telling them that she had no intention of incommod-
ing them: she had come merely to return the money which had
been borrowed from them: and she laid two banknotes on the
table and asked for a receipt. They changed their tone at once,
and pretended to be unwilling to accept it: they were feeling
for her that sudden affection which comes to the creditor for
the debtor, who, after many years, returns the loan which he
had ceased to reckon upon. They inquired where she was living with her brother, and how they lived. She did not reply,
asked once more for the receipt, said that she was in a hurry,
bowed coldly, and went away. The Poyets were horrified at
the girl's ingratitude.

Then, when she was rid of that obsession, Antoinette went on
with the same sparing existence, but now it was entirely for her
brother's sake. Only she concealed it more to prevent his
knowing it: she economized on her clothes and sometimes on
her food, to keep her brother well-dressed and amused, and to
make his life pleasanter and gayer, and to let him go every now
and then to a concert, or to the opera, which was Olivier's
greatest joy. He was unwilling to go without her, but she
would always make excuses for not going so that he should
feel no remorse: she would pretend that she was too tired and
did not want to go out: she would even go so far as to say
that music bored her. Her fond quibbles would not deceive
him: but his boyish selfishness would be too strong for him.
He would go to the theater: once inside, he would be filled
with remorse, and it would haunt him all through the piece,
and spoil his pleasure. One Sunday, when she had packed
him off to the *Châtelet* concert, he returned half an hour later,
and told Antoinette that when he reached the Saint Michel

Bridge he had not the heart to go any farther: the concert did not interest him: it hurt him too much to have any pleasure without her. Nothing was sweeter to Antoinette, although she was sorry that her brother should be deprived of his Sunday entertainment because of her. But Olivier never regretted it: when he saw the joy that lit up his sister's face as he came in, a joy that she tried in vain to conceal, he felt happier than the most lovely music in the world could ever have made him. They spent the afternoon sitting together by the window, he with a book in his hand, she with her work, hardly reading at all, hardly sewing at all, talking idly of things that interested neither of them. Never had they had so delightful a Sunday. They agreed that they would never go alone to a concert again: they could never enjoy anything alone.

She managed secretly to save enough money to surprise and delight Olivier with a hired piano, which, on the hire-purchase system became their property at the end of a certain number of months. The payments for it were a heavy burden for her to shoulder! It often haunted her dreams, and she ruined her health in screwing together the necessary money. But, folly as it was, it did assure them both so much happiness. Music was their Paradise in their hard life. It filled an enormous place in their existence. They steeped themselves in music so as to forget the rest of the world. There was danger in it too. Music is one of the great modern dissolvents. Its languorous warmth, like the heat of a stove, or the enervating air of autumn, excites the senses and destroys the will. But it was a relaxation for a creature forced into excessive, joyless activity as was Antoinette. The Sunday concert was the only ray of light that shone through the week of unceasing toil. They lived in the memory of the last concert and the eager anticipation of the next, in those few hours spent outside Paris and out of the vile weather. After a long wait outside in the rain, or the snow, or the wind and the cold, clinging together, and trembling lest all the places should be taken, they would pass into the theater, where they were lost in the throng, and sit on dark uncomfortable benches. They were crushed and stifling, and often on the point of fainting from the heat and discomfort of it all:—but they were happy, happy in their own and in each other's pleasure, happy to feel coursing through their veins the flood of kindness, light, and strength, that surged forth from the great souls of Beethoven and Wagner, happy, each of them, to see the dear, dear face light up—the poor, pale face worn by suffering and premature anxieties. Antoinette would feel so tired and as though loving arms were about her, holding her to a motherly breast! She would nestle in its softness and warmth: and she would weep quietly. Olivier would press her hand. No one noticed them in the dimness of the vast hall, where they were not the only suffering souls taking refuge under the motherly wing of Music.

Antoinette had her religion to support her. She was very pious, and every day never missed saying her prayers fervently and at length, and every Sunday she never missed going to Mass. Even in the injustice of her wretched life she could not help believing in the love of the divine Friend, who suffers with you, and, some day, will console you. Even more than with God, she was in close communion with the beloved dead, and she used secretly to share all her trials with them. But she was of an independent spirit and a clear intelligence: she stood apart from other Catholics, who did not regard her altogether favorably: they thought her possessed of an evil spirit: they were not far from regarding her as a Free Thinker, or on the way to it, because, like the honest little Frenchwoman she was, she had no intention of renouncing her own independent judgment: she believed not from obedience, like the base rabble, but from love.

Olivier no longer believed. The slow disintegration of his faith, which had set in during his first months in Paris, had ended in its complete destruction. He had suffered cruelly: for he was not of those who are strong enough or commonplace enough to dispense with faith: and so he had passed through crises of mental agony. But he was at heart a mystic: and, though he had lost his belief, yet no ideas could be closer to his own than those of his sister. They both lived in a religious atmosphere. When they came home in the evening after the day's parting their little flat was to them a haven, an inviolable refuge, poor, bitterly cold, but pure. How far removed they felt there from the noise and the corrupt thoughts of Paris! . . .

They never talked much of their doings: for when one comes home tired one has hardly the heart to revive the memory of a painful day by the tale of its happenings. Instinctively they set themselves to forget it. Especially during the first hour when they met again for dinner they avoided questions of all kinds. They would greet each other with their eyes: and sometimes they would not speak a word all through the meal. Antoinette would look at her brother as he sat dreaming, just as he used to do when he was a little boy. She would gently touch his hand:

" Come ! " she would say, with a smile. " Courage ! "

He would smile too and go on eating. So dinner would pass without their trying to talk. They were hungry for silence. Only when they had done would their tongues be loosed a little, when they felt rested, and when each of them in the comfort of the understanding love of the other had wiped out the impure traces of the day.

Olivier would sit down at the piano. Antoinette was out of practice from letting him play always: for it was the only relaxation that he had: and he would give himself up to it wholeheartedly. He had a fine temperament for music: his feminine nature, more suited to love than to action, with loving sympathy could catch the thoughts of the musicians whose works he played, and merge itself in them and with passionate fidelity render the finest shades,—at least, within the limitations of his physical strength, which gave out before the Titanic effort of *Tristan,* or the later sonatas of Beethoven. He loved best to take refuge in Mozart or Gluck, and theirs was the music that Antoinette preferred.

Sometimes she would sing too, but only very simple songs, old melodies. She had a light mezzo voice, plaintive and delicate. She was so shy that she could never sing in company, and hardly even before Olivier: her throat used to contract. There was an air of Beethoven set to some Scotch words, of which she was particularly fond: *Faithful Johnnie:* it was calm, so calm . . . and with what a depth of tenderness! . . . It was like herself. Olivier could never hear her sing it without the tears coming to his eyes.

But she preferred listening to her brother. She would hurry through her housework and leave the door of the kitchen open the better to hear Olivier: but in spite of all her care he would complain impatiently of the noise she made with her pots and pans. Then she would close the door; and, when she had finished, she would come and sit in a low chair, not near the piano —(for he could not bear any one near him when he was playing),—but near the fireplace: and there she would sit curled up like a cat, with her back to the piano, and her eyes fixed on the golden eyes of the fire, in which a lump of coal was smoldering, and muse over her memories of the past. When nine o'clock rang she would have to pull herself together to remind Olivier that it was time to stop. It would be hard to drag him, and to drag herself, away from dreams: but Olivier would still have some work to do. And he must not go to bed too late. He would not obey her at once: he always needed a certain time in which to shake free of the music before he could apply himself seriously to his work. His thoughts would be off wandering. Often it would be half-past nine before he could shake free of his misty dreams. Antoinette, bending over her work at the other side of the table, would know that he was doing nothing: but she dared not look in his direction too often for fear of irritating him by seeming to be watching him.

He was at the ungrateful age—the happy age—when a boy saunters dreamily through his days. He had a clear forehead, girlish eyes, deep and trustful, often with dark circles round them, a wide mouth with rather thick pouting lips, a rather

crooked smile, vague, absent, taking: he wore his hair long
so that it hung down almost to his eyes, and made a great bunch
at the back of his neck, while one rebellious lock stuck up at
the back: a neckerchief loosely tied round his neck—(his sister
used to tie it carefully in a bow every morning):—a waistcoat
which was always buttonless, although she was for ever sewing
them on: no cuffs: large hands with bony wrists. He had a
heavy, sleepy, bantering expression, and he was always wool-
gathering. His eyes would blink and wander round Antoinette's room:—(his work-table was in her room):—they
would light on the little iron bed, above which hung an ivory
crucifix, with a sprig of box,—on the portraits of his father
and mother,—on an old photograph of the little provincial town
with its tower mirrored in its waters. And when they reached
his sister's pallid face, bending in silence over her work, he
would be filled with an immense pity for her and anger with
himself: then he would shake himself in annoyance at his own
indolence: and he would work furiously to make up for lost
time.

He spent his holidays in reading. They would read together
each with a separate book. In spite of their love for each
other they could not read aloud. That hurt them as an offense
against modesty. A fine book was to them as a secret which
should only be murmured in the silence of the heart. When
a passage delighted them, instead of reading it aloud, they
would hand the book over, with a finger marking the place: and
they would say:

"Read that."

Then, while the other was reading, the one who had already
read would with shining eyes gaze into the dear face to see
what emotions were roused and to share the enjoyment of it.

But often with their books open in front of them they would
not read: they would talk. Especially towards the end of the
evening they would feel the need of opening their hearts, and
they would have less difficulty in talking. Olivier had sad
thoughts: and in his weakness he had to rid himself of all that

tortured him by pouring out his troubles to some one else. He was a prey to doubt. Antoinette had to give him courage, to defend him against himself: it was an unceasing struggle, which began anew each day. Olivier would say bitter, gloomy things: and when he had said them he would be relieved: but he never troubled to think how they might hurt his sister. Only very late in the day did he see how he was exhausting her: he was sapping her strength and infecting her with his own doubts. Antoinette never let it appear how she suffered. She was by nature valiant and gay, and she forced herself to maintain a show of gaiety, even when that gracious quality was long since dead in her. She had moments of utter weariness, and revolt against the life of perpetual sacrifice to which she had pledged herself. But she condemned such thoughts and would not analyze them: they came to her in spite of herself, and she would not accept them. She found help in prayer, except when her heart could not pray—(as sometimes happens)—when it was, as it were, withered and dry. Then she could only wait in silence, feverish and ashamed, for the return of grace. Olivier never had the least suspicion of the agony she suffered. At such times Antoinette would make some excuse and go away and lock herself in her room: and she would not appear again until the crisis was over: then she would be smiling, sorrowful, more tender than ever, and, as it were, remorseful for having suffered.

Their rooms were adjoining. Their beds were placed on either side of the same wall: they could talk to each other through it in whispers: and when they could not sleep they would tap gently on the wall to say:

"Are you asleep? I can't sleep."

The partition was so thin that it was almost as though they shared the same room. But the door between their rooms was always locked at night, in obedience to an instinctive and profound modesty,—a sacred feeling:—it was only left open when Olivier was ill, as too often happened.

He did not gain in health. Rather he seemed to grow

weaker. He was always ailing: throat, chest, head or heart: if he caught the slightest cold there was always the danger of its turning to bronchitis: he caught scarlatina and almost died of it: but even when he was not ill he would betray strange symptoms of serious illnesses, which fortunately did not come to anything: he would have pains in his lungs or his heart. One day the doctor who examined him diagnosed pericarditis, or peripneumonia, and the great specialist who was then consulted confirmed his fears. But it came to nothing. It was his nerves that were wrong, and it is common knowledge that disorders of the nerves take the most unaccountable shapes: they are got rid of at the cost of days of anxiety. But such days were terrible for Antoinette, and they gave her sleepless nights. She would lie in a state of terror in her bed, getting up every now and then to listen to her brother's breathing. She would think that perhaps he was dying, she would feel sure, convinced of it: she would get up, trembling, and clasp her hands, and hold them fast against her lips to keep herself from crying out.

"Oh! God! Oh! God!" she would moan. "Take him not from me! Not that . . . not that. You have no right! . . . Not that, oh! God, I beg! . . . Oh, mother, mother! Come to my aid! Save him: let him live! . . ."

She would lie at full stretch.

"Ah! To die by the way, when so much has been done, when we were nearly there, when he was going to be happy . . . no: that could not be: it would be too cruel! . . ."

It was not long before Olivier gave her other reasons for anxiety.

He was profoundly honest, like herself, but he was weak of will and too open-minded and too complex not to be uneasy, skeptical, indulgent towards what he knew to be evil, and attracted by pleasure. Antoinette was so pure that it was some time before she understood what was going on in her brother's mind. She discovered it suddenly, one day.

Olivier thought she was out. She usually had a lesson at

that hour: but at the last moment she had received word from
her pupil, telling her that she could not have her that day.
She was secretly pleased, although it meant a few francs less in
that week's earnings: but she was very tired and she lay down
on her bed: she was very glad to be able to rest for once without
reproaching herself. Olivier came in from school bringing
another boy with him. They sat down in the next room and
began to talk. She could hear everything they said: they
thought they were alone and did not restrain themselves. Antoinette smiled as she heard her brother's merry voice. But
soon she ceased to smile, and her blood ran cold. They were
talking of dirty things with an abominable crudity of expression: they seemed to revel in it. She heard Olivier, her
boy Olivier, laughing: and from his lips, which she had
thought so innocent, there came words so obscene that the
horror of it chilled her. Keen anguish stabbed her to the heart.
It went on and on: they could not stop talking, and she could
not help listening. At last they went out, and Antoinette was
left alone. Then she wept: something had died in her: the
ideal image that she had fashioned of her brother—of her boy—
was plastered with mud: it was a mortal agony to her. She
did not say anything to him when they met again in the evening. He saw that she had been weeping and he could not think
why. He could not understand why she had changed her
manner towards him. It was some time before she was able
to recover herself.

But the worst blow of all for her was one evening when he
did not come home. She did not go to bed, but sat up waiting
for him. It was not only her moral purity that was hurt:
her suffering went down to the most mysterious inner depths
of her heart—those same depths where there lurked the most
awful feelings of the human heart, feelings over which she cast
a veil, to hide them from her sight.

Olivier's first aim had been the declaration of his independence. He returned in the morning, casting about for the proper
attitude and quite prepared to fling some insolent remark at his

sister if she had said anything to him. He stole into the flat on tiptoe so as not to waken her. But when he saw her standing there, waiting for him, pale, red-eyed from weeping, when he saw that, instead of making any effort to reproach him, she only set about silently cooking his breakfast, before he left for school, and that she had nothing to say to him, but was overwhelmed, so that she was, in herself, a living reproach, he could hold out no longer: he flung himself down before her, buried his face in her lap, and they both wept. He was ashamed of himself, sick at the thought of what he had done: he felt degraded. He tried to speak, but she would not let him and laid her hand on his lips: and he kissed her hand. They said no more: they understood each other. Olivier vowed that he would never again do anything to hurt Antoinette, and that he would be in all things what she wanted him to be. But though she tried bravely she could not so easily forget so sharp a wound: she recovered from it slowly. There was a certain awkwardness between them. Her love for him was just the same: but in her brother's soul she had seen something that was foreign to herself, and she was fearful of it.

She was the more overwhelmed by the glimpse she had had into Olivier's inmost heart, in that, about the same time, she had to put up with the unwelcome attentions of certain men. When she came home in the evening at nightfall, and especially when she had to go out after dinner to take or fetch her copying, she suffered agonies from her fear of being accosted, and followed (as sometimes happened) and forced to listen to insulting advances. She took her brother with her whenever she could under pretext of making him take a walk: but he only consented grudgingly and she dared not insist: she did not like to interrupt his work. She was so provincial and so pure that she could not get used to such ways. Paris at night was to her like a dark forest in which she felt that she was being tracked by dreadful, savage beasts: and she was afraid to leave the house. But she had to go out. She would put off going out as long as possible: she was always fearful. And when she thought that her Olivier would be—was perhaps—like one of those men who pursued her, she could hardly hold out her hand to him when she came in. He could not think what he had done to change her so, and she was angry with herself.

She was not very pretty, but she had charm, and attracted attention though she did nothing to do so. She was always very simply dressed, almost always in black: she was not very tall, graceful, frail-looking; she rarely spoke: she tripped quietly through the crowded streets, avoiding attention, which, however, she attracted in spite of herself by the sweetness of the expression of her tired eyes and her pure young lips. Sometimes she saw that she had attracted notice: and though it put her to confusion she was pleased all the same. Who can say what gentle and chaste pleasure in itself there may be in so innocent a creature at feeling herself in sympathy with others? All that she felt was shown in a slight awkwardness in her movements, a timid, sidelong glance: and it was sweet to see and very touching. And her uneasiness added to her attraction. She excited interest, and, as she was a poor girl, with none to protect her, men did not hesitate to tell her so.

Sometimes she used to go to the house of some rich Jews, the Nathans, who took an interest in her because they had met her at the house of some friends of theirs where she gave lessons: and, in spite of her shyness, she had not been able to avoid accepting invitations to their parties. M. Alfred Nathan was a well-known professor in Paris, a distinguished scientist, and at the same time he was very fond of society, with that strange mixture of learning and frivolity which is so common among the Jews. Madame Nathan was a mixture in equal proportions of real kindliness and excessive worldliness. They were both generous, with loud-voiced, sincere, but intermittent sympathy for Antoinette.—Generally speaking Antoinette had found more kindness among the Jews than among the members of her own sect. They have many faults: but they have one great quality—perhaps the greatest of all: they are alive, and human: nothing human is foreign to them and they are interested in every living being. Even when they lack real, warm sympathy they feel a perpetual curiosity which makes them seek out men and ideas that are of worth, however different from themselves they may be. Not that, generally speaking, they do anything much to help them, for they are interested in too many things at once and much more a prey to the vanities of the world than other people, while they pretend to be immune from them. But at least they do something: and that is saying a great deal in the present apathetic condition of society. They are an active balm in society, the very leaven of life.—-Antoinette who, among the Catholics, had been brought sharp up against a wall of icy indifference, was keenly alive to the worth of the interest, however superficial it might be, which the Nathans took in her. Madame Nathan had marked Antoinette's life of devoted sacrifice: she was sensible of her physical and moral charm: and she made a show of taking her under her protection. She had no children: but she loved young people and often had gatherings of them in her house: and she insisted on Antoinette's coming also, and breaking away from her solitude, and having some amusement in her life. And as she had no difficulty in guessing that Antoinette's shyness was in part the result of her poverty, she even went so far as to offer to give her a pretty frock or two, which Antoinette refused proudly: but her kindly patroness found a way of forcing her to accept a few of those little presents which are so dear to a woman's innocent vanity. Antoinette was both grateful and embarrassed. She forced herself to go to Madame Nathan's parties from time to time: and being young she managed to enjoy herself in spite of everything.

But in that rather mixed society of all sorts of young people Madame Nathan's protégée, being poor and pretty, became at once the mark of two or three young gentlemen, who with perfect confidence in themselves picked her out for their attentions. They calculated how far her timidity would go: they even made bets about her.

One day she received certain anonymous letters—or rather letters signed with a noble pseudonym—which conveyed a declaration of love: at first they were love-letters, flattering, ardent, appointing a rendezvous: then they quickly became bolder, threatening, and soon insulting and basely slanderous: they stripped her, exposed her, besmirched her with their coarse expressions of desire: they tried to play upon Antoinette's simplicity by making her fearful of a public insult if she did not go to the appointed rendezvous. She wept bitterly at the thought of having called down on herself such base proposals: and these insults scorched her pride. She did not know what to do. She did not like to speak to her brother about it: she knew that he would feel it too keenly and that he would make the affair even more serious than it was. She had no friends. The police? She would not do that for fear of scandal. But somehow she had to make an end of it. She felt that her silence would not sufficiently defend her, that the blackguard who was pursuing her would hold to the chase and that he would go on until to go farther would be dangerous.

He had just sent her a sort of ultimatum commanding her to meet him next day at the Luxembourg. She went.—By racking her brains she had come to the conclusion that her persecutor must have met her at Madame Nathan's. In one of his letters he had alluded to something which could only have happened there. She begged Madame Nathan to do her a great favor and to drive her to the door of the gallery and to wait for her outside. She went in. In front of the appointed picture her tormentor accosted her triumphantly and began to talk to her with affected politeness. She stared straight at him without a word. When he had finished his remark he asked her jokingly why she was staring at him. She replied:

"You are a coward."

He was not put out by such a trifle as that, and became familiar in his manner. She said:

"You have tried to threaten me with a scandal. Very well, I have come to give you your scandal. You have asked for it!"

She was trembling all over, and she spoke in a loud voice to show him that she was quite equal to attracting attention to themselves. People had already begun to watch them. He felt that she would stick at nothing. He lowered his voice. She said once more, for the last time:

"You are a coward," and turned her back on him.

Not wishing to seem to have given in he followed her. She left the gallery with the fellow following hard on her heels. She walked straight to the carriage waiting there, wrenched the door open, and her pursuer found himself face to face with Madame Nathan, who recognized him and greeted him by name. His face fell and he bolted.

Antoinette had to tell the whole story to her companion. She was unwilling to do so, and only hinted roughly at the facts. It was painful to her to reveal to a stranger the intimate secrets of her life, and the sufferings of her injured modesty. Madame Nathan scolded her for not having told her before. Antoinette begged her not to tell anybody. That was the end of it: and Madame Nathan did not even need to strike the fellow off her visiting list: for he was careful not to appear again.

About the same time another sorrow of a very different kind came to Antoinette.

At the Nathans' she met a man of forty, a very good fellow, who was in the Consular service in the Far East, and had come home on a few months' leave. He fell in love with her. The meeting had been planned unknown to Antoinette, by Madame Nathan, who had taken it into her head that she must find a husband for her little friend. He was a Jew. He was not good-looking and he was no longer young. He was rather bald and round-shouldered: but he had kind eyes, an affectionate way with him, and he could feel for and understand suffering, for he had suffered himself. Antoinette was no longer the romantic girl, the spoiled child, dreaming of life as a lovely day's walk on her lover's arm: now she saw the hard struggle of life, which began again every day, allowing no time for rest, or, if rest were taken, it might be to lose in one mo-

ment all the ground that had been gained, inch by inch, through
years of striving: and she thought it would be very sweet to be
able to lean on the arm of a friend, and share his sorrows
with him, and be able to close her eyes for a little, while he
watched over her. She knew that it was a dream: but she had
not had the courage to renounce her dream altogether. In her
heart she knew quite well that a dowerless girl had nothing to
hope for in the world in which she lived. The old French middle-classes are known throughout the world for the spirit of
sordid interest in which they conduct their marriages. The
Jews are far less grasping with money. Among the Jews it is
no uncommon thing for a rich young man to choose a poor
girl, or a young woman of fortune to set herself passionately
to win a man of intellect. But in the French middle-classes,
Catholic and provincial in their outlook, almost always money
woos money. And to what end? Poor wretches, they have
none but dull commonplace desires: they can do nothing but
eat, yawn, sleep—save. Antoinette knew them. She had observed their ways from her childhood on. She had seen them
with the eyes of wealth and the eyes of poverty. She had no
illusions left about them, nor about the treatment she had to
expect from them. And so the attentions of this man who
had asked her to marry him came as an unhoped for treasure in
her life. At first she did not think of him as a lover, but
gradually she was filled with gratitude and tenderness towards
him. She would have accepted his proposal if it had not meant
following him to the colonies and consequently leaving her
brother. She refused: and though her lover understood the
magnanimity of her reason for doing so, he could not forgive
her: love is so selfish, that the lover will not hear of being
sacrificed even to those virtues which are dearest to him in the
beloved. He gave up seeing her: when he went away he never
wrote: she had no news of him at all until, five or six months
later, she received a printed intimation, addressed in his hand,
that he had married another woman.

Antoinette felt it deeply. She was broken-hearted, and she

offered up her suffering to God: she tried to persuade herself
that she was justly punished for having for one moment lost
sight of her one duty, to devote herself to her brother: and she
grew more and more wrapped up in it.

She withdrew from the world altogether. She even dropped
going to the Nathans', for they were a little cold towards her
after she refused the marriage which they had arranged for her:
they too refused to see any justification for her. Madame
Nathan had decided that the marriage should take place, and
her vanity was hurt at its missing fire through Antoinette's
fault. She thought her scruples certainly quite praiseworthy,
but exaggerated and sentimental: and thereafter she lost interest
in the silly little goose. It was necessary for her always to be
helping people, with or without their consent, and she quickly
found another protégée to absorb, for the time being, all the interest and devotion which she had to expend.

Olivier knew nothing of his sister's sad little romance. He
was a sentimental, irresponsible boy, living in his dreams and
fancies. It was impossible to depend on him in spite of his
intelligence and charm and his very real tenderheartedness.
Often he would fling away the results of months of work by his
irresponsibility, or in a fit of discouragement, or by some boyish
freak, or some fancied love affair, in which he would waste all
his time and energy. He would fall in love with a pretty face,
that he had seen once, with coquettish little girls, whom perhaps
he once met out somewhere, though they never paid any attention to him. He would be infatuated with something he had
read, a poet, or a musician: he would steep himself in their
works for months together, to the exclusion of everything else
and the detriment of his studies. He had to be watched always,
though great care had to be taken that he did not know it, for he
was easily wounded. There was always a danger of a seizure.
He had the feverish excitement, the want of balance, the uneasy
trepidation, that are often found in those who have a consumptive tendency. The doctor had not concealed the danger from
Antoinette. The sickly plant, transplanted from the provinces

to Paris, needed fresh air and light. Antoinette could not provide them. They had not enough money to be able to go away
from Paris during the holidays. All the rest of their year every
day in the week was full, and on Sundays they were so tired that
they never wanted to go out, except to a concert.

There were Sundays in the summer when Antoinette would
make an effort and drag Olivier off to the woods outside Paris,
near Chaville or Saint-Cloud. But the woods were full of noisy
couples, singing music-hall songs, and littering the place with
greasy bits of paper: they did not find the divine solitude which
purifies and gives rest. And in the evening when they turned
homewards they had to suffer the roar and clatter of the trains,
the dirty, crowded, low, narrow, dark carriages of the suburban
lines, the coarseness of certain things they saw, the noisy, singing, shouting, smelly people, and the reek of tobacco smoke.
Neither Antoinette nor Olivier could understand the people, and
they would return home disgusted and demoralized. Olivier
would beg Antoinette not to go for Sunday walks again:
and for some time Antoinette would not have the heart to go
again. And then she would insist, though it was even more
disagreeable to her than to Olivier: but she thought it necessary
for her brother's health. She would force him to go out once
more. But their new experience would be no better than the
last, and Olivier would protest bitterly. So they stayed shut
up in the stifling town, and, in their prison-yard, they sighed
for the open fields.

Olivier had reached the end of his schooldays. The examinations for the *École Normale* were over. It was quite time.
Antoinette was very tired. She was counting on his success:
her brother had everything in his favor. At school he was
regarded as one of the best pupils: and all his masters were
agreed in praising his industry and intelligence, except for a
certain want of mental discipline which made it difficult for him
to bend to any sort of plan. But the responsibility of it
weighed on Olivier so heavily that he lost his head as the exam-

ination came near. He was worn out, and paralyzed by the
fear of failure, and a morbid shyness that crept over him. He
trembled at the thought of appearing before the examiners in
public. He had always suffered from shyness: in class he would
blush and choke when he had to speak: at first he could hardly
do more than answer his name. And it was much more easy
for him to reply impromptu than when he knew that he was
going to be questioned: the thought of it made him ill: his
mind rushed ahead picturing every detail of the ordeal as it
would happen: and the longer he had to wait, the more he was
obsessed by it. It might be said that he passed every examination at least twice: for he passed it in his dreams on the
night before and expended all his energy, so that he had none
left for the real examination.

But he did not even reach the *viva voce,* the very thought
of which had sent him into a cold sweat the night before. In
the written examination on a philosophical subject, which at
any ordinary time would have sent him flying off, he could not
even manage to squeeze out a couple of pages in six hours. For
the first few hours his brain was empty; he could think of
nothing, nothing. It was like a blank wall against which he
hurled himself in vain. Then, an hour before the end, the
wall was rent and a few rays of light shone through the crevices.
He wrote an excellent short essay, but it was not enough to
place him. When Antoinette saw the despair on his face as he
came out, she foresaw the inevitable blow, and she was as
despairing as he: but she did not show it. Even in the most
desperate situations she had always an inexhaustible capacity
for hope.

Olivier was rejected.

He was crushed by it. Antoinette pretended to smile as
though it were nothing of any importance: but her lips
trembled. She consoled her brother, and told him that it was
an easily remedied misfortune, and that he would be certain to
pass next year, and win a better place. She did not tell him
how vital it was to her that he should have passed, that year,

or how utterly worn out she felt in soul and body, or how uneasy she felt about fighting through another year like that. But she had to go on. If she were to go away before Olivier had passed he would never have the courage to go on fighting alone: he would succumb.

She concealed her weariness from him, and even redoubled her efforts. She wore herself to skin and bone to let him have amusement and change during the holidays so that he might resume work with greater energy and confidence. But at the very outset her small savings had to be broken into, and, to make matters worse, she lost some of her most profitable pupils.

Another year! . . . Within sight of the final ordeal they were almost at breaking-point. Above all, they had to live, and discover some other means of scraping along. Antoinette accepted a situation as a governess in Germany which had been offered her through the Nathans. It was the very last thing she would have thought of, but nothing else offered at the time, and she could not wait. She had never left her brother for a single day during the last six years: and she could not imagine what life would be like without seeing and hearing him from day to day. Olivier was terrified when he thought of it: but he dared not say anything: it was he who had brought it about: if he had passed Antoinette would not have been reduced to such an extremity: he had no right to say anything, or to take into account his own grief at the parting: it was for her to decide.

They spent the last days together in dumb anguish, as though one of them were about to die: they hid away from each other when their sorrow was too much for them. Antoinette gazed into Olivier's eyes for counsel. If he had said to her: "Don't go!" she would have stayed, although she had to go. Up to the very last moment, in the cab in which they drove to the station, she was prepared to break her resolution: she felt that she could never go through with it. At a word from him, one word! . . . But he said nothing. Like her, he set his teeth and would not budge.—She made him promise to write to

her every day, and to conceal nothing from her, and to send for
her if he were ever in the least danger.

They parted. While Olivier returned with a heavy heart to
his school, where it had been agreed that he should board, the
train carried Antoinette, crushed and sorrowful, towards Germany. Lying awake and staring through the night they felt
the minutes dragging them farther and farther apart, and
they called to each other in whispering voices.

Antoinette was fearful of the new world to which she was
going. She had changed much in six years. She who had
once been so bold and afraid of nothing had grown so used to
silence and isolation that it hurt her to go out into the world
again. The laughing, gay, chattering Antoinette of the old
happy times had passed away with them. Unhappiness had
made her sensitive and shy. No doubt living with Olivier had
infected her with his timidity. She had had hardly anybody
to talk to except her brother. She was scared by the least
little thing, and was really in a panic when she had to pay a
call. And so it was a nervous torture to her to think that she
was now going to live among strangers, to have to talk to them,
to be always with them. The poor girl had no more real vocation for teaching than her brother: she did her work conscientiously, but her heart was not in it, and she had not the support
of feeling that there was any use in it. She was made to love
and not to teach. And no one cared for her love.

Nowhere was her capacity for love less in demand than in
her new situation in Germany. The Grünebaums, whose children she was engaged to teach French, took not the slightest
interest in her. They were haughty and familiar, indifferent
and indiscreet: they paid fairly well: and, as a result, they
regarded everybody in their payment as being under an obligation to them, and thought they could do just as they liked.
They treated Antoinette as a superior sort of servant and allowed her hardly any liberty. She did not even have a room

to herself: she slept in a room adjoining that of the children and had to leave the door open all night. She was never alone. They had no respect for her need of taking refuge every now and then within herself—the sacred right of every human being to preserve an inner sanctuary of solitude. The only happiness she had lay in correspondence and communion with her brother: she made use of every moment of liberty she could snatch. But even that was encroached upon. As soon as she began to write they would prowl about in her room and ask her what she was writing. When she was reading a letter they would ask her what was in it: by their persistent impertinent curiosity they found out about her "little brother." She had to hide from them. Too shameful sometimes were the expedients to which she had to resort, and the holes and crannies in which she had to hide, in order to be able to read Olivier's letters unobserved. If she left a letter lying in her room she was sure it would be read: and as she had nothing she could lock except her box, she had to carry any papers she did not want to have read about with her: they were always prying into her business and her intimate affairs, and they were always fishing for her secret thoughts. It was not that the Grünebaums were really interested in her, only they thought that, as they paid her, she was their property. They were not malicious about it: indiscretion was with them an incurable habit: they were never offended with each other.

Nothing could have been more intolerable to Antoinette than such espionage, such a lack of moral modesty, which made it impossible for her to escape even for an hour a day from their curiosity. The Grünebaums were hurt by the haughty reserve with which she treated them. Naturally they found highly moral reasons to justify their vulgar curiosity, and to condemn Antoinette's desire to be immune from it.

"It was their duty," they thought, "to know the private life of a girl living under their roof, as a member of their household, to whom they had intrusted the education of their children: they were responsible for her."—(That is the sort of thing that so many mistresses say of their servants, mistresses whose "responsibility" does not go so far as to spare the unhappy girls any fatigue or work that must revolt them, but is entirely limited to denying them every sort of pleasure.)— "And that Antoinette should refuse to acknowledge that duty, imposed on them by conscience, could only show," they concluded, "that she was conscious of being not altogether beyond reproach: an honest girl has nothing to conceal."

So Antoinette lived under a perpetual persecution, against which she was always on her guard, so that it made her seem even more cold and reserved than she was.

Every day her brother wrote her a twelve-page letter: and she contrived to write to him every day even if it were only a few lines. Olivier tried hard to be brave and not to show his grief too clearly. But he was bored and dull. His life had always been so bound up with his sister's that, now that she was torn from him, he seemed to have lost part of himself: he could not use his arms, or his legs, or his brains, he could not walk, or play the piano, or work, or do anything, not even dream—except through her. He slaved away at his books from morning to night: but it was no good: his thoughts were elsewhere: he would be suffering, or thinking of her, or of the morrow's letter: he would sit staring at the clock, waiting for the day's letter: and when it arrived his fingers would tremble with joy— with fear, too—as he tore open the envelope. Never did lover tremble with more tenderness and anxiety at a letter from his mistress. He would hide away, like Antoinette, to read his letters: he would carry them about with him: and at night he always had the last letter under his pillow, and he would touch it from time to time to make sure that it was still there, during the long, sleepless nights when he lay awake dreaming of his dear sister. How far removed from her he felt! He felt that most dreadfully when Antoinette's letters were delayed by the post and came a day late. Two days, two nights, between them! . . . He exaggerated the time and the distance because he had never traveled. His imagination would take fire:

"Heavens! If she were to fall ill! There would be time
for her to die before he could see her. . . . Why had she
not written to him, just a line or two, the day before? . . .
Was she ill? . . . Yes. She was surely ill. . . ." He
would choke.—More often still he would be terrified of dying
away from her, dying alone, among people who did not care,
in the horrible school, in grim, gray Paris. He would make
himself ill with the thought of it. . . . "Should he write
and tell her to come back?"—But then he would be ashamed
of his cowardice. Besides, as soon as he began to write to
her it gave him such joy to be in communion with her that
for a moment he would forget his suffering. It seemed to him
that he could see her, hear her voice: he would tell her everything: never had he spoken to her so intimately, so passionately,
when they had been together: he would call her "my true, brave,
dear, kind, beloved, little sister," and say, "I love you so."
Indeed they were real love-letters.

Their tenderness was sweet and comforting to Antoinette:
they were all the air she had to breathe. If they did not come
in the morning at the usual time she would be miserable. Once
or twice it happened that the Grünebaums, from carelessness, or
—who knows?—from a wicked desire to tease, forgot to give
them to her until the evening, and once even until the next
morning: and she worked herself into a fever.—On New Year's
Day they had the same idea, without telling each other: they
planned a surprise, and each sent a long telegram—(at vast expense)—and their messages arrived at the same time.—Olivier
always consulted Antoinette about his work and his troubles:
Antoinette gave him advice, and encouragement, and fortified
him with her strength, though indeed she had not really enough
for herself.

She was stifled in the foreign country, where she knew nobody, and nobody was interested in her, except the wife of a
professor, lately come to the town, who also felt out of her
element. The good creature was kind and motherly, and sympathetic with the brother and sister who loved each other so

and had to live apart—(for she had dragged part of her story
out of Antoinette) :—but she was so noisy, so commonplace, she
was so lacking—though quite innocently—in tact and discretion that aristocratic little Antoinette was irritated and drew
back. She had no one in whom she could confide and so all
her troubles were pent up, and weighed heavily upon her: sometimes she thought she must give way under them: but she set
her teeth and struggled on. Her health suffered: she grew
very thin. Her brother's letters became more and more down-
hearted. In a fit of depression he wrote:

"Come back, come back, come back! . . ."

But he had hardly sent the letter off than he was ashamed
of it and wrote another begging Antoinette to tear up the first
and give no further thought to it. He even pretended to be in
good spirits and not to be wanting his sister. It hurt his um-
brageous vanity to think that he might seem incapable of doing
without her.

Antoinette was not deceived: she read his every thought: but
she did not know what to do. One day she almost went to him:
she went to the station to find out what time the train left for
Paris. And then she said to herself that it was madness: the
money she was earning was enough to pay for Olivier's board:
they must hold on as long as they could. She was not strong
enough to make up her mind: in the morning her courage would
spring forth again: but as the day dragged towards evening her
strength would fail her and she would think of flying to him.
She was homesick,—longing for the country that had treated
her so hardly, the country that enshrined all the relics of her
past life,—and she was aching to hear the language that her
brother spoke, the language in which she told her love for
him.

Then it was that a company of French actors passed through
the little German town. Antoinette, who rarely visited the
theater—(she had neither time nor taste for it)—was seized
with an irresistible longing to hear her own language spoken,
to take refuge in France.

The rest is known.[1]

There were no seats left in the theater: she met the young musician, Jean-Christophe, whom she did not know, and he, seeing her disappointment, offered to share with her a box which he had to give away: in her confusion she accepted. Her presence with Christophe set tongues wagging in the little town: and the malicious rumors came at once to the ears of the Grünebaums, who, being already inclined to believe anything ill of the young Frenchwoman, and furious with Christophe as a result of certain events which have been narrated elsewhere, dismissed Antoinette without more ado.

She, who was so chaste and modest, she, whose whole life had been absorbed by her love for her brother and never yet had been besmirched with one thought of evil, nearly died of shame, when she understood the nature of the charge against her. Not for one moment was she resentful against Christophe. She knew that he was as innocent as she, and that, if he had injured her, he had meant only to be kind: she was grateful to him. She knew nothing of him, save that he was a musician, and that he was much maligned: but, in her ignorance of life and men, she had a natural intuition about people, which unhappiness had sharpened, and in her queer, boorish companion she had recognized a quality of candor equal to her own, and a sturdy kindness, the mere memory of which was comforting and good to think on. The evil she had heard of him did not at all affect the confidence which Christophe had inspired in her. Being herself a victim she had no doubt that he was in the same plight, suffering, as she did, though for a longer time, from the malevolence of the townspeople who insulted him. And as she always forgot herself in the thought of others the idea of what Christophe must have suffered distracted her mind a little from her own torment. Nothing in the world could have induced her to try to see him again, or to write to him: her modesty and pride forbade it. She told herself that he did

[1] See *Jean-Christophe*—I, " Revolt. "

not know the harm he had done, and, in her gentleness, she
hoped that he would never know it.

She left Germany. An hour away from the town it chanced
that the train in which she was traveling passed the train by
which Christophe was returning from a neighboring town where
he had been spending the day.

For a few minutes their carriages stopped opposite each
other, and in the silence of the night they saw each other, but
did not speak. What could they have said save a few trivial
words? That would have been a profanation of the indefinable
feeling of common pity and mysterious sympathy which had
sprung up in them, and was based on nothing save the sure-
ness of their inward vision. During those last moments, when,
still strangers, they gazed into each other's eyes, they saw in
each other things which never had appeared to any other soul
among the people with whom they lived. Everything must pass:
the memory of words, kisses, passionate embraces: but the contact of souls, which have once met and hailed each other amid
the throng of passing shapes, that never can be blotted out.
Antoinette bore it with her in the innermost recesses of her
heart—that poor heart, so swathed about with sorrow and sad
thoughts, from out the midst of which there smiled a misty
light, which seemed to steal sweetly from the earth, a pale and
tender light like that which floods the Elysian Shades of Gluck.

She returned to Olivier. It was high time she returned to
him. He had just fallen ill: and the poor, nervous, unhappy
little creature who trembled at the thought of illness before it
came—now that he was really ill, refused to write to his sister
for fear of upsetting her. But he called to her, prayed for her
coming as for a miracle.

When the miracle happened he was lying in the school infirmary, feverish and wandering. When he saw her he made
no sound. How often had he seen her enter in his fevered
fancy! . . . He sat up in bed, gaping, and trembling lest it
should be once more only an illusion. And when she sat down

on the bed by his side, when she took him in her arms and he
had taken her in his, when he felt her soft cheek against his
lips, and her hands still cold from traveling by night in his,
when he was quite, quite sure that it was his dear sister he began to weep. He could do nothing else: he was still the "little
cry-baby" that he had been when he was a child. He clung
to her and held her close for fear she should go away from
him again. How changed they were! How sad they looked!
. . . No matter! They were together once more: everything
was lit up, the infirmary, the school, the gloomy day: they clung
to each other, they would never let each other go. Before she
had said a word he made her swear that she would not go
away again. He had no need to make her swear: no, she would
never go away again: they had been too unhappy away from
each other: their mother was right: anything was better than
being parted. Even poverty, even death, so only they were
together.

They took rooms. They wanted to take their old little flat,
horrible though it was: but it was occupied. Their new rooms
also looked out on to a yard: but above a wall they could see
the top of a little acacia and grew fond of it at once, as a
friend from the country, a prisoner like themselves, in the
paved wilderness of the city. Olivier quickly recovered his
health, or rather, what he was pleased to call his health:—
(for what was health to him would have been illness to a
stronger boy).—Antoinette's unhappy stay in Germany had
helped her to save a little money: and she made some more by
the translation of a German book which a publisher accepted.
For a time, then, they were free of financial anxiety: and all
would be well if Olivier passed his examination at the end of the
year.—But if he did not pass?

No sooner had they settled down to the happiness of being
together again than they were once more obsessed by the prospect of the examination. They tried hard not to think about
it, but in vain, they were always coming back to it. The fixed
idea haunted them, even when they were seeking distraction

from their thoughts: at concerts it would suddenly leap out at them in the middle of the performance: at night when they woke up it would lie there like a yawning gulf before them. In addition to his eagerness to please his sister and repay her for the sacrifice of her youth that she had made for his sake, Olivier lived in terror of his military service which he could not escape if he were rejected:—(at that time admission to the great schools was still admitted as an exemption from service).— He had an invincible disgust for the physical and moral promiscuity, the kind of intellectual degradation, which, rightly or wrongly, he saw in barrack-life. Every pure and aristocratic quality in him revolted from such compulsion, and it seemed to him that death would be preferable. In these days it is permitted to make light of such feelings, and even to decry them in the name of a social morality which, for the moment, has become a religion: but they are blind who deny it: there is no more profound suffering than that of the violation of moral solitude by the coarse liberal Communism of the present day.

The examinations began. Olivier was almost incapable of going in: he was unwell, and he was so fearful of the torment he would have to undergo, whether he passed or not, that he almost longed to be taken seriously ill. He did quite well in the written examination. But he had a cruel time waiting to hear the results. Following the immemorial custom of the country of Revolutions, which is the worst country in the world for red-tape and routine, the examinations were held in July during the hottest days of the year, as though it were deliberately intended to finish off the luckless candidates, who were already staggering under the weight of cramming a monstrous list of subjects, of which even the examiners did not know a tenth part. The written examinations were held on the day after the holiday of the 14th July, when the whole city was upside down, and making merry, to the undoing of the young men who were by no means inclined to be merry, and asked for nothing but silence. In the square outside the house booths were set up, rifles cracked at the miniature ranges, merry-go-rounds creaked and grunted, and hideous steam organs roared from morning till night. The idiotic noise went on for a week. Then a President of the Republic, by way of maintaining his popularity, granted the rowdy merry-makers another three days' holiday. It cost him nothing: he did not hear the row. But Olivier and Antoinette were distracted and appalled by the noise, and had to keep their windows shut, so that their rooms were stifling, and stop their ears, trying vainly to escape the shrill, insistent, idiotic tunes which were ground out from morning till night and stabbed through their brains like daggers, so that they were reduced to a pitiful condition.

The *viva voce* examination began immediately after the publication of the first results. Olivier begged Antoinette not to go. She waited at the door,—much more anxious than he. Of course he never told her what he thought of his performance. He tormented her by telling her what he had said and what he had not said.

At last the final results were published. The names of the candidates were posted in the courtyard of the Sorbonne. Antoinette would not let Olivier go alone. As they left the house, they thought, though they did not say it, that when they came back they would *know*, and perhaps they would regret their present fears, when at least there was still hope. When they came in sight of the Sorbonne they felt their legs give way under them. Brave little Antoinette said to her brother:

"Please not so fast. . . ."

Olivier looked at his sister, and she forced a smile. He said:

"Shall we sit down for a moment on the seat here?"

He would gladly have gone no further. But, after a moment, she pressed his hand and said:

"It's nothing, dear. Let us go on."

They could not find the list at first. They read several others in which the name of Jeannin did not appear. When at last they saw it, they did not take it in at first: they read it several times and could not believe it. Then when they were quite sure that it was true that Jeannin was Olivier, that Jeannin had passed, they could say nothing: they hurried home: she took his arm, and held his wrist, and leaned her weight on him: they almost ran, and saw nothing of what was going on about them: as they crossed the boulevard they were almost run over. They said over and over again:

"Dear. . . . Darling. . . . Dear. . . . Dear. . . ."

They tore upstairs to their rooms and then they flung their arms round each other. Antoinette took her brother's hand and led him to the photographs of their father and mother, which hung on the wall near her bed, in a corner of her room, which was a sort of sanctuary to her: they knelt down before them: and with tears in their eyes they prayed.

Antoinette ordered a jolly little dinner: but they could not eat a morsel: they were not hungry. They spent the evening, Olivier kneeling by his sister's side while she petted him like a child. They hardly spoke at all. They could not even be happy, for they were too worn out. They went to bed before nine o'clock and slept the sleep of the just.

Next day Antoinette had a frightful headache, but there was such a load taken from her heart! Olivier felt, for the first time in his life, that he could breathe freely. He was saved, she was saved, she had accomplished her task: and he had shown himself to be not unworthy of his sister's expectations! . . . For the first time for years and years they allowed themselves a little laziness. They stayed in bed till twelve talking through the wall, with the door between their rooms open: when they looked in the mirror they saw their faces happy and tired-looking: they smiled, and threw kisses to each other, and dozed off again, and watched each other's sleep, and lay weary and worn with hardly the strength to do more than mutter tender little scraps of words.

Antoinette had always put by a little money, sou by sou, so as to have some small reserve in case of illness. She did not tell her brother the surprise she had in store for him. The day after his success she told him that they were going to spend a month in Switzerland to make up for all their years of trouble and hardship. Now that Olivier was assured of three years at the *École Normale* at the expense of the State, and then, when he left the *École,* of finding a post, they could be extravagant and spend all their savings. Olivier shouted for joy when she told him. Antoinette was even more happy than he,—happy in her brother's happiness,—happy to think that she was going to see the country once more: she had so longed for it.

It took them some time to get ready for the journey, but the work of preparation was an unending joy. It was well on in August when they set out. They were not used to traveling. Olivier did not sleep the night before. And he did not sleep in the train. The whole day they had been fearful of missing the train. They were in a feverish hurry, they had been jostled about at the station, and finally huddled into a second-class carriage, where they could not even lean back to go to sleep:— (that is one of the privileges of which the eminently democratic French companies deprive poor travelers, so that rich travelers may have the pleasure of thinking that they have a monopoly of it).—Olivier did not sleep a wink: he was not sure that they were in the right train, and he looked out for the name of every station. Antoinette slept lightly and woke up very frequently: the jolting of the train made her head bob. Olivier watched her by the light of the funereal lamp, which shone at the top of the moving sarcophagus: and he was suddenly struck by the change in her face. Her eyes were hollow: her childish lips were half-open from sheer weariness: her skin was sallow, and there were little wrinkles on her cheeks, the marks of the sad years of sorrow and disillusion. She looked old and ill.— And, indeed, she was so tired! If she had dared she would have postponed their journey. But she did not like to spoil her brother's pleasure: she tried to persuade herself that she was only tired, and that the country would make her well again. She was fearful lest she should fall ill on the way.—She felt that he was looking at her: and she suddenly flung off the drowsiness that was creeping over her, and opened her eyes,—eyes still young, still clear and limpid, across which, from time to time, there passed an involuntary look of pain, like shadows on a little lake. He asked her in a whisper, anxiously and tenderly, how she was: she pressed his hand and assured him that she was well. A word of love revived her.

Then, when the rosy dawn tinged the pale country between Dôle and Pontarlier, the sight of the waking fields, and the gay sun rising from the earth,—the sun, who, like themselves, had escaped from the prison of the streets, and the grimy houses, and the thick smoke of Paris:—the waving fields wrapped in the light mist of their milk-white breath: the little things they passed: a little village belfry, a glimpse of a winding stream, a blue line of hills hovering on the far horizon: the tinkling, moving sound of the angelus borne from afar on the wind, when the train stopped in the midst of the sleeping country: the solemn shapes of a herd of cows browsing on a slope above the railway,—all absorbed Antoinette and her brother, to whom it all seemed new. They were like parched trees, drinking in ecstasy the rain from heaven.

Then, in the early morning, they reached the Swiss Customs, where they had to get out. A little station in a bare country-side. They were almost worn out by their sleepless night, and the cold, dewy freshness of the dawn made them shiver: but it was calm, and the sky was clear, and the fragrant air of the fields was about them, upon their lips, on their tongues, down their throats, flowing down into their lungs like a cooling stream: and they stood by a table, out in the open air, and drank comforting hot coffee with creamy milk, heavenly sweet, and tasting of the grass and the flowers of the fields.

They climbed up into the Swiss carriage, the novel arrangement of which gave them a childish pleasure. But Antoinette was so tired! She could not understand why she should feel so ill. Why was everything about her so beautiful, so absorbing, when she could take so little pleasure in it? Was it not all just what she had been dreaming for years: a journey with her brother, with all anxiety for the future left behind, dear mother Nature? . . . What was the matter with her? She was annoyed with herself, and forced herself to admire and share her brother's naïve delight.

They stopped at Thun. They were to go up into the mountains next day. But that night in the hotel, Antoinette was stricken with a fever, and violent illness, and pains in her head. Olivier was at his wits' ends, and spent a night of frightful anxiety. He had to send for a doctor in the morning —(an unforeseen expense which was no light tax on their slender purse).—The doctor could find nothing immediately serious, but said that she was run down, and that her constitution was undermined. There could be no question of their going on. The doctor forbade Antoinette to get up all day: and he thought they would perhaps have to stay at Thun for some time. They were very downcast—though very glad to have got off so cheaply after all their fears. But it was hard to have come so far to be shut up in a nasty hotel-room into which the sunlight poured so that it was like a hothouse. Antoinette insisted on her brother going out. He went a few yards from the hotel, saw the beautiful green Aar, and, hovering in the distance against the sky, a white peak: he bubbled over with joy: but he could not keep it to himself. He rushed back to his sister's room, and told her excitedly what he had just seen: and when she expressed her surprise at his coming back so soon and made him promise to go out again, he said, as once before he had said when he came back from the *Châtelet* concert:

"No, no. It is too beautiful: it hurts me to see it without you."

That feeling was not new to them: they knew that they had to be together to enjoy anything wholly. But they always loved to hear it said. His tender words did Antoinette more good than any medicine. She smiled now, languidly, happily. —And after a good night, although it was not very wise to go on so soon, she decided that they would get away very early, without telling the doctor, who would only want to keep them back.

The pure air and the joy of seeing so much beauty made her stronger, so that she did not have to pay for her rashness, and without any further misadventure they reached the end of their journey—a mountain village, high above the lake, some distance away from Spiez.

There they spent three or four weeks in a little hotel. Antoinette did not have any further attack of fever, but she never got really well. She still felt a heaviness, an intolerable weight, in her head, and she was always unwell. Olivier often asked her about her health: he longed to see her grow less pale: but he was intoxicated by the beauty of the country, and instinctively avoided all melancholy thoughts: when she assured him that she was really quite well, he tried to believe that it was true,—although he knew perfectly well that it was not so. And she enjoyed to the full her brother's exuberance and the fine air, and the all-pervading peace. How good it was to rest at last after those terrible years!

Olivier tried to induce her to go for walks with him: she would have been happy to join him: but on several occasions when she had bravely set out, she had been forced to stop after twenty minutes, to regain her breath, and rest her heart. So he went out alone,—climbing the safe peaks, though they filled her with terror until he came home again. Or they would go for little walks together: she would lean on his arm, and walk slowly, and they would talk, and he would suddenly begin to chatter, and laugh, and discuss his plans, and make quips and jests. From the road on the hillside above the valley they would watch the white clouds reflected in the still lake, and the boats moving like insects on the surface of a pond: they would drink in the warm air and the music of the goat-bells, borne on the gusty wind, and the smell of the new-mown hay and the warm resin. And they would dream together of the past and the future, and the present which seemed to them to be the most unreal and intoxicating of dreams. Sometimes Antoinette would be infected with her brother's jolly childlike humor: they would chase each other and roll about on the grass. And one

day he saw her laughing as she used to do when they were
children, madly, carelessly, laughter clear and bubbling as a
spring, such as he had not heard for many years.

But, most often, Olivier could not resist the pleasure of
going for long walks. He would be sorry for it at once, and
later he had bitterly to regret that he had not made enough
of those dear days with his sister. Even in the hotel he would
often leave her alone. There was a party of young men and
girls in the hotel, from whom they had at first kept apart.
Then Olivier was attracted by them, and shyly joined their
circle. He had been starved of friendship: outside his sister
he had hardly known any one but his rough schoolfellows and
their girls, who repelled him. It was very sweet to him to
be among well-mannered, charming, merry boys and girls of
his own age. Although he was very shy, he was naïvely curious,
sentimental, and affectionate, and easily bewitched by the little
burning, flickering fires that shine in a woman's eyes. And in
spite of his shyness, women liked him. His frank longing to
love and be loved gave him, unknown to himself, a youthful
charm, and made him find words and gestures and affectionate
little attentions, the very awkwardness of which made them all
the more attractive. He had the gift of sympathy. Although
in his isolation his intelligence had taken on an ironical tinge
which made him see the vulgarity of people and their defects,
which he often loathed,—yet in their presence he saw nothing
but their eyes, in which he would see the expression of a living being, who one day would die, a being who had only one
life, even as he, and, even as he, would lose it all too soon:
then of that creature he would involuntarily be fond: in that
moment nothing in the world could make him do anything to
hurt: whether he liked it or not, he had to be kind and amiable.
He was weak: and, in being so, he was sure to please the
"world" which pardons every vice, and even every virtue,—
except one: force, on which all the rest depend.

Antoinette did not join them. Her health, her tiredness, her
apparently causeless moral collapse, paralyzed her. Through

the long years of anxiety and ceaseless toil, exhausting body and soul, the positions of the brother and sister had been inverted: now it was she who felt far removed from the world, far from everything and everybody, so far! . . . She could not break down the wall between them: all their chatter, their noise, their laughter, their little interests, bored her, wearied her, almost hurt her. It hurt her to be so: she would have loved to go with the other girls, to share their interests and laugh with them. . . . But she could not! . . . Her heart ached; she seemed to be as one dead. In the evening she would shut herself up in her room; and often she would not even turn on the light: she would sit there in the dark, while downstairs Olivier would be amusing himself, surrendering to the current of one of those romantic little love affairs to which he so easily succumbed. She would only shake off her torpor when she heard him coming upstairs, laughing and talking to the girls, hanging about saying good-night outside their rooms, being unable to tear himself away. Then in the darkness Antoinette would smile, and get up to turn on the light. The sound of her brother's laughter revived her.

Autumn was setting in. The sun was dying down. Nature was a-weary. Under the thick mists and clouds of October the colors were fading fast; snow fell on the mountains: mists descended upon the plains. The visitors went away one by one, and then several at a time. And it was sad to see even the friends of a little while going away, but sadder still to see the passing of the summer, the time of peace and happiness which had been an oasis in their lives. They went for a last walk together, on a cloudy autumn day, through the forest on the mountain-side. They did not speak: they mused sadly, as they walked along with the collars of their cloaks turned up, clinging close together: their hands were locked. There was silence in the wet woods, and in silence the trees wept. From the depths there came the sweet plaintive cry of a solitary bird who felt the coming of winter. Through the mist came the clear tinkling of the goat-bells, far away, so faint they could hardly hear it, so faint it was as though it came up from their inmost hearts. . . .

They returned to Paris. They were both sad. Antoinette was no better.

They had to set to work to prepare Olivier's wardrobe for the *École*. Antoinette spent the last of her little store of money, and even sold some of her jewels. What did it matter? He would repay her later on. And then, she would need so little when he was gone from her! . . . She tried not to think of what it would be like when he was gone: she worked away at his clothes, and put into the work all the tenderness she had for her brother, and she had a presentiment that it would be the last thing she would do for him.

During the last days together they were never apart: they were fearful of wasting the tiniest moment. On their last evening they sat up very late by the fireside, Antoinette occupying the only armchair, and Olivier a stool at her feet, and she made a fuss of him like the spoiled child he was. He was dreading—though he was curious about it, too—the new life upon which he was to enter. Antoinette thought only that it was the end of their dear life together, and wondered fearfully what would become of her. As though he were trying to make the thought even more bitter for her, he was more tender than ever he had been, with the innocent instinctive coquetry of those who always wait until they are just going to show themselves at their best and most charming. He went to the piano and played her their favorite passages from Mozart and Gluck— those visions of tender happiness and serene sorrow with which so much of their past life was bound up.

When the time came for them to part, Antoinette accompanied Olivier as far as the gates of the *École*. Then she returned. Once more she was alone. But now it was not, as when she had gone away to Germany, a separation which she could bring to an end at will when she could bear it no longer. Now it was she who remained behind, he who went away: it was he who had gone away, for a long, long time—perhaps for life. And yet her love for him was so maternal that at first she thought less of herself than of him: she thought only of how different the first few days would be for him, of the strict rules of the *École,* and was preoccupied with those harmless little worries which so easily assume alarming proportions in the minds of people who live alone and are always tormenting themselves about those whom they love. Her anxiety did at least have this advantage, that it distracted her thoughts from her own loneliness. She had already begun to think of the half-hour when she would be able to see him next day in the visitors' room. She arrived a quarter of an hour too soon. He was very nice to her, but he was altogether taken up with all the new things he had seen. And during the following days, when she went to see him, full of the most tender anxiety, the contrast between what those meetings meant for her and what they meant for him was more and more marked. For her they were her whole life. For Olivier—no doubt he loved Antoinette dearly: but it was too much to expect him to think only of her, as she thought of him. Once or twice he came down late to the visitors' room. One day, when she asked him if he were at all unhappy, he said that he was nothing of the kind. Such little things as that stabbed Antoinette to the heart.—She was angry with herself for being so sensitive, and accused herself of selfishness: she knew quite well that it would be absurd, even wrong and unnatural, for him to be unable to do without her, and for her to be unable to do without him, and to have no other object in life. Yes: she knew all that. But what was the good of her knowing it? She could not help it if for the last ten years her whole life had been bound up in that one idea: her brother. Now that the one interest of her life had been torn from her, she had nothing left.

She tried bravely to keep herself occupied and to take up her music and read her beloved books. . . . But alas! how empty were Shakespeare and Beethoven without Olivier! . . .—Yes: no doubt they were beautiful. . . . But Olivier was not there. What is the good of beautiful things if the eyes of the beloved are not there to see them? What is the use of beauty, what is the use even of joy, if they cannot be won through the heart of the beloved?

If she had been stronger she would have tried to build up her life anew, and give it another object. But she was at the end of her tether. Now that there was nothing to force her to hold on, at all costs, the effort of will to which she had subjected herself snapped: she collapsed. The illness, which had been gaining grip on her for over a year, during which she had fought it down by force of will, was now left to take its course.

She spent her evenings alone in her room, by the spent fire, a prey to her thoughts: she had neither the courage to light the fire again, nor the strength to go to bed: she would sit there far into the night, dozing, dreaming, shivering. She would live through her life again, and summon up the beloved dead and her lost illusions: and she would be terribly sad at the thought of her lost youth, without love or hope of love. A dumb, aching sorrow, obscure, unconfessed. . . . A child laughed in the street: its little feet pattered up to the floor below. . . . Its little feet trampled on her heart. . . . She would be beset with doubts and evil thoughts; her soul in its weakness would be contaminated by the soul of that city of selfish pleasure.—— She would fight down her regrets, and burn with shame at certain longings which she thought evil and wicked: she could not understand what it was that hurt her so, and attributed it to her evil instincts. Poor little Ophelia, devoured by a mysterious evil, she felt with horror dark and uneasy desires mounting from the depths of her being, from the very pit of life. She could not work, and she had given up most of her pupils: she, who was so plucky, and had always risen so early, now lay in bed sometimes until the afternoon: she had no more reason for getting up than for going to bed: she ate little or nothing. Only on her brother's holidays—Thursday afternoons and Sundays—she would make an effort to be her old self with him.

He saw nothing. He was too much taken up with his new
life to notice his sister much. He was at that period of boy-
hood when it was difficult for him to be communicative, and
he always seemed to be indifferent to things outside himself
which would only be his concern in later days.—People of riper
years sometimes seem to be more open to impressions, and
to take a simpler delight in life and Nature, than young people
between twenty and thirty. And so it is often said that young
people are not so young in heart as they were, and have lost all
sense of enjoyment. That is often a mistaken idea. It is not
because they have no sense of enjoyment that they seem less
sensitive. It is because their whole being is often absorbed by
passion, ambition, desire, some fixed idea. When the body is
worn and has no more to expect from life, then the emotions
become disinterested and fall into their place; and then once
more the source of childish tears is reopened.—Olivier was preoccupied with a thousand little things, the most outstanding of
which was an absurd little passion,—(he was always a victim
to them),—which so obsessed him as to make him blind and indifferent to everything else.—Antoinette did not know what was
happening to her brother: she only saw that he was drawing
away from her. That was not altogether Olivier's fault. Sometimes when he came he would be glad to see her and start talking. He would come in. Then all of a sudden he would dry
up. Her affectionate anxiety, the eagerness with which she clung
to him, and drank in his words, and overwhelmed him with little attentions,—all her excess of tenderness and querulous devotion would deprive him utterly of any desire to be warm and
open with her. He might have seen that Antoinette was not in
a normal condition. Nothing could be farther from her usual
tact and discretion. But he never gave a thought to it. He
would reply to her questions with a curt " Yes " or " No." He
would grow more stiff and surly, the more she tried to win him
over: sometimes even he would hurt her by some brusque reply.
Then she would be crushed and silent. Their day together

would slip by, wasted. But hardly had he set foot outside the house on his way back to the *École* than he would be heartily ashamed of his treatment of her. He would torture himself all night as he lay awake thinking of the pain he had caused her. Sometimes even, as soon as he reached the *École,* he would write an effusive letter to his sister.—But next morning, when he read it through, he would tear it up. And Antoinette would know nothing at all about it. She would go on thinking that he had ceased to love her.

She had—if not one last joy—one last flutter of tenderness and youth, when her heart beat strongly once more; one last awakening of love in her, and hope of happiness, hope of life. It was quite ridiculous, so utterly unlike her tranquil nature! It could never have been but for her abnormal condition, the state of fear and over-excitement which was the precursor of illness.

She went to a concert at the *Châtelet* with her brother. As he had just been appointed musical critic to a little Review, they were in better places than those they occupied in old days, but the people among whom they sat were much more apathetic. They had stalls near the stage. Christophe Krafft was to play. Neither of them had ever heard of the German musician. When she saw him come on, the blood rushed to her heart. Although her tired eyes could only see him through a mist, she had no doubt when he appeared: he was the unknown young man of her unhappy days in Germany. She had never mentioned him to her brother: and she had hardly even admitted his existence to her thoughts: she had been entirely absorbed by the anxieties of her life since then. Besides, she was a reasonable little Frenchwoman, and refused to admit the existence of an obscure feeling which she could not trace to its source, while it seemed to lead nowhere. There was in her a whole region of the soul, of unsuspected depths, wherein there slept many other feelings which she would have been ashamed to behold: she knew that they were there: but she looked away

from them in a sort of religious terror of that Being within
herself which lies beyond the mind's control.

When she had recovered a little, she borrowed her brother's
glasses to look at Christophe: she saw him in profile at the conductor's stand, and she recognized his expression of forceful
concentration. He was wearing a shabby old coat which fitted
him very badly.—Antoinette sat in silent agony through the
vagaries of that lamentable concert when Christophe joined
issue with the unconcealed hostility of his audience, who were
at the time ill-disposed towards German artists, and actively
bored by his music. And when he appeared, after a symphony
which had seemed unconscionably long, to play some piano
music, he was received with cat-calls which left no room for
doubt as to their displeasure at having to put up with him
again. However, he began to play in the face of the bored
resignation of his audience: but the uncomplimentary remarks
exchanged in a loud voice by two men in the gallery went on,
to the great delight of the rest of the audience. Then he broke
off: and in a childish fit of temper he played *Malbrouck s'en va
t'en guerre* with one finger, got up from the piano, faced the
audience, and said:

"That is all you are fit for."

The audience were for a moment so taken aback that they
did not quite take in what the musician meant. Then there
was an outburst of angry protests. Followed a terrible uproar.
They hissed and shouted:

"Apologize! Make him apologize!"

They were all red in the face with anger, and they blew out
their fury—tried to persuade themselves that they were really
enraged: as perhaps they were, but the chief thing was that
they were delighted to have a chance of making a row, and letting themselves go: they were like schoolboys after a few hours
in school.

Antoinette could not move: she was petrified: she sat still
tugging at one of her gloves. Ever since the last bars of
the symphony she had had a growing presentiment of what

would happen: she felt the blind hostility of the audience, felt it growing: she read Christophe's thoughts, and she was sure he would not go through to the end without an explosion: she sat waiting for the explosion while agony grew in her: she stretched every nerve to try to prevent it; and when at last it came, it was so exactly what she had foreseen that she was overwhelmed by it, as by some fatal catastrophe against which there was nothing to be done. And as she gazed at Christophe, who was staring insolently at the howling audience, their eyes met. Christophe's eyes recognized her, greeted her, for the space of perhaps a second: but he was in such a state of excitement that his mind did not recognize her (he had not thought of her for long enough). He disappeared while the audience yelled and hissed.

She longed to cry out: to say or do something: but she was bound hand and foot, and could not stir; it was like a nightmare. It was some comfort to her to hear her brother at her side, and to know that, without having any idea of what was happening to her, he had shared her agony and indignation. Olivier was a thorough musician, and he had an independence of taste which nothing could encroach upon: when he liked a thing, he would have maintained his liking in the face of the whole world. With the very first bars of the symphony, he had felt that he was in the presence of something big, something the like of which he had never in his life come across. He went on muttering to himself with heartfelt enthusiasm:

"That's fine! That's beautiful! Beautiful!" while his sister instinctively pressed close to him, gratefully. After the symphony he applauded loudly by way of protest against the ironic indifference of the rest of the audience. When it came to the great fiasco, he was beside himself: he stood up, shouted that Christophe was right, abused the booers, and offered to fight them: it was impossible to recognize the timid Olivier. His voice was drowned in the uproar: he was told to shut up: he was called a "snotty little kid," and told to go to bed. An-

toinette saw the futility of standing up to them, and took his
arm and said:

"Stop! Stop! I implore you! Stop!"

He sat down in despair, and went on muttering:

"It's shameful! Shameful! The swine! . . ."

She said nothing and bore her suffering in silence: he thought
she was insensible to the music, and said:

"Antoinette, don't *you* think it beautiful?"

She nodded. She was frozen, and could not recover herself.
But when the orchestra began another piece, she suddenly got
up, and whispered to her brother in a tone of savage hatred:

"Come, come! I can't bear the sight of these people!"

They hurried out. They walked along arm-in-arm, and
Olivier went on talking excitedly. Antoinette said nothing.

All that day and the days following she sat alone in her
room, and a feeling crept over her which at first she refused
to face: but then it went on and took possession of her thoughts,
like the furious throbbing of the blood in her aching temples.

Some time afterwards Olivier brought her Christophe's collection of songs, which he had just found at a publisher's. She
opened it at random. On the first page on which her eyes fell
she read in front of a song this dedication in German:

"*To my poor dear little victim,*" together with a date.

She knew the date well.—She was so upset that she could
read no farther. She put the book down and asked her brother
to play, and went and shut herself up in her room. Olivier,
full of his delight in the new music, began to play without remarking his sister's emotion. Antoinette sat in the adjoining
room, striving to repress the beating of her heart. Suddenly
she got up and looked through a cupboard for a little account-
book in which was written the date of her departure from Germany, and the mysterious date. She knew it already: yes, it
was the evening of the performance at the theater to which she
had been with Christophe. She lay down on her bed and closed
her eyes, blushing, with her hands folded on her breast, while

she listened to the dear music. Her heart was overflowing with gratitude. . . . Ah! Why did her head hurt her so?

When Olivier saw that his sister had not come back, he went into her room after he had done playing, and found her lying there. He asked her if she were ill. She said she was rather tired, and got up to keep him company. They talked: but she did not answer his questions at once: her thoughts seemed to be far away: she smiled, and blushed, and said, by way of excuse, that her headache was making her stupid. At last Olivier went away. She had asked him to leave the book of songs. She sat up late reading them at the piano, without playing, just lightly touching a note here and there, for fear of annoying her neighbors. But for the most part she did not even read: she sat dreaming: she was carried away by a feeling of tenderness and gratitude towards the man who had pitied her, and had read her mind and soul with the mysterious intuition of true kindness. She could not fix her thoughts. She was happy and sad—sad! . . . Ah! How her head ached!

She spent the night in sweet and painful dreams, a crushing melancholy. During the day she tried to go out for a little to shake off her drowsiness. Although her head was still aching, to give herself something to do, she went and made a few purchases at a great shop. She hardly gave a thought to what she was doing. Her thoughts were always with Christophe, though she did not admit it to herself. As she came out, worried and mortally sad, through the crowd of people she saw Christophe go by on the other side of the street. He saw her, too, at the same moment. At once,—(suddenly and without thinking), she held out her hands towards him. Christophe stopped: this time he recognized her. He sprang forward to cross the road to Antoinette: and Antoinette tried to go to meet him. But the insensate current of the passing throng carried her along like a windlestraw, while the horse of an omnibus, falling on the slippery asphalt, made a sort of dyke in front of Christophe, by which the opposing streams of carriages were dammed, so that for a few moments there was an impassable barrier. Christophe tried to force his way through in spite of everything: but he was trapped in the middle of the traffic, and could not move either way. When at last he did extricate himself and managed to reach the place where he had seen Antoinette, she was gone: she had struggled vainly against the human torrent that carried her along: then she yielded to it— gave up the struggle. She felt that she was dogged by some fatality which forbade the possibility of her ever meeting Christophe: against Fate there was nothing to be done. And when she did succeed in escaping from the crowd, she made no attempt to go back: she was suddenly ashamed: what could she dare to say to him? What had she done? What must he have thought of her? She fled away home.

She did not regain assurance until she reached her room. Then she sat by the table in the dark, and had not even the strength to take off her hat or her gloves. She was miserable at having been unable to speak to him: and at the same time there glowed a new light in her heart: she was unconscious of the darkness, and unconscious of the illness that was upon her. She went on and on turning over and over every detail of the scene in the street: and she changed it about and imagined what would have happened if certain things had turned out differently. She saw herself holding out her arms to Christophe, and Christophe's expression of joy as he recognized her, and she laughed and blushed. She blushed: and then in the darkness of her room, where there was no one to see her, and she could hardly see herself, once more she held out her arms to him. Her need was too strong for her: she felt that she was losing ground, and instinctively she sought to clutch at the strong vivid life that passed so near her, and gazed so kindly at her. Her heart was full of tenderness and anguish, and through the night she cried:

"Help me! Save me!"

All in a fever she got up and lit the lamp, and took pen and paper. She wrote to Christophe. Her illness was full upon her, or she would never even have thought of writing to him, so proud she was and timid. She did not know what she wrote. She was no longer mistress of herself. She called to him, and told him that she loved him. . . . In the middle of her letter she stopped, appalled. She tried to write it all over again: but her impulse was gone: her mind was a blank, and her head was aching: she had a horrible difficulty in finding words: she was utterly worn out. She was ashamed. . . . What was the good of it all? She knew perfectly well that she was trying to trick herself, and that she would never send the letter. . . . Even if she had wished to do so, how could she? She did not know Christophe's address. . . . Poor Christophe! And what could he do for her? Even if he knew all and were kind to her, what could he do? . . . It was too late! No, no: it was all in vain, the last dying struggle of a bird, blindly, desperately beating its wings. She must be resigned to it. . . .

So for a long time she sat there by the table, lost in thought, unable to move hand or foot. It was past midnight when she struggled to her feet—bravely. Mechanically she placed the loose sheets of her letter in one of her few books, for she had the strength neither to put them in order nor to tear them up. Then she went to bed, shivering and shaking with fever. The key to the riddle lay near at hand: she felt that the will of God was to be fulfilled.—And a great peace came upon her.

On Sunday morning when Olivier came he found Antoinette in bed, delirious. A doctor was called in. He said it was acute consumption.

Antoinette had known how serious her condition was: she had discovered the cause of the moral turmoil in herself which had so alarmed her. She had been dreadfully ashamed, and it was some consolation to her to think that not she herself but her illness was the cause of it. She had managed to take a few precautions and to burn her papers and to write a letter to Madame Nathan: she appealed to her kindness to look after

her brother during the first few weeks after her "death"—
(she dared not write the word). . . .

The doctor could do nothing: the disease was too far gone,
and Antoinette's constitution had been wrecked by the years of
hardship and unceasing toil.

Antoinette was quite calm. Since she had known that there
was no hope her agony and torment had left her. She lay
turning over in her mind all the trials and tribulations through
which she had passed: she saw that her work was done and her
dear Olivier saved: and she was filled with unutterable joy.
She said to herself:

"I have achieved that."

And then she turned in shame from her pride and said:

"I could have done nothing alone. God has given me His
aid."

And she thanked God that He had granted her life until she
had accomplished her task. There was a catch at her heart as
she thought that now she had to lay down her life: but she
dared not complain: that would have been to feel ingratitude
towards God, who might have called her away sooner. And
what would have happened if she had passed away a year
sooner?—She sighed, and humbled herself in gratitude.

In spite of her weakness and oppression she did not complain,—except when she was sleeping heavily, when every now
and then she moaned like a little child. She watched things and
people with a calm smile of resignation. It was always a joy
to her to see Olivier. She would move her lips to call him,
though she made no sound: she would want to hold his hand in
hers: she would bid him lay his head on the pillow near hers,
and then, gazing into his eyes, she would go on looking at him
in silence. At last she would raise herself up and hold his face
in her hands and say:

"Ah! Olivier! . . . Olivier! . . ."

She took the medal that she wore round her neck, and hung
it on her brother's. She commended her beloved Olivier to
the care of her confessor, her doctor, everybody. It seemed as

though she was to live henceforth in him, that, on the point of
death, she was taking refuge in his life, as upon some island
in uncharted seas. Sometimes she seemed to be uplifted by
a mystic exaltation of tenderness and faith, and she forgot her
illness, and sadness changed to joy in her,—a joy divine indeed
that shone upon her lips and in her eyes. Over and over again
she said:

"I am happy. . . ."

Her senses grew dim. In her last moments of consciousness
her lips moved and it seemed that she was repeating something to herself. Olivier went to her bedside and bent down
over her. She recognized him once more and smiled feebly up
at him: her lips went on moving and her eyes were filled with
tears. They could not make out what she was trying to say.
. . . But faintly Olivier heard her breathe the words of the
dear old song they used to love so much, the song she was always singing:

"*I will come again, my sweet and bonny, I will come again.*"

Then she relapsed into unconsciousness. So she passed away.

Unconsciously she had aroused a profound sympathy in
many people whom she did not even know: in the house in
which she lived she did not even know the names of the other
tenants. Olivier received expressions of sympathy from people
who were strangers to him. Antoinette was not taken to her
grave unattended as her mother had been. Her body was followed to the cemetery by friends and schoolfellows of her
brother, and members of the families whose children she had
taught, and people whom she had met without saying a word
of her own life or hearing a word from them, though they admired her secretly, knowing her devotion, and many of the
poor, and the housekeeper who had helped her, and even many
of the small tradesmen of the neighborhood. Madame Nathan
had taken Olivier under her wing on the day of his sister's
death, and she had carried him off in spite of himself, and done
her best to turn his thoughts away from his grief.

If it had come later in his life he could never have borne
up against such a catastrophe,—but now it was impossible for
him to succumb absolutely to his despair. He had just begun a
new life; he was living in a community, and had to live the
common life whatever he might be feeling. The full busy life
of the *École,* the intellectual pressure, the examinations, the
struggle for life, all kept him from withdrawing into himself:
he could not be alone. He suffered, but it proved his salvation.
A year earlier, or a few years earlier, he must have succumbed.

And yet he did as far as possible retire into isolation in
the memory of his sister. It was a great sorrow to him that he
could not keep the rooms where they had lived together: but
he had no money. He hoped that the people who seemed to
be interested in him would understand his distress at not being
able to keep the things that had been hers. But nobody seemed
to understand. He borrowed some money and made a little
more by private tuition and took an attic in which he stored all
that he could preserve of his sister's furniture: her bed, her
table, and her armchair. He made it the sanctuary of her
memory. He took refuge there whenever he was depressed.
His friends thought he was carrying on an intrigue. He would
stay there for hours dreaming of her with his face buried in his
hands: unhappily he had no portrait of her except a little photograph, taken when she was a child, of the two of them together.
He would talk to her and weep. . . . Where was she? Ah!
if she had been at the other end of the world, wherever she
might be and however inaccessible the spot,—with what great
joy and invincible ardor he would have rushed forth in search
of her, though a thousand sufferings lay in wait for him,
though he had to go barefoot, though he had to wander for
hundreds of years, if only it might be that every step would
bring him nearer to her! . . . Yes, even though there were
only one chance in a thousand of his ever finding her. . . .
But there was nothing. . . . Nowhere to go. . . . No way
of ever finding her again. . . . How utterly lonely he was
now! Now that she was no longer there to love and counsel

and console him, inexperienced and childish as he was, he was flung into the waters of life, to sink or swim! . . . He who has once had the happiness of perfect intimacy and boundless friendship with another human being has known the divinest of all joys,—a joy that will make him miserable for the remainder of his life. . . .

Nessun maggior dolore che ricordarsi del tempo felice nella miseria. . . .

For a weak and tender soul it is the greatest of misfortunes ever to have known the greatest happiness.

But though it is sad indeed to lose the beloved at the beginning of life, it is even more terrible later on when the springs of life are running dry. Olivier was young: and, in spite of his inborn pessimism, in spite of his misfortune, he had to live his life. As often seems to happen after the loss of those dear to us, it was as though when Antoinette passed away she had breathed part of her soul into her brother's life. And he believed it was so. Though he had not such faith as hers, yet he did arrive at a vague conviction that his sister was not dead, but lived on in him, as she had promised. There is a Breton superstition that those who die young are not dead, but stay and hover over the places where they lived until they have fulfilled the normal span of their existence.—So Antoinette lived out her life in Olivier.

He read through the papers he had found in her room. Unhappily she had burned most of them. Besides, she was not the sort of woman to keep notes and tallies of her inner life. She was too modest to uncloak her inmost thoughts in morbid babbling indiscretion. She only kept a little notebook which was almost unintelligible to anybody else—a bare record in which she had written down without remark certain dates, and certain small events in her daily life, which had given her joys and emotions, which she had no need to write down in detail to keep alive. Almost all these dates were connected with some event in Olivier's life. She had kept every letter he had ever written to her, without exception.—Alas! He had not been so careful: he had lost almost all the letters she had written to him. What need had he of letters? He thought he would have his sister always with him: that dear fount of tenderness seemed inexhaustible: he thought that he would always be able to quench his thirst of lips and heart at it: he had most prodigally squandered the love he had received, and now he was eager to gather up the smallest drops. . . . What was his emotion when, as he skimmed through one of Antoinette's books, he found these words written in pencil on a scrap of paper:

"Olivier, my dear Olivier! . . ."

He almost swooned. He sobbed and kissed the invisible lips that so spoke to him from the grave.—Thereafter he took down all her books and hunted through them page by page to see if she had not left some other words of him. He found the fragment of the letter to Christophe, and discovered the unspoken romance which had sprung to life in her: so for the first time he happed upon her emotional life, that he had never known in her and never tried to know: he lived through the last passionate days, when, deserted by himself, she had held out her arms to the unknown friend. She had never told him that she had seen Christophe before. Certain words in her letter revealed the fact that they had met in Germany. He understood that Christophe had been kind to Antoinette, in circumstances the details of which were unknown to him, and that Antoinette's feeling for the musician dated from that day, though she had kept her secret to the end.

Christophe, whom he loved already for the beauty of his art, now became unutterably dear to him. She had loved him: it seemed to Olivier that it was she whom he loved in Christophe. He moved heaven and earth to meet him. It was not an easy matter to trace him. After his rebuff Christophe had been lost in the wilderness of Paris: he had shunned all society and no one gave a thought to him.—After many months it chanced that Olivier met Christophe in the street: he was pale and sunken from the illness from which he had only just recovered. But Olivier had not the courage to stop him. He followed him home at a distance. He wanted to write to him, but could not screw himself up to it. What was there to say? Olivier was not alone: Antoinette was with him: her love, her modesty had become a part of him: the thought that his sister had loved Christophe made him as bashful in Christophe's presence as though he had been Antoinette. And yet how he longed to talk to him of her!—But he could not. Her secret was a seal upon his lips.

He tried to meet Christophe again. He went everywhere where he thought Christophe might be. He was longing to shake hands with him. And when he saw him he tried to hide so that Christophe should not see him.

At last Christophe saw him at the house of some mutual friends where they both happened to be one evening. Olivier stood far away from him and said nothing: but he watched him. And no doubt the spirit of Antoinette was hovering near Olivier that night: for Christophe saw her in Olivier's eyes: and it was her image, so suddenly evoked, that made him cross the room and go towards the unknown messenger, who, like a young Hermes, brought him the melancholy greeting of the blessed dead.

THE HOUSE

I

I HAVE a friend! . . . Oh! The delight of having found
a kindred soul to which to cling in the midst of torment,
a tender and sure refuge in which to breathe again while
the fluttering heart beats slower! No longer to be alone,
no longer never to unarm, no longer to stay on guard with
straining, burning eyes, until from sheer fatigue he should
fall into the hands of his enemies! To have a dear companion into whose hands all his life should be delivered—
the friend whose life was delivered into his! At last to
taste the sweetness of repose, to sleep while the friend watches,
watch while the friend sleeps. To know the joy of protecting
a beloved creature who should trust in him like a little child.
To know the greater joy of absolute surrender to that friend,
to feel that he is in possession of all secrets, and has power
over life and death. Aging, worn out, weary of the burden
of life through so many years, to find new birth and fresh
youth in the body of the friend, through his eyes to see the
world renewed, through his senses to catch the fleeting love-
liness of all things by the way, through his heart to enjoy
the splendor of living. . . . Even to suffer in his suffering.
. . . Ah! Even suffering is joy if it be shared!

I have a friend! . . . Away from me, near me, in me
always. I have my friend, and I am his. My friend loves
me. I am my friend's, the friend of my friend. Of our two
souls love has fashioned one.

Christophe's first thought, when he awoke the day after
the Roussins' party, was for Olivier Jeannin. At once he
felt an irresistible longing to see him again. He got up and

went out. It was not yet eight o'clock. It was a heavy and rather oppressive morning. An April day before its time: stormy clouds were hovering over Paris.

Olivier lived below the hill of Sainte-Geneviève, in a little street near the *Jardin des Plantes.* The house stood in the narrowest part of the street. The staircase led out of a dark yard, and was full of divers unpleasant smells. The stairs wound steeply up and sloped down towards the wall, which was disfigured with scribblings in pencil. On the third floor a woman, with gray hair hanging down, and in petticoat-bodice, gaping at the neck, opened the door when she heard footsteps on the stairs, and slammed it to when she saw Christophe. There were several flats on each landing, and through the ill-fitting doors Christophe could hear children romping and squalling. The place was a swarming heap of dull base creatures, living as it were on shelves, one above the other, in that low-storied house, built round a narrow, evil-smelling yard. Christophe was disgusted, and wondered what lusts and covetous desires could have drawn so many creatures to this place, far from the fields, where at least there is air enough for all, and what it could profit them in the end to be in the city of Paris, where all their lives they were condemned to live in such a sepulcher.

He reached Olivier's landing. A knotted piece of string was his bell-pull. Christophe tugged at it so mightily that at the noise several doors on the staircase were half opened. Olivier came to the door. Christophe was struck by the careful simplicity of his dress: and the neatness of it, which at any other time would have been little to his liking, was in that place an agreeable surprise: in such an atmosphere of foulness there was something charming and healthy about it. And at once he felt just as he had done the night before when he gazed into Olivier's clear, honest eyes. He held out his hand: but Olivier was overcome with shyness, and murmured:

"You. . . . You here!"

Christophe was engrossed in catching at the lovable quality of the man as it was revealed to him in that fleeting moment of embarrassment, and he only smiled in answer. He moved forward and forced Olivier backward, and entered the one room in which he both slept and worked. An iron bedstead stood against the wall near the window; Christophe noticed the pillows heaped up on the bolster. There were three chairs, a black-painted table, a small piano, bookshelves and books, and that was all. The room was cramped, low, ill-lighted: and yet there was in it a ray of the pure light that shone in the eyes of its owner. Everything was clean and tidy, as though a woman's hands had dealt with it: and a few roses in a vase brought spring-time into the room, the walls of which were decorated with photographs of old Florentine pictures.

"So. . . . You. . . . You have come to see me?" said Olivier warmly.

"Good Lord, I had to!" said Christophe. "You would never have come to me?"

"You think not?" replied Olivier.

Then, quickly:

"Yes, you are right. But it would not be for want of thinking of it."

"What would have stopped you?"

"Wanting to too much."

"That's a fine reason!"

"Yes. Don't laugh. I was afraid you would not want it as much as I."

"A lot that's worried me! I wanted to see you, and here I am. If it bores you, I shall know at once."

"You will have to have good eyes."

They smiled at each other.

Olivier went on:

"I was an ass last night. I was afraid I might have offended you. My shyness is absolutely a disease: I can't get a word out."

"I shouldn't worry about that. There are plenty of talkers

in your country: one is only too glad to meet a man who is silent occasionally, even though it be only from shyness and in spite of himself."

Christophe laughed and chuckled over his own gibe.

"Then you have come to see me because I can be silent?"

"Yes. For your silence, the sort of silence that is yours. There are all sorts: and I like yours, and that's all there is to say."

"But how could you sympathize with me? You hardly saw me."

"That's my affair. It doesn't take me long to make up my mind. When I see a face that I like in the crowd, I know what to do: I go after it: I simply have to know the owner of it."

"And don't you ever make mistakes when you go after them?"

"Often."

"Perhaps you have made a mistake this time."

"We shall see."

"Ah! In that case I'm done! You terrify me. If I think you are watching me, I shall lose what little wits I have."

With fond and eager curiosity Christophe watched the sensitive, mobile face, which blushed and went pale by turns. Emotion showed fleeting across it like the shadows of clouds on a lake.

"What a nervous youngster it is!" he thought. "He is like a woman."

He touched his knee.

"Come, come!" he said. "Do you think I should come to you with weapons concealed about me? I have a horror of people who practise their psychology on their friends. I only ask that we should both be open and sincere, and frankly and without shame, and without being afraid of committing ourselves finally to anything or of any sort of contradiction, be true to what we feel. I ask only the right to love now, and next minute, if needs must, to be out of love. There's loyalty and manliness in that, isn't there?"

Olivier gazed at him with serious eyes, and replied:

"No doubt. It is the more manly part, and you are strong enough. But I don't think I am."

"I'm sure you are," said Christophe; "but in a different way. And then, I've come just to help you to be strong, if you want to be so. For what I have just said gives me leave to go on and say, with more frankness than I should otherwise have had, that—without prejudice for to-morrow—I love you."

Olivier blushed hotly. He was struck dumb with embarrassment, and could not speak.

Christophe glanced round the room.

"It's a poor place you live in. Haven't you another room?"

"Only a lumber-room."

"Ugh! I can't breathe. How do you manage to live here?"

"One does it somehow."

"I couldn't—never."

Christophe unbuttoned his waistcoat and took a long breath.

Olivier went and opened the window wide.

"You must be very unhappy in a town, M. Krafft. But there's no danger of my suffering from too much vitality. I breathe so little that I can live anywhere. And yet there are nights in summer when even I am hard put to it to get through. I'm terrified when I see them coming. Then I stay sitting up in bed, and I'm almost stifled."

Christophe looked at the heap of pillows on the bed, and from them to Olivier's worn face: and he could see him struggling there in the darkness.

"Leave it," he said. "Why do you stay?"

Olivier shrugged his shoulders and replied carelessly:

"It doesn't matter where I live."

Heavy footsteps padded across the floor above them. In the

room below a shrill argument was toward. And always, without ceasing, the walls were shaken by the rumbling of the buses in the street.

"And the house!" Christophe went on. "The house reeking of filth, the hot dirtiness of it all, the shameful poverty—how can you bring yourself to come back to it night after night? Don't you lose heart with it all? I couldn't live in it for a moment. I'd rather sleep under an arch."

"Yes. I felt all that at first, and suffered. I was just as disgusted as you are. When I went for walks as a boy, the mere sight of some of the crowded dirty streets made me ill. They gave me all sorts of fantastic horrors, which I dared not speak of. I used to think: 'If there were an earthquake now, I should be dead, and stay here for ever and ever'; and that seemed to me the most appalling thing that could happen. I never thought that one day I should live in one of them of my own free-will, and that in all probability I shall die there. And then it became easier to put up with: it had to. It still revolts me: but I try not to think of it. When I climb the stairs I close my eyes, and stop my ears, and hold my nose, and shut off all my senses and withdraw utterly into myself. And then, over the roof there, I can see the tops of the branches of an acacia. I sit here in this corner so that I don't see anything else: and in the evening when the wind rustles through them I fancy that I am far away from Paris: and the mighty roar of a forest has never seemed so sweet to me as the gentle murmuring of those few frail leaves at certain moments."

"Yes," said Christophe. "I've no doubt that you are always dreaming; but it's all wrong to waste your fancy in such a struggle against the sordid things of life, when you might be using it in the creation of other lives."

"Isn't it the common lot? Don't you yourself waste energy in anger and bitter struggles?"

"That's not the same thing. It's natural to me: what I was born for. Look at my arms and hands! Fighting is the breath of life to me. But you haven't any too much strength: that's obvious."

Olivier looked sadly down at his thin wrists, and said:

" Yes. I am weak: I always have been. But what can I do? One must live? "

" How do you make your living? "

" I teach."

" Teach what? "

" Everything—Latin, Greek, history. I coach for degrees. And I lecture on Moral Philosophy at the Municipal School."

" Lecture on what? "

" Moral Philosophy."

" What in thunder is that? Do they teach morality in French schools? "

Olivier smiled:

" Of course."

" Is there enough in it to keep you talking for ten minutes? "

" I have to lecture for twelve hours a week."

" Do you teach them to do evil, then? "

" What do you mean? "

" There's no need for so much talk to find out what good is."

" Or to leave it undiscovered either."

" Good gracious, yes! Leave it undiscovered. There are worse ways of doing good than knowing nothing about it. Good isn't a matter of knowledge: it's a matter of action. It's only your neurasthenics who go haggling about morality: and the first of all moral laws is not to be neurasthenic. Rotten pedants! They are like cripples teaching people how to walk."

" But they don't do their talking for such as you. You *know:* but there are so many who do not know! "

" Well, let them crawl like children until they learn how to walk by themselves. But whether they go on two legs or on all fours, the first thing, the only thing you can ask is that they should walk somehow."

He was prowling round and round and up and down the room, though less than four strides took him across it. He stopped in front of the piano, opened it, turned over the pages of some music, touched the keys, and said:

" Play me something."

Olivier started.

" I ! " he said. " What an idea ! "

" Madame Roussin told me you were a good musician. Come: play me something."

" With you listening? Oh ! " he said, " I should die."

The sincerity and simplicity with which he spoke made Christophe laugh: Olivier, too, though rather bashfully.

" Well," said Christophe, " is that a reason for a Frenchman ? "

Olivier still drew back.

" But why? Why do you want me to ? "

" I'll tell you presently. Play ! "

" What ? "

" Anything you like."

Olivier sat down at the piano with a sigh, and, obedient to the imperious will of the friend who had sought him out, he began to play the beautiful *Adagio in B Minor* of Mozart. At first his fingers trembled so that he could hardly make them press down the keys: but he regained courage little by little: and, while he thought he was but repeating Mozart's utterance, he unwittingly revealed his inmost heart. Music is an indiscreet confidant: it betrays the most secret thoughts of its lovers to those who love it. Through the godlike scheme of the *Adagio* of Mozart Christophe could perceive the invisible lines of the character, not of Mozart, but of his new friend sitting there by the piano: the serene melancholy, the timid, tender smile of the boy, so nervous, so pure, so full of love, so ready to blush. But he had hardly reached the end of the air, the topmost point where the melody of sorrowful love ascends and snaps, when a sudden irrepressible feeling of shame and modesty overcame Olivier, so that he could not go on: his fingers would

not move, and his voice failed him. His hands fell by his side,
and he said:

"I can't play any more. . . ."

Christophe was standing behind him, and he stooped and
reached over him and finished the broken melody: then he
said:

"Now I know the music of your soul."

He held his hands, and stayed for a long time gazing into
his face. At last he said:

"How queer it is! . . . I have seen you before. . . . I
know you so well, and I have known you so long! . . ."

Olivier's lips trembled: he was on the point of speaking. But
he said nothing.

Christophe went on gazing at him for a moment or two
longer. Then he smiled and said no more, and went away.

He went down the stairs with his heart filled with joy. He
passed two ugly children going up, one with bread, the other
with a bottle of oil. He pinched their cheeks jovially. He
smiled at the scowling porter. When he reached the street he
walked along humming to himself until he came to the Luxembourg. He lay down on a seat in the shade, and closed his eyes.
The air was still and heavy: there were only a few passers-by.
Very faintly he could hear the irregular trickling of the fountain, and every now and then the scrunching of the gravel as
footsteps passed him by. Christophe was overcome with drowsiness, and he lay basking like a lizard in the sun: his face had
been out of the shadow of the trees for some time: but he could
not bring himself to stir. His thoughts wound about and about:
he made no attempt to hold and fix them: they were all steeped
in the light of happiness. The Luxembourg clock struck: he
did not listen to it: but, a moment later, he thought it must
have been striking twelve. He jumped up to realize that he had
been lounging for a couple of hours, had missed an appointment with Hecht, and wasted the whole morning. He laughed,
and went home whistling. He composed a *Rondo* in canon on

the cry of a peddler. Even sad melodies now took on the charm of the gladness that was in him. As he passed the laundry in his street, as usual, he glanced into the shop, and saw the little red-haired girl, with her dull complexion flushed with the heat, and she was ironing with her thin arms bare to the shoulder and her bodice open at the neck: and, as usual, she ogled him brazenly: for the first time he was not irritated by her eyes meeting his. He laughed once more. When he reached his room he was free of all the obsessions from which he had suffered. He flung his hat, coat, and vest in different directions, and sat down to work with an all-conquering zest. He gathered together all his scattered scraps of music, which were lying all over the room, but his mind was not in his work: he only read the script with his eyes: and a few minutes later he fell back into the happy somnolence that had been upon him in the Luxembourg Gardens; his head buzzed, and he could not think. Twice or thrice he became aware of his condition, and tried to shake it off: but in vain. He swore light-heartedly, got up, and dipped his head in a basin of cold water. That sobered him a little. He sat down at the table again, sat in silence, and smiled dreamily. He was wondering:

" What is the difference between that and love? "

Instinctively he had begun to think in whispers, as though he were ashamed. He shrugged his shoulders.

" There are not two ways of loving. . . . Or, rather, yes, there are two ways: there is the way of those who love with every fiber of their being, and the way of those who only give to love a part of their superfluous energy. God keep me from such cowardice of heart! "

He stopped in his thought, from a sort of shame and dread of following it any farther. He sat for a long time smiling at his inward dreams. His heart sang through the silence:

Du bist mein, und nun ist das Meine Meiner als jemals . . .

(" Thou art mine, and now I am mine, more mine than I have ever been. . . .")

He took a sheet of paper, and with tranquil ease wrote down the song that was in his heart.

They decided to take rooms together. Christophe wanted to take possession at once without worrying about the waste of half a quarter. Olivier was more prudent, though not less ardent in their friendship, and thought it better to wait until their respective tenancies had expired. Christophe could not understand such parsimony. Like many people who have no money, he never worried about losing it. He imagined that Olivier was even worse off than himself. One day when his friend's poverty had been brought home to him he left him suddenly and returned a few hours later in triumph with a few francs which he had squeezed in advance out of Hecht. Olivier blushed and refused. Christophe was put out and made to throw them to an Italian who was playing in the yard. Olivier withheld him. Christophe went away, apparently offended, but really furious with his own clumsiness to which he attributed Olivier's refusal. A letter from his friend brought balm to his wounds. Olivier could write what he could not express by word of mouth: he could tell of his happiness in knowing him and how touched he was by Christophe's offer of assistance. Christophe replied with a crazy, wild letter, rather like those which he wrote when he was fifteen to his friend Otto: it was full of *Gemüth* and blundering jokes: he made puns in French and German, and even translated them into music.

At last they went into their rooms. In the Montparnasse quarter, near the *Place Denfert,* on the fifth floor of an old house they had found a flat of three rooms and a kitchen, all very small, and looking on to a tiny garden inclosed by four high walls. From their windows they looked out over the opposite wall, which was lower than the rest, on to one of those large convent gardens which are still to be found in Paris, hidden and unknown. Not a soul was to be seen in the deserted avenues. The old trees, taller and more leafy than those in the Luxembourg Gardens, trembled in the sunlight: troops of birds sang: in the early dawn the blackbirds fluted, and then there came the riotously rhythmic chorus of the sparrows: and in summer in the evening the rapturous cries of the swifts cleaving the luminous air and skimming through the heavens. And at night, under the moon, like bubbles of air mounting to the surface of a pond, there came up the pearly notes of the toads. Almost they might have forgotten the surrounding presence of Paris but that the old house was perpetually shaken by the heavy vehicles rumbling by, as though the earth beneath were shivering in a fever.

One of the rooms was larger and finer than the rest, and there was a struggle between the friends as to who should not have it. They had to toss for it: and Christophe, who had made the suggestion, contrived not to win with a dexterity of which he found it hard to believe himself capable.

Then for the two of them there began a period of absolute happiness. Their happiness lay not in any one thing, but in all things at once: their every thought, their every act, were steeped in it, and it never left them for a moment.

During this honeymoon of their friendship, the first days of deep and silent rejoicing, known only to him "who in all the universe can call one soul his own" . . . *Ja, wer auch nur eine Seele sein nennt auf dem Erdenrund* . . . they hardly spoke to each other, they dared hardly breathe a word; it was enough for them to feel each other's nearness, to exchange a look, a word in token that their thoughts, after long periods of silence, still ran in the same channel. Without probing or inquiring, without even looking at each other, yet unceasingly they watched each other. Unconsciously the lover takes for model the soul of the beloved: so great is his desire to give no hurt, to be in all things as the beloved, that with mysterious and sudden intuition he marks the imperceptible movements in the depths of his soul. One friend to another is crystal-clear: they exchange entities. Their features are assimilated. Soul imitates soul,—until that day comes when deep-moving force, the spirit of the race, bursts his bonds and rends asunder the web of love in which he is held captive.

Christophe spoke in low tones, walked softly, tried hard to make no noise in his room, which was next to that of the silent Olivier: he was transfigured by his friendship: he had an expression of happiness, confidence, youth, such as he had never worn before. He adored Olivier. It would have been easy for the boy to abuse his power if he had not been so timorous in feeling that it was a happiness undeserved: for he thought himself much inferior to Christophe, who in his turn was no less humble. This mutual humility, the product of their great love for each other, was an added joy. It was a pure delight—even with the consciousness of unworthiness—for each to feel that he filled so great a room in the heart of his friend. Each to other they were tender and filled with gratitude.

Olivier had mixed his books with Christophe's: they made no distinction. When he spoke of them he did not say " *my* book," but " *our* book." He kept back only a few things from the common stock: those which had belonged to his sister or were bound up with her memory. With the quick perception of love Christophe was not slow to notice this: but he did not know the reason of it. He had never dared to ask Olivier about his family: he only knew that Olivier had lost his parents: and to the somewhat proud reserve of his affection, which forbade his prying into his friend's secrets, there was added a fear of calling to life in him the sorrows of the past. Though he might long to do so, yet he was strangely timid and never dared to look closely at the photographs on Olivier's desk, portraits of a lady and a gentleman stiffly posed, and a little girl of twelve with a great spaniel at her feet.

A few months after they had taken up their quarters Olivier caught cold and had to stay in bed. Christophe, who had become quite motherly, nursed him with fond anxiety: and the doctor, who, on examining Olivier, had found a little inflammation at the top of the lungs, told Christophe to smear the invalid's chest with tincture of iodine. As Christophe was gravely acquitting himself of the task he saw a confirmation medal hanging from Olivier's neck. He was familiar enough with Olivier to know that he was even more emancipated in matters of religion than himself. He could not refrain from showing his surprise. Olivier colored and said:

"It is a souvenir. My poor sister Antoinette was wearing it when she died."

Christophe trembled. The name of Antoinette struck him like a flash of lightning.

"Antoinette?" he said.

"My sister," said Olivier.

Christophe repeated:

"Antoinette . . . Antoinette Jeannin. . . . She was your sister? . . . But," he said, as he looked at the photograph on the desk, "she was quite a child when you lost her?"

Olivier smiled sadly.

"It is a photograph of her as a child," he said. "Alas! I have no other. . . . She was twenty-five when she left me."

"Ah!" said Christophe, who was greatly moved. "And she was in Germany, was she not?"

Olivier nodded.

Christophe took Olivier's hands in his.

"I knew her," he said.

"Yes, I know," replied Olivier.

And he flung his arms round Christophe's neck.

"Poor girl! Poor girl!" said Christophe over and over again.

They were both in tears.

Christophe remembered then that Olivier was ill. He tried to calm him, and made him keep his arms inside the bed, and tucked the clothes up round his shoulders, and dried his eyes for him, and then sat down by the bedside and looked long at him.

"You see," he said, "that is how I knew you. I recognized you at once, that first evening."

(It were hard to tell whether he was speaking of the present or the absent friend.)

"But," he went on a moment later, "you knew? . . . Why didn't you tell me?"

And through Olivier's eyes Antoinette replied:

"I could not tell you. You had to see it for yourself."

They said nothing for some time: then, in the silence of the night, Olivier, lying still in bed, in a low voice told Christophe, who held his hand, poor Antoinette's story:—but he did not tell him what he had no right to tell; the secret that she had kept locked,—the secret that perhaps Christophe knew already without needing to be told.

From that time on the soul of Antoinette was ever near them. When they were together she was with them. They had no need to think of her: every thought they shared was shared with her too. Her love was the meeting-place wherein their two hearts were united.

Often Olivier would conjure up the image of her: scraps of memory and brief anecdotes. In their fleeting light they gave a glimpse of her shy, gracious gestures, her grave, young smile, the pensive, wistful grace that was so natural to her. Christophe would listen without a word and let the light of the unseen friend pierce to his very soul. In obedience to the law of his own nature, which everywhere and always drank in life more greedily than any other, he would sometimes hear in Olivier's words depths of sound which Olivier himself could not hear: and more than Olivier he would assimilate the essence of the girl who was dead.

Instinctively he supplied her place in Olivier's life: and it was a touching sight to see the awkward German hap unwittingly on certain of the delicate attentions and little mothering ways of Antoinette. Sometimes he could not tell whether it was Olivier that he loved in Antoinette or Antoinette in Olivier. Sometimes on a tender impulse, without saying anything, he would go and visit Antoinette's grave and lay flowers on it. It was some time before Olivier had any idea of it. He did not discover it until one day when he found fresh flowers on the grave: but he had some difficulty in proving that it was Christophe who had laid them there. When he tried bashfully to speak about it Christophe cut him short roughly and abruptly. He did not want Olivier to know: and he stuck to it until one day when they met in the cemetery at Ivry.

Olivier, on his part, used to write to Christophe's mother without letting him know. He gave Louisa news of her son, and told her how fond he was of him and how he admired him. Louisa would send Olivier awkward, humble letters in which she thanked him profusely: she used always to write of her son as though he were a little boy.

After a period of fond semi-silence—"a delicious time of peace and enjoyment without knowing why,"—their tongues were loosed. They spent hours in voyages of discovery, each in the other's soul.

They were very different, but they were both pure metal. They loved each other because they were so different though so much the same.

Olivier was weak, delicate, incapable of fighting against difficulties. When he came up against an obstacle he drew back, not from fear, but something from timidity, and more from disgust with the brutal and coarse means he would have to employ to overcome it. He earned his living by giving classes, and writing art-books, shamefully underpaid, as usual, and occasionally articles for reviews, in which he never had a free hand and had to deal with subjects in which he was not greatly interested:—there was no demand for the things that did interest him: he was never asked for the sort of thing he could do best: he was a poet and was asked for criticism: he knew something about music and he had to write about painting: he knew quite well that he could only say mediocre things, which was just what people liked, for there he could speak to mediocre minds in a language which they could understand. He grew disgusted with it all and refused to write. He had no pleasure except in writing for certain obscure periodicals, which never paid anything, and, like so many other young men, he devoted his talents to them because they left him a free hand. Only in their pages could he publish what was worthy of publicity.

He was gentle, well-mannered, seemingly patient, though he was excessively sensitive. A harsh word drew blood: injustice overwhelmed him: he suffered both on his own account and for others. Certain crimes, committed ages ago, still had the power to rend him as though he himself had been their victim. He would go pale, and shudder, and be utterly miserable as he thought how wretched he must have been who suffered them, and how many ages cut him off from his sympathy. When any unjust deed was done before his eyes he would be wild with indignation and tremble all over, and sometimes become quite ill and lose his sleep. It was because he knew his weakness that he drew on his mask of calmness: for when he was angry he knew that he went beyond all limits and was apt to say unpardonable things. People were more resentful with him than with Christophe, who was always violent, because it seemed that in moments of anger Olivier, much more than Christophe, expressed exactly what he thought: and that was true. He judged men and women without Christophe's blind exaggeration, but lucidly and without his illusions. And that is precisely what people do pardon the least readily. In such cases he would say nothing and avoid discussion, knowing its futility. He had suffered from this restraint. He had suffered more from his timidity, which sometimes led him to betray his thoughts, or deprived him of the courage to defend his thoughts conclusively, and even to apologize for them, as had happened in the argument with Lucien Lévy-Cœur about Christophe. He had passed through many crises of despair before he had been able to strike a compromise between himself and the rest of the world. In his youth and budding manhood, when his nerves were not hopelessly out of order, he lived in a perpetual alternation of periods of exaltation and periods of depression which came and went with horrible suddenness. Just when

he was feeling most at his ease and even happy he was very
certain that sorrow was lying in wait for him. And suddenly
it would lay him low without giving any warning of its coming.
And it was not enough for him to be unhappy: he had to blame
himself for his unhappiness, and hold an inquisition into his
every word and deed, and his honesty, and take the side of other
people against himself. His heart would throb in his bosom, he
would struggle miserably, and he would scarcely be able to
breathe.—Since the death of Antoinette, and perhaps thanks to
her, thanks to the peace-giving light that issues from the beloved dead, as the light of dawn brings refreshment to the
eyes and soul of those who are sick, Olivier had contrived, if
not to break away from these difficulties, at least to be resigned
to them and to master them. Very few had any idea of his inward struggles. The humiliating secret was locked up in his
breast, all the immoderate excitement of a weak, tormented
body, surveyed serenely by a free and keen intelligence which
could not master it, though it was never touched by it,—
*" the central peace which endures amid the endless agitation of
the heart."*

Christophe marked it. This it was that he saw in Olivier's
eyes. Olivier had an intuitive perception of the souls of
men, and a mind of a wide, subtle curiosity that was open to
everything, denied nothing, hated nothing, and contemplated
the world and things with generous sympathy: that freshness
of outlook, which is a priceless gift, granting the power to taste
with a heart that is always new the eternal renewal and re-birth.
In that inward universe, wherein he knew himself to be free,
vast, sovereign, he could forget his physical weakness and
agony. There was even a certain pleasure in watching from
a great height, with ironic pity, that poor suffering body which
seemed always so near the point of death. So there was no
danger of his clinging to *his* life, and only the more passionately
did he hug life itself. Olivier translated into the region of
love and mind all the forces which in action he had abdicated.
He had not enough vital sap to live by his own substance,

He was as ivy: it was needful for him to cling. He was never so rich as when he gave himself. His was a womanish soul with its eternal need of loving and being loved. He was born for Christophe, and Christophe for him. Such are the aristocratic and charming friends who are the escorts of the great artists and seem to have come to flower in the lives of their mighty souls: Beltraffio, the friend of Leonardo: Cavalliere of Michael Angelo: the gentle Umbrians, the comrades of young Raphael: Aërt van Gelder, who remained faithful to Rembrandt in his poor old age. They have not the greatness of the masters: but it is as though all the purity and nobility of the masters in their friends were raised to a yet higher spiritual power. They are the ideal companions for men of genius.

Their friendship was profitable to both of them. Love lends wings to the soul. The presence of the beloved friend gives all its worth to life: a man lives for his friend and for his sake defends his soul's integrity against the wearing force of time.

Each enriched the other's nature. Olivier had serenity of mind and a sickly body. Christophe had mighty strength and a stormy soul. They were in some sort like a blind man and a cripple. Now that they were together they felt sound and strong. Living in the shadow of Christophe Olivier recovered his joy in the light: Christophe transmitted to him something of his abounding vitality, his physical and moral robustness, which, even in sorrow, even in injustice, even in hate, inclined to optimism. He took much more than he gave, in obedience to the law of genius, which gives in vain, but in love always takes more than it gives, *quia nominor leo,* because it is genius, and genius half consists in the instinctive absorption of all that is great in its surroundings and making it greater still. The vulgar saying has it that riches go to the rich. Strength goes to the strong. Christophe fed on Olivier's ideas: he impregnated himself with his intellectual calmness and mental detachment, his lofty outlook, his silent understanding and mastery of things. But when they were transplanted into him, the richer soil, the virtues of his friend grew with a new and other energy.

They both marveled at the things they discovered in each other. There were so many things to share! Each brought vast treasures of which till then he had never been conscious: the moral treasure of his nation: Olivier the wide culture and the psychological genius of France: Christophe the innate music of Germany and his intuitive knowledge of nature.

Christophe could not understand how Olivier could be a Frenchman. His friend was so little like all the Frenchmen he had met! Before he found Olivier he had not been far from taking Lucien Lévy-Cœur as the type of the modern French mind, Lévy-Cœur who was no more than the caricature of it. And now through Olivier he saw that there might be in Paris minds just as free, more free indeed than that of Lucien Lévy-Cœur, men who remained as pure and stoical as any in Europe. Christophe tried to prove to Olivier that he and his sister could not be altogether French.

"My poor dear fellow," said Olivier, "what do you know of France?"

Christophe avowed the trouble he had taken to gain some knowledge of the country: he drew up a list of all the Frenchmen he had met in the circle of the Stevens and the Roussins: Jews, Belgians, Luxemburgers, Americans, Russians, Levantines, and here and there a few authentic Frenchmen.

"Just what I was saying," replied Olivier. "You haven't seen a single Frenchman. A group of debauchees, a few beasts of pleasure, who are not even French, men-about-town, politicians, useless creatures, all the fuss and flummery which passes over and above the life of the nation without even touching it. You have only seen the swarms of wasps attracted by a fine autumn and the rich meadows. You haven't noticed the busy hives, the industrious city, the thirst for knowledge."

"I beg pardon," said Christophe, "I've come across your intellectual élite as well."

"What? A few dozen men of letters? They're a fine lot!

Nowadays when science and action play so great a part literature has become superficial, no more than the bed where the thought of the people sleeps. And in literature you have only come across the theater, the theater of luxury, an international kitchen where dishes are turned out for the wealthy customers of the cosmopolitan hotels. The theaters of Paris? Do you think a working-man even knows what is being done in them? Pasteur did not go to them ten times in all his life! Like all foreigners you attach an exaggerated importance to our novels, and our boulevard plays, and the intrigues of our politicians. . . . If you like I will show you women who never read novels, girls in Paris who have never been to the theater, men who have never bothered their heads about politics,—yes, even among our intellectuals. You have not come across either our men of science or our poets. You have not discovered the solitary artists who languish in silence, nor the burning flame of our revolutionaries. You have not seen a single great believer, or a single great skeptic. As for the people, we won't talk of them. Outside the poor woman who looked after you, what do you know of them? Where have you had a chance of seeing them? How many Parisians have you met who have lived higher than the second or third floor? If you do not know these people, you do not know France. You know nothing of the brave true hearts, the men and women living in poor lodgings, in the garrets of Paris, in the dumb provinces, men and women who, through a dull, drab life, think grave thoughts, and live in daily sacrifice,—the little Church, which has always existed in France—small in numbers, great in spirit, almost unknown, having no outward or apparent force of action, though it is the very force of France, that might which endures in silence, while the so-called élite rots away and springs to life again unceasingly. . . . You are amazed when you find a Frenchman who lives not for the sake of happiness, happiness at all costs, but to accomplish or to serve his faith? There are thousands of men like myself, men more worthy than myself, more pious, more humble, men who to their dying day live un-

failingly to serve an ideal, a God, who vouchsafes them no reply
You know nothing of the thrifty, methodical, industrious, tranquil middle-class living with a quenchless dormant flame in their
hearts—the people betrayed and sacrificed who in old days defended 'my country' against the selfish arrogance of the
great, the blue-eyed ancient race of Vauban. You do not know
the people, you do not know the élite. Have you read a single
one of the books which are our faithful friends, the companions
who support us in our lives? Do you even know of the existence of our young reviews in which such great faith and
devotion are expressed? Have you any idea of the men of
moral might and worth who are as the sun to us, the sun whose
voiceless light strikes terror to the army of the hypocrites?
They dare not make a frontal attack: they bow before them,
the better to betray them. The hypocrite is a slave, and there
is no slave but he has a master. You know only the slaves:
you know nothing of the masters. . . . You have watched
our struggles and they have seemed to you brutish and un-
meaning because you have not understood their aim. You
see the shadow, the reflected light of day: you have never seen
the inward day, our age-old immemorial spirit. Have you ever
tried to perceive it? Have you ever heard of our heroic deeds
from the Crusades to the Commune? Have you ever seen and
felt the tragedy of the French spirit? Have you ever stood at
the brink of the abyss of Pascal? How dare you slander a people who for more than a thousand years have been living in
action and creation, a people that has graven the world in its
own image through Gothic art, and the seventeenth century,
and the Revolution,—a people that has twenty times passed
through the ordeal of fire, and plunged into it again, and twenty
times has come to life again and never yet has perished! . . .
—You are all the same. All your countrymen who come
among us see only the parasites who suck our blood, literary,
political, and financial adventurers, with their minions and
their hangers-on and their harlots: and they judge France by
these wretched creatures who prey on her. Not one of you has

any idea of the real France living under oppression, or of the reserve of vitality in the French provinces, or of the great mass of the people who go on working heedless of the uproar and pother made by their masters of a day. . . . Yes: it is only natural that you should know nothing of all this: I do not blame you: how could you? Why, France is hardly at all known to the French. The best of us are bound down and held captive to our native soil. . . . No one will ever know all that we have suffered, we who have guarded as a sacred charge the light in our hearts which we have received from the genius of our race, to which we cling with all our might, desperately defending it against the hostile winds that strive blusteringly to snuff it out;—we are alone and in our nostrils stinks the pestilential atmosphere of these harpies who have swarmed about our genius like a thick cloud of flies, whose hideous grubs gnaw at our minds and defile our hearts:—we are betrayed by those whose duty it is to defend us, our leaders, our idiotic and cowardly critics, who fawn upon the enemy, to win pardon for being of our race:—we are deserted by the people who give no thought to us and do not even know of our existence. . . . By what means can we make ourselves known to them? We cannot reach them. . . . Ah! that is the hardest thing of all! We know that there are thousands of men in France who all think as we do, we know that we speak in their name, and we cannot gain a hearing! Everything is in the hands of the enemy: newspapers, reviews, theaters. . . . The Press scurries away from ideas or admits them only as an instrument of pleasure or a party weapon. The cliques and coteries will only suffer us to break through on condition that we degrade ourselves. We are crushed by poverty and overwork. The politicians, pursuing nothing but wealth, are only interested in that section of the public which they can buy. The middle-class is selfish and indifferent, and unmoved sees us perish. The people know nothing of our existence: even those who are fighting the same fight like us are cut off by silence and do not know that we exist, and we do not know that they exist. . . .

Ill-omened Paris! No doubt good also has come of it—by
gathering together all the forces of the French mind and genius.
But the evil it has done is at least equal to the good: and in a
time like the present the good quickly turns to evil. A pseudo-
élite fastens on Paris and blows the loud trumpet of publicity
and the voices of all the rest of France are drowned. More
than that: France herself is deceived by it: she is scared and
silent and fearfully locks away her own ideas. . . . There
was a time when it hurt me dreadfully. But now, Christophe, I
can bear it calmly. I know and understand my own strength
and the might of my people. We must wait until the flood dies
down. It cannot touch or change the bed-rock of France. I
will make you feel that bed-rock under the mud that is borne
onward by the flood. And even now, here and there, there are
lofty peaks appearing above the waters. . . ."

Christophe discovered the mighty power of idealism which
animated the French poets, musicians, and men of science of
his time. While the temporary masters of the country with
their coarse sensuality drowned the voice of the French genius,
it showed itself too aristocratic to vie with the presumptuous
shouts of the rabble and sang on with burning ardor in its own
praise and the praise of its God. It was as though in its desire
to escape the revolting uproar of the outer world it had with-
drawn to the farthest refuge in the innermost depths of its
castle-keep.

The poets—that is, those only who were worthy of that
splendid name, so bandied by the Press and the Academies
and doled out to divers windbags greedy of money and flattery—
the poets, despising impudent rhetoric and that slavish realism
which nibbles at the surface of things without penetrating to
reality, had intrenched themselves in the very center of the
soul, in a mystic vision into which was drawn the universe of
form and idea, like a torrent falling into a lake, there to take
on the color of the inward life. The very intensity of this
idealism, which withdrew into itself to recreate the universe,
made it inaccessible to the mob. Christophe himself did not

understand it at first. The transition was too abrupt after the market-place. It was as though he had passed from a furious rush and scramble in the hot sunlight into silence and the night. His ears buzzed. He could see nothing. At first, with his ardent love of life, he was shocked by the contrast. Outside was the roaring of the rushing streams of passion overturning France and stirring all humanity. And at the first glance there was not a trace of it in this art of theirs. Christophe asked Olivier:

"You have been lifted to the stars and hurled down to the depths of hell by your Dreyfus affair. Where is the poet in whose soul the height and depth of it were felt? Now, at this very moment, in the souls of your religious men and women there is the mightiest struggle there has been for centuries between the authority of the Church and the rights of conscience. Where is the poet in whose soul this sacred agony is reflected? The working classes are preparing for war, nations are dying, nations are springing to new life, the Armenians are massacred, Asia, awaking from its sleep of a thousand years, hurls down the Muscovite colossus, the keeper of the keys of Europe: Turkey, like Adam, opens its eyes on the light of day: the air is conquered by man: the old earth cracks under our feet and opens: it devours a whole people. . . . All these prodigies, accomplished in twenty years, enough to supply material for twenty *Iliads:* but where are they, where shall their fiery traces be found in the books of your poets? Are they of all men unable to see the poetry of the world?"

"Patience, my friend, patience!" replied Olivier. "Be silent, say nothing, listen. . . ."

Slowly the creaking of the axle-tree of the world died away and the rumbling over the stones of the heavy car of action was lost in the distance. And there arose the divine song of silence. . . .

The hum of bees, and the perfume of the limes. . . .
The wind,
With his golden lips kissing the earth of the plains. . . .
The soft sound of the rain and the scent of the roses.

There rang out the hammer and chisel of the poets carving the sides of a vase with

The fine majesty of simple things,

solemn, joyous life,

With its flutes of gold and flutes of ebony,

religious joy, faith welling up like a fountain of souls

For whom the very darkness is clear, . . .

and great sweet sorrow, giving comfort and smiling,

*With her austere face from which there shines
A clearness beyond nature, . . .*

and

Death serene with her great, soft eyes.

A symphony of harmonious and pure voices. Not one of them had the full sonorousness of such national trumpets as were Corneille and Hugo: but how much deeper and more subtle in expression was their music! The richest music in Europe of to-day.

Olivier said to Christophe, who was silent:

"Do you understand now?"

Christophe in his turn bade him be silent. In spite of himself, and although he preferred more manly music, yet he drank in the murmuring of the woods and fountains of the soul which came whispering to his ears. Amid the passing struggles of the nations they sang the eternal youth of the world, the

Sweet goodness of Beauty.

While humanity,

*Screaming with terror and yelping its complaint
Marched round and round a barren gloomy field,*

while millions of men and women wore themselves out in wrangling for the bloody rags of liberty, the fountains and the woods sang on:

"Free! . . . Free! . . . *Sanctus, Sanctus. . . .*"

And yet they slept not in any dream selfishly serene. In the choir of the poets there were not wanting tragic voices: voices of pride, voices of love, voices of agony.

A blind hurricane, mad, intoxicated

With its own rough force or gentleness profound,

tumultuous forces, the epic of the illusions of those who sing the wild fever of the crowd, the conflicts of human gods, the breathless toilers,

Faces inky black and golden peering through darkness and
*   mist,*
Muscular backs stretching, or suddenly crouching
Round mighty furnaces and gigantic anvils . . .

forging the City of the Future.

In the flickering light and shadow falling on the glaciers of the mind there was the heroic bitterness of those solitary souls which devour themselves with desperate joy.

Many of the characteristics of these idealists seemed to the German more German than French. But all of them had the love for the " fine speech of France " and the sap of the myths of Greece ran through their poetry. Scenes of France and daily life were by some hidden magic transformed in their eyes into visions of Attica. It was as though antique souls had come to life again in these twentieth-century Frenchmen, and longed to fling off their modern garments to appear again in their lovely nakedness.

Their poetry as a whole gave out the perfume of a rich civilization that has ripened through the ages, a perfume such as could not be found anywhere else in Europe. It were impossible to forget it once it had been breathed. It attracted foreign artists from every country in the world. They became French poets, almost bigotedly French: and French classical art had no more fervent disciples than these Anglo-Saxons and Flemings and Greeks.

Christophe, under Olivier's guidance, was impregnated with
the pensive beauty of the Muse of France, while in his heart
he found the aristocratic lady a little too intellectual for his
liking, and preferred a pretty girl of the people, simple, healthy,
robust, who thinks and argues less, but is more concerned with
love.

The same *odor di bellezza* arose from all French art, as
the scent of ripe strawberries and raspberries ascends from
autumn woods warmed by the sun.   French music was like one
of those little strawberry plants, hidden in the grass, the scent
of which sweetens all the air of the woods.   At first Christophe had passed it by without seeing it, for in his own country
he had been used to whole thickets of music, much fuller and
bearing more brilliant fruits.   But now the delicate perfume
made him turn: with Olivier's help among the stones and
brambles and dead leaves which usurped the name of music,
he discovered the subtle and ingenuous art of a handful of
musicians.   Amid the marshy fields and the factory chimneys
of democracy, in the heart of the Plaine-Saint-Denis, in a little
magic wood fauns were dancing blithely.   Christophe was
amazed to hear the ironic and serene notes of their flutes which
were like nothing he had ever heard:

> " *A little reed sufficed for me*
> *To make the tall grass quiver,*
> *And all the meadow,*
> *The willows sweet,*
> *And the singing stream also :*
> *A little reed sufficed for me*
> *To make the forest sing.*"

Beneath the careless grace and the seeming dilettantism of
their little piano pieces, and songs, and French chamber-music,
which German art never deigned to notice, while Christophe
himself had hitherto failed to see the poetic accomplishment of
it all, he now began to see the fever of renovation, and the
uneasiness,—unknown on the other side of the Rhine,—with

which French musicians were seeking in the untilled fields of their art the germs from which the future might grow. While German musicians sat stolidly in the encampments of their forebears, and arrogantly claimed to stay the evolution of the world at the barrier of their past victories, the world was moving onwards: and in the van the French plunged onward to discovery: they explored the distant realms of art, dead suns and suns lit up once more, and vanished Greece, and the Far East, after its age-long slumber, once more opening its slanting eyes, full of vasty dreams, upon the light of day. In the music of the West, run off into channels by the genius of order and classic reason, they opened up the sluices of the ancient fashions: into their Versailles pools they turned all the waters of the universe: popular melodies and rhythms, exotic and antique scales, new or old beats and intervals. Just as, before them, the impressionist painters had opened up a new world to the eyes,—Christopher Columbuses of light,—so the musicians were rushing on to the conquest of the world of Sound; they pressed on into mysterious recesses of the world of Hearing: they discovered new lands in that inward ocean. It was more than probable that they would do nothing with their conquests. As usual the French were the harbingers of the world.

Christophe admired the initiative of their music born of yesterday and already marching in the van of art. What valiance there was in the elegant tiny little creature! He found indulgence for the follies that he had lately seen in her. Only those who attempt nothing never make mistakes. But error struggling on towards the living truth is more fruitful and more blessed than dead truth.

Whatever the results, the effort was amazing. Olivier showed Christophe the work done in the last thirty-five years, and the amount of energy expended in raising French music from the void in which it had slumbered before 1870: no symphonic school, no profound culture, no traditions, no masters, no public: the whole reduced to poor Berlioz, who died of suf-

focation and weariness. And now Christophe felt a great respect for those who had been the laborers in the national revival: he had no desire now to jeer at their esthetic narrowness
or their lack of genius. They had created something much
greater than music: a musical people. Among all the great
toilers who had forged the new French music one man was especially dear to him: César Franck, who died without seeing the
victory for which he had paved the way, and yet, like old Schütz,
through the darkest years of French art, had preserved intact
the treasure of his faith and the genius of his race. It was
a moving thing to see: amid pleasure-seeking Paris, the angelic
master, the saint of music, in a life of poverty and work
despised, preserving the unimpeachable serenity of his patient
soul, whose smile of resignation lit up his music in which is
such great goodness.

To Christophe, knowing nothing of the depths of the life of
France, this great artist, adhering to his faith in the midst
of a country of atheists, was a phenomenon, almost a miracle.

But Olivier would gently shrug his shoulders and ask if
any other country in Europe could show a painter so wholly
steeped in the spirit of the Bible as François Millet;—a man
of science more filled with burning faith and humility than the
clear-sighted Pasteur, bowing down before the idea of the infinite, and, when that idea possessed his mind, " in bitter agony "
—as he himself has said—" praying that his reason might be
spared, so near it was to toppling over into the sublime madness of Pascal." Their deep-rooted Catholicism was no more
a bar in the way of the heroic realism of the first of these two
men, than of the passionate reason of the other, who, sure of
foot and not deviating by one step, went his way through " the
circles of elementary nature, the great night of the infinitely
little, the ultimate abysses of creation, in which life is born."
It was among the people of the provinces, from which they
sprang, that they had found this faith, which is for ever brooding on the soil of France, while in vain do windy demagogues

struggle to deny it. Olivier knew well that faith: it had lived in his own heart and mind.

He revealed to Christophe the magnificent movement towards a Catholic revival, which had been going on for the last twenty-five years, the mighty effort of the Christian idea in France to wed reason, liberty, and life: the splendid priests who had the courage, as one of their number said, "to have themselves baptized as men," and were claiming for Catholicism the right to understand everything and to join in every honest idea: for "every honest idea, even when it is mistaken, is sacred and divine": the thousands of young Catholics banded by the generous vow to build a Christian Republic, free, pure, in brotherhood, open to all men of good-will: and, in spite of the odious attacks, the accusations of heresy, the treachery on all sides, right and left,—(especially on the right),—which these great Christians had to suffer, the intrepid little legion advancing towards the rugged defile which leads to the future, serene of front, resigned to all trials and tribulations, knowing that no enduring edifice can be built, except it be welded together with tears and blood.

The same breath of living idealism and passionate liberalism brought new life to the other religions in France. The vast slumbering bodies of Protestantism and Judaism were thrilling with new life. All in generous emulation had set themselves to create the religion of a free humanity which should sacrifice neither its power for reason, nor its power for enthusiasm.

This religious exaltation was not the privilege of the religious: it was the very soul of the revolutionary movement. There it assumed a tragic character. Till now Christophe had only seen the lowest form of socialism,—that of the politicians who dangled in front of the eyes of their famished constituents the coarse and childish dreams of Happiness, or, to be frank, of universal Pleasure, which Science in the hands of Power could, according to them, procure. Against such revolting optimism Christophe saw the furious mystic reaction of the élite arise to lead the Syndicates of the working-classes on to battle. It

was a summons to " war, which engenders the sublime," to heroic
war " which alone can give the dying worlds a goal, an aim, an
ideal." These great Revolutionaries, spitting out such
" bourgeois, peddling, peace-mongering, English " socialism,
set up against it a tragic conception of the universe, " whose
law is antagonism," since it lives by sacrifice, perpetual sacrifice,
eternally renewed.—If there was reason to doubt that the army,
which these leaders urged on to the assault upon the old world,
could understand such warlike mysticism, which applied both
Kant and Nietzsche to violent action, nevertheless it was a stirring sight to see the revolutionary aristocracy, whose blind pessimism, and furious desire for heroic life, and exalted faith in
war and sacrifice, were like the militant religious ideal of some
Teutonic Order or the Japanese Samurai.

And yet they were all Frenchmen: they were of a French
stock whose characteristics have endured unchanged for centuries. Seeing with Olivier's eyes Christophe marked them in
the tribunes and proconsuls of the Convention, in certain of the
thinkers and men of action and French reformers of the *Ancien
Régime*. Calvinists, Jansenists, Jacobins, Syndicalists, in all
there was the same spirit of pessimistic idealism, struggling
against nature, without illusions and without loss of courage:—
the iron bands which uphold the nation.

Christophe drank in the breath of these mystic struggles, and
he began to understand the greatness of that fanaticism, into
which France brought uncompromising faith and honesty, such
as were absolutely unknown to other nations more familiar
with *combinazioni*. Like all foreigners it had pleased him at
first to be flippant about the only too obvious contradiction between the despotic temper of the French and the magic formula,
which their Republic wrote up on the walls of their buildings.
Now for the first time he began to grasp the meaning of the
bellicose Liberty which they adored as the terrible sword of
Reason. No: it was not for them, as he had thought, mere
sounding rhetoric and vague ideology. Among a people for
whom the demands of reason transcend all others the fight for

reason dominated every other. What did it matter whether the fight appeared absurd to nations who called themselves practical? To eyes that see deeply it is no less vain to fight for empire, or money, or the conquest of the world: in a million years there will be nothing left of any of these things. But if it is the fierceness of the fight that gives its worth to life, and uplifts all the living forces to the point of sacrifice to a superior Being, then there are few struggles that do more honor life than the eternal battle waged in France for or against reason. And for those who have tasted the bitter savor of it the much-vaunted apathetic tolerance of the Anglo-Saxons is dull and unmanly. The Anglo-Saxons paid for it by finding elsewhere an outlet for their energy. Their energy is not in their tolerance, which is only great when, between factions, it becomes heroism. In Europe of to-day it is most often indifference, want of faith, want of vitality. The English, adapting a saying of Voltaire, are fain to boast that " diversity of belief has produced more tolerance in England " than the Revolution has done in France.—The reason is that there is more faith in the France of the Revolution than in all the creeds of England.

From the circle of brass of militant idealism and the battles of Reason,—like Virgil leading Dante, Olivier led Christophe by the hand to the summit of the mountain where, silent and serene, dwelt the small band of the elect of France who were really free.

Nowhere in the world are there men more free. They have the serenity of a bird soaring in the still air. On such a height the air was so pure and rarefied that Christophe could hardly breathe. There he met artists who claimed the absolute and limitless liberty of dreams,—men of unbridled subjectivity, like Flaubert, despising " the poor beasts who believe in the reality of things ":—thinkers, who, with supple and many-sided minds, emulating the endless flow of moving things, went on " ceaselessly trickling and flowing," staying nowhere, nowhere coming in contact with stubborn earth or rock, and " depicted not the essence of life, but the *passage*," as Montaigne said, " the eternal passage, from day to day, from minute to minute ";— men of science who knew the emptiness and void of the universe, wherein man has builded his idea, his God, his art, his science, and went on creating the world and its laws, that vivid day's dream. They did not demand of science either rest, or happiness, or even truth:—for they doubted whether it were attainable: they loved it for itself, because it was beautiful, because it alone was beautiful, and it alone was real. On the topmost pinnacles of thought these men of science, passionately Pyrrhonistic, indifferent to all suffering, all deceit, almost indifferent to reality, listened, with closed eyes, to the silent music of souls, the delicate and grand harmony of numbers and forms. These great mathematicians, these free philosophers,— the most rigorous and positive minds in the world,—had reached the uttermost limit of mystic ecstasy: they created a void about themselves, they hung over the abyss, they were drunk with its dizzy depths: into the boundless night with joy sublime they flashed the lightnings of thought.

Christophe leaned forward and tried to look over as they did: and his head swam. He who thought himself free because he had broken away from all laws save those of his own conscience, now became fearfully conscious of how little he was free compared with these Frenchmen who were emancipated from every absolute law of mind, from every categorical imperative, from every reason for living. Why, then, did they live?

" For the joy of being free," replied Olivier.

But Christophe, who was unsteadied by such liberty, thought regretfully of the mighty spirit of discipline and German authoritarianism: and he said:

" Your joy is a snare, the dream of an opium-smoker. You make yourselves drunk with liberty, and forget life. Absolute liberty means madness to the mind, anarchy to the State . . . Liberty! What man is free in this world? What man in your

Republic is free?—Only the knaves. You, the best of the nation, are stifled. You can do nothing but dream. Soon you will not be able even to dream."

"No matter!" said Olivier. "My poor dear Christophe, you cannot know the delight of being free. It is worth while paying for it with so much danger, and suffering, and even death. To be free, to feel that every mind about you—yes, even the knave's—is free, is a delicious pleasure which it is impossible to express: it is as though your soul were soaring through the infinite air. It could not live otherwise. What should I do with the security you offer me, and your order and your impeccable discipline, locked up in the four walls of your Imperial barracks? I should die of suffocation. Air! give me air, more and more of it! Liberty, more and more of that!"

"There must be law in the world," replied Christophe. "Sooner or later the master cometh."

But Olivier laughed and reminded Christophe of the saying of old Pierre de l'Estoile:

It is as little in the power of all the
dominions of the earth to curb the French
liberty of speech, as
to bury the sun in the earth
or to shut it up
inside a
hole.

Gradually Christophe grew accustomed to the air of boundless liberty. From the lofty heights of French thought, where those minds dream that are all light, he looked down upon the slopes of the mountain at his feet, where the heroic elect, fighting for a living faith, whatever faith it be, struggle eternally to reach the summit:—those who wage the holy war against ignorance, disease, and poverty: the fever of invention, the mental delirium of the modern Prometheus and Icarus conquering the light and marking out roads in the air: the

Titanic struggle between Science and Nature, being tamed;—
lower down, the little silent band, the men and women of good
faith, those brave and humble hearts, who, after a thousand
efforts, have climbed half-way, and can climb no farther, being
held bound in a dull and difficult existence, while in secret
they burn away in obscure devotion:—lower still, at the foot
of the mountain, in a narrow gorge between rocky crags, the
endless battle, the fanatics of abstract ideas and blind instincts,
fiercely wrestling, with never a suspicion that there may be
something beyond, above the wall of rocks which hems them in:
—still lower, swamps and brutish beasts wallowing in the mire.
—And everywhere, scattered about the sides of the mountain,
the fresh flowers of art, the scented strawberry-plants of music,
the song of the streams and the poet birds.

And Christophe asked Olivier:

"Where are your people? I see only the elect, all sorts, good
and bad."

Olivier replied:

"The people? They are tending their gardens. They never
bother about us. Every group and faction among the elect
strives to engage their attention. They pay no heed to any
one. There was a time when it amused them to listen to the
humbug of the political mountebanks. But now they never
worry about it. There are several millions who do not even
make use of their rights as electors. The parties may break
each other's heads as much as they like, and the people don't
care one way or another so long as they don't trample the crops
in their wrangling: if that happens then they lose their tempers,
and smash the parties indiscriminately. They do not act: they
react in one way or another against all the exaggerations which
disturb their work and their rest. Kings, Emperors, republics,
priests, Freemasons, Socialists, whatever their leaders may be,
all that they ask of them is to be protected against the great
common dangers: war, riots, epidemics,—and, for the rest, to be
allowed to go on tending their gardens. When all is said and
done they think:

" ' Why won't these people leave us in peace? '

" But the politicians are so stupid that they worry the people, and won't leave off until they are pitched out with a fork,—as will happen some day to our members of Parliament. There was a time when the people were embarked upon great enterprises. Perhaps that will happen again, although they sowed their wild oats long ago: in any case their embarkations are never for long: very soon they return to their age-old companion: the earth. It is the soil which binds the French to France, much more than the French. There are so many different races who for centuries have been tilling that brave soil side by side, that it is the soil which unites them, the soil which is their love. Through good times and bad they cultivate it unceasingly: and it is all good to them, even the smallest scrap of ground."

Christophe looked down. As far as he could see, along the road, around the swamps, on the slopes of rocky hills, over the battlefields and ruins of action, over the mountains and plains of France, all was cultivated and richly bearing: it was the great garden of European civilization. Its incomparable charm lay no less in the good fruitful soil than in the blind labors of an indefatigable people, who for centuries have never ceased to till and sow and make the land ever more beautiful.

A strange people! They are always called inconstant: but nothing in them changes. Olivier, looking backward, saw in Gothic statuary all the types of the provinces of to-day: and so in the drawings of a Clouet and a Dumoustier, the weary ironical faces of worldly men and intellectuals: or in the work of a Lenain the clear eyes of the laborers and peasants of Île-de-France or Picardy. And the thoughts of the men of old days lived in the minds of the present day. The mind of Pascal was alive, not only in the elect of reason and religion, but in the brains of obscure citizens or revolutionary Syndicalists. The art of Corneille and Racine was living for the people even more than for the elect, for they were less attainted by foreign influences: a humble clerk in Paris would feel more sympathy

with a tragedy of the time of Louis XIV than with a novel of
Tolstoi or a drama of Ibsen. The chants of the Middle Ages,
the old French *Tristan*, would be more akin to the modern
French than the *Tristan* of Wagner. The flowers of thought,
which since the twelfth century have never ceased to blossom in
French soil, however different they may be, were yet kin one to
another, though utterly different from all the flowers about
them.

Christophe knew too little of France to be able to grasp
how these characteristics had endured. What struck him most
of all in all the wide expanse of country was the extremely
small divisions of the earth. As Olivier said, every man had his
garden: and each garden, each plot of land, was separated from
the rest by walls, and quickset hedges, and inclosures of all
sorts. At most there were only a few woods and fields in common, and sometimes the dwellers on one side of a river were
forced to live nearer to each other than to the dwellers on the
other. Every man shut himself up in his own house: and it
seemed that this jealous individualism, instead of growing
weaker after centuries of neighborhood, was stronger than ever.
Christophe thought:

"How lonely they all are!"

In that sense nothing could have been more characteristic
than the house in which Christophe and Olivier lodged. It
was a world in miniature, a little France, honest and industrious, without any bond which could unite its divers elements. A five-storied house, a shaky house, leaning over to
one side, with creaking floors and crumbling ceilings. The
rain came through into the rooms under the roof in which
Christophe and Olivier lived: they had had to have the workmen in to botch up the roof as best they could: Christophe
could hear them working and talking overhead. There was one
man in particular who amused and exasperated him: he never
stopped talking to himself, and laughing, and singing, and
babbling nonsense, and whistling inane tunes, and holding long

conversations with himself all the time he was working: he was incapable of doing anything without proclaiming exactly what it was:

"I'm going to put in another nail. Where's my hammer? I'm putting in a nail, two nails. One more blow with the hammer! There, old lady, that's it. . . ."

When Christophe was playing he would stop for a moment and listen, and then go on whistling louder than ever: during a stirring passage he would beat time with his hammer on the roof. At last Christophe was so exasperated that he climbed on a chair, and poked his head through the skylight of the attic to rate the man. But when he saw him sitting astride the roof, with his jolly face and his cheek stuffed out with nails, he burst out laughing, and the man joined in. And not until they had done laughing did he remember why he had come to the window:

"By the way," he said, "I wanted to ask you: my playing doesn't interfere with your work?"

The man said it did not: but he asked Christophe to play something faster, because, as he worked in time to the music, slow tunes kept him back. They parted very good friends. In a quarter of an hour they had exchanged more words than in six months Christophe had spoken to the other inhabitants of the house.

There were two flats on each floor, one of three rooms, the other of only two. There were no servants' rooms: each household did its own housework, except for the tenants of the ground floor and the first floor, who occupied the two flats thrown into one.

On the fifth floor Christophe and Olivier's next-door neighbor was the Abbé Corneille, a priest of some forty years old, a learned man, an independent thinker, broad-minded, formerly a professor of exegesis in a great seminary, who had recently been censured by Rome for his modernist tendency. He had accepted the censure without submitting to it, in silence: he made no attempt to dispute it and refused every opportunity offered to him of publishing his doctrine: he shrank from a noisy publicity and would rather put up with the ruin of his ideas than figure in a scandal. Christophe could not understand that sort of revolt in resignation. He had tried to talk to the priest, who, however, was coldly polite and would not speak of the things which most interested him, and seemed to prefer as a matter of dignity to remain buried alive.

On the floor below in the flat corresponding to that of the two friends there lived a family of the name of Elie Elsberger: an engineer, his wife, and their two little girls, seven and ten years old: superior and sympathetic people who kept themselves very much to themselves, chiefly from a sort of false shame of their straitened means. The young woman who kept her house most pluckily was humiliated by it: she would have put up with twice the amount of worry and exhaustion if she could have prevented anybody knowing their condition: and that too was a feeling which Christophe could not understand. They belonged to a Protestant family and came from the East of France. Both man and wife, a few years before, had been bowled over by the storm of the Dreyfus affair: both of them had taken the affair passionately to heart, and, like thousands of French people, they had suffered from the frenzy brought on by the turbulent wind of that exalted fit of hysteria which lasted for seven years. They had sacrificed everything to it, rest, position, relations: they had broken off many dear friendships through it: they had almost ruined their health. For months at a time they did not sleep nor act, but went on bringing forward the same arguments over and over again with the monotonous insistence of the insane: they screwed each other up to a pitch of excitement: in spite of their timidity and their dread of ridicule, they had taken part in demonstrations and spoken at meetings, from which they returned with minds bewildered and aching hearts, and they would weep together through the night. In the struggle they had expended so much enthusiasm and passion that when at last victory was theirs they had not enough of either to rejoice: it left them dry of energy and broken for life. Their hopes had been so high, their eagerness for sacrifice had been so pure, that triumph when it came had seemed a mockery compared with what they had dreamed. To such single-minded creatures for whom there could exist but one truth, the bargaining of politics, the compromises of their heroes had been a bitter disappointment. They had seen their comrades in arms, men whom they had thought inspired with the same single passion for justice,—once the enemy was overcome, swarming about the loot, catching at power, carrying off honors and positions, and, in their turn, trampling justice underfoot. Only a mere handful of men held steadfast to their faith, and, in poverty and isolation, rejected by every party, rejecting every party, they remained in obscurity, cut off one from the other, a prey to sorrow and neurasthenia, left hopeless and disgusted with men and utterly weary of life. The engineer and his wife were among these wretched victims.

They made no noise in the house: they were morbidly afraid of disturbing their neighbors, the more so as they suffered from their neighbors' noises, and they were too proud to complain. Christophe was sorry for the two little girls, whose outbursts of merriment, and natural need of shouting, jumping about and laughing, were continually being suppressed. He adored children, and he made friendly advances to his little neighbors when he met them on the stairs. The little girls were shy at first, but were soon on good terms with Christophe, who always had some funny story to tell them or sweetmeats in his pockets: they told their parents about him: and, though at first they had been inclined to look askance at his advances, they were won over by the frank open manners of their noisy neighbor, whose pianoplaying and terrific disturbance overhead had often made them curse:—(for Christophe used to feel stifled in his room and take to pacing up and down like a caged bear).—They did not find it easy to talk to him. Christophe's rather boorish and abrupt manners sometimes made Elie Elsberger shudder. But it was all in vain for the engineer to try to keep up the wall of reserve, behind which he had taken shelter, between himself and the German: it was impossible to resist the impetuous good humor of the man whose eyes were so honest and affectionate and so free from any ulterior motive. Every now and then Christophe managed to squeeze a little confidence out of his neighbor. Elsberger was a queer man, full of courage, yet apathetic, sorrowful, and yet resigned. He had energy enough to bear a life of difficulty with dignity, but not enough to change it. It was as though he took a delight in justifying his own pessimism. Just at that time he had been offered a post in Brazil as manager of an undertaking: but he had refused as he was afraid of the climate and fearful of the health of his wife and children.

"Well, leave them," said Christophe. "Go alone and make their fortune."

"Leave them!" cried the engineer. "It's easy to see that you have no children."

"I assure you that, if I had, I should be of the same opinion."

"Never! Never! . . . Leave the country! . . . No. I would rather suffer here."

To Christophe it seemed an odd way of loving one's country and one's wife and children to sit down and vegetate with them. Olivier understood.

"Just think," he said, "of the risk of dying out there, in a strange unknown country, far away from those you love! Anything is better than the horror of that. Besides, it isn't worth while taking so much trouble for the few remaining years of life! . . ."

"As though one had always to be thinking of death!" said Christophe with a shrug. "And even if that does happen, isn't it better to die fighting for the happiness of those one loves than to flicker out in apathy?"

On the same landing in the smaller flat on the fourth floor lived a journeyman electrician named Aubert.—If he lived entirely apart from the other inhabitants of the house it was not altogether his fault. He had risen from the lower class and had a passionate desire not to sink back into it. He was small and weakly-looking; he had a harsh face, and his forehead bulged over his eyes, which were keen and sharp and bored into you like a gimlet: he had a fair mustache, a satirical mouth, a sibilant way of speaking, a husky voice, a scarf round his neck, and he had always something the matter with his throat, in which irritation was set up by his perpetual habit of smoking: he was always feverishly active and had the consumptive temperament. He was a mixture of conceit, irony, and bitterness, cloaking a mind that was enthusiastic, bombastic, and naïve, while it was always being taken in by life. He was the bastard of some burgess whom he had never known, and was brought up by a mother whom it was impossible to respect, so that in his childhood he had seen much that was sad and degrading. He had plied all sorts of trades and had traveled much in France. He had an admirable desire for education, and had taught himself with frightful toil and labor: he read everything: history, philosophy, decadent poets: he was up-to-date in everything: theaters, exhibitions, concerts: he had a touching veneration for art, literature, and middle-class ideas: they fascinated him. He had imbibed the vague and ardent ideology which intoxicated the middle-classes in the first days of the Revolution. He had a definite belief in the infallibility of reason, in boundless progress,—*quo non ascendam?*—in the near advent of happiness on earth, in the omnipotence of science, in Divine Humanity, and in France, the eldest daughter of Humanity. He had an enthusiastic and credulous sort of anti-clericalism which made him lump together religion—especially Catholicism—and obscurantism, and see in priests the natural foe of light. Socialism, individualism, Chauvinism jostled each other in his brain. He was a humanitarian in mind, despotic in temperament, and an anarchist in fact. He was proud and knew the gaps in his education, and, in conversation, he was very cautious: he turned to account everything that was said in his presence, but he would never ask advice: that humiliated him; now, though he had intelligence and cleverness, these things could not altogether supply the defects of his education. He had taken it into his head to write. Like so many men in France who have not been taught, he had the gift of style, and a clear vision: but he was a confused thinker. He had shown a few pages of his productions to a successful journalist in whom he believed, and the man made fun of him. He was profoundly humiliated, and from that time on never told a soul what he was doing. But he went on writing: it fed his need of expansion and gave him pride and delight. In his heart he was immensely pleased with his eloquent passages and philosophic ideas, which were not worth a brass farthing. And he set no store by his observation of real life, which was excellent. It was his crank to fancy himself as a philosopher, and he wished to write sociological plays and novels of ideas. He had no difficulty in solving all sorts of insoluble questions, and at every turn he discovered America. When in due course he found that America was already discovered, he was disappointed, humiliated, and rather bitter: he was never far from scenting injustice and intrigue. He was consumed by a thirst for fame and a burning capacity for devotion which suffered from finding no means or direction of employment: he would have loved to be a great man of letters. a member of that literary élite, who in his eyes were adorned with a supernatural prestige. In spite of his longing to deceive himself he had too much good sense and was too ironical not to know that there was no chance of its coming to pass. But he would at least have liked to live in that atmosphere of art and middle-class ideas which at a distance seemed to him so brilliant and pure and chastened of mediocrity. This innocent longing had the unfortunate result of making the society of the people with whom his condition in life forced him to live intolerable to him. And as the middle-class society which he wished to enter closed its doors to him. the result was that he never saw anybody. And so Christophe had no difficulty in making his acquaintance. On the contrary he had very soon to bolt and bar against him: otherwise Aubert would more often have been in Christophe's rooms, than Christophe in his. He was only too happy to find an artist to whom he could talk about music, plays, etc. But, as one would imagine, Christophe did not find them so interesting: he would rather have discussed the people with a man who was of the people. But that was just what Aubert would not and could not discuss.

In proportion as he went lower in the house relations between Christophe and the other tenants became naturally more distant. Besides, some secret magic, some *Open Sesame,* would have been necessary for him to reach the inhabitants of the third floor.—In the one flat there lived two ladies who were under the self-hypnotism of grief for a loss that was already some years old: Madame Germain, a woman of thirty-five who had lost her husband and daughter, and lived in seclusion with her aged and devout mother-in-law.—On the other side of the landing there dwelt a mysterious character of uncertain age, anything between fifty and sixty, with a little girl of ten. He was bald, with a handsome, well-trimmed beard, a soft way of speaking, distinguished manners, and aristocratic hands. He was called M. Watelet. He was said to be an anarchist, a revolutionary, a foreigner, from what country was not known, Russia or Belgium. As a matter of fact he was a Northern Frenchman and was hardly at all revolutionary: but he was living on his past reputation. He had been mixed up with the Commune of '71 and condemned to death: he had escaped, how he did not know: and for ten years he had lived for a short time in every country in Europe. He had seen so many ill-deeds during the upheaval in Paris, and afterwards, and also in exile, and also since his return, ill-deeds done by his former comrades now that they were in power, and also by men in every rank of the revolutionary parties, that he had broken with them, peacefully keeping his convictions to himself useless and untarnished. He read much, wrote a few mildly incendiary books, pulled— (so it was said)—the wires of anarchist movements in distant places, in India or the Far East, busied himself with the universal revolution, and, at the same time, with researches no less universal but of a more genial aspect, namely with a universal language, a new method of popular instruction in music. He never came in contact with anybody in the house: when he met any of its inmates he did no more than bow to them with exaggerated politeness. However, he condescended to tell Christophe a little about his musical method. Christophe was not the least interested in it: the symbols of his ideas mattered very little to him: in any language he would have managed somehow to express them. But Watelet was not to be put off, and went on explaining his system gently but firmly: Christophe could not find out anything about the rest of his life. And so he gave up stopping when he met him on the stairs and only looked at the little girl who was always with him: she was fair, pale, anemic: she had blue eyes, rather a sharp profile, a thin little figure—she was always very neatly dressed—and she looked sickly and her face was not very expressive. Like everybody else he thought she was Watelet's daughter. She was an orphan, the daughter of poor parents, whom Watelet had adopted when she was four or five, after the death of her father and mother in an epidemic. He had an almost boundless love for the poor, especially for poor children. It was a sort of mystic tenderness with him as with Vincent de Paul. He distrusted official charity, and knew exactly what philanthropic institutions were worth, and therefore he set about doing charity alone: he did it by stealth, and took a secret joy in it. He had learned medicine so as to be of some use in the world. One day when he went to the house of a working-man in the district and found sickness there, he turned to and nursed the invalids: he had some medical knowledge and turned it to account. He could not bear to see a child suffer: it broke his heart. But, on the other hand, what a joy it was when he had succeeded in tearing one of these poor little creatures from the clutches of sickness, and the first pale smile appeared on the little pinched face! Then Watelet's heart would melt. Those were his moments of Paradise. They made him forget the trouble he often had with his protégés: for they very rarely showed him much gratitude. And the housekeeper was furious at seeing so many people with dirty boots going up her stairs, and she would complain bitterly. And the proprietor would watch uneasily these meetings of anarchists, and make remarks. Watelet would contemplate leaving his flat: but that hurt him: he had his little whimsies: he was gentle and obstinate, and he put up with the proprietor's observations.

Christophe won his confidence up to a certain point by the love he showed for children. That was their common bond. Christophe never met the little girl without a catch at his heart: for, though he did not know why, by one of those mysterious similarities in outline, which the instinct perceives immediately and subconsciously, the child reminded him of Sabine's little girl. Sabine, his first love, now so far away, the silent grace of whose fleeting shadow had never faded from his heart. And so he took an interest in the pale-faced little girl whom he never saw romping, or running, whose voice he hardly ever heard, who had no little friend of her own age, who was always alone, mum, quietly amusing herself with lifeless toys, a doll or a block of wood, while her lips moved as she whispered some story to herself. She was affectionate and a little offhanded in manner: there was a foreign and uneasy quality in her, but her adopted father never saw it: he loved her too much. Alas! Does not that foreign and uneasy quality exist even in the children of our own flesh and blood? . . :— Christophe tried to make the solitary little girl friends with the engineer's children. But with both Elsberger and Watelet he met with a polite but categorical refusal. These people seemed to make it a point of honor to bury themselves alive, each in his own mausoleum. If it came to a point each would have been ready to help the other: but each was afraid of it being thought that he himself was in need of help: and as they were both equally proud and vain,—and the means of both were equally precarious,—there was no hope of either of them being the first to hold out his hand to the other.

The larger flat on the second floor was almost always empty. The proprietor of the house reserved it for his own use: and he was never there. He was a retired merchant who had closed down his business as soon as he had made a certain fortune, the figure of which he had fixed for himself. He spent the greater part of the year in some hotel on the Riviera, and the summer at some watering-place in Normandy, living as a gentleman with private means who enjoys the illusion of luxury cheaply by watching the luxury of others, and, like them, leading a useless existence.

The smaller flat was let to a childless couple: M. and Madame Arnaud. The husband, a man of between forty and forty-five, was a master at a school. He was so overworked with lectures, and correcting exercises, and giving classes, that he had never been able to find time to write his thesis: and at last he had given it up altogether. The wife was ten years younger, pretty, and very shy. They were both intelligent, well read, in love with each other: they knew nobody, and never went out. The husband had no time for it. The wife had too much time: but she was a brave little creature, who fought down her fits of depression when they came over her, and hid them, by occupying herself as best she could, trying to learn, taking notes for her husband, copying out her husband's notes, mending her husband's clothes, making frocks and hats for herself. She would have liked to go to the theater from time to time: but Arnaud did not care about it: he was too tired in the evening. And she resigned herself to it.

Their great joy was music. They both adored it. He could not play, and she dared not although she could: when she played before anybody, even before her husband, it was like a child strumming. However, that was good enough for them: and Gluck, Mozart, Beethoven, whom they stammered out, were as friends to them: they knew their lives in detail, and their sufferings filled them with love and pity. Books, too, beautiful, fine books, which they read together, gave them happiness. But

there are few such books in the literature of to-day: authors do
not worry about those people who can bring them neither reputation, nor pleasure, nor money, such humble readers who
are never seen in society, and do not write in any journal,
and can only love and say nothing. The silent light of art,
which in their upright and religious hearts assumed almost a
supernatural character, and their mutual affection, were enough
to make them live in peace, happy enough, though a little sad—
(there is no gainsaying that),—very lonely, a little bruised in
spirit. They were both much superior to their position in life.
M. Arnaud was full of ideas: but he had neither the time nor
enough courage left to write them down. It meant such a lot of
trouble to get articles and books published: it was not worth
it: futile vanity! Anything he could do was so small in com-
parison with the thinkers he loved! He had too true a love
for the great works of art to want to produce art himself: it
would have seemed to him pretentious, impertinent, and
ridiculous. It seemed to be his lot to spread their influence.
He gave his pupils the benefit of his ideas: they would turn
them into books later on,—without mentioning his name of
course.—Nobody spent more money than he in subscribing
to various publications. The poor are always the most generous: they do buy their books: the rich would take it as a slur
upon themselves if they did not somehow manage to get them
for nothing. Arnaud ruined himself in buying books: it was
his weakness—his vice. He was ashamed of it, and concealed it
from his wife. But she did not blame him for it: she would
have spent just as much.—And with it all they were always
making fine plans for saving, with a view to going to Italy
some day—though, as they knew quite well, they never would
go: and they were the first to laugh at their incapacity for
keeping money. Arnaud would console himself. His dear wife
was enough for him, and his life of work and inward joys.
Was it not also enough for her?—She said it was. She dared
not say how dear it would have been to her if her husband could
have some reputation, which would in some sort be reflected

upon herself, and brighten her life, and give her ease and comfort: inward joys are beautiful: but a little ray of light from without shining in from time to time is sweet. and does so much good! . . . But she never said anything, because she was timid: and besides, she knew that even if he wished to make a reputation it was by no means certain that he would succeed: it was too late! . . . Their greatest sorrow was that they had no children. Each hid that sorrow from the other: and they were only the more tender with each other: it was as though the poor creatures were striving to win one another's forgiveness. Madame Arnaud was kind and affectionate: she would gladly have been friends with Madame Elsberger. But she dared not: she was never approached. As for Christophe, husband and wife would have asked nothing better than to know him: they were fascinated by the music that they could hear faintly when he was playing. But nothing in the world could have induced them to make the first move: they would have thought it indiscreet.

The whole of the first floor was occupied by M. and Madame Félix Weil. They were rich Jews, and had no children. and they spent six months of the year in the country near Paris. Although they had lived in the house for twenty years—(they stayed there as a matter of habit, although they could easily have found a flat more in keeping with their fortune)—they were always like passing strangers. They had never spoken a word to any of their neighbors. and no one knew any more about them than on the day of their arrival. But that was no reason why the other tenants should not pass judgment on them: on the contrary. They were not liked. And no doubt they did nothing to win popularity. And yet they were worthy of more acquaintance: they were both excellent people and remarkably intelligent. The husband, a man of sixty, was an Assyriologist, well known through his famous excavations in Central Asia: like most of his race he was open-minded and curious, and did not confine himself to his special studies: he was interested in an infinite number of things: the arts, social questions, every manifestation of contemporary thought. But these were not enough to occupy his mind: for they all amused him, and none of them roused passionate interest. He was very intelligent, too intelligent, too much emancipated from all ties, always ready to destroy with one hand what he had constructed with the other: for he was constructive, always producing books and theories: he was a great worker: as a matter of habit and spiritual health he was always patiently plowing his deep furrow in the field of knowledge, without having any belief in the utility of what he was doing. He had always had the misfortune to be rich, so that he had never had the interest of the struggle for life, and, since his explorations in the East, of which he had grown tired after a few years, he had not accepted any official position. Outside his own personal work, however, he busied himself with clairvoyance, contemporary problems, social reforms of a practical and pressing nature, the reorganization of public education in France: he flung out ideas and created lines of thought: he would set great intellectual machines working, and would immediately grow disgusted with them. More than once he had scandalized people, who had been converted to a cause by his arguments, by producing the most incisive and discouraging criticisms of the cause itself. He did not do it deliberately: it was a natural necessity for him: he was very nervous and ironical in temper, and found it hard to bear with the foibles of things and people which he saw with the most disconcerting clarity. And, as there is no good cause, nor any good man, who, seen at a certain angle or with a certain distortion, does not present a ridiculous aspect, there was nothing that, with his ironic disposition, he could go on respecting for long. All this was not calculated to make him friends. And yet he was always well-disposed towards people, and inclined to do good: he did much good: but no one was ever grateful to him: even those whom he had helped could not in their hearts forgive him, because they had seen that they were ridiculous in his eyes. It was necessary

for him not to see too much of men if he were to love them.
Not that he was a misanthrope. He was not sure enough of
himself to be that. Face to face with the world at which he
mocked, he was timid and bashful: at heart he was not at all sure
that the world was not right and himself wrong: he endeavored
not to appear too different from other people, and strove to base
his manners and apparent opinions on theirs. But he strove in
vain: he could not help judging them: he was keenly sensible
of any sort of exaggeration and anything that was not simple:
and he could never conceal his irritation. He was especially
sensible of the foibles of the Jews, because he knew them best:
and as, in spite of his intellectual freedom, which did not admit of barriers between races, he was often brought up sharp
against those barriers which men of other races raised against
him,—as, in spite of himself, he was out of his element among
Christian ideas, he retired with dignity into his ironic labors
and the profound affection he had for his wife.

Worst of all, his wife was not secure against his irony. She
was a kindly, busy woman, anxious to be useful, and always
taken up with various charitable works. Her nature was much
less complex than that of her husband, and she was cramped
by her moral benevolence and the rather rigidly intellectual,
though lofty, idea of duty that she had begotten. Her whole
life, which was sad enough, without children, with no great joy
nor great love, was based on this moral belief of hers, which
was more than anything else the will to believe. Her husband's irony had, of course, seized on the element of voluntary
self-deception in her faith, and—(it was too strong for him)—
he had made much fun at her expense. He was a mass of contradictions. He had a feeling for duty no less lofty than his
wife's, and, at the same time, a merciless desire to analyze, to
criticize, and to avoid deception, which made him dismember
and take to pieces his moral imperative. He could not see
that he was digging away the ground from under his wife's
feet: he used cruelly to discourage her. When he realized that
he had done so, he suffered even more than she: but the harm

was done. It did not keep them from loving each other faithfully, and working and doing good. But the cold dignity of the wife was not more kindly judged than the irony of the husband: and as they were too proud to publish abroad the good they did, or their desire to do good, their reserve was regarded as indifference, and their isolation as selfishness. And the more conscious they became of the opinion that was held of them, the more careful were they to do nothing to dispute it. Reacting against the coarse indiscretion of so many of their race they were the victims of an excessive reserve which covered a vast deal of pride.

As for the ground floor, which was a few steps higher than the little garden, it was occupied by Commandant Chabran, a retired officer of the Colonial Artillery: he was still young, a man of great vigor, who had fought brilliantly in the Soudan and Madagascar: then suddenly, he had thrown the whole thing up, and buried himself there: he did not even want to hear the army mentioned, and spent his time in digging his flower-beds, and practising the flute without making any progress, and growling about politics, and scolding his daughter, whom he adored: she was a young woman of thirty, not very pretty, but quite charming, who devoted herself to him, and had not married so as not to leave him. Christophe used often to see them leaning out of the window: and, naturally, he paid more attention to the daughter than the father. She used to spend part of the afternoon in the garden, sewing, dreaming, digging, always in high good humor with her grumbling old father. Christophe could hear her soft clear voice laughingly replying to the growling tones of the Commandant, whose footsteps ground and scrunched on the gravel-paths: then he would go in, and she would stay sitting on a seat in the garden, and sew for hours together, never stirring, never speaking, smiling vaguely, while inside the house the bored old soldier played flourishes on his shrill flute, or, by way of a change, made a broken-winded old harmonium squeal and groan, much to Christophe's amusement—or exasperation—(which, depended on the day and his mood).

All these people went on living side by side in that house with its walled-in garden sheltered from all the buffets of the world, hermetically sealed even against each other.   Only Christophe, with his need of expansion and his great fullness of life, unknown to them, wrapped them about with his vast sympathy, blind, yet all-seeing.   He could not understand them.   He had no means of understanding them.   He lacked Olivier's psychological insight and quickness.   But he loved them.   Instinctively he put himself in their place.   Slowly, mysteriously, there crept through him a dim consciousness of these lives so near him and yet so far removed, the stupefying sorrow of the mourning woman, the stoic silence of all their proud thoughts, the priest, the Jew, the engineer, the revolutionary: the pale and gentle flame of tenderness and faith which burned in silence in the hearts of the two Arnauds: the naïve aspirations towards the light of the man of the people: the suppressed revolt and fertile activity which were stifled in the bosom of the old soldier: and the calm resignation of the girl dreaming in the shade of the lilac.   But only Christophe could perceive and hear the silent music of their souls: they heard it not: they were all absorbed in their sorrow and their dreams.

They all worked hard, the skeptical old scientist, the pessimistic engineer, the priest, the anarchist, and all these proud or dispirited creatures.   And on the roof the mason sang.

In the district round the house among the best of the people Christophe found the same moral solitude—even when the people were banded together.

Olivier had brought him in touch with a little review for which he wrote. It was called *Ésope*, and had taken for its motto this quotation from Montaigne:

"*Æsop was put up for sale with two other slaves. The purchaser inquired of the first what he could do: and he, to put a price upon himself, described all sorts of marvels; the second said as much for himself, or more.   When it came to Æsop's turn, and he was asked what he could do:—Nothing, he said, for these two have taken everything: they can do everything."*

Their attitude was that of pure reaction against "the impudence," as Montaigne says, "of those who profess knowledge and their overweening presumption!"   The self-styled skeptics of the *Ésope* review were at heart men of the firmest faith. But their mask of irony and haughty ignorance, naturally enough, had small attraction for the public: rather it repelled. The people are only with a writer when he brings them words of simple, clear, vigorous, and assured life.   They prefer a sturdy lie to an anemic truth.   Skepticism is only to their liking when it is the covering of lusty naturalism or Christian idolatry. The scornful Pyrrhonism in which the *Ésope* clothed itself could only be acceptable to a few minds—"*acme sdegnose*,"—who knew the solid worth beneath it.   It was force absolutely lost upon action and life.

There was no help for it.   The more democratic France became, the more aristocratic did her ideas, her art, her science seem to grow.   Science securely lodged behind its special languages, in the depths of its sanctuary, wrapped about with a triple veil, which only the initiate had the power to draw, was less accessible than at the time of Buffon and the Encyclopedists.   Art,—that art at least which had some respect for itself and the worship of beauty,—was no less hermetically sealed: it despised the people.   Even among writers who cared less for beauty than for action, among those who gave moral ideas precedence over esthetic ideas, there was often a strange dominance of the aristocratic spirit.   They seemed to be more intent upon preserving the purity of their inward flame than to communicate its warmth to others.   It was as though they desired not to make their ideas prevail but only to affirm them.

And yet among these writers there were some who applied themselves to popular art.   Among the most sincere some hurled

into their writings destructive anarchical ideas, truths of the
distant future, which might be beneficent in a century or so, but
for the time being, corroded and scorched the soul: others wrote
bitter or ironical plays, robbed of all illusion, sad to the last degree.   Christophe was left in a state of collapse, ham-strung
for a day or two after he read them.

"And you give that sort of thing to the people?" he would
ask, feeling sorry for the poor audiences who had come to forget
their troubles for a few hours, only to be presented with these
lugubrious entertainments.   "It's enough to make them all go
and drown themselves!"

"You may be quite easy on that score," said Olivier, laughing
"The people don't go."

"And a jolly good thing too!   You're mad.   Are you trying
to rob them of every scrap of courage to live?"

"Why?   Isn't it right to teach them to see the sadness of
things, as we do, and yet to go on and do their duty without
flinching?"

"Without flinching?   I doubt that.   But it's very certain
that they'll do it without pleasure.   And you don't go very far
when you've destroyed a man's pleasure in living."

"What else can one do?   One has no right to falsify the
truth."

"Nor have you any right to tell the whole truth to everybody."

"You say that?   You who are always shouting the truth
aloud, you who pretend to love truth more than anything in
the world!"

"Yes: truth for myself and those whose backs are strong
enough to bear it.   But it is cruel and stupid to tell it to the
rest.   Yes.   I see that now.   At home that would never have
occurred to me: in Germany people are not so morbid about
the truth as they are here: they're too much taken up with living: very wisely they see only what they wish to see.   I love you
for not being like that: you are honest and go straight ahead
But you are inhuman.   When you think you have unearthed

a truth, you let it loose upon the world, without stopping to
think whether, like the foxes in the Bible with their burning
tails, it will not set fire to the world. I think it is fine of you
to prefer truth to your happiness. But when it comes to the
happiness of other people. . . . Then I say, 'Stop!' You
are taking too much upon yourselves. Thou shalt love truth
more than thyself, but thy neighbor more than truth."

"Is one to lie to one's neighbor?"

Christophe replied with the words of Goethe:

"We should only express those of the highest truths which
will be to the good of the world. The rest we must keep to ourselves: like the soft rays of a hidden sun, they will shed their
light upon all our actions."

But they were not moved by these scruples. They never
stopped to think whether the bow in their hands shot "*ideas
or death*," or both together. They were too intellectual. They
lacked love. When a Frenchman has ideas he tries to impose
them on others. He tries to do the same thing when he has
none. And when he sees that he cannot do it he loses interest in
other people, he loses interest in action. That was the chief
reason why this particular group took so little interest in politics,
save to moan and groan. Each of them was shut up in his
faith, or want of faith.

Many attempts had been made to break down their individualism and to form groups of these men: but the majority
of these groups had immediately resolved themselves into literary clubs, or split up into absurd factions. The best of them
were mutually destructive. There were among them some first-
rate men of force and faith, men well fitted to rally and guide
those of weaker will. But each man had his following, and
would not consent to merging it with that of other men. So
they were split up into a number of reviews, unions, associations,
which had all the moral virtues, save one: self-denial; for not
one of them would give way to the others: and, while they
wrangled over the crumbs that fell from an honest and well-
meaning public, small in numbers and poor in purse, they

vegetated for a short time, starved and languished, and at last
collapsed never to rise again, not under the assault of the enemy,
but—(most pitiful!)—under the weight of their own quarrels.
—The various professions,—men of letters, dramatic authors,
poets, prose writers, professors, members of the Institute, jour-
nalists were divided up into a number of little castes, which
they themselves split up again into smaller castes, each one of
which closed its doors against the rest. There was no sort of
mutual interchange. There was no unanimity on any subject
in France, except at those very rare moments when unanimity
assumed an epidemic character, and, as a rule, was in the wrong:
for it was morbid. A crazy individualism predominated in
every kind of French activity: in scientific research as well as in
commerce, in which it prevented business men from combining
and organizing working agreements. This individualism was
not that of a rich and bustling vitality, but that of obstinacy
and self-repression. To be alone, to owe nothing to others, not
to mix with others for fear of feeling their inferiority in their
company, not to disturb the tranquillity of their haughty isolation: these were the secret thoughts of almost all these men who
founded "outside" reviews, "outside" theaters, "outside"
groups: reviews, theaters, groups, all most often had no other
reason for existing than the desire not to be with the general
herd, and an incapacity for joining with other people in a common idea or course of action, distrust of other people, or, at
the very worst, party hostility, setting one against the other
the very men who were most fitted to understand each other.

Even when men who thought highly of each other were
united in some common task, like Olivier and his colleagues
on the *Ésope* review, they always seemed to be on their guard
with each other: they had nothing of that open-handed geni-
ality so common in Germany, where it is apt to become a
nuisance. Among these young men there was one especially
who attracted Christophe because he divined him to be a man of
exceptional force: he was a writer of inflexible logic and will,
with a passion for moral ideas, in the service of which he was

absolutely uncompromising and ready in their cause to sacrifice
the whole world and himself: he had founded and conducted
almost unaided a review in which to uphold them: he had sworn
to impose on Europe and on France the idea of a pure, heroic,
and free France: he firmly believed that the world would one
day recognize that he was responsible for one of the boldest
pages in the history of French thought:—and he was not mistaken. Christophe would have been only too glad to know him
better and to be his friend. But there was no way of bringing it
about. Although Olivier had a good deal to do with him
they saw very little of each other except on business: they never
discussed any intimate matter, and never got any farther than
the exchange of a few abstract ideas: or rather—(for, to be
exact, there was no exchange, and each adhered to his own
ideas)—they soliloquized in each other's company in turn. However, they were comrades in arms and knew their worth.

There were innumerable reasons for this reservedness, reasons
difficult to discern, even for their own eyes. The first reason
was a too great critical faculty, which saw too clearly the un-
alterable differences between one mind and another, backed by
an excessive intellectualism which attached too much importance
to those differences: they lacked that puissant and naïve sympathy whose vital need is of love, the need of giving out its
overflowing love. Then, too, perhaps overwork, the struggle
for existence, the fever of thought, which so taxes strength
that by the evening there is none left for friendly intercourse,
had a great deal to do with it. And there was that terrible
feeling, which every Frenchman is afraid to admit, though too
often it is stirring in his heart, the feeling of *not being of one
race,* the feeling that the nation consists of different races
established at different epochs on the soil of France, who,
though all bound together, have few ideas in common, and
therefore ought not, in the common interest, to ponder them
too much. But above all the reason was to seek in the intoxicating and dangerous passion for liberty, to which, when a
man has once tasted it, there is nothing that he will not

sacrifice. Such solitary freedom is all the more precious for having been bought by years of tribulation. The select few have taken refuge in it to escape the slavishness of the mediocre. It is a reaction against the tyranny of the political and religious masses, the terrific crushing weight which overbears the individual in France: the family, public opinion, the State, secret societies, parties, coteries, schools. Imagine a prisoner who, to escape, has to scale twenty great walls hemming him in. If he manages to clear them all without breaking his neck, and, above all, without losing heart, he must be strong indeed. A rough schooling for free-will! But those who have gone through it bear the marks of it all their life in the mania for independence, and the impossibility of their ever living in the lives of others.

Side by side with this loneliness of pride, there was the loneliness of renunciation. There were many, many good men in France whose goodness and pride and affection came to nothing in withdrawal from life! A thousand reasons, good and bad, stood in the way of action for them. With some it was obedience, timidity, force of habit. With others human respect, fear of ridicule, fear of being conspicuous, of being a mark for the comments of the gallery, of meddling with things that did not concern them, of having their disinterested actions attributed to motives of interest. There were men who would not take part in any political or social struggle, women who declined to undertake any philanthropic work, because there were too many people engaged in these things who lacked conscience and even common sense, and because they were afraid of the taint of these charlatans and fools. In almost all such people there are disgust, weariness, dread of action, suffering, ugliness, stupidity, risks, responsibilities: the terrible " What's the use? " which destroys the good-will of so many of the French of to-day. They are too intelligent,—(their intelligence has no wide sweep of the wings),—they are too intent upon reasons for and against. They lack force. They lack vitality. When a man's life beats strongly he never wonders why he goes on living: he lives for the sake of living,—because it is a splendid thing to be alive!

In fine, the best of them were a mixture of sympathetic and average qualities: a modicum of philosophy, moderate desires, fond attachment to the family, the earth, moral custom: discretion, dread of intruding, of being a nuisance to other people: modesty of feeling, unbending reserve. All these amiable and charming qualities could, in certain cases, be brought into line with serenity, courage, and inward joy: but at bottom there was a certain connection between them and poverty in the blood, the progressive ebb of French vitality.

The pretty garden, beneath the house in which Christophe and Olivier lived, tucked away between the four walls, was symbolical of that part of the life of France. It was a little patch of green earth shut off from the outer world. Only now and then did the mighty wind of the outer air, whirling down, bring to the girl dreaming there the breath of the distant fields and the vast earth.

Now that Christophe was beginning to perceive the hidden resources of France he was furious that she should suffer the oppression of the rabble. The half-light, in which the select and silent few were huddled away, stifled him. Stoicism is a fine thing for those whose teeth are gone. But he needed the open air, the great public, the sunshine of glory, the love of thousands of men and women: he needed to hold close to him those whom he loved, to pulverize his enemies, to fight and to conquer.

"You can," said Olivier. "You are strong. You were born to conquer through your faults—(forgive me!)—as well as through your qualities. You are lucky enough not to belong to a race and a nation which are too aristocratic. Action does not repel you. If need be you could even become a politician. —Besides, you have the inestimable good fortune to write music. Nobody understands you, and so you can say anything and everything. If people had any idea of the contempt for them-

selves which you put into your music, and your faith in what
they deny, and your perpetual hymn in praise of what they
are always trying to kill, they would never forgive you, and
you would be so fettered, and persecuted, and harassed, that you
would waste most of your strength in fighting them: when you
had beaten them back you would have no breath left for going
on with your work: your life would be finished. The great men
who triumph have the good luck to be misunderstood. They
are admired for the very opposite of what they are."

"Pooh!" said Christophe. "You don't understand how
cowardly your masters are. At first I thought you were alone,
and I used to find excuses for your inaction. But, as a matter
of fact, there's a whole army of you all of the same mind.
You are a hundred times stronger than your oppressors, you are
a thousand times more worthy, and you let them impose on you
with their effrontery! I don't understand you. You live in a
most beautiful country, you are gifted with the finest intelligence
and the most human quality of mind, and with it all you do
nothing: you allow yourselves to be overborne and outraged and
trampled underfoot by a parcel of fools. Good Lord! Be yourselves! Don't wait for Heaven or a Napoleon to come to your
aid! Arise, band yourselves together! Get to work, all of you!
Sweep out your house!"

But Olivier shrugged his shoulders, and said, wearily and
ironically:

"Grapple with them? No. That is not our game: we
have better things to do. Violence disgusts me. I know only
too well what would happen. All the old embittered failures,
the young Royalist idiots, the odious apostles of brutality and
hatred, would seize on anything I did and bring it to dishonor. Do you want me to adopt the old device of hate: *Fuori
Barbari,* or: *France for the French?*"

"Why not?" asked Christophe.

"No. Such a device is not for the French. Any attempt
to propagate it among our people under cover of patriotism
must fail. It is good enough for barbarian countries! But

our country has no use for hatred. Our genius never yet asserted itself by denying or destroying the genius of other countries, but by absorbing them. Let the troublous North and the loquacious South come to us. . . ."

"And the poisonous East?"

"And the poisonous East: we will absorb it with the rest: we have absorbed many others! I just laugh at the air of triumph they assume, and the pusillanimity of some of my fellow-countrymen. They think they have conquered us, they strut about our boulevards, and in our newspapers and reviews, and in our theaters and in the political arena. Idiots! It is they who are conquered! They will be assimilated after having fed us. Gaul has a strong stomach: in these twenty centuries she has digested more than one civilization. We are proof against poison. . . . It is meet that you Germans should be afraid! You must be pure or impure. But with us it is not a matter of purity but of universality. You have an Emperor: Great Britain calls herself an Empire: but, in fact, it is our Latin Genius that is Imperial. We are the citizens of the City of the Universe. *Urbis, Orbis.*"

"That is all very well," said Christophe, "as long as the nation is healthy and in the flower of its manhood. But there will come a day when its energy declines: and then there is a danger of its being submerged by the influx of foreigners. Between ourselves, does it not seem as though that day had arrived?"

"People have been saying that for ages. Again and again our history has given the lie to such fears. We have passed through many different trials since the days of the Maid of Orleans, when Paris was deserted, and bands of wolves prowled through the streets. Neither in the prevalent immorality, nor the pursuit of pleasure, nor the laxness, nor the anarchy of the present day, do I see any cause for fear. Patience! Those who wish to live must endure in patience. I am sure that presently there will be a moral reaction,—which will not be much better, and will probably lead to an equal degree of folly; those who are now living on the corruptness of public life will not be the least clamorous in the reaction! . . . But what does that matter to us? All these movements do not touch the real people of France. Rotten fruit does not corrupt the tree. It falls. Besides, all these people are such a small part of the nation! What does it matter to us whether they live or die? Why should I bother to organize leagues and revolutions against them? The existing evil is not the work of any form of government. It is the leprosy of luxury, a contagion spread by the parasites of intellectual and material wealth. Such parasites will perish."

"After they have sapped your vitality."

"It is impossible to despair of such a race. There is in it such hidden virtue, such a power of light and practical idealism, that they creep into the veins even of those who are exploiting and ruining the nation. Even the grasping, self-seeking politicians succumb to its fascination. Even the most mediocre of men when they are in power are gripped by the greatness of its Destiny: it lifts them out of themselves: the torch is passed on from hand to hand among them: one after another they resume the holy war against darkness. They are drawn onward by the genius of the people: willy-nilly they fulfil the law of the God whom they deny. *Gesta Dei per Francos.* . . . O my beloved country, I will never lose my faith in thee! And though in thy trials thou didst perish, yet would I find in that only a reason the more for my proud belief, even to the bitter end, in our mission in the world. I will not have my beloved France fearfully shutting herself up in a sickroom, and closing every inlet to the outer air. I have no mind to prolong a sickly existence. When a nation has been so great as we have been, then it were far better to die rather than to sink from greatness. Therefore let the ideas of the world rush into the channels of our minds! I am not afraid. The flood will go down of its own accord after it has enriched the soil of France with its ooze."

"My poor dear fellow," said Christophe, "but it's a grim

prospect in the meanwhile. Where will you be when your France emerges from the Nile? Don't you think it would be better to fight against it? You wouldn't risk anything except defeat, and you seem inclined to impose that on yourself as long as you like."

"I should be risking much more than defeat," said Olivier. "I should be running the risk of losing my peace of mind, which I prize far more than victory. I will not be a party to hatred. I will be just to all my enemies. In the midst of passion I wish to preserve the clarity of my vision, to understand and love everything."

But Christophe, to whom this love of life, detached from life, seemed to be very little different from resignation and acceptance of death, felt in his heart, as in Empedocles of old, the stirring of a hymn to Hatred and to Love, the brother of Hate, fruitful Love, tilling and sowing good seed in the earth. He did not share Olivier's calm fatalism: he had no such confidence in the continuance of a race which did not defend itself, and his desire was to appeal to all the healthy forces of the nation, to call forth and band together all the honest men in the whole of France.

Just as it is possible to learn more of a human being in one minute of love than in months of observation, so Christophe had learned more about France in a week of intimacy with Olivier, hardly ever leaving the house, than during a whole year of blind wandering through Paris, and standing at attention at various intellectual and political gatherings. Amid the universal anarchy in which he had been floundering, a soul like that of his friend seemed to him veritably to be the "*Île de France*"— the island of reason and serenity in the midst of the ocean. The inward peace which was in Olivier was all the more striking, inasmuch as it had no intellectual support,—as it existed amid unhappy circumstances,—(in poverty and solitude, while the country of its birth was decadent),—and as its body was weak.

sickly, and nerve-ridden. That serenity was apparently not the fruit of any effort of will striving to realize it,—(Olivier had little will) ;—it came from the depths of his being and his race. In many of the men of Olivier's acquaintance Christophe perceived the distant light of that σωφροσύνη,—" the silent calm of the motionless sea ";—and he, who knew, none better, the stormy, troublous depths of his own soul, and how he had to stretch his will-power to the utmost to maintain the balance in his lusty nature, marveled at its veiled harmony.

What he had seen of the inner France had upset all his preconceived ideas about the character of the French. Instead of a gay, sociable, careless, brilliant people, he saw men of a headstrong and close temper, living in isolation, wrapped about with a seeming optimism, like a gleaming mist, while they were in fact steeped in a deep-rooted and serene pessimism, possessed by fixed ideas, intellectual passions, indomitable souls, which it would have been easier to destroy than to alter. No doubt these men were only the select few among the French: but Christophe wondered where they could have come by their stoicism and their faith. Olivier told him:

"In defeat. It is you, my dear Christophe, who have forged us anew. Ah! But we suffered for it, too. You can have no idea of the darkness in which we grew up in a France humiliated and sore, which had come face to face with death, and still felt the heavy weight of the murderous menace of force. Our life, our genius, our French civilization, the greatness of a thousand years,—we were conscious that France was in the hands of a brutal conqueror who did not understand her, and hated her in his heart, and at any moment might crush the life out of her for ever. And we had to live for that and no other destiny! Have you ever thought of the French children born in houses of death in the shadow of defeat, fed with ideas of discouragement, trained to strike for a bloody, fatal, and perhaps futile revenge: for even as babies, the first thing they learned was that there was no justice, there was no justice in the world: might prevailed against right! For a child to open its

eyes upon such things is for its soul to be degraded or uplifted
for ever. Many succumbed: they said: 'Since it is so, why
struggle against it? Why do anything? Everything is nothing.
We'll not think of it. Let us enjoy ourselves.'—But those who
stood out against it are proof against fire: no disillusion can
touch their faith: for from their earliest childhood they have
known that their road could never lead them near the road to
happiness, and that they had no choice but to follow it: else
they would suffocate. Such assurance is not come by all at
once. It is not to be expected of boys of fifteen. There is
bitter agony before it is attained, and many tears are shed. But
it is well that it should be so. It must be so. . . .

"*O Faith, virgin of steel* . . .

"Dig deep with thy lance into the downtrodden hearts of the
peoples! . . ."

In silence Christophe pressed Olivier's hand.

"Dear Christophe," said Olivier, "your Germany has made
us suffer indeed."

And Christophe begged for forgiveness almost as though he
had been responsible for it.

"There's nothing for you to worry about," said Olivier, smiling. "The good it has unintentionally done us far outweighs
the ill. You have rekindled our idealism, you have revived in
us the keen desire for knowledge and faith, you have filled our
France with schools, you have raised to the highest pitch the
creative powers of a Pasteur, whose discoveries are alone worth
more than your indemnity of two hundred million; you have
given new life to our poetry, our painting, our music: to you
we owe the new awakening of the consciousness of our race.
We have reward enough for the effort needed to learn to set our
faith before our happiness: for, in doing so, we have come
by a feeling of such moral force, that, amid the apathy of the
world, we have no doubt, even of victory in the end. Though
we are few in number, my dear Christophe, though we seem
so weak,—a drop of water in the ocean of German power—we
believe that the drop of water will in the end color the whole

ocean. The Macedonian phalanx will destroy the mighty armies of the plebs of Europe."

Christophe looked down at the puny Olivier, in whose eyes there shone the light of faith, and he said:

"Poor weakly little Frenchmen! You are stronger than we are."

"O beneficent defeat," Olivier went on. "Blessed be that disaster! We will no more deny it! We are its children."

II

DEFEAT new-forges the chosen among men: it sorts out the people: it winnows out those who are purest and strongest, and makes them purer and stronger. But it hastens the downfall of the rest, or cuts short their flight. In that way it separates the mass of the people, who slumber or fall by the way, from the chosen few who go marching on. The chosen few know it and suffer: even in the most valiant there is a secret melancholy, a feeling of their own impotence and isolation. Worst of all,— cut off from the great mass of their people, they are also cut off from each other. Each must fight for his own hand. The strong among them think only of self-preservation. *O man, help thyself!* . . . They never dream that the sturdy saying means: *O men, help yourselves!* In all there is a want of confidence, they lack free-flowing sympathy, and do not feel the need of common action which makes a race victorious, the feeling of overflowing strength, of reaching upward to the zenith.

Christophe and Olivier knew something of all this. In Paris, full of men and women who could have understood them, in the house peopled with unknown friends, they were as solitary as in a desert of Asia.

They were very poor. Their resources were almost nil. Christophe had only the copying and transcriptions of music given him by Hecht. Olivier had very unwisely thrown up his

post at the University during the period of depression following on his sister's death, which had been accentuated by an
unhappy love affair with a young lady he had met at Madame
Nathan's:—(he had never mentioned it to Christophe, for he
was modest about his troubles: part of his charm lay in the
little air of mystery which he always preserved about his private affairs, even with his friend, from whom, however, he made
no attempt to conceal anything).—In his depressed condition
when he had longed for silence his work as a lecturer became intolerable to him. He had never cared for the profession, which
necessitates a certain amount of showing off, and thinking aloud,
while it gives a man no time to himself. If teaching in a
school is to be at all a noble thing it must be a matter of a sort
of apostolic vocation, and that Olivier did not possess in the
slightest degree: and lecturing for any of the Faculties means
being perpetually in contact with the public, which is a grim
fate for a man, like Olivier, with a desire for solitude. On
several occasions he had had to speak in public: it gave him a
singular feeling of humiliation. At first he loathed being ex-
hibited on a platform. He *saw* the audience, felt it, as with
antennæ, and knew that for the most part it was composed of
idle people who were there only for the sake of having something to do: and the rôle of official entertainer was not at all to
his liking. Worst of all, speaking from a platform is almost
bound to distort ideas: if the speaker does not take care there
is a danger of his passing gradually from a certain theatricality
in gesture, diction, attitude, and the form in which he presents
his ideas—to mental trickery. A lecture is a thing hovering
in the balance between tiresome comedy and polite pedantry.
For an artist who is rather bashful and proud, a lecture, which
is a monologue shouted in the presence of a few hundred unknown, silent people, a ready-made garment warranted to fit all
sizes, though it actually fits no one, is a thing intolerably false.
Olivier, being more and more under the necessity of withdrawing into himself and saying nothing which was not wholly the
expression of his thought, gave up the profession of teaching,

which he had had so much difficulty in entering: and, as he
no longer had his sister to check him in his tendency to dream,
he began to write. He was naïve enough to believe that his un-
doubted worth as an artist could not fail to be recognized without
his doing anything to procure recognition.

He was quickly undeceived. He found it impossible to get
anything published. He had a jealous love of liberty, which
gave him a horror of everything that might impinge on it, and
made him live apart, like a poor starved plant, among the solid
masses of the political churches whose baleful associations divided the country and the Press between them. He was just as
much cut off from all the literary coteries and rejected by
them. He had not, nor could he have, a single friend among
them. He was repelled by the hardness, the dryness, the egoism
of the intellectuals—(except for the very few who were following a real vocation, or were absorbed by a passionate enthusiasm
for scientific research). That man is a sorry creature who has
let his heart atrophy for the sake of his mind—when his mind
is small. In such a man there is no kindness, only a brain
like a dagger in a sheath: there is no knowing but it will one
day cut your throat. Against such a man it is necessary to be
always armed. Friendship is only possible with honest men,
who love fine things for their own sake, and not for what they
can make out of them,—those who live outside their art. The
majority of men cannot breathe the atmosphere of art. Only
the very great can live in it without loss of love, which is the
source of life.

Olivier could only count on himself. And that was a very
precarious support. Any fresh step was a matter of extreme
difficulty to him. He was not disposed to accept humiliation
for the sake of his work. He went hot with shame at the base
and obsequious homage which young authors forced themselves
to pay to a well-known theater manager, who took advantage
of their cowardice, and treated them as he would never dare to
treat his servants. Olivier could never have done that to save
his life. He just sent his manuscripts by post, or left them

at the offices of the theaters or the reviews, where they lay
for months unread. However, one day by chance he met one
of his old schoolfellows, an amiable loafer, who had still a sort
of grateful admiration for him for the ease and readiness with
which Olivier had done his exercises: he knew nothing at all
about literature: but he knew several literary men, which was
much better: he was rich and in society, something of a snob,
and so he let them, discreetly, exploit him. He put in a word
for Olivier with the editor of an important review in which he
was a shareholder: and at once one of his forgotten manuscripts
was disinterred and read: and, after much temporization,—(for,
if the article seemed to be worth something, the author's name,
being unknown, was valueless),—they decided to accept it.
When he heard the good news Olivier thought his troubles were
over. They were only just beginning.

It is comparatively easy to have an article accepted in Paris:
but getting it published is quite a different matter. The unhappy writer has to wait and wait, for months, if need be for
life, if he has not acquired the trick of flattering people, or
bullying them, and showing himself from time to time at the
receptions of these petty monarchs, and reminding them of his
existence, and making it clear that he means to go on being a
nuisance to them as long as they make it necessary. Olivier
just stayed at home, and wore himself out with waiting. At best
he would write a letter or two which were never answered. He
would lose heart, and be unable to work. It was quite absurd,
but there was nothing to be done. He would wait for post after
post, sitting at his desk, with his mind blanketed by all sorts of
vague injuries: then he would get up and go downstairs to the
porter's room, and look hopefully in his letter-box, only to meet
with disappointment: he would walk blindly about with no
thought in his head but to go back and look again: and when
the last post had gone, when the silence of his room was broken
only by the heavy footsteps of the people in the room above,
he would feel strangled by the cruel indifference of it all. Only
a word of reply, only a word! Could that be refused him if only

in charity? And yet those who refused him that had no idea
of the hurt they were dealing him. Every man sees the world
in his own image. Those who have no life in their hearts see
the universe as withered and dry: and they never dream of the
anguish of expectation, hope, and suffering which rends the
hearts of the young: or if they give it a thought, they judge them
coldly, with the weary, ponderous irony of those who are surfeited and beyond the freshness of life.

At last the article appeared. Olivier had waited so long that
it gave him no pleasure: the thing was dead for him. And yet
he hoped desperately that it would be a living thing for others.
There were flashes of poetry and intelligence in it which could
not pass unnoticed. It fell upon absolute silence.—He made
two or three more attempts. Being attached to no clique he met
with silence or hostility everywhere. He could not understand
it. He had thought simply that everybody must be naturally
well-disposed towards the work of a new man, even if it was
not very good. It always represents such an amount of work,
and surely people would be grateful to a man who has tried
to give others a little beauty, a little force, a little joy. But he
only met with indifference or disparagement. And yet he knew
that he could not be alone in feeling what he had written, and
that it must be in the minds of other good men. He did not
know that such good men did not read him, and had nothing to
do with literary opinion, or with anything, or with anything.
If here and there there were a few men whom his words had
reached, men who sympathized with him, they would never
tell him so: they remained immured in their unnatural silence.
Just as they refrained from voting, so they took no share in
art: they did not read books, which shocked them: they did
not go to the theater, which disgusted them: but they let their
enemies vote, elect their enemies, engineer a scandalous success and a vulgar celebrity for books and plays and ideas which
only represented an impudent minority of the people of
France.

Since Olivier could not count on those who were mentally

akin to himself, as they did not read, he was delivered up to the hosts of the enemy, to the mercy of men of letters, who were for the most part hostile to his ideas, and the critics who were at their beck and call.

His first bouts with them left him bleeding. He was as sensitive to criticism as old Bruchner, who could not bear to have his work performed, because he had suffered so much from the malevolence of the Press. He did not even win the support of his former colleagues at the University, who, thanks to their profession, did preserve a certain sense of the intellectual traditions of France, and might have understood him. But for the most part these excellent young men, cramped by discipline, absorbed in their work, often rather embittered by their thankless duties, could not forgive Olivier for trying to break away and do something else. Like good little officials, many of them were inclined only to admit the superiority of talent when it was consonant with hierarchic superiority.

In such a position three courses were open to him: to break down resistance by force: to submit to humiliating compromises: or to make up his mind to write only for himself. Olivier was incapable of the two first: he surrendered to the third. To make a living he went through the drudgery of teaching and went on writing, and as there was no possibility of his work attaining full growth in publicity, it became more and more involved, chimerical, and unreal.

Christophe dropped like a thunderbolt into the midst of his dim crepuscular life. He was furious at the wickedness of people and Olivier's patience.

"Have you no blood in your veins?" he would say. "How can you stand such a life? You know your own superiority to these swine, and yet you let them squeeze the life out of you without a murmur!"

"What can I do?" Olivier would say. "I can't defend myself. It revolts me to fight with people I despise: I know that they can use every weapon against me: and I can't. Not only should I loathe to stoop to use the means they employ, but I should be afraid of hurting them. When I was a boy I used to let my schoolfellows beat me as much as they liked. They used to think me a coward, and that I was afraid of being hit. I was more afraid of hitting than of being hit. I remember some one saying to me one day, when one of my tormentors was bullying me: 'Why don't you stop it once and for all, and give him a kick in the stomach?' That filled me with horror. I would much rather be thrashed."

"There's no blood in your veins," said Christophe. "And on top of that, all sorts of Christian ideas! . . . Your religious education in France is reduced to the Catechism: the emasculate Gospel, the tame, boneless New Testament. . . . Humanitarian clap-trap, always tearful. . . . And the Revolution, Jean-Jacques, Robespierre, '48, and, on top of that, the Jews! . . . Take a dose of the full-blooded Old Testament every morning."

Olivier protested. He had a natural antipathy for the Old Testament, a feeling which dated back to his childhood, when he used secretly to pore over an illustrated Bible, which had been in the library at home, where it was never read, and the children were even forbidden to open it. The prohibition was useless! Olivier could never keep the book open for long. He used quickly to grow irritated and saddened by it, and then he would close it: and he would find consolation in plunging into the *Iliad,* or the *Odyssey,* or the *Arabian Nights.*

"The gods of the *Iliad* are men, beautiful, mighty, vicious: I can understand them," said Olivier. "I like them or dislike them: even when I dislike them I still love them: I am in love with them. More than once, with Patroclus, I have kissed the lovely feet of Achilles as he lay bleeding. But the God of the Bible is an old Jew, a maniac, a monomaniac, a raging madman, who spends his time in growling and hurling threats, and howling like an angry wolf, raving to himself in the confinement of that cloud of his. I don't understand him. I don't love him; his perpetual curses make my head ache, and his savagery fills me with horror:

" The burden of Moab. . . .
" The burden of Damascus. . . .
" The burden of Babylon. . . .
" The burden of Egypt. . . .
" The burden of the desert of the sea. . . .
" The burden of the valley of vision. . . .

He is a lunatic who thinks himself judge, public prosecutor, and executioner rolled into one, and, even in the courtyard of his prison, he pronounces sentence of death on the flowers and the pebbles. One is stupefied by the tenacity of his hatred, which fills the book with bloody cries . . .—'a cry of destruction, . . . the cry is gone round about the borders of Moab: the howling thereof unto Eglaim, and the howling thereof unto Beerelim. . . .'

" Every now and then he takes a rest, and looks round on his massacres, and the little children done to death, and the women outraged and butchered: and he laughs like one of the captains of Joshua, feasting after the sack of a town:

" ' *And the Lord of hosts shall make unto all people a feast of fat things, a feast of wine on the lees, of fat things full of marrow, of wine on the lees well refined. . . . The sword of the Lord is filled with blood, it is made fat with fatness, with the fat of the kidneys of rams. . . .'*

" But worst of all is the perfidy with which this God sends his prophet to make men blind, so that in due course he may have a reason for making them suffer:

" ' *Make the heart of this people fat, and make their ears heavy and shut their eyes: lest they see with their eyes and hear with their ears and understand with their heart, and convert, and be healed.—Lord, how long?—Until the cities be wasted without inhabitants, and the houses without men, and the land be utterly desolate. . . .'* Oh! I have never found a man so evil as that! . . .

" I'm not so foolish as to deny the force of the language. But I cannot separate thought and form: and if I do occasionally admire this Hebrew God, it is with the same sort of admiration that I feel for a viper, or a . . .—(I'm trying in vain to find a Shakespearean monster as an example: I can't find one: even Shakespeare never begat such a hero of Hatred—saintly and virtuous Hatred). Such a book is a terrible thing. Madness is always contagious. And that particular madness is all the more dangerous inasmuch as it sets up its own murderous pride as an instrument of purification. England makes me shudder when I think that her people have for centuries been nourished on no other fare. . . . I'm glad to think that there is the dike of the Channel between them and me. I shall never believe that a nation is altogether civilized as long as the Bible is its staple food."

"In that case," said Christophe, "you will have to be just as much afraid of me, for I get drunk on it. It is the very marrow of a race of lions. Stout hearts are those which feed on it. Without the antidote of the Old Testament the Gospel is tasteless and unwholesome fare. The Bible is the bone and sinew of nations with the will to live. A man must fight, and he must hate."

"I hate hatred," said Olivier.

"I only wish you did!" retorted Christophe.

"You're right. I'm too weak even for that. What would you? I can't help seeing the arguments in favor of my enemies. And I say to myself over and over again, like Chardin: 'Gentleness! Gentleness!' . . ."

"What a silly sheep you are!" said Christophe. "But whether you like it or not, I'm going to make you leap the ditch you're shying at, and I'm going to drag you on and beat the big drum for you."

In the upshot he took Olivier's affairs in hand and set out to do battle for him. His first efforts were not very successful. He lost his temper at the very outset, and did his friend much harm by pleading his cause: he recognized what he had done very quickly, and was in despair at his own clumsiness.

Olivier did not stand idly by. He went and fought for Christophe. In spite of his fear and dislike of fighting, in spite of his lucid and ironical mind, which scorned any sort of exaggeration in word and deed, when it came to defending Christophe he was far more violent than anybody else, and even than Christophe himself. He lost his head. Love makes a man irrational, and Olivier was no exception to the rule.—However, he was cleverer than Christophe. Though he was uncompromising and clumsy in handling his own affairs, when it came to promoting Christophe's success he was politic and even tricky: he displayed an energy and ingenuity well calculated to win support: he succeeded in interesting various musical critics and Mæcenases in Christophe, though he would have been utterly ashamed to approach them with his own work.

In spite of everything they found it very difficult to better their lot. Their love for each other made them do many stupid things. Christophe got into debt over getting a volume of Olivier's poems published secretly, and not a single copy was sold. Olivier induced Christophe to give a concert, and hardly anybody came to it. Faced with the empty hall, Christophe consoled himself bravely with Handel's quip: " Splendid! My music will sound all the better. . . ." But these bold attempts did not repay the money they cost: and they would go back to their rooms full of indignation at the indifference of the world.

In their difficulties the only man who came to their aid was a Jew, a man of forty, named Taddée Mooch. He kept an art-photograph shop: but although he was interested in his trade and brought much taste and skill to bear on it, he was interested in so many things outside it that he was apt to neglect his business for them. When he did attend to his business he was chiefly engaged in perfecting technical devices, and he would lose his head over new reproduction processes, which, in spite of their ingenuity, hardly ever succeeded, and always cost him a great deal of money. He was a voracious reader, and was always hard on the heels of every new idea in philosophy, art, science, and politics: he had an amazing knack of finding out men of originality and independence of character: it was as though he answered to their magnetism.   He was a sort of connecting-link between Olivier's friends, who were all as isolated as himself, and all working in their several directions.   He used to go from one to the other, and through him there was established between them a complete circuit of ideas, though neither he nor they had any notion of it.

When Olivier first proposed to introduce him to Christophe, Christophe refused: he was sick of his experiences with the tribe of Israel.   Olivier laughed and insisted on it, saying that he knew no more of the Jews than he did of France.   At last Christophe consented, but when he saw Taddée Mooch he made a face.   In appearance Mooch was extraordinarily Jewish: he was the Jew as he is drawn by those who dislike the race: short, bald, badly built, with a greasy nose and heavy eyes goggling behind large spectacles: his face was hidden by a rough, black, scrubby beard: he had hairy hands, long arms, and short bandy legs: a little Syrian Baal.   But he had such a kindly expression that Christophe was touched by it.   Above all, he was very simple, and never talked too much.   He never paid exaggerated compliments, but just dropped the right word, pat.   He was very eager to be of service, and before any kindness was asked of him it would be done.   He came often, too often; and he almost always brought good news: work for one or other of them, a commission for an article or a lecture for Olivier, or music-lessons for Christophe.   He never stayed long.   It was a sort of affectation with him never to intrude.   Perhaps he saw Christophe's irritation, for his first impulse was always towards an ejaculation of impatience when he saw the bearded face of the Carthaginian idol,—(he used to call him "Moloch")—appear round the door: but the next moment it would be gone, and he would feel nothing but gratitude for his perfect kindness.

Kindness is not a rare quality with the Jews: of all the virtues it is the most readily admitted among them, even when they do not practise it. Indeed, in most of them it remains negative or neutral: indulgence, indifference, dislike for hurting anybody, ironic tolerance. With Mooch it was an active passion. He was always ready to devote himself to some cause or person: to his poor co-religionists, to the Russian refugees, to the oppressed of every nation, to unfortunate artists, to the alleviation of every kind of misfortune, to every generous cause. His purse was always open: and however thinly lined it might be, he could always manage to squeeze a mite out of it: when it was empty he would squeeze the mite out of some one else's purse: if he could do any one a service no pains were too great for him to take, no distance was too far for him to go. He did it simply—with exaggerated simplicity. He was a little apt to talk too much about his simplicity and sincerity: but the great thing was that he was both simple and sincere.

Christophe was torn between irritation and sympathy with Mooch, and one day he said an innocently cruel thing, though he said it with the air of a spoiled child. Mooch's kindness had touched him, and he took his hands affectionately and said:

"What a pity! . . . What a pity it is that you are a Jew!"

Olivier started and blushed, as though the shaft had been leveled at himself. He was most unhappy, and tried to heal the wound his friend had dealt.

Mooch smiled, with sad irony, and replied calmly:

"It is an even greater misfortune to be a man."

To Christophe the remark was nothing but the whim of a moment. But its pessimism cut deeper than he imagined: and Olivier, with his subtle perception, felt it intuitively. Beneath the Mooch of their acquaintance there was another different Mooch, who was in many ways exactly the opposite. His apparent nature was the result of a long struggle with his real nature. Though he was apparently so simple he had a distorted mind: when he gave way to it he was forced to complicate simple things and to endow his most genuine feelings with a deliberately ironical character. Though he was apparently modest and, if anything, too humble, at heart he was proud,

and knew it, and strove desperately to whip it out of himself.
His smiling optimism, his incessant activity, his perpetual business in helping others, were the mask of a profound nihilism, a
deadly despondency which dared not see itself face to face.
Mooch made a show of immense faith in all sorts of things: in
the progress of humanity, in the future of the pure Jewish spirit,
in the destiny of France, the soldier of the new spirit——(he was
apt to identify the three causes).   Olivier was not taken in by
it, and used to say to Christophe:

"At heart he believes in nothing."

With all his ironical common sense and calmness Mooch was
a neurasthenic who dared not look upon the void within himself.
He had terrible moments when he felt his nothingness: sometimes he would wake suddenly in the middle of the night
screaming with terror.   And he would cast about for things
to do, like a drowning man clinging to a life-buoy.

It is a costly privilege to be a member of a race which is ex-
ceeding old.   It means the bearing of a frightful burden of the
past, trials and tribulations, weary experience, disillusion of
mind and heart,—all the ferment of immemorial life, at the
bottom of which is a bitter deposit of irony and boredom. . . .
Boredom, the immense boredom of the Semites, which has
nothing in common with our Aryan boredom, though that, too,
makes us suffer; while it is at least traceable to definite causes,
and vanishes when those causes cease to exist: for in most cases
it is only the result of regret that we cannot have what we want.
But in some of the Jews the very source of joy and life is tainted
with a deadly poison.   They have no desire, no interest in anything: no ambition, no love, no pleasure.   Only one thing con-
tinues to exist, not intact, but morbid and fine-drawn, in these
men uprooted from the East, worn out by the amount of energy
they have had to give out for centuries, longing for quietude,
without having the power to attain it: thought, endless analysis,
which forbids the possibility of enjoyment, and leaves them no
courage for action.   The most energetic among them set themselves parts to play, and play them, rather than act on their

own account. It is a strange thing that in many of them—
and not in the least intelligent or the least seriously minded—
this lack of interest in life prompts the impulse, or the un-
avowed desire, to act a part, to play at life,—the only means
they know of living!

Mooch was an actor after his fashion. He rushed about to
try to deaden his senses. But whereas most people only bestir
themselves for selfish reasons, he was restlessly active in pro-
curing the happiness of others. His devotion to Christophe was
both touching and a bore. Christophe would snub him and
then immediately be sorry for it. But Mooch never bore him
any ill-will. Nothing abashed him. Not that he had any
ardent affection for Christophe. It was devotion that he loved
rather than the men to whom he devoted himself. They were
only an excuse for doing good, for living.

He labored to such effect that he managed to induce Hecht to
publish Christophe's *David* and some other compositions. Hecht
appreciated Christophe's talent, but he was in no hurry to
reveal it to the world. It was not until he saw that Mooch
was on the point of arranging the publication at his own expense with another firm that he took the initiative out of vanity.

And on another occasion, when things were very serious and
Olivier was ill and they had no money, Mooch thought of going
to Félix Weil, the rich archeologist, who lived in the same
house. Mooch and Weil were acquainted, but had little sympathy with one another. They were too different: Mooch's restlessness and mysticism and revolutionary ideas and "vulgar"
manners, which, perhaps, he exaggerated, were an incentive to
the irony of Félix Weil, with his calm, mocking temper, his distinguished manners and conservative mind. They had only one
thing in common: they were both equally lacking in any profound interest in action: and if they did indulge in action, it
was not from faith, but from their tenacious and mechanical
vitality. But neither was prepared to admit it: they preferred
to give their minds to the parts they were playing, and their
different parts had very little in common. And so Mooch was

quite coldly received by Weil: when he tried to interest him in
the artistic projects of Olivier and Christophe, he was brought
up sharp against a mocking skepticism. Mooch's perpetual embarkations for one Utopia or another were a standing joke in
Jewish society, where he was regarded as a dangerous visionary.
But on this occasion, as on so many others, he was not put out:
and he went on speaking about the friendship of Christophe
and Olivier until he roused Weil's interest. He saw that and
went on.

He had touched a responsive chord. The friendless solitary
old man worshiped friendship: the one great love of his life
had been a friendship which he had left behind him: it was his
inward treasure: when he thought of it he felt a better man.
He had founded institutions in his friend's name, and had
dedicated his books to his memory. He was touched by what
Mooch told him of the mutual tenderness of Christophe and
Olivier. His own story had been something like it. His lost
friend had been a sort of elder brother to him, a comrade of
youth, a guide whom he had idolized. That friend had been
one of those young Jews, burning with intelligence and generous ardor, who suffer from the hardness of their surroundings,
and set themselves to uplift their race, and, through their race,
the world, and burn hotly into flame, and, like a torch of resin,
flare for a few hours and then die. The flame of his life had
kindled the apathy of young Weil. He had raised him from
the earth. While his friend was alive Weil had marched by
his side in the shining light of his stoical faith,—faith in
science, in the power of the spirit, in a future happiness,—the
rays of which were shed upon everything with which that mes-
sianic soul came in contact. When he was left alone, in his
weakness and irony, Weil fell from the heights of that idealism
into the sands of that Book of Ecclesiastes, which exists in the
mind of every Jew and saps his spiritual vitality. But he had
never forgotten the hours spent in the light with his friend:
jealously he guarded its clarity, now almost entirely faded.
He had never spoken of him to a soul, not even to his wife,

whom he loved: it was a sacred thing. And the old man, who was considered prosaic and dry of heart, and nearing the end of his life, used to say to himself the bitter and tender words of a Brahmin of ancient India:

" The poisoned tree of the world puts forth two fruits sweeter than the waters of the fountain of life: one is poetry, the other, friendship."

From that time on he took an interest in Christophe and Olivier. He knew how proud they were, and got Mooch, without saying anything, to send him Olivier's volume of poems, which had just been published: and, without the two friends having anything to do with it, without their having even the smallest idea of what he was up to, he managed to get the Academy to award the book a prize, which came in the nick of time to help them in their difficulty.

When Christophe discovered that such unlooked-for assistance came from a man of whom he was inclined to think ill, he regretted all the unkind things he had said or thought of him: he gulped down his dislike of calling, and went and thanked him. His good intentions met with no reward. Old Weil's irony was excited by Christophe's young enthusiasm, although he tried hard to conceal it from him, and they did not get on at all well.

That very day, when Christophe returned, irritated, though still grateful, to his attic, after his interview with Weil, he found Mooch there, doing Olivier some fresh act of service, and also a review containing a disparaging article on his music by Lucien Lévy-Cœur;—it was not written in a vein of frank criticism, but took the insultingly kindly line of chaffing him and banteringly considering him alongside certain third-rate and fourth-rate musicians whom he loathed.

"You see," said Christophe to Olivier, after Mooch had gone, "we always have to deal with Jews, nothing but Jews! Perhaps we're Jews ourselves? Do tell me that we're not. We seem to attract them. We're always knocking up against them, both friends and foes."

"The reason is," said Olivier, "that they are more intelligent than the rest. The Jews are almost the only people in France to whom a free man can talk of new and vital things. The rest are stuck fast in the past among dead things. Unfortunately the past does not exist for the Jews, or at least it is not the same for them as for us. With them we can only talk about the things of to-day: with our fellow-countrymen we can only discuss the things of yesterday. Look at the activity of the Jews in every kind of way: commerce, industry, education, science, philanthropy, art. . . ."

"Don't let's talk about art," said Christophe.

"I don't say that I am always in sympathy with what they do: very often I detest it. But at least they are alive, and can understand men who are alive. It is all very well for us to criticise and make fun of the Jews, and speak ill of them. We can't do without them."

"Don't exaggerate," said Christophe jokingly. "I could do without them perfectly."

"You might go on living perhaps. But what good would that be to you if your life and your work remained unknown, as they probably would without the Jews? Would the members of your own religion come to your assistance? The Catholic Church lets the best of its members perish without raising a hand to help them. Men who are religious from the very bottom of their hearts, men who give their lives in the defense of God,—if they have dared to break away from Catholic dominion and shake off the authority of Rome,—at once find the unworthy mob who call themselves Catholic not only indifferent, but hostile: they condemn them to silence, and abandon them to the mercy of the common enemy. If a man of independent spirit, be he never so great and Christian at heart, is not a Christian as a matter of obedience, it is nothing to the Catholics that in him is incarnate all that is most pure and most truly divine in their faith. He is not of the pack, the blind and deaf sect which refuses to think for itself. He is cast out, and the rest rejoice to see him suffering alone, torn to pieces by the

enemy, and crying for help to those who are his brothers, for
whose faith he is done to death.   In the Catholicism of to-day
there is a horrible, death-dealing power of inertia.   It would
find it far easier to forgive its enemies than those who wish to
awake it and restore it to life. . . .   My dear Christophe,
where should we be, and what should we do—we, who are
Catholics by birth, we, who have shaken free, without the little
band of free Protestants and Jews?   The Jews in Europe of
to-day are the most active and living agents of good and evil.
They carry hither and thither the pollen of thought.   Have not
your worst enemies and your friends from the very beginning
been Jews?"

"That's true," said Christophe.   "They have given me encouragement and help, and said things to me which have given
me new life for the struggle, by showing me that I was understood.   No doubt very few of my friends have remained faithful to me: their friendship was but a fire of straw.   No matter!
That fleeting light is a great thing in darkness.   You are right:
we mustn't be ungrateful."

"We must not be stupid, either," replied Olivier.   "We must
not mutilate our already diseased civilization by lopping off
some of its most living branches.   If we were so unfortunate as
to have the Jews driven from Europe, we should be left so poor
in intelligence and power for action that we should be in danger
of utter bankruptcy.   In France especially, in the present condition of French vitality, their expulsion would mean a more
deadly drain on the blood of the nation than the expulsion of
the Protestants in the seventeenth century.—No doubt, for the
time being, they do occupy a position out of all proportion to
their true merit.   They do take advantage of the present moral
and political anarchy, which in no small degree they help to
aggravate, because it suits them, and because it is natural to
them to do so.   The best of them, like our friend Mooch, make
the mistake, in all sincerity, of identifying the destiny of France
with their Jewish dreams, which are often more dangerous than
useful.   But you can't blame them for wanting to build France

in their own image: it means that they love the country. If
their love becomes a public danger, all we have to do is to defend ourselves and keep them in their place, which, in France,
is the second. Not that I think their race inferior to ours:—
(all these questions of the supremacy of races are idiotic and disgusting).—But we cannot admit that a foreign race which has
not yet been fused into our own, can possibly know better than
we do what suits us. The Jews are well off in France: I am
glad of it: but they must not think of turning France into
Judea! An intelligent and strong Government which was able
to keep the Jews in their place would make them one of the
most useful instruments for the building of the greatness of
France: and it would be doing both them and us a great
service. These hypernervous, restless, and unsettled creatures
need the restraint of law and the firm hand of a just master, in
whom there is no weakness, to curb them. The Jews are like
women: admirable when they are reined in; but, with the Jews
as with women, their use of mastery is an abomination, and
those who submit to it present a pitiful and absurd spectacle."

In spite of their love for each other, and the intuitive knowledge that came with it, there were many things which Christophe
and Olivier could not understand in each other, things, too,
which shocked them. In the beginning of their friendship,
when each tried instinctively only to suffer the existence of
those qualities in himself which were most like the qualities
of his friend, they never remarked them. It was only gradually that the different aspects of their two nationalities appeared
on the surface again, more sharply defined than before: for
being in contrast, each showed the other up. There were moments of difficulty, moments when they clashed, which, with all
their fond indulgence, they could not altogether avoid.

Sometimes they misunderstood each other. Olivier's mind
was a mixture of faith, liberty, passion, irony, and universal
doubt, for which Christophe could not find any working formula.

Olivier, on his part, was distressed by Christophe's lack of psychology: being of an old intellectual stock, and therefore aristocratic, he was moved to smile at the awkwardness of such a vigorous, though lumbering and single mind, which had no power of self-analysis, and was always being taken in by others and by itself. Christophe's sentimentality, his noisy outbursts, his facile emotions, used sometimes to exasperate Olivier, to whom they seemed absurd. Not to speak of a certain worship of force, the German conviction of the excellence of fist-morality, *Faustrecht,* to which Olivier and his countrymen had good reason for not subscribing.

And Christophe could not bear Olivier's irony, which used sometimes to make him furious with exasperation: he could not bear his mania for arguing, his perpetual analysis, and the curious intellectual immorality, which was surprising in a man who set so much store by moral purity as Olivier, and arose from the very breadth of his mind, to which every kind of negation was detestable,—so that he took a delight in the contemplation of ideas the opposite of his own. Olivier's outlook on things was in some sort historical and panoramic: it was so necessary for him to understand everything that he always saw reasons both for and against, and supported each in turn, according as the opposite thesis was put forward: and so amid such contradictions he lost his way. He would leave Christophe hopelessly perplexed. It was not that he had any desire to contradict or any taste for paradox: it was an imperious need in him for justice and common sense: he was exasperated by the stupidity of any assumption, and he had to react against it. The crudeness with which Christophe judged immoral men and actions, by seeing everything as much coarser and more brutal than it really was, distressed Olivier, who was just as moral, but was not of the same unbending steel; he allowed himself to be tempted, colored, and molded by outside influences. He would protest against Christophe's exaggerations and fly off into exaggeration in the opposite direction. Almost every day this perverseness of mind would make him take up the cudgels for his adversaries against his friends. Christophe would lose his

temper. He would cry out upon Olivier's sophistry and his indulgence of hateful things and people. Olivier would smile: he
knew the utter absence of illusion that lay behind his indulgence:
he knew that Christophe believed in many more things than
he did, and had a greater power of acceptance! But Christophe would look neither to the right hand nor the left, but
went straight ahead. He was especially angry with Parisian
" kindness."

"Their great argument, of which they are so proud, in
favor of 'pardoning' rascals, is," he would say, "that all
rascals are sufficiently unhappy in their wickedness, or that they
are irresponsible or diseased. . . . In the first place, it is
not true that those who do evil are unhappy. That's a moral
idea in action, a silly melodramatic idea, stupid, empty
optimism, such as you find in Scribe and Capus,—(Scribe and
Capus, your Parisian great men, artists of whom your pleasure-
seeking, vulgar society is worthy, childish hypocrites, too
cowardly to face their own ugliness).—It is quite possible for a
rascal to be a happy man. He has every chance of being so.
And as for his irresponsibility, that is an idiotic idea. Do
have the courage to face the fact that Nature does not care a
rap about good and evil, and is so far malevolent that a man may
easily be a criminal and yet perfectly sound in mind and body.
Virtue is not a natural thing. It is the work of man. It is
his duty to defend it. Human society has been built up by a
few men who were stronger and greater than the rest. It is
their duty to see that the work of so many ages of frightful
struggles is not spoiled by the cowardly rabble."

At bottom there was no great difference between these ideas
and Olivier's: but, by a secret instinct for balance and proportion, he was never so dilettante as when he heard provocative
words thrown out.

"Don't get so excited, my friend," he would say to Christophe. "Let the world hug its vices. Like the friends in the
'Decameron,' let us breathe in peace the balmy air of the
gardens of thought, while under the cypress-hill and the tall,

shady pines, twined about with roses, Florence is devastated by the black plague."

He would amuse himself for days together by pulling to pieces art, science, philosophy, to find their hidden wheels: so he came by a sort of Pyrrhonism, in which everything that was became only a figment of the mind, a castle in the air, which had not even the excuse of the geometric symbols, of being necessary to the mind. Christophe would rage against his pulling the machine to pieces:

"It was going quite well: you'll probably break it. Then how will you be better off? What are you trying to prove? That nothing is nothing? Good Lord! I know that. It is because nothingness creeps in upon us from every side that we fight. Nothing exists? I exist. There's no reason for doing anything? I'm doing what I can. If people like death, let them die! For my part, I'm alive, and I'm going to live. My life is in one scale of the balance, my mind and thought in the other. . . . To hell with thought!"

He would fly off with his usual violence, and in their argument he would say things that hurt. Hardly had he said them than he was sorry. He would long to withdraw them: but the harm was done. Olivier was very sensitive: his skin was easily barked: a harsh word, especially if it came from some one he loved, hurt him terribly. He was too proud to say anything, and would retire into himself. And he would see in his friend those sudden flashes of unconscious egoism which appear in every great artist. Sometimes he would feel that his life was no great thing to Christophe compared with a beautiful piece of music:— (Christophe hardly troubled to disguise the fact).—He would understand and see that Christophe was right: but it made him sad.

And then there were in Christophe's nature all sorts of disordered elements which eluded Olivier and made him uneasy. He used to have sudden fits of a freakish and terrible humor. For days together he would not speak: or he would break out in diabolically malicious moods and try deliberately to hurt.

Sometimes he would disappear altogether and be seen no more for the rest of the day and part of the night. Once he stayed away for two whole days. God knows what he was up to! He was not very clear about it himself. . . . The truth was that his powerful nature, shut up in that narrow life, and those small rooms, as in a hen-coop, every now and then reached bursting-point. His friend's calmness maddened him: then he would long to hurt him, to hurt some one. He would have to rush away, and wear himself out. He would go striding through the streets of Paris and the outskirts in the vague quest of adventure, which sometimes he found: and he would not have been sorry to meet with some rough encounter which would have given him the opportunity of expending some of his superfluous energy in a brawl. . . . It was hard for Olivier, with his poor health and weakness of body, to understand. Christophe was not much nearer understanding it. He would wake up from his aberrations as from an exhausting dream,—a little uneasy and ashamed of what he had been doing and might yet do. But when the fit of madness was over he would feel like a great sky washed by the storm, purged of every taint, serene, and sovereign of his soul. He would be more tender than ever with Olivier, and bitterly sorry for having hurt him. He would give up trying to account for their little quarrels. The wrong was not always on his side: but he would take all the blame upon himself, and put it down to his unjust passion for being right; and he would think it better to be wrong with his friend than to be right, if right were not on his side.

Their misunderstandings were especially grievous when they occurred in the evening, so that the two friends had to spend the night in disunion, which meant that both of them were morally upset. Christophe would get up and scribble a note and slip it under Olivier's door: and next day as soon as he woke up he would beg his pardon. Sometimes, even, he would knock at his door in the middle of the night: he could not bear to wait for the day to come before he humbled himself. As a rule, Olivier would be just as unable to sleep. He knew that Christophe loved him, and had not wished to hurt him: but he wanted to hear him say so. Christophe would say so, and then the whole thing would be forgotten. Then they would be pacified. Delightful state! How well they would sleep for the rest of the night!

"Ah!" Olivier would sigh. "How difficult it is to understand each other!"

"But is it necessary always to understand each other?" Christophe would ask. "I give it up. We only need love each other."

All these petty quarrels which, with anxious tenderness, they would at once find ways of mending, made them almost dearer to each other than before. When they were hotly arguing Antoinette would appear in Olivier's eyes. The two friends would pay each other womanish attentions. Christophe never let Olivier's birthday go by without celebrating it by dedicating a composition to him, or by the gift of flowers, or a cake, or a little present, bought Heaven knows how!—(for they often had no money in the house)—Olivier would tire his eyes out with copying out Christophe's scores at night and by stealth.

Misunderstandings between friends are never very serious so long as a third party does not come between them.—But that was bound to happen: there are too many people in this world ready to meddle in the affairs of others and make mischief between them.

Olivier knew the Stevens, whom Christophe rarely visited, and he too had been attracted by Colette. The reason why Christophe had not met him in the girl's little court was that just at that time Olivier was suffering from his sister's death, and had shut himself up with his grief and saw no one. Colette, on her part, did not go out of her way to see him: she liked Olivier, but she did not like unhappy people: she used to declare that she was so sensitive that she could not bear the sight of sorrow: she waited until Olivier's sorrow was over before she remembered his existence. When she heard that he seemed to be himself again, and that there was no danger of infection, she made bold to beckon him to her. Olivier did not need much inducement to go. He was shy but he liked society, and he was easily led: and he had a weakness for Colette. When he told Christophe of his intention of going back to her, Christophe, who had too much respect for his friend's liberty to express any adverse opinion, just shrugged his shoulders and said jokingly:

"Go, dear boy, if it amuses you."

But nothing would have induced him to follow his example. He had made up his mind to have nothing more to do with a coquette like Colette or the world she lived in. Not that he was a misogynist: far from it. He had a very tender feeling for all the young women who worked for their living, the factory-hands, and typists, and Government clerks, who are to be seen every morning, half awake, always a little late, hurrying to their workshops and offices. It seemed to him that a woman was only in possession of all her senses when she was working and struggling for her own individual existence, by earning her daily bread and her independence. And it seemed to him that only then did she possess all her charm, her alert suppleness of movement, the awakening of all her senses, her integrity of life and will. He detested the idle, pleasure-seeking woman, who seemed to him to be only an overfed animal, perpetually in the act of digestion, bored, browsing over unwholesome dreams. Olivier, on the contrary, adored the *far niente* of women, their charm, like the charm of flowers, living only to be beautiful and to perfume the air about them. He was more of an artist: Christophe was more human. Unlike Colette, Christophe loved other people in proportion as they shared in the suffering of the world. So, between him and them there was a bond of brotherly compassion.

Colette was particularly anxious to see Olivier again, after she heard of his friendship with Christophe: for she was curious to hear the details. She was rather angry with Christophe for the disdainful manner in which he seemed to have forgotten her: and, though she had no desire for revenge,—(it was not worth the trouble: and revenge does mean a certain amount of trouble),—she would have been very glad to pay him out. She was like a cat that bites the hand that strokes it. She had an ingratiating way with her, and she had no difficulty in getting Olivier to talk. Nobody could be more clear-sighted than he, or less easily taken in by people, when he was away from them: but nobody could be more naïvely confiding than he when he was with a woman whose eyes smiled kindly at him. Colette displayed so genuine an interest in his friendship with Christophe that he went so far as to tell her the whole story, and even about certain of their amicable misunderstandings, which, at a distance, seemed amusing, and he took the whole blame for them on himself. He also confided to Colette Christophe's artistic projects, and also some of his opinions—which were not altogether flattering—concerning France and the French. Nothing that he told her was of any great importance in itself, but Colette repeated it all at once, and adapted it partly to make the story more spicy, and partly to satisfy her secret feeling of malice against Christophe. And as the first person to receive her confidence was naturally her inseparable Lucien Lévy-Cœur, who had no reason for keeping it secret, the story went the rounds, and was embellished by the way: a note of ironic pity for Olivier, who was represented as a victim, was introduced, and he cut rather a sorry figure. It seemed unlikely that the story could be very interesting to anybody, since the heroes of it were very little known: but a Parisian takes an interest in everything that does not concern him. So much so, that one day Christophe heard the story from the lips of Madame Roussin. She met him one day at a concert, and asked him if it were true that he had quarreled with that poor Olivier Jeannin: and she asked about his work, and alluded to things which he believed were known only to himself and Olivier. And when he asked her how she had come by her information, she said she had had it from Lucien Lévy-Cœur, who had had it direct from Olivier.

The blow overwhelmed Christophe. Violent and uncritical as he was, it never occurred to him to think how utterly fantastic the story was: he only saw one thing: his secrets which he had confided to Olivier had been betrayed—betrayed to Lucien Lévy-Cœur. He could not stay to the end of the concert: he left the hall at once. Around him all was blank and dark. In the street he narrowly escaped being run over. He said to himself over and over again: " My friend has betrayed me! . . ."

Olivier was with Colette. Christophe locked the door of his room, so that when Olivier came in he could not have his usual talk with him. He heard him come in a few moments later and try to open the door, and whisper " Good-night " through the keyhole: he did not stir. He was sitting on his bed in the dark, holding his head in his hands, and saying over and over again: " My friend has betrayed me! . . .": and he stayed like that half through the night. Then he felt how dearly he loved Olivier: for he was not angry with him for having betrayed him: he only suffered. Those whom we love have absolute rights over us, even the right to cease loving us. We cannot bear them any ill-will; we can only be angry with ourselves for being so unworthy of love that it must desert us. There is mortal anguish in such a state of mind—anguish which destroys the will to live.

Next morning, when he saw Olivier, he did not tell him anything: he so detested the idea of reproaching him,—reproaching him for having abused his confidence and flung his secrets into the enemy's maw,—that he could not find a single word to say to him. But his face said what he could not speak: his expression was icy and hostile. Olivier was struck dumb: he could not understand it. He tried timidly to discover what Christophe had against him. Christophe turned away from him brutally, and made no reply. Olivier was hurt in his turn, and said no more, and gulped down his distress in silence. They did not see each other again that day.

Even if Olivier had made him suffer a thousand times more,

Christophe would never have done anything to avenge himself, and he would have done hardly anything to defend himself: Olivier was sacred to him. But it was necessary that the indignation he felt should be expended upon some one: and since that some one could not be Olivier, it was Lucien Lévy-Cœur. With his usual passionate injustice he put upon him the responsibility for the ill-doing which he attributed to Olivier: and he suffered intolerable pangs of jealousy in the thought that such a man as that could have robbed him of his friend's affection, just as he had previously ousted him from his friendship with Colette Stevens. To bring his exasperation to a head, that very day he happened to see an article by Lucien Lévy-Cœur on a performance of *Fidelio*. In it he spoke of Beethoven in a bantering way, and poked fun at his heroine. Christophe was as alive as anybody to the absurdities of the opera, and even to certain mistakes in the music. He had not always displayed an exaggerated respect for the acknowledged master himself. But he set no store by always agreeing with his own opinions, nor had he any desire to be Frenchily logical. He was one of those men who are quite ready to admit the faults of their friends, but cannot bear anybody else to do so. And, besides, it was one thing to criticise a great artist, however bitterly, from a passionate faith in art, and even—(one may say)— from an uncompromising love for his fame and intolerance of anything mediocre in his work,—and another thing, as Lucien Lévy-Cœur did, only to use such criticism to flatter the baseness of the public, and to make the gallery laugh, by an exhibition of wit at the expense of a great man. Again, free though Christophe was in his judgments, there had always been a certain sort of music which he had tacitly left alone and shielded: music which was not to be tampered with: that music, which was higher and better than music, the music of an absolutely pure soul, a great health-giving soul, to which a man could turn for consolation, strength, and hope. Beethoven's music was in the category. To see a puppy like Lévy-Cœur insulting Beethoven made him blind with anger. It was no longer a .

question of art, but a question of honor; everything that makes life rare, love, heroism, passionate virtue, the good human longing for self-sacrifice, was at stake. The Godhead itself was imperiled! There was no room for argument. It is as impossible to suffer that to be besmirched as to hear the woman you respect and love insulted: there is but one thing to do, to hate and kill. . . . What is there to say when the insulting blackguard was, of all men, the one whom Christophe most despised?

And, as luck would have it, that very evening the two men came face to face.

To avoid being left alone with Olivier, contrary to his habit, Christophe went to an At Home at the Roussins'. He was asked to play. He consented unwillingly. However, after a moment or two he became absorbed in the music he was playing, until, glancing up, he saw Lucien Lévy-Cœur standing in a little group, watching him with an ironical stare. He stopped short in the middle of a bar: he got up and turned away from the piano. There was an awkward silence. Madame Roussin came up to Christophe in her surprise and smiled forcedly; and, very cautiously,—for she was not sure whether the piece was finished or not,—she asked him:

"Won't you go on, Monsieur Krafft?"

"I've finished," he replied curtly.

He had hardly said it than he became conscious of his rudeness: but, instead of making him more restrained, it only excited him the more. He paid no heed to the amused attention of his auditors, but went and sat in a corner of the room from which he could follow Lucien Lévy-Cœur's movements. His neighbor, an old general, with a pinkish, sleepy face, light-blue eyes, and a childish expression, thought it incumbent on him to compliment him on the originality of his music. Christophe bowed irritably, and growled out a few inarticulate sounds. The general went on talking with effusive politeness and a gentle, meaningless smile: and he wanted Christophe to explain how he could play such a long piece of music from memory. Christophe fidgeted impatiently, and thought wildly of knocking the old gentleman off the sofa. He wanted to hear what Lucien Lévy-Cœur was saying: he was waiting for an excuse for attacking him. For some moments past he had been conscious that he was going to make a fool of himself: but no power on earth could have kept him from it.—Lucien Lévy-Cœur, in his high falsetto voice, was explaining the aims and secret thoughts of great artists to a circle of ladies. During a moment of silence Christophe heard him talking about the friendship of Wagner and King Ludwig, with all sorts of nasty innuendoes.

"Stop!" he shouted, bringing his fist down on the table by his side.

Everybody turned in amazement. Lucien Lévy-Cœur met Christophe's eyes and paled a little, and said:

"Were you speaking to me?"

"You hound! . . . Yes," said Christophe.

He sprang to his feet.

"You soil and sully everything that is great in the world," he went on furiously. "There's the door! Get out, you cur, or I'll fling you through the window!"

He moved towards him. The ladies moved aside screaming. There was a moment of general confusion. Christophe was surrounded at once. Lucien Lévy-Cœur had half risen to his feet: then he resumed his careless attitude in his chair. He called a servant who was passing and gave him a card: and he went on with his remarks as though nothing had happened: but his eyelids were twitching nervously, and his eyes blinked as he looked this way and that to see how people had taken it. Roussin had taken his stand in front of Christophe, and he took him by the lapel of his coat and urged him in the direction of the door. Christophe hung his head in his anger and shame, and his eyes saw nothing but the wide expanse of shirt-front, and kept on counting the diamond studs: and he could feel the big man's breath on his cheek.

"Come, come, my dear fellow!" said Roussin. "What's the

matter with you? Where are your manners? Control your-self! Do you know where you are? Come, come, are you mad?"

"I'm damned if I ever set foot in your house again!" said Christophe, breaking free: and he reached the door.

The people prudently made way for him. In the cloak-room a servant held out a salver. It contained Lucien Lévy-Cœur's card. He took it without understanding what it meant, and read it aloud: then, suddenly, snorting with rage, he fumbled in his pockets: mixed up with a varied assortment of things, he pulled out three or four crumpled dirty cards:

"There! There!" he said, flinging them on the salver so violently that one of them fell to the ground.

He left the house.

Olivier knew nothing about it. Christophe chose as his wit-nesses the first men of his acquaintance who turned up, the musical critic, Théophile Goujart, and a German, Doctor Barth, an honorary lecturer in a Swiss University, whom he had met one night in a café; he had made friends with him, though they had little in common: but they could talk to each other about Germany. After conferring with Lucien Lévy-Cœur's wit-nesses, pistols were chosen. Christophe was absolutely ignorant about the use of arms, and Goujart told him it would not be a bad thing for him to go and have a few lessons: but Christophe refused, and while he was waiting for the day to come went on with his work.

But his mind was distracted. He had a fixed idea, of which he was dimly conscious, while it kept buzzing in his head like a bad dream. . . . "It was unpleasant, yes, very unpleasant. . . . What was unpleasant?—Oh! the duel to-morrow. . . . Just a joke! Nobody is ever hurt. . . . But it was pos-sible. . . . Well, then, afterwards? . . . Afterwards, that was it, afterwards. . . . A cock of the finger by that swine who hates me may wipe out my life. . . . So be it! . . .— Yes, to-morrow, in a day or two, I may be lying in the loathsome soil of Paris. . . .—Bah! Here or anywhere, what does it matter! . . . Oh! Lord: I'm not going to play the coward!— No, but it would be monstrous to waste the mighty world of ideas that I feel springing to life in me for a moment's folly. . . . What rot it is, these modern duels in which they try to equalize the chances of the two opponents! That's a fine sort of equality that sets the same value on the life of a mountebank as on mine! Why don't they let us go for each other with fists and cudgels? There'd be some pleasure in that. But this cold-blooded shooting! . . . And, of course, he knows how to shoot, and I have never had a pistol in my hand. . . . They are right: I must learn. . . . He'll try to kill me. I'll kill him."

He went out. There was a range a few yards away from the house. Christophe asked for a pistol, and had it explained how he ought to hold it. With his first shot he almost killed his instructor: he went on with a second and a third, and fared no better: he lost patience, and went from bad to worse. A few young men were standing by watching and laughing. He paid no heed to them. With his German persistency he went on trying, and was so indifferent to their laughter and so determined to succeed that, as always happens, his blundering patience roused interest, and one of the spectators gave him advice. In spite of his usual violence he listened to everything with childlike docility; he managed to control his nerves, which were making his hand tremble: he stiffened himself and knit his brows: the sweat was pouring down his cheeks: he said not a word: but every now and then he would give way to a gust of anger, and then go on shooting. He stayed there for a couple of hours. At the end of that time he hit the bull's-eye. Few things could have been more absorbing than the sight of such a power of will mastering an awkward and rebellious body. It inspired respect. Some of those who had scoffed at the outset had gone, and the others were silenced one by one, and had not been able to tear themselves away. They took off their hats to Christophe when he went away.

When he reached home Christophe found his friend Mooch waiting anxiously. Mooch had heard of the quarrel, and had come at once: he wanted to know how it had originated. In spite of Christophe's reticence and desire not to attach any blame to Olivier, he guessed the reason. He was very cool-headed, and knew both the friends, and had no doubt of Olivier's innocence of the treachery ascribed to him. He looked into the matter, and had no difficulty in finding out that the whole trouble arose from the scandal-mongering of Colette and Lucien Lévy-Cœur. He rushed back with his evidence to Christophe, thinking that he could in that way prevent the duel. But the result was exactly the opposite of what he expected: Christophe was only the more rancorous against Lévy-Cœur when he learned that it was through him that he had come to doubt his friend. To get rid of Mooch, who kept on imploring him not to fight, he promised him everything he asked. But he had made up his mind. He was quite happy now: he was going to fight for Olivier, not for himself!

A remark made by one of the seconds as the carriage was going along a road through the woods suddenly caught Christophe's attention. He tried to find out what they were thinking, and saw how little they really cared about him. Professor Barth was wondering when the affair would be over, and whether he would be back in time to finish a piece of work he had begun on the manuscripts in the *Bibliothèque Nationale*. Of Christophe's three companions, he was the most interested in the result of the encounter as a matter of German national pride. Goujart paid no attention either to Christophe or the other German, but discussed certain scabrous subjects in connection with the coarser branches of physiology with Dr. Jullien, a young physician from Toulouse, who had recently come to live next door to Christophe, and occasionally borrowed his spirit-lamp, or his umbrella, or his coffee-cups, which he invariably returned broken. In return he gave him free consultations, tried medicines on him, and laughed at his simplicity. Under his impassive manner, that would have well become a Castilian hidalgo, there was a perpetual love of teasing. He was highly delighted with the adventure of the duel, which struck him as sheer burlesque: and he was amusing himself with fancying the mess that Christophe would make of it. He thought it a great joke to be driving through the woods at the expense of good old Krafft.—That, clearly, was what was in the minds of the trio: they regarded it as a jolly excursion which cost them nothing. Not one of them attached the least importance to the duel. But, on the other hand, they were just as calmly prepared for anything that might come of it.

They reached the appointed spot before the others. It was a little inn in the heart of the forest. It was a pleasure-resort, more or less unclean, to which Parisians used to resort to cleanse their honor when the dirt on it became too apparent. The hedges were bright with the pure flowers of the eglantine. In the shade of the bronze-leaved oak-trees there were rows of little tables. At one of these tables were seated three bicyclists: a painted woman, in knickerbockers, with black socks: and two men in flannels, who were stupefied by the heat, and every now and then gave out growls and grunts as though they had forgotten how to speak.

The arrival of the carriage produced a little buzz of excitement in the inn. Goujart, who knew the house and the people of old, declared that he would look after everything. Barth dragged Christophe into an arbor and ordered beer. The air was deliciously warm and soft, and resounding with the buzzing of bees. Christophe forgot why he had come. Barth emptied the bottle, and said, after a short silence:

"I know what I'll do."

He drank and went on:

"I shall have plenty of time: I'll go on to Versailles when it's all over."

Goujart was heard haggling with the landlady over the price of the dueling-ground. Jullien had not been wasting his time: as he passed near the bicyclists he broke into noisy and ecstatic comment on the woman's bare legs: and there was exchanged a perfect deluge of filthy epithets in which Jullien did not come off worst. Barth said in a whisper:

"The French are a low-minded lot. Brother, I drink to your victory."

He clinked his glass against Christophe's. Christophe was dreaming: scraps of music were floating in his mind, mingled with the harmonious humming of insects. He was very sleepy.

The wheels of another carriage crunched over the gravel of the drive. Christophe saw Lucien Lévy-Cœur's pale face, with its inevitable smile: and his anger leaped up in him. He got up, and Barth followed him.

Lévy-Cœur, with his neck swathed in a high stock, was dressed with a scrupulous care which was strikingly in contrast with his adversary's untidiness. He was followed by Count Bloch, a sportsman well known for his mistresses, his collection of old pyxes, and his ultra-Royalist opinions,—Léon Mouey, another man of fashion, who had reached his position as Deputy through literature, and was a writer from political ambition: he was young, bald, clean-shaven, with a lean bilious face: he had a long nose, round eyes, and a head like a bird's,—and Dr. Emmanuel, a fine type of Semite, well-meaning and cold, a member of the Academy of Medicine, a chief-surgeon in a hospital, famous for a number of scientific books, and the medical skepticism which made him listen with ironic pity to the plaints of his patients without making the least attempt to cure them.

The newcomers saluted the other three courteously. Christophe barely responded, but was annoyed by the eagerness and the exaggerated politeness with which they treated Lévy-Cœur's seconds. Jullien knew Emmanuel, and Goujart knew Mouey, and they approached them obsequiously smiling. Mouey greeted them with cold politeness and Emmanuel jocularly and without ceremony. As for Count Bloch, he stayed by Lévy-Cœur, and with a rapid glance he took in the condition of the clothes and linen of the three men of the opposing camp, and, hardly opening his lips, passed abrupt humorous comment on them with his friend,—and both of them stood calm and correct.

Lucien Lévy-Cœur stood at his ease waiting for Count Bloch, who had the ordering of the duel, to give the signal. He regarded the affair as a mere formality. He was an excellent shot, and was fully aware of his adversary's want of skill. He would not be foolish enough to make use of his advantage and hit him, always supposing, as was not very probable, that the seconds did not take good care that no harm came of the encounter: for he knew that nothing is so stupid as to let an enemy appear to be a victim, when a much surer and better method is to wipe him out of existence without any fuss being made. But Christophe stood waiting, stripped to his shirt, which was open to reveal his thick neck, while his sleeves were rolled up to show his strong wrists, head down, with his eyes glaring at Lévy-Cœur: he stood taut, with murder written implacably on every feature: and Count Bloch, who watched him carefully, thought what a good thing it was that civilization had as far as possible suppressed the risks of fighting.

After both men had fired, of course without result, the seconds hurried forward and congratulated the adversaries. Honor was satisfied.—Not so Christophe. He stayed there, pistol in hand, unable to believe that it was all over. He was quite ready to repeat his performance at the range the evening before, and go on shooting until one or other of them had hit the target. When he heard Goujart proposing that he should shake hands with his adversary, who advanced chivalrously towards him with his perpetual smile, he was exasperated by the pretense of the whole thing. Angrily he hurled his pistol away, pushed Goujart aside, and flung himself upon Lucien Lévy-Cœur. They were hard put to it to keep him from going on with the fight with his fists.

The seconds intervened while Lévy-Cœur escaped. Christophe broke away from them, and, without listening to their laughing expostulation, he strode along in the direction of the forest, talking loudly and gesticulating wildly. He did not even notice that he had left his hat and coat on the dueling-ground. He plunged into the woods. He heard his seconds laughing and calling him: then they tired of it, and did not worry about him any more. Very soon he heard the wheels of the carriages rumbling away and away, and knew that they had gone. He was left alone among the silent trees. His fury had subsided. He flung himself down on the ground and sprawled on the grass.

Shortly afterwards Mooch arrived at the inn. He had been pursuing Christophe since the early morning. He was told that his friend was in the woods, and went to look for him. He beat all the thickets, and awoke all the echoes, and was going away in despair when he heard him singing: he found his way by the voice, and at last came upon him in a little clearing with his arms and legs in the air, rolling about like a young calf. When Christophe saw him he shouted merrily, called him "dear old Moloch," and told him how he had shot his adversary full of holes until he was like a sieve: he made him tuck in his tuppenny, and then join him in a game of leap-frog: and when he jumped over him he gave him a terrific thump. Mooch was not very good at it, but he enjoyed the game almost as much as Christophe.—They returned to the inn arm-in-arm, and caught the train back to Paris at the nearest station.

Olivier knew nothing of what had happened. He was surprised at Christophe's tenderness: he could not understand his sudden change. It was not until the next day, when he saw the newspapers, that he knew that Christophe had fought a duel. It made him almost ill to think of the danger that Christophe had run. He wanted to know why the duel had been fought. Christophe refused to tell him anything. When he was pressed he said with a laugh:

"It was for you."

Olivier could not get a word more out of him. Mooch told him all about it. Olivier was horrified, quarreled with Colette, and begged Christophe to forgive his imprudence. Christophe was incorrigible, and quoted for his benefit an old French saying, which he adapted so as to infuriate poor Mooch, who was present to share in the happiness of the friends:

"My dear boy, let this teach you to be careful. . . .

> " *From an idle chattering girl,*
> *From a wheedling, hypocritical Jew,*
> *From a painted friend,*
> *From a familiar foe,*
> *And from flat wine,*
> *Libera Nos, Domine!* "

Their friendship was re-established. The danger of losing it, which had come so near, made it only the more dear. Their small misunderstandings had vanished: the very differences between them made them more attractive to each other. In his own soul Christophe embraced the souls of the two countries, harmoniously united. He felt that his heart was rich and full: and, as usual with him, his abundant happiness expressed itself in a flow of music.

Olivier marveled at it. Being too critical in mind, he was never far from believing that music, which he adored, had said its last word. He was haunted by the morbid idea that decadence must inevitably succeed a certain degree of progress: and he trembled lest the lovely art, which made him love life, should stop short, and dry up, and disappear into the ground. Christophe would scoff at such pusillanimous ideas. In a spirit of contradiction he would pretend that nothing had been done before he appeared on the scene, and that everything remained to be done. Olivier would instance French music, which seemed to have reached a point of perfection and ultimate civilization beyond which there could not possibly be anything. Christophe would shrug his shoulders:

"French music? . . . There has never been any. . . . And yet you have such fine things to do in the world! You can't really be musicians, or you would have discovered that. Ah! if only I were a Frenchman! . . . ."

And he would set out all the things that a Frenchman might turn into music:

"You involve yourselves in forms which do not suit you, and you do nothing at all with those which are admirably fitted for your use. You are a people of elegance, polite poetry, beautiful gestures, beautiful walking movements, beautiful attitudes, fashion, clothes, and you never write ballets nowadays, though you ought to be able to create an inimitable art of poetic dancing. . . .—You are a people of laughter and comedy, and you never write comic operas, or else you leave it to minor musicians, the confectioners of music. Ah! if I were a Frenchman I would set Rabelais to music, I would write comic epics. . . .—You are a people of story-tellers, and you never write novels in music: (for I don't count the feuilletons of Gustave Charpentier). You make no use of your gift of psychological analysis, your insight into character. Ah! if I were a Frenchman I would give you portraits in music. . . . (Would you like me to sketch the girl sitting in the garden under the lilac?). . . . I would write you Stendhal for a string quartet. . . .—You are the greatest democracy in Europe, and you have no theater for the people, no music for the people. Ah! if I were a Frenchman, I would set your Revolution to music: the 14th July, the 10th August. Valmy, the Federation, I would express the people in music! Not in the false form of Wagnerian declamation. I want symphonies, choruses, dances. Not speeches! I'm sick of them. There's no reason why people should always be talking in a music drama! Bother the words! Paint in bold strokes, in vast symphonies with choruses, immense landscapes in music, Homeric and Biblical epics, fire, earth, water, and sky, all bright and shining, the fever which makes hearts burn, the stirring of the instincts and destinies of a race, the triumph of Rhythm, the emperor of the world, who enslaves thousands of men, and hurls armies down to death. . . . Music everywhere, music in everything! If you were musicians you would have music for every one of your public holidays, for your official ceremonies, for the trades

unions, for the student associations, for your family festivals.
. . . But, above all, above all, if you were musicians, you
would make pure music, music which has no definite meaning,
music which has no definite use, save only to give warmth,
and air, and life. Make sunlight for yourselves! *Sat prata.*
. . . (What is that in Latin?). . . . There has been rain
enough. Your music gives me a cold. One can't see in it:
light your lanterns. . . . You complain of the Italian
porcherie, who invade your theaters and conquer the public,
and turn you out of your own house? It is your own fault!
The public are sick of your crepuscular art, your harmonized
neurasthenia, your contrapuntal pedantry. The public goes
where it can find life, however coarse and gross. Why do you
run away from life? Your Debussy is a bad man, however
great he may be as an artist. He aids and abets you in your
torpor. You want roughly waking up."

"What about Strauss?"

"No better. Strauss would finish you off. You need the
digestion of my fellow-countrymen to be able to bear such immoderate drinking. And even they cannot bear it. . . .
Strauss's *Salome!* . . . A masterpiece. . . . I should not
like to have written it. . . . I think of my old grandfather and uncle Gottfried, and with what respect and loving
tenderness they used to talk to me about the lovely art of
sound! . . . But to have the handling of such divine powers,
and to turn them to such uses! . . . A flaming, consuming
meteor! An Isolde, who is a Jewish prostitute. Bestial and
mournful lust. The frenzy of murder, pillage, incest, and un-
trammeled instincts which is stirring in the depths of German
decadence. . . . And, on the other hand, the spasm of a
voluptuous and melancholy suicide, the death-rattle which sounds
through your French decadence. . . . On the one hand, the
beast: on the other, the prey. Where is man? . . . Your
Debussy is the genius of good taste: Strauss is the genius of
bad taste. Debussy is rather insipid. But Strauss is very unpleasant. One is a silvery thread of stagnant water, losing it-

self in the reeds, and giving off an unhealthy aroma. The other is a mighty muddy flood. . . . Ah! the musty base Italianism and neo-Meyerbeerism, the filthy masses of sentiment which are borne on by the torrent! . . . An odious masterpiece! . . . Salome, the daughter of Ysolde. . . . And whose mother will Salome be in her turn?"

"Yes," said Olivier, "I wish we could jump fifty years. This headlong gallop towards the precipice must end one way or another: either the horse must stop or fall. Then we shall breathe again. Thank Heaven, the earth will not cease to flower, nor the sky to give light, with or without music! What have we to do with an art so inhuman! . . . The West is burning away. . . . Soon. . . . Very soon. . . . I see other stars arising in the furthest depths of the East."

"Bother the East!" said Christophe. "The West has not said its last word yet. Do you think I am going to abdicate? I have enough to say to keep you going for centuries. Hurrah for life! Hurrah for joy! Hurrah for the courage which drives us on to struggle with our destiny! Hurrah for love which maketh the heart big! Hurrah for friendship which rekindles our faith,—friendship, a sweeter thing than love! Hurrah for the day! Hurrah for the night! Glory be to the sun! *Laus Deo,* the God of joy, the God of dreams and actions, the God who created music! Hosannah! . . ."

With that he sat down at his desk and wrote down everything that was in his head, without another thought for what he had been saying.

At that time Christophe was in a condition in which all the elements of his life were perfectly balanced. He did not bother his head with esthetic discussions as to the value of this or that musical form, nor with reasoned attempts to create a new form: he did not even have to cast about for subjects for translation into music. One thing was as good as another. The flood of music welled forth without Christophe knowing exactly what feeling he was expressing. He was happy: that was all: happy in expanding, happy in having expanded, happy in feeling within himself the pulse of universal life.

His fullness of joy was communicated to those about him.

The house with its closed garden was too small for him. He had the view out over the garden of the neighboring convent with the solitude of its great avenues and century-old trees: but it was too good to last. In front of Christophe's windows they were building a six-story house, which shut out the view and completely hemmed him in. In addition, he had the pleasure of hearing the creaking of pulleys, the chipping of stones, the hammering of nails, all day long from morning to night. Among the workmen he found his old friend the slater, whose acquaintance he had made on the roof. They made signs to each other, and once, when he met him in the street, he took the man to a wineshop, and they drank together, much to the surprise of Olivier, who was a little scandalized. He found the man's drollery and unfailing good-humor very entertaining, but did not curse him any the less, with his troop of workmen and stupid idiots who were raising a barricade in front of the house and robbing him of air and light. Olivier did not complain much: he could quite easily adapt himself to a limited horizon: he was like the stove of Descartes, from which the suppressed ideas darted upward to the free sky. But Christophe needed more air. Shut up in that confined space, he avenged himself by expanding into the lives of those about him. He drank in their inmost life, and turned it into music. Olivier used to tell him that he looked like a lover.

"If I were in love," Christophe would reply, "I should see nothing, love nothing, be interested in nothing outside my love."

"What is the matter with you, then?"

"I'm very well. I'm hungry."

"Lucky Christophe!" Olivier would sigh. "I wish you could hand a little of your appetite over to us."

Health, like sickness, is contagious. The first to feel the benefit of Christophe's vitality was naturally Olivier. Vitality

was what he most lacked. He retired from the world because
its vulgarity revolted him. Brilliantly clever though he was,
and in spite of his exceptional artistic gifts, he was too delicate
to be a great artist. Great artists do not feel disgust: the first
law for every healthy being is to live: and that law is even more
imperative for a man of genius: for such a man lives more.
Olivier fled from life: he drifted along in a world of poetic fic-
tions that had no body, no flesh and blood, no relation to reality.
He was one of those literary men who, in quest of beauty, have
to go outside time, into the days that are no more, or the days
that have never been. As though the wine of life were not as
intoxicating, and its vintages as rich nowadays as ever they
were! But men who are weary in soul recoil from direct contact with life: they can only bear to see it through the veil of
visions spun by the backward movement of time, and hear it
in the echo which sends back and distorts the dead words of
those who were once alive.—Christophe's friendship gradually
dragged Olivier out of this Limbo of art. The sun's rays
pierced through to the innermost recesses of his soul in which he
was languishing.

Elsberger, the engineer, also succumbed to Christophe's contagious optimism. It was not shown in any change in his
habits: they were too inveterate: and it was too much to expect
him to become enterprising enough to leave France and go and
seek his fortune elsewhere. But he was shaken out of his
apathy: he recovered his taste for research, and reading, and
the scientific work which he had long neglected. He would
have been much astonished had he been told that Christophe
had something to do with his new interest in his work: and
certainly no one would have been more surprised than
Christophe.

But of all the inhabitants of the house, Christophe was the
soonest intimate with the little couple on the second floor.
More than once as he passed their door he had stopped to listen

to the sound of the piano which Madame Arnaud used to play quite well when she was alone. Then he gave them tickets for his concert, for which they thanked him effusively. And after that he used to go and sit with them occasionally in the evening. He had never heard Madame Arnaud playing again: she was too shy to play in company: and even when she was alone, now that she knew she could be heard on the stairs, she kept the soft pedal down. But Christophe used to play to them, and they would talk about it for hours together. The Arnauds used to speak of music with such eagerness and freshness of feeling that he was enchanted with them. He had not thought it possible for French people to care so much for music.

"That," Olivier would say, "is because you have only come across musicians."

"I'm perfectly aware," Christophe would reply, "that professed musicians are the very people who care least for music: but you can't make me believe that there are many people like you in France."

"A few thousands at any rate."

"I suppose it's an epidemic, the latest fashion."

"It is not a matter of fashion," said Arnaud. *"He who does not rejoice to hear a sweet accord of instruments, or the sweetness of the natural voice, and is not moved by it, and does not tremble from head to foot with its sweet ravishment, and is not taken completely out of himself, does thereby show himself to have a twisted, vicious, and depraved soul, and of such an one we should beware as of a man ill-born. . . ."*

"I know that," said Christophe. "It is my friend Shakespeare."

"No," said Arnaud gently. "It is a Frenchman who lived before him, Ronsard. That will show you that, if it is the fashion in France to care for music, it is no new thing."

But what astonished Christophe was not so much that people in France should care for music, as that almost without exception they cared for the same music as the people in Germany.

In the world of Parisian snobs and artists, in which he had moved at first, it had been the mode to treat the German masters as distinguished foreigners, by all means to be admired, but to be kept at a distance: they were always ready to poke fun at the dullness of a Gluck, and the barbarity of a Wagner: against them they set up the subtlety of the French composers. And in the end Christophe had begun to wonder whether a Frenchman could have the least understanding of German music, to judge by the way it was rendered in France. Only a short time before he had come away perfectly scandalized from a performance of an opera of Gluck's: the ingenious Parisians had taken it into their heads to deck the old fellow up, and cover him with ribbons, and pad out his rhythms, and bedizen his music with impressionistic settings, and charming little dancing girls, forward and wanton. . . . Poor Gluck! There was nothing left of his eloquent and sublime feeling, his moral purity, his naked sorrow. Was it that the French could not understand these things?—And now Christophe could see how deeply and tenderly his new friends loved the very inmost quality of the Germanic spirit, and the old German *lieder,* and the German classics. And he asked them if it was not the fact that the great Germans were as foreigners to them, and that a Frenchman could only really love the artists of his own nationality.

"Not at all!" they protested. "It is only the critics who take upon themselves to speak for us. They always follow the fashion, and they want us to follow it too. But we don't worry about them any more than they worry about us. They're funny little people, trying to teach us what is and is not French—us, who are French of the old stock of France! . . . They come and tell us that our France is in Rameau,—or Racine,—and nowhere else. As though we did not know,—(and thousands like us in the provinces, and in Paris). How often Beethoven, Mozart, and Gluck, have sat with us by the fireside, and watched with us by the bedside of those we love, and shared our troubles, and revived our hopes, and been one of ourselves! If we dared say exactly what we thought, it is much more likely that the French artists, who are set up on a pedestal by our Parisian critics, are strangers among us."

"The truth is," said Olivier, "that if there are frontiers in art, they are not so much barriers between races as barriers between classes. I'm not so sure that there is a French art or a German art: but there is certainly one art for the rich and another for the poor. Gluck was a great man of the middle-classes: he belongs to our class. A certain French artist, whose name I won't mention, is not of our class: though he was of the middle-class by birth, he is ashamed of us, and denies us: and we deny him."

What Olivier said was true. The better Christophe got to know the French, the more he was struck by the resemblance between the honest men of France and the honest men of Germany. The Arnauds reminded him of dear old Schulz with his pure, disinterested love of art, his forgetfulness of self, his devotion to beauty. And he loved them in memory of Schulz.

At the same time as he realized the absurdity of moral frontiers between the honest men of different nationalities, Christophe began to see the absurdity of the frontiers that lay between the different ideas of honest men of the same nationality. Thanks to him, though without any deliberate effort on his part, the Abbé Corneille and M. Watelet, two men who seemed very far indeed from understanding each other, made friends.

Christophe used to borrow books from both of them and, with a want of ceremony which shocked Olivier, he used to lend their books in turn to the other. The Abbé Corneille was not at all scandalized: he had an intuitive perception of the quality of a man: and, without seeming to do so, he had marked the generous and even unconsciously religious nature of his young neighbor. A book by Kropotkin, which had been borrowed from M. Watelet, and for different reasons had given great pleasure to all three of them, began the process of bringing them to-

gether. It chanced one evening that they met in Christophe's
room. At first Christophe was afraid that they might be rude to
each other: but, on the contrary, they were perfectly polite.
They discussed various sage subjects: their travels, and their experience of men. And they discovered in each other a fund
of gentleness and the spirit of the Gospels, and chimerical
hopes, in spite of the many reasons that each had for despair.
They discovered a mutual sympathy, mingled with a little
irony. Their sympathy was of a very discreet nature. They
never revealed their fundamental beliefs. They rarely met and
did not try to meet: but when they did so they were glad to see
each other.

Of the two men the Abbé Corneille was not the least independent of mind, though Christophe would never have thought
it. He gradually came to perceive the greatness of the religious
and yet free ideas, the immense, serene, and unfevered mysticism which permeated the priest's whole mind, the every action
of his daily life, and his whole outlook on the world,—leading
him to live in Christ, as he believed that Christ had lived in
God.

He denied nothing, no single element of life. To him the
whole of Scripture, ancient and modern, lay and religious, from
Moses to Berthelot, was certain, divine, the very expression of
God. Holy Writ was to him only its richest example, just as the
Church was the highest company of men united in the brotherhood of God: but in neither of them was the spirit confined
in any fixed, unchanging truth. Christianity was the living
Christ. The history of the world was only the history of the
perpetual advance of the idea of God. The fall of the Jewish
Temple, the ruin of the pagan world, the repulse of the Crusades,
the humiliation of Boniface VIII, Galileo flinging the world
back into giddy space, the infinitely little becoming more mighty
than the great, the downfall of kingdoms, and the end of the
Concordats, all these for a time threw the minds of men out
of their reckoning. Some clung desperately to the passing
order: some caught at a plank and drifted. The Abbé Cor-

neille only asked: "Where do we stand as men? Where is that which makes us live?" For he believed: "Where life is, there is God."—And that was why he was in sympathy with Christophe.

For his part, Christophe was glad once more to hear the splendid music of a great religious soul. It awoke in him echoes distant and profound. Through the feeling of perpetual reaction, which is in vigorous natures a vital instinct, the instinct of self-preservation, the stroke which preserves the quivering balance of the boat, and gives it a new drive onward,—his surfeit of doubts and his disgust with Parisian sensuality had for the last two years been slowly restoring God to his place in Christophe's heart. Not that he believed in God. He denied God. But he was filled with the spirit of God. The Abbé Corneille used to tell him with a smile, that like his namesake, the sainted giant, he bore God on his shoulders without knowing it.

"How is it that I don't see it then?" Christophe would ask.

"You are like thousands of others: you see God every day, and never know that it is He. God reveals Himself to all, in every shape,—to some He appears in their daily life, as He did to Saint Peter in Galilee,—to others (like your friend M. Watelet), as He did to Saint Thomas, in wounds and suffering that call for healing,—to you in the dignity of your ideal: *Noli me tangere.* . . . Some day you will know it."

"I will never surrender," said Christophe. "I am free. Free I shall remain."

"Only the more will you live in God," replied the priest calmly.

But Christophe would not submit to being made out a Christian against his will. He defended himself ardently and simply, as though it mattered in the least whether one label more than another was plastered on to his ideas. The Abbé Corneille would listen with a faint ecclesiastical irony, that was hardly perceptible, while it was altogether kindly. He had an inexhaustible fund of patience, based on his habit of faith. It had been tempered by the trials to which the existing Church had exposed him: while it had made him profoundly melancholy, and had even dragged him through terrible moral crises, he had not really been touched by it all. It was cruel to suffer the oppression of his superiors, to have his every action spied upon by the Bishops, and watched by the free-thinkers, who were endeavoring to exploit his ideas, to use him as a weapon against his own faith, and to be misunderstood and attacked both by his co-religionists and the enemies of his religion. It was impossible for him to offer any resistance: for submission was enforced upon him. It was impossible for him to submit in his heart: for he knew that the authorities were wrong. It was agony for him to hold his peace. It was agony for him to speak and to be wrongly interpreted. Not to mention the soul for which he was responsible, he had to think of those, who looked to him for counsel and help, while he had to stand by and see them suffer. . . . The Abbé Corneille suffered both for them and for himself, but he was resigned. He knew how small a thing were the days of trial in the long history of the Church.—Only, by dint of being turned in upon himself in his silent resignation, slowly he lost heart, and became timid and afraid to speak, so that it became more and more difficult for him to do anything, and little by little the torpor of silence crept over him. Meeting Christophe had given him new courage. His neighbor's youthful ardor and the affectionate and simple interest which he took in his doings, his sometimes indiscreet questions, did him a great deal of good. Christophe forced him to mix once more with living men and women.

Aubert, the journeyman electrician, once met him in Christophe's room. He started back when he saw the priest, and found it hard to conceal his feeling of dislike. Even when he had overcome his first inclination, he was uncomfortable and oddly embarrassed at finding himself in the company of a man in a cassock, a creature to whom he could attach no exact definition. However, his sociable instincts and the pleasure he always found in talking to educated men were stronger than his anti-clericalism. He was surprised by the pleasant relations existing between M. Watelet and the Abbé Corneille: he was no less surprised to find a priest who was a democrat, and a revolutionary who was an aristocrat: it upset all his preconceived ideas. He tried vainly to classify them in any social category: for he always had to classify people before he could begin to understand them. It was not easy to find a pigeon-hole for the peaceful freedom of mind of a priest who had read Anatole France and Renan, and was prepared to discuss them calmly, justly, and with some knowledge. In matters of science the Abbé Corneille's way was to accept the guidance of those who knew, rather than of those who laid down the law. He respected authority, but in his eyes it stood lower than knowledge. The flesh, the spirit, and charity: the three orders, the three rungs of the divine ladder, the ladder of Jacob. —Of course, honest Aubert was far, indeed, from understanding, or even from dreaming, of the possibility of such a state of mind. The Abbé Corneille used to tell Christophe that Aubert reminded him of certain French peasants whom he had seen one day. A young Englishwoman had asked them the way, in English. They listened solemnly, but did not understand. Then they spoke in French. She did not understand. Then they looked at each other pityingly, and wagged their heads, and went on with their work, and said:

"What a pity! What a pity! Such a pretty girl, too! . . ."

As though they had thought her deaf, or dumb, or soft in the head. . . .

At first Aubert was abashed by the knowledge and distinguished manners of the priest and M. Watelet, and sat mum, listening intently to what they said. Then, little by little, he joined in the conversation, giving way to the naïve pleasure that he found in hearing himself speak. He paraded his generous store of rather vague ideas. The other two would listen politely, and smile inwardly. Aubert was delighted, and could not hold himself in: he took advantage of, and presently abused, the inexhaustible patience of the Abbé Corneille. He read his literary productions to him. The priest listened resignedly; and it did not bore him overmuch, for he listened not so much to the words as to the man. And then he would reply to Christophe's commiseration:

"Bah! I hear so many of them!"

Aubert was grateful to M. Watelet and the Abbé Corneille: and, without taking much trouble to understand each other's ideas, or even to find out what they were, the three of them became very good friends without exactly knowing why. They were very surprised to find themselves so intimate. They would never have thought it.—Christophe was the bond between them.

He had other innocent allies in the three children, the two little Elsbergers and M. Watelet's adopted daughter. He was great friends with them: they adored him. He told each of them about the other, and gave them an irresistible longing to know each other. They used to make signs to each other from the windows, and spoke to each other furtively on the stairs. Aided and abetted by Christophe, they even managed to get permission sometimes to meet in the Luxembourg Gardens. Christophe was delighted with the success of his guile, and went to see them there the first time they were together: they were shy and embarrassed, and hardly knew what to make of their new happiness. He broke down their reserve in a moment, and invented games for them, and races, and played hide-and-seek: he joined in as keenly as though he were a child of ten: the passers-by cast amused and quizzical glances at the great big fellow, running and shouting and dodging round trees, with three little girls after him. And as their parents were still suspicious of each other, and showed no great readiness to let these excursions to the Luxembourg Gardens occur very often—(because it kept them too far out of sight)—Christophe managed to get Commandant Chabran, who lived on the ground floor, to invite the children to play in the garden belonging to the house.

Chance had thrown Christophe and the old soldier together:
—(chance always singles out those who can turn it to account).
—Christophe's writing-table was near his window. One day
the wind blew a few sheets of music down into the garden.
Christophe rushed down, bareheaded and disheveled, just as he
was, without even taking the trouble to brush his hair. He
thought he would only have to see a servant. However, the
daughter opened the door to him. He was rather taken aback,
but told her what he had come for. She smiled and let him in:
they went into the garden. When he had picked up his papers
he was for hurrying away, and she was taking him to the door,
when they met the old soldier. The Commandant gazed at his
odd visitor in some surprise. His daughter laughed, and introduced him.

"Ah! So you are the musician?" said the old soldier.
"We are comrades."

They shook hands. They talked in a friendly, bantering
tone of the concerts they gave together, Christophe with his
piano, the Commandant with his flute. Christophe tried to go,
but the old man would not let him: and he plunged blindly into
a disquisition on music. Suddenly he stopped short, and
said:

"Come and see my canons."

Christophe followed him, wondering how anybody could be
interested in anything he might think about French artillery.
The old man showed him in triumph a number of musical
canons, amazing productions, compositions that might just as
well be read upside down, or played as duets, one person playing
the right-hand page, and the other the left. The Commandant was
an old pupil of the Polytechnic, and had always had a taste for
music: but what he loved most of all in it was the mathematical
problem: it seemed to him—(as up to a point it is)—a magnificent mental gymnastic: and he racked his brains in the invention and solution of puzzles in the construction of music,
each more useless and extravagant than the last. Of course, his
military career had not left him much time for the development

of his mania: but since his retirement he had thrown himself
into it with enthusiasm: he expended on it all the energy and
ingenuity which he had previously employed in pursuing the
hordes of negro kings through the deserts of Africa, or avoiding
their traps. Christophe found his puzzles quite amusing, and
set him a more complicated one to solve. The old soldier was
delighted: they vied with one another: they produced a perfect
shower of musical riddles. After they had been playing the
game for some time, Christophe went upstairs to his own room.
But the very next morning his neighbor sent him a new problem,
a regular teaser, at which the Commandant had been working
half the night: he replied with another: and the duel went on
until Christophe, who was getting tired of it, declared himself
beaten: at which the old soldier was perfectly delighted. He
regarded his success as a retaliation on Germany. He invited
Christophe to lunch. Christophe's frankness in telling the old
soldier that he detested his musical compositions, and shouting
in protest when Chabran began to murder an *andante of* Haydn
on his harmonium, completed the conquest. From that time
on they often met to talk. But not about music. Christophe
could not summon up any great interest in his neighbor's
crotchety notions about it, and much preferred getting him to
talk about military subjects. The Commandant asked nothing
better: music was only a forced amusement for the unhappy
man: in reality, he was fretting his life out.

He was easily led on to yarn about his African campaigns.
Gigantic adventures worthy of the tales of a Pizarro and a
Cortez! Christophe was delighted with the vivid narrative of
that marvelous and barbaric epic, of which he knew nothing,
and almost every Frenchman is ignorant: the tale of the twenty
years during which the heroism, and courage, and inventive-
ness, and superhuman energy of a conquering handful of Frenchmen were spent far away in the depths of the Black Continent,
where they were surrounded by armies of negroes, where they
were deprived of the most rudimentary arms of war, and yet, in
the face of public opinion and a panic-stricken Government, in

spite of France, conquered for France an empire greater than France itself. There was the flavor of a mighty joy, a flavor of blood in the tale, from which, in Christophe's mind's eye, there sprang the figures of modern *condottieri*, heroic adventurers, unlooked for in the France of to-day, whom the France of to-day is ashamed to own, so that she modestly draws a veil over them. The Commandant's voice would ring out bravely as he recalled it all: and he would jovially recount, with learned descriptions—(oddly interpolated in his epic narrative)—of the geological structure of the country, in cold, precise terms, the story of the tremendous marches, and the charges at full gallop, and the man-hunts, in which he had been hunter and quarry, turn and turn about, in a struggle to the death.— Christophe would listen and watch his face, and feel a great pity for such a splendid human animal, condemned to inaction, and forced to spend his time in playing ridiculous games. He wondered how he could ever have become resigned to such a lot. He asked the old man how he had done it. The Commandant was at first not at all inclined to let a stranger into his confidence as to his grievances. But the French are naturally loquacious, especially when they have a chance of pitching into each other:

"What on earth should I do," he said, "in the army as it is to-day? The marines write books. The infantry study sociology. They do everything but make war. They don't even prepare for it: they prepare never to go to war again: they study the philosophy of war. . . . The philosophy of war! That's a game for beasts of burden wondering how much thrashing they are going to get! . . . Discussing, philosophizing, no, that's not my work. Much better stay at home and go on with my canons!"

He was too much ashamed to air the most serious of his grievances: the suspicion created among the officers by the appeal to informers, the humiliation of having to submit to the insolent orders of certain crass and mischievous politicians, the army's disgust at being put to base police duty, taking inventories

of the churches, putting down industrial strikes, at the bidding
of capital and the spite of the party in power—the petty burgess
radicals and anti-clericals—against the rest of the country.
Not to speak of the old African's disgust with the new Colonial
Army, which was for the most part recruited from the lowest
elements of the nation, by way of pandering to the egoism and
cowardice of the rest, who refuse to share in the honor and the
risks of securing the defense of "greater France"—France beyond the seas.

Christophe was not concerned with these French quarrels:
they were no affair of his: but he sympathized with the old soldier. Whatever he might think of war, it seemed to him that
an army was meant to produce soldiers, as an apple-tree to
produce apples, and that it was a strange perversion to graft on
to it politicians, esthetes, and sociologists. And yet he could
not understand how a man of such vigor could give way to his
adversaries. It is to be his own worst enemy for a man not to
fight his enemies. In all French people of any worth at all there
was a spirit of surrender, a strange temper of renunciation.—
To Christophe it was even more profound, and even more
touching as it existed in the old soldier's daughter.

Her name was Céline. She had beautiful hair, plaited and
braided so as to set off her high, round forehead and her rather
pointed ears, her thin cheeks, and her pretty chin: she was like
a country girl, with fine intelligent dark eyes, very trustful,
very soft, rather shortsighted: her nose was a little too large,
and she had a tiny mole on her upper lip by the corner of her
mouth, and she had a quiet smile which made her pout prettily
and thrust out her lower lip, which was a little protruding. She
was kind, active, clever, but she had no curiosity of mind. She
read very little, and never any of the newest books, never went
to the theater, never traveled,—(for traveling bored her father,
who had had too much of it in the old days),—never had anything to do with any polite charitable work,—(her father used
to condemn all such things),—made no attempt to study,—(he
used to make fun of blue stockings),—hardly ever left her little

patch of garden inclosed by its four high walls, so that it was
like being at the bottom of a deep well. And yet she was not
really bored. She occupied her time as best she could, and was
good-tempered and resigned. About her and about the setting
which every woman unconsciously creates for herself wherever
she may be, there was a Chardinesque atmosphere: the same
soft silence, the same tranquil expression, the same attitude of
absorption—(a little drowsy and languid)—in the common
task: the poetry of the daily round, of the accustomed way of
life, with its fixed thoughts and actions, falling into exactly the
same place at exactly the same time—thoughts and actions
which are cherished none the less with an all-pervading tranquil
gentleness: the serene mediocrity of the fine-souled women of
the middle-class: honest, conscientious, truthful, calm—calm in
their pleasures, unruffled in their labors, and yet poetic in all
their qualities. They are healthy and neat and tidy, clean in
body and mind: all their lives are sweetened with the scent of
good bread, and lavender, and integrity, and kindness. There
is peace in all that they are and do, the peace of old houses and
smiling souls. . . .

Christophe, whose affectionate trustfulness invited trust, had
become very friendly with her: they used to talk quite frankly:
and he even went so far as to ask her certain questions, which
she was surprised to find herself answering: she would tell
him things which she had not told anybody, even her most intimate friends.

"You see," Christophe would say, "you're not afraid of me.
There's no danger of our falling in love with each other: we're
too good friends for that."

"You're very polite!" she would answer with a laugh.

Her healthy nature recoiled as much as Christophe's from
philandering friendship, that form of sentimentality dear to
equivocal men and women, who are always juggling with their
emotions. They were just comrades one to another.

He asked her one day what she was doing in the afternoons,
when he saw her sitting in the garden with her work on her

knees, never touching it, and not stirring for hours together. She blushed, and protested that it was not a matter of hours, but only a matter of a few minutes, perhaps a quarter of an hour, during which she " went on with her story."

" What story? "

" The story I am always telling myself."

" You tell yourself stories?   Oh, tell them to me! "

She told him that he was too curious. She would only go so far as to intimate that they were stories of which she was not the heroine.

He was surprised at that:

" If you are going to tell yourself stories, it seems to me that it would be more natural if you told your own story with embellishments, and lived in a happier dream-life."

" I couldn't," she said. " If I did that, I should become desperate."

She blushed again at having revealed even so much of her inmost thoughts: and she went on:

" Besides, when I am in the garden and a gust of wind reaches me, I am happy. Then the garden becomes alive for me. And when the wind blusters and comes from a great distance, he tells me so many things! "

In spite of her reserve, Christophe could see the hidden depths of melancholy that lay behind her good-humor, and the restless activity which, as she knew perfectly well, led nowhere. Why did she not try to break away from her condition and emancipate herself? She would have been so well fitted for a useful and active life!—But she alleged her affection for her father, who would not hear of her leaving him. In vain did Christophe tell her that the old soldier was perfectly vigorous and energetic, and had no need of her, and that a man of his stamp could quite well be left alone, and had no right to make a sacrifice of her. She would begin to defend her father: by a pious fiction she would pretend that it was not her father who was forcing her to stay, but she herself who could not bear to leave him.—And, up to a point, what she said was true. It seemed to have been accepted from time immemorial by herself, and her father, and all their friends that their life had to be thus and thus, and not otherwise. She had a married brother, who thought it quite natural that she should devote her life to their father in his stead. He was entirely wrapped up in his children. He loved them jealously, and left them no will of their own. His love for his children was to him, and especially to his wife, a voluntary bondage which weighed heavily on their life, and cramped all their movements: his idea seemed to be that as soon as a man has children, his own life comes to an end, and he has to stop short in his own development: he was still young, active, and intelligent, and there he was reckoning up the years he would have still to work before he could retire.—Christophe saw how these good people were weighed down by the atmosphere of family affection, which is so deep-rooted in France—deep-rooted, but stifling and destructive of vitality. And it has become all the more oppressive since families in France have been reduced to the minimum: father, mother, one or two children, and here and there, perhaps, an uncle or an aunt. It is a cowardly, fearful love, turned in upon itself, like a miser clinging tightly to his hoard of gold.

A fortuitous circumstance gave Christophe a yet greater interest in the girl, and showed him the full extent of the suppression of the emotions of the French, their fear of life, of letting themselves go, and claiming their birthright.

Elsberger, the engineer, had a brother ten years younger than himself, likewise an engineer. He was a very good fellow, like thousands of others, of the middle-class, and he had artistic aspirations: he was one of those people who would like to practise an art, but are afraid of compromising their reputation and position. As a matter of fact, it is not a very difficult problem, and most of the artists of to-day have solved it without any great danger to themselves. But it needs a certain amount of will-power: and not everybody is capable of even that much expenditure of energy: such people are not sure enough of wanting what they really want: and as their position in life grows more

assured, they submit and drift along, without any show of revolt
or protest.   They cannot be blamed if they become good citizens
instead of bad artists.   But their disappointment too often
leaves behind it a secret discontent, a *qualis artifex pereo*, which
as best it can assumes a crust of what is usually called philosophy, and spoils their lives, until the wear and tear of daily
life and new anxieties have erased all trace of the old bitterness.
Such was the case of André Elsberger.   He would have liked
to be a writer: but his brother, who was very self-willed, had
made him follow in his footsteps and enter upon a scientific
career.   André was clever, and quite well equipped for scientific
work—or for literature, for that matter: he was not sure enough
of being an artist, and he was too sure that he was middle-
class: and so, provisionally at first,—(one knows what that
means)—he had bowed to his brother's wishes: he entered the
Centrale, high up in the list, and passed out equally high, and
since then he had practised his profession as an engineer conscientiously, but without being interested in it.   Of course, he
had lost the little artistic quality that he had possessed, and he
never spoke of it except ironically.

"And then," he used to say—(Christophe recognized Olivier's
pessimistic tendency in his arguments)—"life is not good
enough to make one worry about a spoiled career.   What does a
bad poet more or less matter! . . ."

The brothers were fond of one another: they were of the
same stamp morally: but they did not get on well together.
They had both been Dreyfus-mad.   But André was attracted
by syndicalism, and was an anti-militarist: and Elie was a
patriot.

From time to time André would visit Christophe without going to see his brother: and that astonished Christophe: for
there was no great sympathy between himself and André, who
used hardly ever to open his mouth except to gird at something or somebody,—which was very tiresome: and when Christophe said anything, André would not listen.   Christophe made
no effort to conceal the fact that he found his visits a nuisance:

but André did not mind, and seemed not to notice it. At last Christophe found the key to the riddle one day when he found his visitor leaning out of the window, and paying much more attention to what was happening in the garden below than to what he was saying. He remarked upon it, and André was not reluctant to admit that he knew Mademoiselle Chabran, and that she had something to do with his visits to Christophe. And, his tongue being loosed, he confessed that he had long been attached to the girl, and perhaps something more than that: the Elsbergers had long ago been in close touch with the Chabrans: but, though they had been very intimate, politics and recent events had separated them: and thereafter they saw very little of each other. Christophe did not disguise his opinion that it was an idiotic state of things. Was it impossible for people to think differently, and yet to retain their mutual esteem? André said he thought it was, and protested that he was very broad-minded: but he would not admit the possibility of tolerance in certain questions, concerning which, he said, he could not admit any opinion different from his own: and he instanced the famous Affair. On that, as usual, he became wild. Christophe knew the sort of thing that happened in that connection, and made no attempt to argue: but he asked whether the Affair was never going to come to an end, or whether its curse was to go on and on to the end of time, descending even unto the third and fourth generation. André began to laugh: and without answering Christophe, he fell to tender praise of Céline Chabran, and protested against her father's selfishness, who thought it quite natural that she should be sacrificed to him.

"Why don't you marry her," asked Christophe, "if you love her and she loves you?"

André said mournfully that Céline was clerical. Christophe asked what he meant by that. André replied that he meant that she was religious, and had vowed a sort of feudal service to God and His bonzes.

"But how does that affect you?"

"I don't want to share my wife with any one."

"What! You are jealous even of your wife's ideas? Why, you're more selfish even than the Commandant!"

"It's all very well for you to talk: would you take a woman who did not love music?"

"I have done so."

"How can a man and a woman live together if they don't think the same?"

"Don't you worry about what you think! Ah! my dear fellow, ideas count for so little when one loves. What does it matter to me whether the woman I love cares for music as much as I do? She herself is music to me! When a man has the luck, as you have, to find a dear girl whom he loves, and she loves him, she must believe what she likes, and he must believe what he likes! When all is said and done, what do your ideas amount to? There is only one truth in the world, there is only one God: love."

"You speak like a poet. You don't see life as it is. I know only too many marriages which have suffered from such a want of union in thought."

"Those husbands and wives did not love each other enough. You have to know what you want."

"Wanting does not do everything in life. Even if I wanted to marry Mademoiselle Chabran, I couldn't."

"I'd like to know why."

André spoke of his scruples: his position was not assured: he had no fortune and no great health. He was wondering whether he had the right to marry in such circumstances. It was a great responsibility. Was there not a great risk of bringing unhappiness on the woman he loved, and himself,—not to mention any children there might be? . . . It was better to wait—or give up the idea.

Christophe shrugged his shoulders.

"That's a fine sort of love! If she loves you, she will be happy in her devotion to you. And as for the children, you French people are absurd. You would like only to bring them into the world when you are sure of turning them out with

comfortable private means, so that they will have nothing to
suffer and nothing to fear. . . . Good Lord! That's nothing
to do with you: your business is only to give them life, love of
life, and courage to defend it. The rest . . . whether they
live or die . . . is the common lot. Is it better to give up
living than to take the risks of life?"

The sturdy confidence which emanated from Christophe affected André, but did not change his mind. He said:

"Yes, perhaps, that is true. . . ."

But he stopped at that. Like all the rest, his will and power
of action seemed to be paralyzed.

Christophe had set himself to fight the inertia which he found
in most of his French friends, oddly coupled with laborious and
often feverish activity. Almost all the people he met in the
various middle-class houses which he visited were discontented.
They had almost all the same disgust with the demagogues and
their corrupt ideas. In almost all there was the same sorrowful
and proud consciousness of the betrayal of the genius of their
race. And it was by no means the result of any personal rancor nor the bitterness of men and classes beaten and thrust
out of power and active life, or discharged officials, or unem-
ployed energy, nor that of an old aristocracy which has returned
to its estates, there to die in hiding like a wounded lion. It
was a feeling of moral revolt, mute, profound, general: it was to
be found everywhere, in a greater or less degree, in the army, in
the magistracy, in the University, in the officers, and in every
vital branch of the machinery of government. But they took
no active measures. They were discouraged in advance: they
kept on saying:

"There is nothing to be done:"

or

"Let us try not to think of it."

Fearfully they dodged anything sad in their thoughts and
conversation: and they took refuge in their home life.

If they had been content to refrain only from political action!

But even in their daily lives these good people had no interest in doing anything definite. They put up with the degrading, haphazard contact with horrible people whom they despised, because they could not take the trouble to fight against them, thinking that any such revolt must of necessity be useless. Why, for instance, should artists, and, in particular, the musicians with whom Christophe was most in touch, unprotestingly put up with the effrontery of the scaramouches of the Press, who laid down the law for them? There were absolute idiots among them, whose ignorance *in omni re scibili* was proverbial, though they were none the less invested with a sovereign authority *in omni re scibili*. They did not even take the trouble to write their articles and books: they had secretaries, poor starving creatures, who would have sold their souls, if they had had such things, for bread or women. There was no secret about it in Paris. And yet they went on riding their high horse and patronizing the artists. Christophe used to roar with anger sometimes when he read their articles.

"They have no heart!" he would say. "Oh! the cowards!"

"Who are you screaming at?" Olivier would ask. "The idiots of the market-place?"

"No. The honest men. These rascals are plying their trade: they lie, they steal, they rob and murder. But it is the others—those who despise them and yet let them go on—that I despise a thousand times more. If their colleagues on the Press, if honest, cultured critics, and the artists on whose backs these harlequins strut and poise themselves, did not put up with it, in silence, from shyness or fear of compromising themselves, or from some shameful anticipation of mutual service, a sort of secret pact made with the enemy so that they may be immune from their attacks,—if they did not let them preen themselves in their patronage and friendship, their upstart power would soon be killed by ridicule. There's the same weakness in everything, everywhere. I've met twenty honest men who have said to me of so-and-so: 'He is a scoundrel.' But there is not one of them who would not refer to him as his 'dear colleague,' and, if he

met him, shake hands with him.—'There are too many of
them!' they say.—Too many cowards. Too many flabby honest
men."

"Eh! What do you want them to do?"

"Be every man his own policeman! What are you waiting
for? For Heaven to take your affairs in hand? Look you, at
this very moment. It is three days now since the snow fell.
Your streets are thick with it, and your Paris is like a sewer of
mud. What do you do? You protest against your Municipal
Council for leaving you in such a state of filth. But do you
yourselves do anything to clear it away? Not a bit of it! You
sit with your arms folded. Not one of you has energy enough
even to clean the pavement in front of his house. Nobody does
his duty, neither the State nor the members of the State: each
man thinks he has done as much as is expected of him by
laying the blame on some one else. You have become so used,
through centuries of monarchical training, to doing nothing
for yourselves that you all seem to spend your time in star-gazing
and waiting for a miracle to happen. The only miracle that
could happen would be if you all suddenly made up your minds
to do something. My dear Olivier, you French people have
plenty of brains and plenty of good qualities: but you lack blood.
You most of all. There's nothing the matter with your mind
or your heart. It's your life that's all wrong. You're sputter-
ing out."

"What can we do? We can only wait for life to return
to us."

"You must want life to return to you. You must want to be
cured. You must *want*, use your will! And if you are to do
that you must first let in some pure air into your houses. If
you won't go out of doors, then at least you must keep your
houses healthy. You have let the air be poisoned by the unwholesome vapors of the market-place. Your art and your
ideas are two-thirds adulterated. And you are so dispirited
that it hardly occasions you any surprise, and rouses you to no
sort of indignation. Some of these good people—(it is pitiful

to see)—are so cowed that they actually persuade themselves that they are wrong and the charlatans are right. Why—even on your *Ésope* review, in which you profess not to be taken in by anything,—I have found unhappy young men persuading themselves that they love an art and ideas for which they have not a vestige of love. They get drunk on it, without any sort of pleasure, simply because they are told to do so: and they are dying of boredom—boredom with the monstrous lie of the whole thing!"

Christophe passed through these wavering and dispirited creatures like a wind shaking the slumbering trees. He made no attempt to force them to his way of thinking: he breathed into them energy enough to make them think for themselves. He used to say:

"You are too humble. The grand enemy is neurasthenia, doubt. A man can and must be tolerant and human. But no man may doubt what he believes to be good and true. A man must believe in what he thinks. And he should maintain what he believes. Whatever our powers may be, we have no right to forswear them. The smallest creature in the world, like the greatest, has his duty. And—(though he is not sufficiently conscious of it)—he has also a power. Why should you think that your revolt will carry so little weight? A sturdy upright conscience which dares assert itself is a mighty thing. More than once during the last few years you have seen the State and public opinion forced to reckon with the views of an honest man, who had no other weapons but his own moral force, which, with constant courage and tenacity, he had dared publicly to assert. . . .

"And if you must go on asking what's the good of taking so much trouble. what's the good of fighting. *what's the good of it all?* . . . Then, I will tell you:—Because France is dying, because Europe is perishing—because, if we did not fight, our civilization, the edifice so splendidly constructed, at the cost of centuries of labor, by our humanity, would crumble away. These

are not idle words. The country is in danger, our European
mother-country,—and more than any, yours, your own native
country, France. Your apathy is killing her. Your silence is
killing her. Each of your energies as it dies, each of your ideas
as it accepts and surrenders, each of your good intentions as it
ends in sterility, every drop of your blood as it dries up, unused, in your veins, means death to her. . . . Up! up! You
must live! Or, if you must die, then you must die fighting like
men."

But the chief difficulty lay not in getting them to do something, but in getting them to act together. There they were
quite unmanageable. The best of them were the most obstinate,
as Christophe found in dealing with the tenants in his own
house: M. Félix Weil, Elsberger, the engineer, and Commandant Chabran, lived on terms of polite and silent hostility.
And yet, though Christophe knew very little of them, he could
see that, underneath their party and racial labels, they all wanted
the same thing.

There were many reasons particularly why M. Weil and the
Commandant should have understood each other. By one of
those contrasts common to thoughtful men, M. Weil, who never
left his books and lived only in the life of the mind, had a
passion for all things military. *"We are all cranks,"* said the
half-Jew Montaigne, applying to mankind in general what is
perfectly true of certain types of minds, like the type of which
M. Weil was an example. The old intellectual had the craze for
Napoleon. He collected books and relics which brought to life
in him the terrible dream of the Imperial epic. Like many
Frenchmen of that crepuscular epoch, he was dazzled by the
distant rays of that glorious sun. He used to go through the
campaigns, fight the battles all over again, and discuss opera-
tions: he was one of those chamber-strategists who swarm in the
Academies and the Universities, who explain Austerlitz and
declare how Waterloo should have been fought. He was the
first to make fun of the " Napoleonite " in himself: it tickled

his irony: but none the less he went on reading the splendid stories with the wild enthusiasm of a child playing a game: he would weep over certain episodes: and when he realized that he had been weak enough to shed tears, he would roar with laughter, and call himself an old fool. As a matter of fact, he was a Napoleonite not so much from patriotism as from a romantic interest and a platonic love of action. However, he was a good patriot, and much more attached to France than many an actual Frenchman. The French anti-Semites are stupid and actively mischievous in casting their insulting suspicions on the feeling for France of the Jews who have settled in the country. Outside the reasons by which any family does of necessity, after a generation or two, become attached to the land of its adoption, where the blood of the soil has become its own, the Jews have especial reason to love the nation which in the West stands for the most advanced ideas of intellectual and moral liberty. They love it because for a hundred years they have helped to make it so, and its liberty is in part their work. How, then, should they not defend it against every menace of feudal reaction? To try—as a handful of unscrupulous politicians and a herd of wrong-headed people would like—to break the bonds which bind these Frenchmen by adoption to France, is to play into the hands of that reaction.

Commandant Chabran was one of those wrong-headed old Frenchmen who are roused to fury by the newspapers, which make out that every immigrant into France is a secret enemy, and, in a human, hospitable spirit, force themselves to suspect and hate and revile them, and deny the brave destiny of the race, which is the conflux of all the races. Therefore, he thought it incumbent on him not to know the tenant of the first floor, although he would have been glad to have his acquaintance. As for M. Weil, he would have been very glad to talk to the old soldier: but he knew him for a nationalist, and regarded him with mild contempt.

Christophe had much less reason than the Commandant for being interested in M. Weil. But he could not bear to hear ill

spoken of anybody unjustly. And he broke many a lance in de-
fence of M. Weil when he was attacked in his presence.

One day, when the Commandant, as usual, was railing against
the prevailing state of things, Christophe said to him:

" It is your own fault. You all shut yourselves up inside
yourselves. When things in France are not going well, to your
way of thinking, you submit to it and send in your resignation.
One would think it was a point of honor with you to admit yourselves beaten. I've never seen anybody lose a cause with such
absolute delight. Come, Commandant, you have made war; is
that fighting, or anything like it? "

" It is not a question of fighting," replied the Commandant.
" We don't fight against France. In such struggles as these we
have to argue, and vote, and mix with all sorts of knaves and
low blackguards: and I don't like it."

" You seem to be profoundly disgusted! I suppose you had
to do with knaves and low blackguards in Africa! "

" On my honor, that did not disgust me nearly so much. Out
there one could always knock them down! Besides, if it's a
question of fighting, you need soldiers. I had my sharpshooters
out there. Here I am all alone."

" It isn't that there is any lack of good men."

" Where are they? "

" Everywhere. All round us."

" Well: what are they doing? "

" Just what you're doing. Nothing. They say there's nothing
to be done."

" Give me an instance."

" Three, if you like, in this very house."

Christophe mentioned M. Weil,—(the Commandant gave an
exclamation),—and the Elsbergers,—(he jumped in his seat):

" That Jew? Those Dreyfusards? "

" Dreyfusards? " said Christophe. " Well: what does that
matter? "

" It is they who have ruined France."

" They love France as much as you do."

"They're mad, mischievous lunatics."

"Can't you be just to your adversaries?"

"I can get on quite well with loyal adversaries who use the same weapons. The proof of that is that I am here talking to you, Monsieur German. I can think well of the Germans, although some day I hope to give them back with interest the thrashing we got from them. But it is not the same thing with our enemies at home: they use underhand weapons, sophistry, and unsound ideas, and a poisonous humanitarianism. . . ."

"Yes. You are in the same state of mind as that of the knights of the Middle Ages, when, for the first time, they found themselves faced with gunpowder. What do you want? There is evolution in war too."

"So be it. But then, let us be frank, and say that war is war."

"Suppose a common enemy were to threaten Europe, wouldn't you throw in your lot with the Germans?"

"We did so, in China."

"Very well, then: look about you. Don't you see that the heroic idealism of your country and every other country in Europe is actually threatened? Don't you see that they are all, more or less, a prey to the adventurers of every class of society? To fight that common enemy, don't you think you should join with those of your adversaries who are of some worth and moral vigor? How can a man like you set so little store by the realities of life? Here are people who uphold an ideal which is different from your own! An ideal is a force, you cannot deny it: in the struggle in which you were recently engaged, it was your adversaries' ideal which defeated you. Instead of wasting your strength in fighting against it, why not make use of it, side by side with your own, against the enemies of all ideals, the men who are exploiting your country and your wealth of ideas, the men who are bringing European civilization to rottenness?"

"For whose sake? One must know where one is. To make our adversaries triumph?"

"When you were in Africa, you never stopped to think whether you were fighting for the King or the Republic. I fancy that not many of you ever gave a thought to the Republic."

"They didn't care a rap."

"Good! And that was well for France. You conquered for her, as well as for yourselves, and for the honor and the joy of it. Why not do the same here? Why not widen the scope of the fight? Don't go haggling over differences in politics and religion. These things are utterly futile. What does it matter whether your nation is the eldest daughter of the Church or the eldest daughter of Reason? The only thing that does matter is that it should live! Everything that exalts life is good. There is only one enemy, pleasure-seeking egoism, which fouls the sources of life and dries them up. Exalt force, exalt the light, exalt fruitful love, the joy of sacrifice, action, and give up expecting other people to act for you. Do, act, combine! Come! . . ."

And he laughed and began to bang out the first bars of the march in *B minor* from the *Choral Symphony*.

"Do you know," he said, breaking off, "that if I were one of your musicians, say Charpentier or Bruneau (devil take the two of them!), I would combine in a choral symphony *Aux armes, citoyens!*, *l'Internationale*, *Vive Henri IV*, and *Dieu Protège la France!*,—(You see, something like this.)—I would make you a soup so hot that it would burn your mouth! It would be unpleasant,—(no worse in any case than what you are doing now):—but I vow it would warm your vitals, and that you would have to set out on the march!"

And he roared with laughter.

The Commandant laughed too:

"You're a fine fellow, Monsieur Krafft. What a pity you're not one of us!"

"But I am one of you! The fight is the same everywhere. Let us close up the ranks!"

The Commandant quite agreed: but there he stayed. Then

Christophe pressed his point and brought the conversation back to M. Weil and the Elsbergers. And the old soldier no less obstinately went back to his eternal arguments against Jews and Dreyfusards, and nothing that Christophe had said seemed to have had the slightest effect on him.

Christophe grew despondent. Olivier said to him:

"Don't you worry about it. One man cannot all of a sudden change the whole state of mind of a nation. That's too much to expect! But you have done a good deal without knowing it."

"What have I done?" said Christophe.

"You are Christophe."

"What good is that to other people?"

"A great deal. Just go on being what you are, my dear Christophe. Don't you worry about us."

But Christophe could not surrender. He went on arguing with Commandant Chabran, sometimes with great vehemence. It amused Céline. She was generally present at their discussions, sitting and working in silence. She took no part in the argument: but it seemed to make her more lively: and quite a different expression would come into her eyes: it was as though it gave her more breathing-space. She began to read, and went out a little more, and found more things to interest her. And one day, when Christophe was battling with her father about the Elsbergers, the Commandant saw her smile: he asked her what she was thinking, and she replied calmly:

"I think M. Krafft is right."

The Commandant was taken aback, and said:

"You . . . you surprise me! . . . However, right or wrong, we are what we are. And there's no reason why we should know these people. Isn't it so, my dear?"

"No, father," she replied. "I would like to know them."

The Commandant said nothing, and pretended that he had not heard. He himself was much less insensible of Christophe's influence than he cared to appear. His vehemence and narrow-mindedness did not prevent his having a proper sense of justice and very generous feelings. He loved Christophe, he loved his frankness and his moral soundness, and he used often bitterly to regret that Christophe was a German. Although he always lost his temper in these discussions, he was always eager for more, and Christophe's arguments did produce an effect on him, though he would never have been willing to admit it. But one day Christophe found him absorbed in reading a book which he would not let him see. And when Céline took Christophe to the door and found herself alone with him, she said:

"Do you know what he was reading? One of M. Weil's books."

Christophe was delighted.

"What does he say about it?"

"He says: 'Beast!' . . . But he can't put it down."

Christophe made no allusion to the fact with the Commandant. It was he who asked:

"Why have you stopped hurling that blessed Jew at my head?"

"Because I don't think there's any need to," said Christophe.

"Why?" asked the Commandant aggressively.

Christophe made no reply, and went away laughing.

Olivier was right. It is not through words that a man can influence other men: but through his life. There are people who irradiate an atmosphere of peace from their eyes, and in their gestures, and through the silent contact with the serenity of their souls. Christophe irradiated life. Softly, softly, like the moist air of spring, it penetrated the walls and the closed windows of the somnolent old house: it gave new life to the hearts of men and women, whom sorrow, weakness, and isolation had for years been consuming, so that they were withered and like dead creatures. What a power there is in one soul over another! Those who wield that power and those who feel it are alike ignorant of its working. And yet the life of the world is in the ebb and flow controlled by that mysterious power of attraction.

On the second floor, below Christophe and Olivier's room, there lived, as we have seen, a young woman of thirty-five, a Madame Germain, a widow of two years' standing, who, the year before, had lost her little girl, a child of seven. She lived with her mother-in-law, and they never saw anybody. Of all the tenants of the house, they had the least to do with Christophe. They had hardly met, and they had never spoken to each other.

She was a tall woman, thin, but with a good figure; she had fine brown eyes, dull and rather inexpressive, though every now and then there glowed in them a hard, mournful light. Her face was sallow and her complexion waxy: her cheeks were hollow and her lips were tightly compressed. The elder Madame Germain was a devout lady, and spent all her time at church. The younger woman lived in jealous isolation in her grief. She took no interest in anything or anybody. She surrounded herself with portraits and pictures of her little girl, and by dint of staring at them she had ceased to see her as she was: the photographs and dead presentments had killed the living image of the child. She had ceased to see her as she was, but she clung to it: she was determined to think of nothing but the child: and so, in the end, she reached a point at which she could not even think of her: she had completed the work of death. There she stopped, frozen, with her heart turned to stone, with no tears to shed, with her life withered. Religion was no aid to her. She went through the formalities, but her heart was not in them, and therefore she had no living faith: she gave money for Masses, but she took no active part in any of the work of the Church: her whole religion was centered in the one thought of seeing her child again. What did the rest matter? God? What had she to do with God? To see her child again, only to see her again. . . . And she was by no means sure that she would do so. She wished to believe it, willed it hardly, desperately: but she was in doubt. . . . She could not bear to see other children, and used to think:

"Why are they not dead too?"

In the neighborhood there was a little girl who in figure and manner was like her own. When she saw her from behind, with her little pigtails down her back, she used to tremble. She would follow her, and, when the child turned round and she saw that it was not *she,* she would long to strangle her. She used to complain that the Elsberger children made a noise below her, though they were very quiet, and even very subdued by their up-bringing: and when the unhappy children began to play about their room, she would send her maid to ask her neighbors to make them be quiet. Christophe met her once as he was coming in with the little girls, and was hurt and horrified by the hard way in which she looked at them.

One summer evening when the poor woman was sitting in the dark in the self-hypnotized condition of the utter emptiness of her living death, she heard Christophe playing. It was his habit to sit at the piano in the half-light, musing and improvising. His music irritated her, for it disturbed the empty torpor into which she had sunk. She shut the window angrily. The music penetrated through to her room. Madame Germain was filled with a sort of hatred for it. She would have been glad to stop Christophe, but she had no right to do so. Thereafter, every day at the same time she sat waiting impatiently and irritably for the music to begin: and when it was later than usual her irritation was only the more acute. In spite of herself, she had to follow the music through to the end, and when it was over she found it hard to sink back into her usual apathy.—And one evening, when she was curled up in a corner of her dark room, and, through the walls and the closed window, the distant music reached her, that light-giving music . . . she felt a thrill run through her, and once more tears came to her eyes. She went and opened the window, and stood there listening and weeping. The music was like rain drop by drop falling upon her poor withered heart, and giving it new life. Once more she could see the sky, the stars, the summer night: within herself she felt the dawning of a new interest in life, as yet only a poor, pale light, vague and sorrowful sympathy for others. And that night, for the first time for many months, the image of her little girl came to her in her dreams.—For the surest road to bring us near the beloved dead, the best means of seeing them again, is not to go with them into death, but to live. They live in our lives, and die with us.

She made no attempt to meet Christophe. Rather she avoided him. But she used to hear him go by on the stairs with the children: and she would stand in hiding behind her door to listen to their babyish prattle, which so moved her heart.

One day, as she was going out, she heard their little padding footsteps coming down the stairs, rather more noisily than usual, and the voice of one of the children saying to her sister :

"Don't make so much noise, Lucette. Christophe says you mustn't because of the sorrowful lady."

And the other child began to walk more quietly and to talk in a whisper. Then Madame Germain could not restrain herself: she opened the door, and took the children in her arms, and hugged them fiercely. They were afraid: one of the children began to cry. She let them go, and went back into her own room.

After that, whenever she met them, she used to try to smile at them, a poor withered smile,—(for she had grown unused to smiling) :—she would speak to them awkwardly and affectionately, and the children would reply shyly in timid, bashful whispers. They were still afraid of the sorrowful lady, more afraid than ever: and now, whenever they passed the door, they used to run lest she should come out and catch them. She used to hide to catch sight of them as they passed. She would have been ashamed to be seen talking to the children. She was ashamed in her own eyes. It seemed to her that she was robbing her own dead child of some of the love to which she only was entitled. She would kneel down and pray for her forgiveness. But now that the instinct for life and love was newly awakened in her, she could not resist it: it was stronger than herself.

One evening, as Christophe came in, he saw that there was an unusual commotion in the house. He met a tradesman, who told him that the tenant of the third floor, M. Watelet, had just died suddenly of angina pectoris. Christophe was filled with pity, not so much for his unhappy neighbor as for the child who was left alone in the world. M. Watelet was not known to have any relations, and there was every reason to believe that he had left the girl almost entirely unprovided for. Christophe raced upstairs, and went into the flat on the third floor, the door of which was open. He found the Abbé Corneille with the body, and the child in tears, crying to her father: the housekeeper was making clumsy efforts to console her. Christophe took the child in his arms and spoke to her tenderly. She clung to him desperately: he could not think of leaving her: he wanted to take her away, but she would not let him. He stayed with her. He sat near the window in the dying light of day, and went on rocking her in his arms and speaking to her softly. The child gradually grew calmer, and went to sleep, still sobbing. Christophe laid her on her bed, and tried awkwardly to undress her and undo the laces of her little shoes. It was nightfall. The door of the flat had been left open. A shadow entered with a rustling of skirts. In the fading light Christophe recognized the fevered eyes of the sorrowful lady. He was amazed. She stood by the door, and said thickly:

" I came. . . . Will you . . . will you let me take her ? "

Christophe took her hand and pressed it. Madame Germain was in tears. Then she sat by the bedside. And, a moment later, she said:

" Let me stay with her. . . ."

Christophe went up to his own room with the Abbé Corneille. The priest was a little embarrassed, and begged his pardon for coming up. He hoped, he said, humbly, that the dead man would have nothing to reproach him with: he had gone, not as a priest, but as a friend. Christophe was too much moved to speak, and left him with an affectionate shake of the hand.

Next morning, when Christophe went down, he found the child with her arms round Madame Germain's neck, with the naïve confidence which makes children surrender absolutely to those who have won their affection. She was glad to go with her new friend. . . . Alas! she had soon forgotten her adopted father. She showed just the same affection for her new mother. That was not very comforting. Did Madame Germain, in the egoism of her love, see it? . . . Perhaps. But what did it matter? The thing is to love. That way lies happiness. . . .

A few weeks after the funeral Madame Germain took the child into the country, far away from Paris. Christophe and Olivier saw them off. The woman had an expression of contentment and secret joy which they had never known in her before. She paid no attention to them. However, just as they were going, she noticed Christophe, and held out her hand, and said:

"It was you who saved me."

"What's the matter with the woman?" asked Christophe in amazement, as they were going upstairs after her departure.

A few days later the post brought him a photograph of a little girl whom he did not know, sitting on a stool, with her little hands sagely folded in her lap, while she looked up at him with clear, sad eyes. Beneath it were written these words:

"With thanks from my dear, dead child."

Thus it was that the breath of life passed into all these people. In the attic on the fifth floor was a great and mighty flame of humanity, the warmth and light of which were slowly filtered through the house.

But Christophe saw it not. To him the process was very slow.

"Ah!" he would sigh, "if one could only bring these good

people together, all these people of all classes and every kind of belief, who refuse to know each other! Can't it be done?"

"What do you want?" said Olivier. "You would need to have mutual tolerance and a power of sympathy which can only come from inward joy,—the joy of a healthy, normal, harmonious existence,—the joy of having a useful outlet for one's activity, of feeling that one's efforts are not wasted, and that one is serving some great purpose. You would need to have a prosperous country, a nation at the height of greatness, or— (better still)—on the road to greatness. And you must also have—(the two things go together)—a power which could employ all the nation's energies, an intelligent and strong power, which would be above party. Now, there is no power above party save that which finds its strength in itself—not in the multitude, that power which seeks not the support of anarchical majorities,—as it does nowadays when it is no more than a well-trained dog in the hands of second-rate men, and bends all to its will by service rendered: the victorious general, the dictatorship of Public Safety, the supremacy of the intelligence . . . what you will. It does not depend on us. You must have the opportunity and the men capable of seizing it: you must have happiness and genius. Let us wait and hope! The forces are there: the forces of faith, knowledge, work, old France and new France, and the greater France. . . . What an upheaval it would be, if the word were spoken, the magic word which should let loose these forces all together! Of course, neither you nor I can say the word. Who will say it? Victory? Glory? . . . Patience! The chief thing is for the strength of the nation to be gathered together, and not to rust away, and not to lose heart before the time comes. Happiness and genius only come to those peoples who have earned them by ages of stoic patience, and labor, and faith."

"Who knows?" said Christophe. "They often come sooner than we think—just when we expect them least. You are counting too much on the work of ages. Make ready. Gird your loins. Always be prepared with your shoes on your feet and your staff in your hand. . . . For you do not know that the Lord will not pass your doors this very night."

The Lord came very near that night. His shadow fell upon the threshold of the house.

Following on a sequence of apparently insignificant events, relations between France and Germany suddenly became strained: and, in a few days, the usual neighborly attitude of banal courtesy passed into the provocative mood which precedes war. There was nothing surprising in this, except to those who were living under the illusion that the world is governed by reason. But there were many such in France: and numbers of people were amazed from day to day to see the vehement Gallophobia of the German Press becoming rampant with the usual quasi-unanimity. Certain of those newspapers which, in the two countries, arrogate to themselves a monopoly of patriotism, and speak in the nation's name, and dictate to the State, sometimes with the secret complicity of the State, the policy it should follow, launched forth insulting ultimatums to France. There was a dispute between Germany and England; and Germany did not admit the right of France not to interfere: the insolent newspapers called upon her to declare for Germany, or else threatened to make her pay the chief expenses of the war: they presumed that they could wrest alliance from her fears, and already regarded her as a conquered and contented vassal,—to be frank, like Austria. It only showed the insane vanity of German Imperialism, drunk with victory, and the absolute incapacity of German statesmen to understand other races, so that they were always applying the simple common measure which was law for themselves: Force, the supreme reason. Naturally, such a brutal demand, made of an ancient nation, rich in its past ages of a glory and a supremacy in Europe, such as Germany had never known, had had exactly the opposite effect to that which Germany expected. It had provoked their slumbering pride: France was shaken from top to base: and even the most diffident of the French roared with anger.

The great mass of the German people had nothing at all to do with the provocation: they were shocked by it: the honest men of every country ask only to be allowed to live in peace: and the people of Germany are particularly peaceful, affectionate, anxious to be on good terms with everybody, and much more inclined to admire and emulate other nations than to go to war with them. But the honest men of a nation are not asked for their opinion: and they are not bold enough to give it. Those who are not virile enough to take public action are inevitably condemned to be its pawns. They are the magnificent and unthinking echo which casts back the snarling cries of the Press and the defiance of their leaders, and swells them into the *Marseillaise,* or the *Wacht am Rhein*.

It was a terrible blow to Christophe and Olivier. They were so used to living in mutual love that they could not understand why their countries did not do the same. Neither of them could grasp the reasons for the persistent hostility, which was now so suddenly brought to the surface, especially Christophe, who, being a German, had no sort of ground for ill-feeling against the people whom his own people had conquered. Although he himself was shocked by the intolerable vanity of some of his fellow-countrymen, and, up to a certain point, was entirely with the French against such a high-handed Brunswicker demand, he could not understand why France should, after all, be unwilling to enter into an alliance with Germany. The two countries seemed to him to have so many deep-seated reasons for being united, so many ideas in common, and such great tasks to accomplish together, that it annoyed him to see them persisting in their wasteful, sterile ill-feeling. Like all Germans, he regarded France as the most to blame for the misunderstanding: for, though he was quite ready to admit that it was painful for her to sit still under the memory of her defeat, yet that was, after all, only a matter of vanity, which should be set aside in the higher interests of civilization and of France herself. He had never taken the trouble to think out the problem of Alsace and Lorraine. At school he had been taught to regard the annexation of those countries as an act of justice, by which, after centuries of foreign subjection, a German province had been restored to the German flag. And so, he was brought down with a run, and he discovered that his friend regarded the annexation as a crime. He had never even spoken to him about these things, so convinced was he that they were of the same opinion: and now he found Olivier, of whose good faith and broadmindedness he was certain, telling him, dispassionately, without anger and with profound sadness, that it was possible for a great people to renounce the thought of vengeance for such a crime, but quite impossible for them to subscribe to it without dishonor.

They had great difficulty in understanding each other. Olivier's historical argument, alleging the right of France to claim Alsace as a Latin country, made no impression on Christophe: there were just as good arguments to the contrary: history can provide politics with every sort of argument in every sort of cause. Christophe was much more accessible to the human, and not only French, aspect of the problem. Whether the Alsatians were or were not Germans was not the question. They did not wish to be Germans: and that was all that mattered. What nation has the right to say: " These people are mine: for they are my brothers"? If the brothers in question renounce that nation, though they be a thousand times in the wrong, the consequences of the breach must always be borne by the party who has failed to win the love of the other, and therefore has lost the right to presume to bind the other's fortunes up with his own. After forty years of strained relations, vexations, patent or disguised, and even of real advantage gained from the exact and intelligent administration of Germany, the Alsatians persist in their refusal to become Germans: and, though they might give in from sheer exhaustion, nothing could ever wipe out the memory of the sufferings of the generations, forced to live in exile from their native land, or, what is even more pitiful, unable to leave it, and compelled to bend under a yoke which was hateful to them, and to submit to the seizure of their country and the slavery of their people.

Christophe naïvely confessed that he had never seen the matter in that light: and he was considerably perturbed by it. And honest Germans always bring to a discussion an integrity which does not always go with the passionate self-esteem of a Latin, however sincere he may be. It never occurred to Christophe to support his argument by the citation of similar crimes perpetrated by all nations all through the history of the world. He was too proud to fall back upon any such humiliating excuse: he knew that, as humanity advances, its crimes become more odious, for they stand in a clearer light. But he knew also that if France were victorious in her turn she would be no more moderate in the hour of victory than Germany had been, and that yet another link would be added to the chain of the crimes of the nations. So the tragic conflict would drag on for ever, in which the best elements of European civilization were in danger. of being lost.

Though the subject was terribly painful for Christophe, it was even more so for Olivier. It meant for him, not only the sorrow of a great fratricidal struggle between the two nations best fitted for alliance together. In France the nation was divided, and one faction was preparing to fight the other. For years pacific and anti-militarist doctrines had been spread and propagated both by the noblest and the vilest elements of the nation. The Government had for a long time held aloof, with the weak-kneed dilettantism with which it handled everything which did not concern the immediate interests of the politicians: and it never occurred to it that it might be less dangerous frankly to maintain the most dangerous doctrines than to leave them free to creep into the veins of the people and ruin their capacity for war, while armaments were being prepared. These doctrines appealed to the Free Thinkers who were dreaming of founding a European brotherhood, working all together to make the world more just and human. They appealed also to the

selfish cowardice of the rabble, who were unwilling to endanger
their skins for anything or anybody.—These ideas had been
taken up by Olivier and many of his friends. Once or twice,
in his rooms, Christophe had been present at discussions which
had amazed him. His friend Mooch, who was stuffed full of
humanitarian illusions, used to say, with eyes blazing, quite
calmly, that war must be abolished, and that the best way of
setting about it was to incite the soldiers to mutiny, and, if
necessary, to shoot down their leaders: and he would insist that
it was bound to succeed. Elie Elsberger would reply, coldly
and vehemently, that, if war were to break out, he and his friends
would not set out for the frontier before they had settled their
account with the enemy at home. André Elsberger would take
Mooch's part. . . . One day Christophe came in for a terrible scene between the two brothers. They threatened to shoot
each other. Although their bloodthirsty words were spoken in
a bantering tone, he had a feeling that neither of them had ut-
tered a single threat which he was not prepared to put into action. Christophe was amazed when he thought of a race of
men so absurd as to be always ready to commit suicide for the
sake of ideas. . . . Madmen. Crazy logicians. And yet
they are good men. Each man sees only his own ideas, and
wishes to follow them through to the end, without turning aside
by a hair's breadth. And it is all quite useless: for they crush
each other out of existence. The humanitarians wage war on
the patriots. The patriots wage war on the humanitarians.
And meanwhile the enemy comes and destroys both country and
humanity in one swoop.

"But tell me," Christophe would ask André Elsberger, "are
you in touch with the proletarians of the rest of the nations?"

"Some one has to begin. And we are the people to do it.
We have always been the first. It is for us to give the
signal!"

"And suppose the others won't follow!"

"They will."

"Have you made treaties, and drawn up a plan?"

"What's the good of treaties? Our force is superior to diplomacy."

"It is not a question of ideas: it's a question of strategy. If you are going to destroy war, you must borrow the methods of war. Draw up your plan of campaign in the two countries. Arrange that on such and such a date in France and Germany your allied troops shall take such and such a step. But, if you go to work without a plan, how can you expect any good to come of it? With chance on the one hand, and tremendous organized forces on the other—the result would never be in doubt: you would be crushed out of existence."

André Elsberger did not listen. He shrugged his shoulders and took refuge in vague threats: a handful of sand, he said, was enough to smash the whole machine, if it were dropped into the right place in the gears.

But it is one thing to discuss at leisure, theoretically, and quite another to have to put one's ideas into practice, especially when one has to make up one's mind quickly. . . . Those are frightful moments when the great tide surges through the depths of the hearts of men! They thought they were free and masters of their thoughts! But now, in spite of themselves, they are conscious of being dragged onwards, onwards. . . . An obscure power of will is set against their will. Then they discover that it is not they who exist in reality, not they, but that unknown Force, whose laws govern the whole ocean of humanity. . . .

Men of the firmest intelligence, men the most secure in their faith, now saw it dissolve at the first puff of reality, and stood turning this way and that, not daring to make up their minds, and often, to their immense surprise, deciding upon a course of action entirely different from any that they had foreseen. Some of the most eager to abolish war suddenly felt a vigorous passionate pride in their country leap into being in their hearts. Christophe found Socialists, and even revolutionary syndicalists, absolutely bowled over by their passionate pride in a duty utterly foreign to their temper. At the very beginning of the upheaval, when as yet he hardly believed that the affair could be serious, he said to André Elsberger, with his usual German want of tact, that now was the moment to apply his theories, unless he wanted Germany to take France. André fumed, and replied angrily:

"Just you try! . . . Swine, you haven't even guts enough to muzzle your Emperor and shake off the yoke, in spite of your thrice-blessed Socialist Party, with its four hundred thousand members and its three million electors. We'll do it for you! Take us? We'll take you. . . ."

And as they were held on and on in suspense, they grew restless and feverish. André was in torment. He knew that his faith was true, and yet he could not defend it! He felt that he was infected by the moral epidemic which spreads among the people of a nation the collective insanity of their ideas, the terrible spirit of war! It attacked everybody about Christophe, and even Christophe himself. They were no longer on speaking terms, and kept themselves to themselves.

But it was impossible to endure such suspense for long. The wind of action willy-nilly sifted the waverers into one group or another. And one day, when it seemed that they must be on the eve of the ultimatum,—when, in both countries, the springs of action were taut, ready for slaughter, Christophe saw that everybody, including the people in his own house, had made up their minds. Every kind of party was instinctively rallied round the detested or despised Government which represented France. Not only the honest men of the various parties: but the esthetes, the masters of depraved art, took to interpolating professions of patriotic faith in their work. The Jews were talking of defending the soil of their ancestors. At the mere mention of the flag tears came to Hamilton's eyes. And they were all sincere: they were all victims of the contagion. André Elsberger and his syndicalist friends, just as much as the rest, and even more: for, being crushed by necessity and pledged to a party that they detested, they submitted with a grim fury and a stormy pessimism which made them crazy for action. Aubert, the artisan, torn between his cultivated humanitarian

ism and his instinctive chauvinism, was almost beside himself.
After many sleepless nights he had at last found a formula
which could accommodate everything: that France was synony-
mous with Humanity. Thereafter he never spoke to Christophe. Almost all the people in the house had closed their doors
to him. Even the good Arnauds never invited him. They
went on playing music and surrounding themselves with art:
they tried to forget the general obsession. But they could not
help thinking of it. When either of them alone happened to
meet Christophe alone, he or she would shake hands warmly,
but hurriedly and furtively. And if, the very same day, Christophe met them together, they would pass him by with a frigid
bow. On the other hand, people who had not spoken to each
other for years now rushed together. One evening Olivier
beckoned to Christophe to go near the window, and, without a
word, he pointed to the Elsbergers talking to Commandant
Chabran in the garden below.

Christophe had no time to be surprised at such a revolution
in the minds of his friends. He was too much occupied with his
own mind, in which there had been an upheaval, the consequences
of which he could not master. Olivier was much calmer than
he, though he had much more reason to be upset. Of all Christophe's acquaintance, he seemed to be the only one to escape
the contagion. Though he was oppressed by the anxious waiting for the outbreak of war, and the dread of schism at home,
which he saw must happen in spite of everything, he knew the
greatness of the two hostile faiths which sooner or later would
come to grips: he knew also that it is the part of France to
be the experimental ground in human progress, and that all
new ideas need to be watered with her blood before they can
come to flower. For his own part, he refused to take part in the
skirmish. While the civilized nations were cutting each other's
throats he was fain to repeat the device of Antigone: "*I am
made for love, and not for hate.*"—For love and for understanding, which is another form of love. His fondness for Christophe was enough to make his duty plain to him. At a time

when millions of human beings were on the brink of hatred, he felt that the duty and happiness of friends like himself and Christophe was to love each other, and to keep their reason uncontaminated by the general upheaval. He remembered how Goethe had refused to associate himself with the liberation movement of 1813, when hatred sent Germany to march out against France.

Christophe felt the same: and yet he was not easy in his mind. He who in a way had deserted Germany, and could not return thither, he who had been fed with the European ideas of the great Germans of the eighteenth century, so dear to his old friend Schulz, and detested the militarist and commercial spirit of New Germany, now found himself the prey of gusty passions: and he did not know whither they would lead him. He did not tell Olivier, but he spent his days in agony, longing for news. Secretly he put his affairs in order and packed his trunk. He did not reason the thing out. It was too strong for him. Olivier watched him anxiously, and guessed the struggle which was going on in his friend's mind: and he dared not question him. They felt that they were impelled to draw closer to each other than ever, and they loved each other more: but they were afraid to speak: they trembled lest they should discover some difference of thought which might come between them and divide them, as their old misunderstanding had done. Often their eyes would meet with an expression of tender anxiety, as though they were on the eve of parting for ever. And they were silent and oppressed.

But still on the roof of the house that was being built on the other side of the yard, all through those days of gloom, with the rain beating down on them, the workmen were putting the finishing touches: and Christophe's friend, the loquacious slater, laughed and shouted across:

"There! The house is finished!"

Happily, the storm passed as quickly as it had come. The chancelleries published bulletins announcing the return of fair weather, barometrically as it were. The howling dogs of the Press were despatched to their kennels. In a few hours the tension was relieved. It was a summer evening, and Christophe had rushed in breathless to convey the good news to Olivier. He was happy, and could breathe again. Olivier looked at him with a little sad smile. And he dared not ask him the question that lay next his heart. He said:

"Well: you have seen them all united, all these people who could not understand each other."

"Yes," said Christophe good-humoredly, "I have seen them united. You're such humbugs! You all cry out upon each other, but at bottom you're all of the same mind."

"You seem to be glad of it," remarked Olivier.

"Why not? Because they were united at my expense? . . . Bah! I'm strong enough for that. . . . Besides, it's a fine thing to feel the mighty torrent rushing you along, and the demons that were let loose in your hearts. . . ."

"They terrify me," said Olivier. "I would rather have eternal solitude than have my people united at such a cost."

They relapsed into silence: and neither of them dared approach the subject which was troubling them. At last Olivier pulled himself together, and, in a choking voice, said:

"Tell me frankly, Christophe: you were going away?"

Christophe replied:

"Yes."

Olivier was sure that he would say it. And yet his heart ached for it. He said:

"Tell me, Christophe: could you . . . could you . . .?"

Christophe drew his hand over his forehead and said:

"Don't let's talk of it. I don't like to think of it."

Olivier went on sorrowfully:

"You would have fought against us?"

"I don't know. I never thought about it."

"But, in your heart, you had decided?"

Christophe said:

"Yes."

"Against me?"

"Never against you. You are mine. Where I am, you are too."

"But against my country?"

"For my country."

"It is a terrible thing," said Olivier. "I love my country, as you do. I love France: but could I slay my soul for her? Could I betray my conscience for her? That would be to betray her. How could I hate, having no hatred, or, without being guilty of a lie, assume a hatred that I did not feel? The modern State was guilty of a monstrous crime—a crime which will prove its undoing—when it presumed to impose its brazen laws on the free Church of those spirits the very essence of whose being is to love and understand. Let Cæsar be Cæsar, but let him not assume the Godhead! Let him take our money and our lives: over our souls he has no rights: he shall not stain them with blood. We are in this world to give it light, not to darken it: let each man fulfil his duty! If Cæsar desires war, then let Cæsar have armies for that purpose, armies as they were in olden times, armies of men whose trade is war! I am not so foolish as to waste my time in vainly moaning and groaning in protest against force. But I am not a soldier in the army of force. I am a soldier in the army of the spirit: with thousands of other men who are my brothers-in-arms I represent France in that army. Let Cæsar conquer the world if he will! We march to the conquest of truth."

"To conquer," said Christophe, "you must vanquish, you must live. Truth is no hard dogma, secreted by the brain, like a stalactite by the walls of a cave. Truth is life. It is not to be found in your own head, but to be sought for in the hearts of others. Attach yourself to them, be one with them. Think as much as you like, but do you every day take a bath of humanity. You must live in the life of others and love and bow to destiny."

"It is our fate to be what we are. It does not depend on us whether we shall or shall not think certain things, even though

they be dangerous.   We have reached such a pitch of civilization
that we cannot turn back."

"Yes, you have reached the farthest limit of the plateau of
civilization, that dizzy height to which no nation can climb
without feeling an irresistible desire to fling itself down.   Religion and instinct are weakened in you.   You have nothing left
but intelligence.   You are machines grinding out philosophy.
Death comes rushing in upon you."

"Death comes to every nation: it is a matter of centuries."

"Have done with your centuries!   The whole of life is a
matter of days and hours.   If you weren't such an infernally
metaphysical lot, you'd never go shuffling over into the absolute,
instead of seizing and holding the passing moment."

"What do you want?   The flame burns the torch away.   You
can't both live and have lived, my dear Christophe."

"You must live."

"It is a great thing to have been great."

"It is only a great thing when there are still men who are
alive enough and great enough to appreciate it."

"Wouldn't you much rather have been the Greeks, who are
dead, than any of the people who are vegetating nowadays?"

"I'd much rather be myself, Christophe, and very much alive."

Olivier gave up the argument.   It was not that he was without
an answer.   But it did not interest him.   All through the discussion he had only been thinking of Christophe.   He said, with
a sigh:

"You love me less than I love you."

Christophe took his hand and pressed it tenderly:

"Dear Olivier," he said, "I love you more than my life.
But you must forgive me if I do not love you more than Life,
the sun of our two races.   I have a horror of the night into
which your false progress drags me.   All your sentiments of renunciation are only the covering of the same Buddhist Nirvana.
Only action is living, even when it brings death.   In this world
we can only choose between the devouring flame and night.
In spite of the sad sweetness of dreams in the hour of twilight,

I have no desire for that peace which is the forerunner of death. The silence of infinite space terrifies me. Heap more fagots upon the fire! More! And yet more! Myself too, if needs must. I will not let the fire dwindle. If it dies down, there is an end of us, an end of everything."

"What you say is old," said Olivier; "it comes from the depths of the barbarous past."

He took down from his shelves a book of Hindoo poetry, and read the sublime apostrophe of the God Krishna:

"*Arise, and fight with a resolute heart. Setting no store by pleasure or pain, or gain or loss, or victory or defeat, fight with all thy might. . .*"

Christophe snatched the book from his hands and read:

"*. . . I have nothing in the world to bid me toil: there is nothing that is not mine: and yet I cease not from my labor. If I did not act, without a truce and without relief, setting an example for men to follow, all men would perish. If for a moment I were to cease from my labors, I should plunge the world in chaos, and I should be the destroyer of life.*"

"Life," repeated Olivier,—"what is life?"

"A tragedy," said Christophe. "Hurrah!"

The panic died down. Every one hastened to forget, with a hidden fear in their hearts. No one seemed to remember what had happened. And yet it was plain that it was still in their thoughts, from the joy with which they resumed their lives, the pleasant life from day to day, which is never truly valued until it is endangered. As usual when danger is past, they gulped it down with renewed avidity.

Christophe flung himself into creative work with tenfold vigor. He dragged Olivier after him. In reaction against their recent gloomy thoughts they had begun to collaborate in a Rabelaisian epic. It was colored by that broad materialism which follows on periods of moral stress. To the legendary heroes—Gargantua, Friar John, Panurge—Olivier had added, on Christophe's inspiration, a new character, a peasant, Jacques

Patience, simple, cunning, sly, resigned, who was the butt of the others, putting up with it when he was thrashed and robbed,—putting up with it when they made love to his wife, and laid waste his fields,—tirelessly putting his house in order and cultivating his land,—forced to follow the others to war, bearing the burden of the baggage, coming in for all the kicks, and still putting up with it,—waiting, laughing at the exploits of his masters and the thrashings they gave him, and saying, " They can't go on for ever," foreseeing their ultimate downfall, looking out for it out of the corner of his eye, and silently laughing at the thought of it, with his great mouth agape. One fine day it turned out that Gargantua and Friar John were drowned while they were away on a crusade. Patience honestly regretted their loss, merrily took heart of grace, saved Panurge, who was drowning also, and said:

" I know that you will go on playing your tricks on me: you don't take me in: but I can't do without you: you drive away the spleen, and make me laugh."

Christophe set the poem to music with great symphonic pictures, with soli and chorus, mock-heroic battles, riotous country fairs, vocal buffooneries, madrigals à la Jannequin, with tremendous childlike glee, a storm at sea, the Island of Bells, and, finally, a pastoral symphony, full of the air of the fields, and the blithe serenity of the flutes and oboes, and the clean-souled folksongs of Old France.—The friends worked away with boundless delight. The weakly Olivier, with his pale cheeks, found new health in Christophe's health. Gusts of wind blew through their garret. The very intoxication of Joy! To be working together, heart to heart with one's friend! The embrace of two lovers is not sweeter or more ardent than such a yoking together of two kindred souls. They were so near in sympathy that often the same ideas would flash upon them at the same moment. Or Christophe would write the music for a scene for which Olivier would immediately find words. Christophe impetuously dragged Olivier along in his wake. His mind swamped that of his friend, and made it fruitful.

The joy of creation was enhanced by that of success. Hecht had just made up his mind to publish the *David:* and the score, well launched, had had an instantaneous success abroad. A great Wagnerian *Kapellmeister,* a friend of Hecht's, who had settled in England, was enthusiastic about it: he had given it at several of his concerts with considerable success, which, with the *Kapellmeister's* enthusiasm, had carried it over to Germany, where also the *David* had been played. The *Kapellmeister* had entered into correspondence with Christophe, and had asked him for more of his compositions, offered to do anything he could to help him, and was engaged in ardent propaganda in his cause. In Germany, the *Iphigenia,* which had originally been hissed, was unearthed, and it was hailed as a work of genius. Certain facts in Christophe's life, being of a romantic nature, contributed not a little to the spurring of public interest. The *Frankfurter Zeitung* was the first to publish an enthusiastic article. Others followed. Then, in France, a few people began to be aware that they had a great musician in their midst. One of the Parisian conductors asked Christophe for his Rabelaisian epic before it was finished: and Goujart, perceiving his approaching fame, began to speak mysteriously of a friend of his who was a genius, and had been discovered by himself. He wrote a laudatory article about the admirable *David.*—entirely forgetting that only the year before he had decried it in a short notice of a few lines. Nobody else remembered it either or seemed to be in the least astonished at his sudden change. There are so many people in Paris who are now loud in their praises of Wagner and César Franck, where formerly they roundly abused them, and actually use the fame of these men to crush those new artists whom to-morrow they will be lauding to the skies!

Christophe did not set any great store on his success. He knew that he would one day win through: but he had not thought that the day could be so near at hand: and he was distrustful of so rapid a triumph. He shrugged his shoulders, and said that he wanted to be left alone. He could have understood people applauding the *David* the year before, when he wrote it: but now he was so far beyond it; he had climbed higher. He was inclined to say to the people who came and talked about his old work:

"Don't worry me with that stuff. It disgusts me. So do you."

And he plunged into his new work again, rather annoyed at having been disturbed. However, he did feel a certain secret satisfaction. The first rays of the light of fame are very sweet. It is good, it is healthy, to conquer. It is like the open window and the first sweet scents of the spring coming into a house.——Christophe's contempt for his old work was of no avail, especially with regard to the *Iphigenia:* there was a certain amount of atonement for him in seeing that unhappy production, which had originally brought him only humiliation, belauded by the German critics, and in great request with the theaters, as he learned from a letter from Dresden, in which the directors stated that they would be glad to produce the piece during their next season.

The very day when Christophe received the news, which, after years of struggling, at last opened up a calmer horizon, with victory in the distance, he had another letter from Germany.

It was in the afternoon. He was washing his face and talking gaily to Olivier in the next room, when the housekeeper slipped an envelope under the door. His mother's writing. . . . He had been just on the point of writing to her, and was happy at the thought of being able to tell her of his success, which would give her so much pleasure. He opened the letter. There were only a few lines. How shaky the writing was!

"*My dear boy, I am not very well. If it were possible, I should like to see you again. Love.*
                                                    " MOTHER."

Christophe gave a groan. Olivier. who was working in the next room, ran to him in alarm. Christophe could not speak, and pointed to the letter on the table. He went on groaning, and did not listen to what Olivier said, who took in the letter at a glance, and tried to comfort him. He rushed to his bed, where he had laid his coat, dressed hurriedly, and without waiting to fasten his collar,—(his hands were trembling too much)— went out. Olivier caught him up on the stairs: what was he going to do? Go by the first train? There wasn't one until the evening. It was much better to wait there than at the station. Had he enough money?—They rummaged through their pockets, and when they counted all that they possessed between them, it only amounted to thirty francs. It was September. Hecht, the Arnauds, all their friends, were out of Paris. They had no one to turn to. Christophe was beside himself, and talked of going part of the way on foot. Olivier begged him to wait for an hour, and promised to procure the money somehow. Christophe submitted: he was incapable of a single idea himself. Olivier ran to the pawnshop: it was the first time he had been there: for his own sake, he would much rather have been left with nothing than pledge any of his possessions, which were all associated with some precious memory: but it was for Christophe, and there was no time to lose. He pawned his watch, for which he was advanced a sum much smaller than he had expected. He had to go home again and fetch some of his books, and take them to a bookseller. It was a great grief to him, but at the time he hardly thought of it: his mind could grasp nothing but Christophe's trouble. He returned, and found Christophe just where he had left him, sitting by his desk, in a state of collapse. With their thirty francs the sum that Olivier had collected was more than enough. Christophe was too upset to think of asking his friend how he had come by it, or whether he had kept enough to live on during his absence. Olivier did not think of it either: he had given Christophe all he possessed. He had to look after Christophe, just like a child, until it was time for him to go. He took him to the station, and never left him until the train began to move.

In the darkness into which he was rushing Christophe sat wide-eyed, staring straight in front of him and thinking:

" Shall I be in time? "

He knew that his mother must have been unable to wait for her to write to him. And in his fevered anxiety he was impatient of the jolting speed of the express. He reproached himself bitterly for having left Louisa. And at the same time he felt how vain were his reproaches: he had no power to change the course of events.

However, the monotonous rocking of the wheels and springs of the carriage soothed him gradually, and took possession of his mind, like tossing waves of music dammed back by a mighty rhythm. He lived through all his past life again from the far-distant days of his childhood: loves, hopes, disillusion, sorrows, —and that exultant force, that intoxication of suffering, enjoying, and creating, that delight in blotting out the light of life and its sublime shadows, which was the soul of his soul, the living breath of the God within him. Now as he looked back on it all was clear. His tumultuous desires, his uneasy thoughts, his faults, mistakes, and headlong struggles, now seemed to him to be the eddy and swirl borne on by the great current of life towards its eternal goal. He discovered the profound meaning of those years of trial: each test was a barrier which was burst by the gathering waters of the river, a passage from a narrow to a wider valley, which the river would soon fill: always he came to a wider view and a freer air. Between the rising ground of France and the German plain the river had carved its way, not without many a struggle, flooding the meadows, eating away the base of the hills, gathering and absorbing all the waters of the two countries. So it flowed between them, not to divide, but to unite them: in it they were wedded. And for the first time Christophe became conscious of his destiny, which was to carry through the hostile peoples, like an artery, all the forces of life of the two sides of the river.—A strange serenity, a sudden calm and clarity, came over him, as sometimes happens in the darkest hours. . . . Then the vision faded, and he saw nothing but the tender, sorrowful face of his old mother.

It was hardly dawn when he reached the little German town. He had to take care not to be recognized, for there was still a warrant of arrest out against him. But nobody at the station took any notice of him: the town was asleep: the houses were shut up and the streets deserted: it was the gray hour when the lights of the night are put out and the light of day is not yet come,—the hour when sleep is sweetest and dreams are lit with the pale light of the east. A little servant-girl was taking down the shutters of a shop and singing an old German folk-song. Christophe almost choked with emotion. O Fatherland! Beloved! . . . He was fain to kiss the earth as he heard the humble song that set his heart aching in his breast; he felt how unhappy he had been away from his country, and how much he loved it. . . . He walked on, holding his breath. When he saw his old home he was obliged to stop and put his hand to his lips to keep himself from crying out. How would he find his mother, his mother whom he had deserted? . . . He took a long breath and almost ran to the door. It was ajar. He pushed it open. No one there. . . . The old wooden stair-case creaked under his footsteps. He went up to the top floor. The house seemed to be empty. The door of his mother's room was shut.

Christophe's heart thumped as he laid his hand on the door-knob. And he had not the strength to open it. . . .

Louisa was alone, in bed, feeling that the end was near. Of her two other sons, Rodolphe, the business man, had settled in Hamburg, the other, Ernest, had emigrated to America, and no one knew what had become of him. There was no one to attend to her except a woman in the house, who came twice a day to see if Louisa wanted anything, stayed for a few minutes, and then went about her business: she was not very punctual, and was often late in coming. To Louisa it seemed quite natural that she should be forgotten, as it seemed to her quite natural to be ill. She was used to suffering, and was as patient as an angel. She had heart disease and palpitations, during which she would think she was going to die: she would lie with her eyes wide open, and her hands clutching the bedclothes, and the sweat dripping down her face. She never complained. She knew that it must be so. She was ready: she had already received the sacrament. She had only one anxiety: lest God should find her unworthy to enter into Paradise. She endured everything else in patience.

In a dark corner of her little room, near her pillow, on the wall of the recess, she had made a little shrine for her relics and trophies: she had collected the portraits of those who were dear to her: her three children, her husband, for whose memory she had always preserved her love in its first freshness, the old grandfather, and her brother, Gottfried: she was touchingly devoted to all those who had been kind to her, though it were never so little. On her coverlet, close to her eyes, she had pinned the last photograph of himself that Christophe had sent her: and his last letters were under her pillow. She had a love of neatness and scrupulous tidiness, and it hurt her to know that everything was not perfectly in order in her room. She listened for the little noises outside which marked the different moments of the day for her. It was so long since she had first heard them! All her life had been spent in that narrow space. . . . She thought of her dear Christophe. How she longed for him to be there, near her, just then! And yet she was resigned even to his absence. She was sure that she would see him again on high. She had only to close her eyes to see him. She spent days and days, half-unconscious, living in the past. . . .

She would see once more the old house on the banks of the Rhine. . . . A holiday. . . . A superb summer day. The window was open: the white road lay gleaming under the sun. They could hear the birds singing. Melchior and the old grandfather were sitting by the front-door smoking, and chatting and laughing uproariously. Louisa could not see them: but she was glad that her husband was at home that day, and that grandfather was in such a good temper. She was in the basement, cooking the dinner: an excellent dinner: she watched over it as

the apple of her eye: there was a surprise: a chestnut cake:
already she could hear the boy's shout of delight. . . . The
boy, where was he? Upstairs: she could hear him practising
at the piano. She could not make out what he was playing,
but she was glad to hear the familiar tinkling sounds, and to
know that he was sitting there with his grave face. . . . What
a lovely day! The merry jingling bells of a carriage went by
on the road. . . . Oh! good heavens! The joint! Perhaps
it had been burned while she was looking out of the window!
She trembled lest grandfather, of whom she was so fond,
though she was afraid of him, should be dissatisfied, and scold
her. . . . Thank Heaven! there was no harm done. There,
everything was ready, and the table was laid. She called
Melchior and grandfather. They replied eagerly. And the
boy? . . . He had stopped playing. His music had ceased
a moment ago without her noticing it. . . .—"Christophe!"
. . . What was he doing? There was not a sound to be
heard. He was always forgetting to come down to dinner:
father was going to scold him. She ran upstairs. . . .—
"Christophe!" . . . He made no sound. She opened the
door of the room where he was practising. No one there. The
room was empty, and the piano was closed. . . . Louisa was
seized with a sudden panic. What had become of him? The
window was open. Oh, Heaven! Perhaps he had fallen out!
Louisa's heart stops. She leans out and looks down. . . .—
"Christophe!" . . . He is nowhere to be found. She
rushes all over the house. Downstairs grandfather shouts to
her: "Come along; don't worry; he'll come back." She will
not go down: she knows that he is there: that he is hiding
for fun, to tease her. Oh, naughty, naughty boy! . . . Yes,
she is sure of it now: she heard the floor creak: he is behind
the door. She tries to open the door. But the key is gone.
The key! She rummages through a drawer, looking for it in a
heap of keys. This one, that. . . . No, not that. . . .
Ah, that's it! . . . She cannot fit it into the lock, her hand
is trembling so. She is in such haste: she must be quick. Why?

She does not know, but she knows that she must be quick, and that if she doesn't hurry she will be too late. She hears Christophe breathing on the other side of the door. . . . Oh, bother the key! . . . At last! The door is opened. A cry of joy. It is he. He flings his arms round her neck. . . . Oh, naughty, naughty, good, darling boy! . . .

She has opened her eyes. He is there, standing by her.

For some time he had been standing looking at her; so changed she was, with her face both drawn and swollen, and her mute suffering made her smile of recognition so infinitely touching: and the silence, and her utter loneliness. . . . It rent his heart. . . .

She saw him. She was not surprised. She smiled all that she could not say, a smile of boundless tenderness. She could not hold out her arms to him, nor utter a single word. He flung his arms round her neck and kissed her, and she kissed him: great tears were trickling down her cheeks. She said in a whisper:

"Wait. . . ."

He saw that she could not breathe.

Neither stirred. She stroked his head with her hands, and her tears went on trickling down her cheeks. He kissed her hands and sobbed, with his face hidden in the coverlet.

When her attack had passed she tried to speak. But she could not find words: she floundered, and he could hardly understand her. But what did it matter? They loved each other, and were together, and could touch each other: that was the main thing.—He asked indignantly why she was left alone. She made excuses for her nurse:

"She cannot always be here: she has her work to do. . . ."

In a faint, broken voice,—she could hardly pronounce her words,—she made a little hurried request about her burial. She told Christophe to give her love to her two other sons who had forgotten her. And she sent a message to Olivier, knowing his love for Christophe. She begged Christophe to tell him that she sent him her blessing—(and then, timidly, she recol-

lected herself, and made use of a more humble expression),—
" her affectionate respects. . . ."

Once more she choked. He helped her to sit up in her bed.
The sweat dripped down her face. She forced herself to smile.
She told herself that she had nothing more to wish for in the
world, now that she had her son's hand clasped in hers.

And suddenly Christophe felt her hand stiffen in his. Louisa
opened her lips. She looked at her son with infinite tenderness:—so the end came.

III

IN the evening of the same day Olivier arrived. He had
been unable to bear the thought of leaving Christophe alone in
those tragic hours of which he had had only too much experience. He was fearful also of the risks his friend was running in
returning to Germany. He wanted to be with him, to look after
him. But he had no money for the journey. When he returned
from seeing Christophe off he made up his mind to sell the few
family jewels that he had left: and as the pawnshop was closed
at that hour, and he wanted to go by the next train, he was
just going out to look for a broker's shop in the neighborhood
when he met Mooch on the stairs. When the little Jew heard
what he was about he was genuinely sorry that Olivier had not
come to him: he would not let Olivier go to the broker's, and
made him accept the necessary money from himself. He was
really hurt to think that Olivier had pawned his watch and sold
his books to pay Christophe's fare, when he would have been
only too glad to help them. In his zeal for doing them a service
he even proposed to accompany Olivier to Christophe's home,
and Olivier had great difficulty in dissuading him.

Olivier's arrival was a great boon to Christophe. He had
spent the day, prostrated with grief, alone by his mother's body.
The nurse had come, performed certain offices, and then had
gone away and had never come back. The hours had passed

in the stillness of death. Christophe sat there, as still as the body: he never took his eyes from his mother's face: he did not weep, he did not think, he was himself as one dead.—Olivier's wonderful act of friendship brought him back to tears and life.

> *"Getrost! Es ist der Schmerzen werth dies haben,*
> *So lang . . . mit uns ein treues Auge weint."*

("Courage! Life is worth all its suffering as long as there are faithful friends to weep with us.")

They clasped each other in a long embrace, and then sat by the dead woman's side and talked in whispers. Night had fallen. Christophe, with his arms on the foot of the bed, told random tales of his childhood's memories, in which his mother's image ever recurred. He would pause every now and then for a few minutes, and then go on again, until there came a pause when he stopped altogether, and his face dropped into his hands: he was utterly worn out: and when Olivier went up to him, he saw that he was asleep. Then he kept watch alone. And presently he, too, was overcome by sleep, with his head leaning against the back of the bed. There was a soft smile on Louisa's face, and she seemed happy to be watching over her two children.

In the early hours of the morning they were awakened by a knocking at the door. Christophe opened it. It was a neighbor, a joiner, who had come to warn Christophe that his presence in the town had been denounced, and that he must go, if he did not wish to be arrested. Christophe refused to fly: he would not leave his mother before he had taken her to her last resting-place. But Olivier begged him to go, and promised that he would faithfully watch over her in his stead: he induced him to leave the house: and, to make sure of his not going back on his decision, went with him to the station. Christophe refused point-blank to go without having a sight of the great river, by which he had spent his childhood, the mighty echo of

which was preserved for ever within his soul as in a sea-shell.
Though it was dangerous for him to be seen in the town, yet
for his whim he disregarded it. They walked along the steep
bank of the Rhine, which was rushing along in its mighty peace
between its low banks, on to its mysterious death in the sands of
the North. A great iron bridge, looming in the mist, plunged
its two arches, like the halves of the wheels of a colossal chariot
into the gray waters. In the distance, fading into the mist
were ships sailing through the meadows along the river's wind-
ings. It was like a dream, and Christophe was lost in it.
Olivier brought him back to his senses, and, taking his arm
led him back to the station. Christophe submitted: he was like
a man walking in his sleep. Olivier put him into the train as it
was just starting, and they arranged to meet next day at the
first French station, so that Christophe should not have to go
back to Paris alone.

The train went, and Olivier returned to the house, where
he found two policemen stationed at the door, waiting for Christophe to come back. They took Olivier for him, and Olivier
did not hurry to explain a mistake so favorable to Christophe's
chances of escape. On the other hand, the police were not in
the least discomfited by their blunder, and showed no great
zest in pursuing the fugitive, and Olivier had an inkling that
at bottom they were not at all sorry that Christophe had gone.

Olivier stayed until the next morning, when Louisa was
buried. Christophe's brother, Rodolphe, the business man, came
by one train and left by the next. That important personage
followed the funeral very correctly, and went immediately it
was over, without addressing a single word to Olivier, either to
ask him for news of his brother or to thank him for what he had
done for their mother. Olivier spent a few hours more in the
town, where he did not know a soul, though it was peopled
for him with so many familiar shadows: the boy Christophe,
those whom he had loved, and those who had made him suffer;
—and dear Antoinette. . . . What was there left of all those
human beings, who had lived in the town, the family of the

Kraffts, that now had ceased to be? Only the love for them that lived in the heart of a stranger.

In the afternoon Olivier met Christophe at the frontier station as they had arranged. It was a village nestling among wooded hills. Instead of waiting for the next train to Paris, they decided to go part of the way on foot, as far as the nearest town. They wanted to be alone. They set out through the silent woods, through which from a distance there resounded the dull thud of an ax. They reached a clearing at the top of a hill. Below them, in a narrow valley, in German territory, there lay the red roof of a forester's house, and a little meadow like a green lake amid the trees. All around there stretched the dark-blue sea of the forest wrapped in cloud. Mists hovered and drifted among the branches of the pines. A transparent veil softened the lines and blurred the colors of the trees. All was still. Neither footsteps nor voices were to be heard. A few drops of rain rang out on the golden copper leaves of the beeches, which had turned to autumn tints. A little stream ran tinkling over the stones. Christophe and Olivier stood still and did not stir. Each was dreaming of those whom he had lost. Olivier was thinking:

"Antoinette, where are you?"

And Christophe:

"What is success to me, now that she is dead?"

But each heard the comforting words of the dead:

"Beloved, weep not for us. Think not of us. Think of Him. . . ."

They looked at each other, and each ceased to feel his own sorrow, and was conscious only of that of his friend. They clasped their hands. In both there was sad serenity. Gently, while no wind stirred, the misty veil was raised: the blue sky shone forth again. The melting sweetness of the earth after rain. . . . So near to us, so tender! . . . The earth takes us in her arms, clasps us to her bosom with a lovely loving smile, and says to us:

"Rest.   All is well. . . ."

The ache in Christophe's heart was gone. He was like a little child. For two days he had been living wholly in the memory of his mother, the atmosphere of her soul : he had lived over again her humble life, with its days one like unto another, solitary, all spent in the silence of the childless house, in the thought of the children who had left her : the poor old woman, infirm but valiant in her tranquil faith, her sweetness of temper, her smiling resignation, her complete lack of selfishness. . . . And Christophe thought also of all the humble creatures he had known. How near to them he felt in that moment ! After all the years of exhausting struggle in the burning heat of Paris, where ideas and men jostle in the whirl of confusion, after those tragic days when there had passed over them the wind of the madness which hurls the nations, cozened by their own hallucinations, murderously against each other, Christophe felt utterly weary of the fevered, sterile world, the conflict between egoisms and ideas, the little groups of human beings deeming themselves above humanity, the ambitious, the thinkers, the artists who think themselves the brain of the world, and are no more than a haunting evil dream. And all his love went out to those thousands of simple souls, of every nation, whose lives burn away in silence, pure flames of kindness, faith, and sacrifice,—the heart of the world.

"Yes," he thought, " I know you; once more I have come to you; you are blood of my blood; you are mine. Like the prodigal son, I left you to pursue the shadows that passed by the wayside. But I have come back to you; give me welcome. We are one; one life is ours, both the living and the dead; where I am there are you also. Now I bear you in my soul, O mother, who bore me. You, too, Gottfried, and you Schulz, and Sabine, and Antoinette, you are all in me, part of me, mine. You are my riches, my joy. We will take the road together. I will never more leave you. I will be your voice. We will join forces : so we shall attain the goal."

A ray of sunlight shot through the dripping branches of the

trees. From the little field down below there came up the voices of children singing an Old German folk-song, frank and moving: the singers were three little girls dancing round the house: and from afar the west wind brought the chiming of the bells of France, like a perfume of roses. . . .

"O peace, Divine harmony, serene music of the soul set free, wherein are mingled joy and sorrow, death and life, the nations at war, and the nations in brotherhood. I love you, I long for you, I shall win you. . . ."

The night drew down her veil. Starting from his dream, Christophe saw the faithful face of his friend by his side. He smiled at him and embraced him. Then they walked on through the forest in silence: and Christophe showed Olivier the way.

> " *Taciti, soli e senza compagnia,*
> *N'andavan l' un dinnanzi, e l' altro dopo,*
> *Come i frati minor vanno per via. . . ."*

The Two Babylons
Alexander Hislop

You may be surprised to learn that many traditions of Roman Catholicism in fact don't come from Christ's teachings but from an ancient Babylonian "Mystery" religion that was centered on Nimrod, his wife Semiramis, and a child Tammuz. This book shows how this ancient religion transformed itself as it incorporated Christ into its teachings....

Religion/History   **Pages:**358

ISBN: *1-59462-010-5*   *MSRP* *$22.95*

QTY

The Go-Getter
Kyne B. Peter

The Go Getter is the story of William Peck.He was a war veteran and amputee who will not be refused what he wants. Peck not only fights to find employment but continually proves himself more than competent at the many difficult test that are throw his way in the course of his early days with the Ricks Lumber Company...

Business/Self Help/Inspirational   **Pages:**68

ISBN: *1-59462-186-1*   *MSRP* *$8.95*

QTY

The Power Of Concentration
Theron Q. Dumont

It is of the utmost value to learn how to concentrate. To make the greatest success of anything you must be able to concentrate your entire thought upon the idea you are working on. The person that is able to concentrate utilizes all constructive thoughts and shuts out all destructive ones...

Self Help/Inspirational   **Pages:**196

ISBN: *1-59462-141-1*   *MSRP* *$14.95*

Self Mastery
Emile Coue

Emile Coue came up with novel way to improve the lives of people. He was a pharmacist by trade and often saw ailing people. This lead him to develop autosuggestion, a form of self-hypnosis. At the time his theories weren't popular but over the years evidence is mounting that he was indeed right all along...

New Age/Self Help   **Pages:**98

ISBN: *1-59462-189-6*   *MSRP* *$7.95*

Rightly Dividing The Word
Clarence Larkin

The "Fundamental Doctrines" of the Christian Faith are clearly outlined in numerous books on Theology, but they are not available to the average reader and were mainly written for students. The Author has made it the work of his ministry to preach the "Fundamental Doctrines." To this end he has aimed to express them in the simplest and clearest manner..

Religion   **Pages:**352

ISBN: *1-59462-334-1*   *MSRP* *$23.45*

The Awful Disclosures Of
Maria Monk

"I cannot banish the scenes and characters of this book from my memory. To me it can never appear like an amusing fable, or lose its interest and importance. The story is one which is continually before me, and must return fresh to my mind with painful emotions as long as I live..."

Religion   **Pages:**232

ISBN: *1-59462-160-8*   *MSRP* *$17.95*

The Law of Psychic Phenomena
Thomson Jay Hudson

"I do not expect this book to stand upon its literary merits; for if it is unsound in principle, felicity of diction cannot save it, and if sound, homeliness of expression cannot destroy it. My primary object in offering it to the public is to assist in bringing Psychology within the domain of the exact sciences. That this has never been accomplished..."

New Age   **Pages:**420

ISBN: *1-59462-124-1*   *MSRP* *$29.95*

As a Man Thinketh
James Allen

"This little volume (the result of meditation and experience) is not intended as an exhaustive treatise on the much-written-upon subject of the power of thought. It is suggestive rather than explanatory, its object being to stimulate men and women to the discovery and perception of the truth that by virtue of the thoughts which they choose and encourage..."

Inspirational/Self Help   **Pages:**80

ISBN: *1-59462-231-0*   *MSRP* *$9.45*

Beautiful Joe
Marshall Saunders

When Marshall visited the Moore family in 1892, she discovered Joe, a dog they had nursed back to health from his previous abusive home to live a happy life. So moved was she, that she wrote this classic masterpiece which won accolades and was recognized as a heartwarming symbol for humane animal treatment...

Fiction   **Pages:**256

ISBN: *1-59462-261-2*   *MSRP* *$18.45*

The Enchanted April
Elizabeth Von Arnim

It began in a woman's club in London on a February afternoon, an uncomfortable club, and a miserable afternoon when Mrs. Wilkins, who had come down from Hampstead to shop and had lunched at her club, took up The Times from the table in the smoking-room...

Fiction   **Pages:**368

ISBN: *1-59462-150-0*   *MSRP* *$23.45*

The Codes Of Hammurabi And
Moses - W. W. Davies

The discovery of the Hammurabi Code is one of the greatest achievements of archaeology, and is of paramount interest, not only to the student of the Bible, but also to all those interested in ancient history...

Religion   **Pages:**132

ISBN: *1-59462-338-4*   *MSRP* *$12.95*

Holland - The History Of Netherlands
Thomas Colley Grattan

Thomas Grattan was a prestigious writer from Dublin who served as British Consul to the US. Among his works is an authoritative look at the history of Holland. A colorful and interesting look at history....

History/Politics   **Pages:**408

ISBN: *1-59462-137-3*   *MSRP* *$26.95*

The Thirty-Six Dramatic Situations
Georges Polti

An incredibly useful guide for aspiring authors and playwrights. This volume categorizes every dramatic situation which could occur in a story and describes them in a list of 36 situations. A great aid to help inspire or formalize the creative writing process...

Self Help/Reference   **Pages:**204

ISBN: *1-59462-134-9*   *MSRP* *$15.95*

A Concise Dictionary of Middle English
A. L. Mayhew
Walter W. Skeat

The present work is intended to meet, in some measure, the requirements of those who wish to make some study of Middle-English, and who find a difficulty in obtaining such assistance as will enable them to find out the meanings and etymologies of the words most essential to their purpose...

Reference/History   **Pages:**332

ISBN: *1-59462-119-5*   *MSRP* *$29.95*